SCOURGE
OF GODS

Book 3

Fire on the Mountain

-by-

Thomas A Farmer

ISBN-13: 978-0-9987679-4-9

ISBN-10: 0-9987679-4-8

Published by: Black Knight Books, 2019

For the Stephanie and Devon, the strongest women I know.

Thanks for supporting me, and for putting up with me, which was the hard part.

Chapter 1

Prosgeiosi and its twin suns shrank into specks before any of the Titans came out of their rooms. After the celebrations, especially the banquet and parade, none of them particularly wanted to spend any more time around crowds than they had to. The first few days of the journey passed by in a blur as each of them made their own personal preparations. Victoria herself exchanged a few notes with the other Titans, but even they were brief.

With the mastigas ship on the move, a trip that should have taken six weeks now barely took a week. Time they should have had to finish honing their skills, or just to socialize and set off the pressure for a few hours, was shorter than anyone expected.

The *Hammer of Ares* was a great skeleton of a vessel, ferrying the Titans and their army alongside the compact escort ships tasked with occupying the mastigas battleship's defenses. Because the other ships had been built with specific functions in mind, they were not intended to be terribly comfortable, and the *Hammer of Ares* contained all of their common and recreational areas, as well as the Titans' personal quarters.

The carrier also had a plethora of training and practice facilities that had been built when the expected destination was the far edge of the system. The massive ship could only reach the Kuiper belt so quickly, and it would have been important for the Titans to keep their skills sharp during the lengthy trip.

Instead, they would be lucky to intercept the mastigas ship before it crossed the frost line. Even at best, that left a very short amount of time before it would reach Dasos itself, laying siege to First Lord Aegesander's world as it did to Kipos five years prior. The mastigas had proven over and over that they would win in ship-to-ship combat, destroying everything sent against it. With Project Titan completed, the goal had become to assault it with the largest force of infantry ever assembled in Technocrat history and end the threat from within.

One of the few pluses to their situation was that the Titans continued to be treated as celebrities by the vast majority of the population. Whatever goals Ouroboros had in trying to discredit the Titans, they quite obviously failed. Victoria, and presumably the others as well, boarded the *Hammer of Ares* to find a number of gifts that had been brought aboard. She also found a complete list of other gifts and things that the ship's captain considered less useful and had forwarded to their homes instead.

Primarily, what she found in her room aboard the carrier were gifts of food and drink, far more than she could use, even taking the return trip into account. Victoria took the first day aboard ship to separate out her favorites and then offered the rest of it to the crew.

For three days, that was all the interaction she had with anyone aboard the ship. She and Pallasophia passed messages back and forth frequently the first day, but even that lessened by the evening of the second day, when the Second Lord had to return to work and begin the decommissioning process for Aphelion.

Pallasophia did promise that she would honor the request Victoria made half-in-jest and save a few pieces of Aphelion for her: sand from the arena where she fought and killed the mastigas elite, an undetermined piece of "something she could smash," and something she could keep as a memento.

Tritogenes did not contact her, which was just as well. Victoria still had not completely decided what she was going to say to him when they had a real chance to sit down and discuss things.

His friend and adviser, one she never met but who held a vague position of equal authority to Pallasophia herself, Philip left Victoria a note on the morning of the fourth day out from Prosgeiosi. It was simple, a set of photographs of Limani and of the Titans themselves, followed by a holo of herself and Pallasophia from the banquet taken by Tritogenes himself.

Philip's note was equally short, a single sentence, typed out rather than voice recorded. "Don't forget what you're fighting for."

Cliche as it was, that message was the thing that finally got Victoria to leave her room and socialize with the others that morning.

Now, she sat on the ship's uppermost deck, an area designed to mimic the look and feel of a park. The captain of the *Hammer* came from Kipos originally, and the cool air and dense foliage was modeled directly on his heavily forested home planet. The larger "trees" around the area were part of the ship itself, conduits and support beams disguised by a thin layer of synthetic bark. Some of the smaller trees and bushes, and the dirt they grew in, were just as real as they would have been planetside.

Rather than blue sky overhead, the common area's dome revealed a crystal canopy of stars drowned out here and there by the manmade lights overhead. Those lights were the only thing breaking the illusion, and even they could be ignored so long as Victoria did not focus on them.

The suns, Prosgeiosi, and several of the other planets were behind them. She knew from the stellar map accessible on her holo that the planets they had yet to pass were off to the "right" of the ship, but at such distances they were little more than specks of starlight themselves.

Ordinarily, she was happy to have the stars overhead. The black infinite gave her a sort of comfort that open blue skies did not. These

3

stars were different, the mastigas ship lurked somewhere out there in that infinite abyss. Every time she glanced up, some still-terrified part of her brain picked out a random star and tried to claim it had not been there before. It was the mastigas, and their time was already up.

The massive ship was hardly stealthy, but space was quite large. Once they drew closer, the hope was that the battleship would be easy to find. If the data from the initial attack at the edge of the Kuiper belt and the observations from Dasos proved wrong, their attack force would have trillions upon trillions of kilometers of space to search.

Victoria did not particularly want to spend the next century of her life searching. Several times, she thought she saw it, but it was too small, too far away to be seen for several more days. The anxiety quickly grew to something more than she wanted to deal with, and she turned away from the stars. They could wait.

Victoria kept her eyes focused on the trees and people around her instead. A hundred or so meters away sat a "shack" where the ship's cooks prepared comfort food for anyone with the clearance to enter the uppermost deck in the first place. Despite the massive size of the ship, only a hundred or so people occupied the verdant dome at any given time, which left rather a lot of space between them.

Victoria was almost more pleased to discover that part of the ship's design than she was to find out how good the food actually was. She was happy to be out and "social," but the open space of the dome allowed her a measure of solitude. The smell of dirt and plants around her was strange, not something she was used to after going straight from Aphelion to Prosgeiosi, but it stirred something primal deep in her brain that spoke joy to a deep piece of her soul.

She finished eating some time ago and the unobtrusive staff quietly came and took her plates and utensils away. Now, she simply sat, lost in thought, reliving things from her very first few days of life deep in the dark bowels of Aphelion.

Ever since *that* night with Pallasophia, the memories of the fighting and death in that dark labyrinth no longer strung in quite the same way. The blood, the *pain*, still came back to her in crystalline detail. That had not changed. Since that night, however, it no longer filled her with the same rush of terror. Now, she could look back on those fights, even the moments she remembered from the previous lives whose programmed and implanted memories helped her survive, and study them.

More importantly, she could use those moments and prepare for the fight ahead.

Most importantly, she could think back on that night with fondness. Hands, lips, all of them caught up in one another with little awareness of where she ended and Pallasophia began. It was much like fighting in that way.

"You're thinking about the mastigas, aren't you?"

She had been so lost in her thoughts that she failed to notice the approaching footsteps. It felt very safe aboard the *Hammer*, and Victoria's guards were not up like they would have been in a public area in Odyssey.

Daniel stood next to her table, carrying a tray with a plate of food and a pair of mugs to the little table where she sat. She looked at her own drink; the dark tea had long since gone cold and forgotten.

She indicated one of the other chairs at the table and he set his tray down, then settled into the chair.

"How can you tell?"

A half smile crossed his lips, nearly lost amid the untamed, early-morning frizz of his beard. "You had the same expression on your face just now that you had before the banquet, when we were talking about training. You and Lelantos both."

She smiled, but the gesture felt cold and empty. "And you recognized it because Enyalios had you fighting mastigas as well."

5

"Yes," he said, then suddenly flicked his eyes away and toward his breakfast. He picked up one of the mugs. "Here. You hadn't touched your coffee since I got in line. They assured me it was fresh."

Victoria briefly considered mentioning to him that she had been drinking tea, but let it slide. He had gone out of his way to do a favor, and she did not dislike the ship's coffee per se. She lifted the mug and took a sip before giving a simple "thank you."

While Daniel started to eat, Victoria turned her attention back to the stars above them. With a friend by her side, even if they were engaged in two different activities at the moment, the terror that open sky represented faded into the background noise of her mind. The mastigas ship remained "out there," but with even one Titan, one of "her people," nearby, that danger suddenly seemed more easily faced.

"Impressive, isn't it?"

She hummed a question in reply.

"That," he pointed with his fork at the stars. "Knowing that somewhere out there is Earth."

"If Earth still exists."

"So you're not an Aterran?" He asked the question with surprising frankness considering the vitriol with which she had heard some of the more fringe cults discussed.

Victoria shook her head. "No," she replied, then cracked a thin smile. "It's hard to describe what I am."

Daniel shrugged. "I wouldn't judge you if you were," he said. "After all, what real proof do we have other than corrupt star charts and stories?"

"Are you...?" she asked, trailing off into silence and leaving the rest unsaid.

"No, just thinking out loud. I was raised a Disciple, actually."

Victoria nodded. Thinking about it for a second, the few times he used the same oaths the other Technocrats did seemed accidental, things that slipped out because everyone around him said them. He certainly did not seem to mean them the way others did. Even Helena, who

6

professed not to believe in anything she had not yet seen, had sworn by the "gods between" more than once.

She had only encountered a few, brief mentions of Disciples in her reading. Between their relatively small size and the frustrating lack of concrete history from before the Technocrats assumed control of the ship named *Odyssey,* there was little to go on.

As far as she could tell, the Disciples were an offshoot, or perhaps even a direct continuation, of an old, Earth-based religion that followed a single god of justice. Some took issue with that, or they had in the past—and with their more unusual mores—but they did not seem to believe anything that explicitly went against what she knew of history. In fact, the Disciples themselves, as a whole, seemed fairly unconcerned with history. Beyond that, she knew very little. She supposed Daniel could tell her more, but she was not particularly in the mood for that sort of talk right then.

Once they were all on their way home, with the blood and violence behind them, she might ask him.

She took another drink of the coffee Daniel had brought. It was strong, the result of the ship's staff trying to accommodate tastes that ranged from cream, sugar, and spices to even hotter and stronger than what she now held. It did the job well enough, however, and the jolt of energy it provided was welcome.

As Daniel finished eating, Lelantos approached. The six of them spent enough time on Prosgeiosi to have similar schedules, though Daniel always seemed to be an early riser and Lelantos a late one.

The bald, thin Titan sat opposite Victoria, placing a tray full of plates and cups in front of him. Victoria's metabolism might have been enhanced by Tritogenes's genetic engineers, but not even she could put away food like Lelantos after a long trip on his chronodrug. He must have been meditating that morning, a task he could accomplish in minutes thanks to the chronodrug's ability to dilate his perception of time.

"Got enough coffee?" Daniel asked. The tone in his voice was friendlier than he had been with Victoria, almost like he was addressing a brother. He made a vague gesture to the two tallest mugs on the other Titan's tray, one of which was capped with a spill-proof lid.

Lelantos smiled in return and, with mock formality, replied, "the first cup does not always suffice, Second Lord. If you and Second Lord Korakti would permit the kitchen staff to serve real coffee rather than hot, brown water, one mug would do the trick, I assure you."

"We all have our burdens to bear," Daniel replied with equal formality. "I do not think I could manage a meal with your sort of drink on top of those fried things you convinced the cooks to call pancakes."

Lelantos turned up his head, sniffed, and looked down his nose at Daniel. "Careful, Second Lord, you insult Kipos's national dish at your own peril."

"Far be it from me to insinuate that Kipos might have misguided priorities when it comes to culinary science," Daniel replied.

Victoria watched the discussion go on for another few minutes. They spoke like Hexarchs debating a corporate acquisition, despite talking about nothing more important than breakfast food. Watching them was almost like watching a pair of fencers or wrestlers going at it, trading barbs and feints until one of them either said the wrong thing or they came to an agreement, at which point the game would be over.

"I cannot help it if the staff routinely burns the espresso," Lelantos said, as Victoria realized that she had been paying more attention to how they were speaking than what they were actually saying. "That fault, I believe, lies with the machine itself."

Daniel raised his nearly-empty mug of coffee. "Hear, hear!"

A moment passed and the atmosphere changed. Lelantos shifted in his seat and clapped Daniel's blue-clad shoulder with his hand. "I'll let you off the hook this time, Daniel."

The other Titan laughed. "I suppose I'll take that. Did you sleep well?"

Lelantos nodded. "As well as I have since leaving Kipos, anyway."

"Before I started traveling much, I used to have the same problems leaving Katarraktes. I suppose we all do." He turned, likely realizing he had been ignoring the very person he came to sit with in the first place. "What about you? Did you miss Limani the first time you left?"

She carefully disguised the long moment she needed to consider her options by taking a drink from her mug. Finally, she settled on the same thing she had been relying on for some time now: a partial truth.

"I've never been to Limani."

Daniel showed more surprise than Lelantos at that, which made her wonder if Daniel was simply the more reactive of the two—which was true—or if Lelantos was the more perceptive. He did not seem like he was using the chronodrug at that moment, so any observational ability was his alone.

Daniel also asked a simple, "really?"

She nodded. "I was born on an outlying facility. I actually spent most of my life under a dome until I came to Prosgeiosi."

"The open sky must have been quite a sight," Lelantos observed.

"It was," she replied. She laughed, mostly at herself, it felt. "If I'm being honest, it took me several minutes to step out of the shuttle the first time. It seems silly, you know, for one of us to be afraid of something like the sky."

Around a mouthful of bacon, Lelantos said, "if it's any consolation, I'm afraid of spiders when I'm sober."

"When you're sober?" Daniel asked.

"They move too fast," Lelantos replied. "When the world is slow, they fascinate me, but it wasn't until that first hit of chrono that I stopped being afraid of them."

The conversation drifted again, moving from topic to topic. Nothing they talked about was important, per se, but for Victoria the very act of the three of them relaxing around one another was enough to put her in a more positive frame of mind.

9

The girl on the holo was twelve years old and clad in the red robe of a Sixth Lord. The caption scrolling across the bottom of the display gave her name as "Alexis" and her homeworld as "Kipos." As the text passed by, it displayed her performance in the day's previous events. While she had not come out on top of every event, her average score put her squarely in third place overall.

First place had been claimed by a fourteen year old Fifth Lord, the previous year's champion. His score was only seven points higher than the second place competitor, another Sixth Lord a year older than Alexis herself.

By contrast, Alexis was over a hundred points down from the second place competitor, but the girl in second place just finished the event Alexis was about to begin. It was possible, if she scored high enough, that Alexis could overtake the second or even first place positions.

The announcer explained all of that in hushed tones that made it seem as though he was down on the field with Alexis, rather than watching a camera feed from inside the studio. He went on to explain—for what had to be the fourth time since Alexis's turn began—that this was the final event of the tournament, at which point he temporarily lost the interest of those watching from the officer's mess aboard the *Abraxas*.

It was lunchtime aboard the *Abraxas*. Indeed, the entire assault force had stopped to eat and watch the finals of this tournament. Titan Victoria had insisted, claiming she met Sixth Lord Alexis before leaving Prosgeiosi.

Second Lord Alcmene shrugged at that thought. She was not going to complain about having an extended lunch break. The *Abraxas* could take care of itself for an hour and half easily enough. To be fair, the battlecruiser could have been left completely unattended until they began attack preparations because the tether to the *Hammer of Ares* handled everything, but leaving the ship completely alone was bad form.

Finally, Alexis signaled someone out of view of the holo's pickup and the first target rose from the gently rolling Limanian countryside. The early evening sun warmed the entire scene and glinted in oranges off the target.

The announcer explained that she had two minutes to hit each target, although such a long time would only really matter once the range really started to open. Second Lord Alcmene rolled her eyes. This was the third time he had given the exact same explanation. The only way she knew it was live and not just a recording played for the third time was little differences in the announcer's voice.

"The difficulty of the next shot depends on how well she does on the one before it. They take accuracy and speed into account when determining the next challenge, and accuracy, speed, and distance when counting score."

That, Alcmene thought, at least was a slightly different comment than the way he explained it before. She supposed someone on set complained, because he had not given that much detail about scoring on the previous two attempts.

The first target was ten meters away and Alexis raised her rifle, inspecting it, a task for which she had ninety seconds. The weapon cost more than the entire kit of a field soldier, but she had to admit it was an impressive piece of hardware. Typically competitors used different weapons, swapping between them as distances changed, but the rifle in Alexis's hands could be adjusted on the go.

Alcmene nodded in appreciation. "Nice gun."

"You said it," replied Second Lord Karolos. If anyone else in the room was the sort to appreciate Alexis's choice of weapon, it was him. Karolos oversaw the *Abraxas*'s armory. The battlecruiser should never see infantry combat, but on the off chance it did, Karolos was the one in charge.

That was just as well for her. If Second Lord Alcmene had to fight, it meant the attackers—or the mastigas—somehow made it into the

11

battlecruiser's magazine. If that happened, she would have bigger problems to worry about than small arms fire.

Conversation sprang up for a moment, mostly talking about the pros and cons of the favored weapons of the officers in the room. None of them agreed on what they liked best. A few came to some sort of consensus about what they did not like, but that was as far as they got before Alexis raised the weapon to her shoulder.

"Quiet!" Alcmene ordered. She did not outrank everyone in the room—in fact she outranked very few of the others present—but they were more interested in the holo than they were in continuing their argument.

Alexis shot the first target quickly, leaving her rifle compact. The second sprang up, followed by a third and then a fourth. Those all went down so quickly that even Second Lord Karolos admitted, "nice shot."

The fifth target popped up at one hundred meters. Alexis took a moment longer to line up her shot, then it too went down. She then took a full fifteen seconds to adjust her rifle, extending and shifting parts around in order to help stabilize it at longer ranges. By the seventh shot, the next target rose at over five hundred meters.

After the tenth shot, with the target at eleven hundred meters, the announcer broke in again to remind the audience that this was the shot where the current second place competitor finally missed his shot. The one in first hit the target, but hit an outer ring rather than the center and went on to miss the shot right after.

Alexis took a full minute to line up the shot, laying down on the ground and using the bipod on her rifle. With it in place, she took another thirty seconds to open her holo and run a series of calculations. The announcer praised her for that, but also warned the audience that those calculations could easily take too much time, and...

Alexis's rifle coughed and hit her shoulder.

The camera switched to a slow-motion view near the target. Her bullet struck halfway to the center, closer than the anyone else had managed.

The announcer said something, but whatever that might have been was drowned out by the cheers in the room.

Still unable to actually hear anything, Alcmene watched the holo. The highlights showed the next target was at a full kilometer and a half.

She quieted the room, shushing ever louder until the message came across. Alexis was already in position, and used that time to further adjust her rifle's bipod and run calculations. With the timer rapidly approaching one-hundred and twenty seconds, she shifted back to the weapon, adjusted her aim...

And the timer hit zero.

Her head fell, but then the announcer pointed out that her previous shot put her squarely in first place. A similar announcement must have gone across the field itself, because she perked back up, smiling.

"Alright, back to work!" barked the stentorian voice of Second Lord Philon, the *Abraxas*'s senior helmsman. Grumbles and groans answered him, but slowly everyone rose and made their way to the mess hall's exits.

Alcmene stood, adjusted her uniform belt, and headed for the lift that would take her back to the ship's magazine. The one advantage of this new battlecruiser design, she reflected as the speedy platform descended, was that nothing was very far from anything else. Her early career, because of some indiscretions at the Academy regarding where and when to partake of certain illicit substances, had been spent aboard the *Tartarus*, where it could take an hour to get from one end of the ship to the other.

The *Tartarus*. She hated that ship. Second Lord Alcmene hated every minute of every day staring at the walls of that glorified flying fortress. One year aboard that ship was a year and a month too long for her tastes. And yet...

The images, finally released after the Titans' assault on Faros, the larger of Prosgeiosi's twin moons, were haunting. The *Tartarus* was too damned large to simply destroy, and the mastigas battleship's weaponry actually blew it apart before picking off the pieces.

"Don't tell me the girl lost."

The voice roused her from her thoughts, and Second Lord Alcmene realized her feet had been operating on autopilot until she reached the magazine. That had probably been a minute or two ago, and since then she had been standing at the observation rail while her feet waited for instructions from her brain.

She looked up to see Second Lord Euphrasia eyeing her from her station, fire control seven. Alcmene raised an eyebrow. "Hmm?"

"You look pissed, Lochagos."

Alcmene shook her head, clearing the fog of memory that settled on it. "No, when I left the mess, she was actually in first."

"I know," Euphrasia replied. She gestured to a small holoprojection above her station. The personal kit was not as high-definition as the one in the mess hall, but it worked well enough for one person. From where she stood, Alcmene could not see the score. She grinned. "Some of us weren't allowed to take a long lunch, ma'am."

Alcmene shrugged, then adjusted the belt of her uniform robe again. Ever since getting promoted to Second Lord when she took the transfer to the *Abraxas*, her new uniform never quite fit right. The military tailors assured her it was the exact same size and cut as her Third Lord's uniform, but she did not find that to be particularly convincing.

When the previous adjustment failed, she unbuckled the belt and rebuckled it. Despite nothing else being different, somehow the stupid thing sat properly.

"Difficulties, Lochagos?"

"You'll tell no one about this, Lochias."

Euphrasia laughed. "As you say. So, if it's not little Sixth Lord Alexis's progress in the tournament, what's on your mind?"

14

Alcmene shook her head. "I was thinking about the *Tartarus*."

Euphrasia flinched dramatically, making an overplayed "oof" noise. "Nothing good there, is there?"

Alcmene shook her head. "No, but it's not even that. I was thinking about what happened to it. I didn't think I would be eager to avenge that hulking monstrosity, but the moment I saw those pictures, I had one thing on my mind."

"Vengeance?"

"Revenge."

"That's the same thing, Lochagos."

"No, this is personal. However you want to phrase it, I've been dreaming about emptying this magazine into that battleship since then."

"It won't be long now, will it?"

Alcmene shook her head. "No," she said. "No, it will not."

***

Second Lord Eleni shouldered her way through the crowd. The areas outside the *Hammer of Ares*'s observation dome were a common area of their own, rife with what passed for bars and cafes aboard an underway warship. By and large, the only way to tell those spots apart from anything else was the crewman-posted signs.

The *Hammer*'s social areas were larger than its working spaces, which was unusual, especially for a ship of its size, but the carrier had been purpose built to accommodate the crews of the troop transports and battlecruisers tethered to its superstructure. For most of the people on the mission, going over to the *Hammer of Ares* was the equivalent of going to town.

Fortunately, unless she vastly underestimated the rate at which the military updated their systems, Eleni possessed what amounted to a pass to the most exclusive club in town.

A few people watched her as she went, wondering where the relatively unassuming Second Lord was headed, and she returned their curious glances with smiles and polite acknowledgments.

At the door to the observation dome, Eleni paused. She opened her holo, and the system automatically pulled up her military ID. The door them compared it against the list of ranking officers who should have access to the lush, foliage-filled dome. It returned a negative, the holo blinked red, and the door remained locked.

She felt an automatic flush across her cheekbones, more in annoyance than embarrassment. Eleni knew her military credentials would not unlock the door and wished the system would have given her the option to use an alternate first.

Once it calmed down and allowed a second attempt, Eleni poked through the menu on her holo and passed across a different set of access codes. The system considered for a moment, and Eleni wondered if it would actually reject this one as well. If it did, she would have no choice but to turn around, admit she was wrong, and walk past everyone else again.

Fortunately, the military had not yet purged the priority access codes given to every high-importance member of Project Titan. The indicator light turned from red to green and the door slid into the wall. The scents of dirt and green life washed over her and heads around her turned in curiosity. Usually, people going to the dome used one of the private access corridors, but getting in through the public area was not unheard of. Her passage would be quickly forgotten.

The dome itself was sparsely filled with people. Off to one side sat the small hut where the warship's VIPs ordered their food. She did not have time to gawk, however, because the surest sign that she was not supposed to be there would be standing and staring at everything in astonishment.

Not that she was not astonished. First Lord Tritogenes himself designed the ship and mandated the social area's setup. While he did not design the system that maintained the real dirt and plants, he commissioned the engineer that did.

Instead, Second Lord Eleni strode purposefully across the area, using her eyes and a gently curving path to find the people she was looking for. Fortunately, the Titans were easy enough to spot, and Eleni found them in just a few minutes. They were not all there, but the one she wanted to speak to was, which meant the whole trip was worth it.

Second Lord Eleni had not seen Victoria, except for news footage, since helping her out of the pits at the bottom of Aphelion. That day, Victoria had been a bruised, bloody wretch. She was strong and determined beneath all that grime, but she had not been eating well or sleeping well. Nearly every waking moment of her life to that point had been spent fighting *for* her life against equally starved mastigas.

Now, she sat straight in her chair, swathed in the black robe that denoted her as a Spatharios, technically outside the normal six-tier social rank of the Technocrats. She wore simple, practical makeup, nothing like the fancy paint of Prosgeiosi's elite social events. A black vine twined around the left side of her face, but little else adorned her skin.

With her sat a thin, heavily tattooed man Eleni recognized from the news. Lelantos turned his large eyes in her direction. No recognition of her identity passed over his expression, only her position and approach. Nothing else about him changed, and he laughed in reaction to something Victoria said, too quiet to carry.

Another woman sat with them, one unusually camera-shy compared to the other Titans. Despite that, Second Lord Helena's glittering implants make her hard to mistake for anyone else. She and Lelantos wore blue robes, hers a brighter shade than his. In contrast to Lelantos's dark blue robe, barely lighter than Victoria's, Helena was draped in a blue approaching sapphire in hue, the height of Dasos fashion.

Having sighted the right table, Eleni went straight for them. When she got close enough for it to be polite, she cleared her throat and asked, "Spatharios?"

"Yes?" Victoria asked automatically. She turned her head, fixing Eleni with her steel-colored eyes. For a moment, the Titan seemed to regard her without recognition, and then a sudden flash crossed her face and Victoria's eyes widened and she smiled. "Eleni!"

"Good afternoon, Spatharios."

Victoria rose, towering over Eleni. She was not particularly tall among normal-sized people, and Victoria had been genetically engineered to be the "perfect soldier." As part of that, she rose to nearly two meters in height, and Eleni felt rather like a very localized eclipse suddenly passed overhead.

She looked up, meeting Victoria's sharp features and smile, and a single thought crossed her brain, drowning out everything else. By the Ten Thousand, Eleni thought, Victoria was beautiful.

"Second Lord Eleni," she said, stiff and formal. It took Eleni a moment to realize that Victoria's mischievous smile remained—the same half-grin she remembered from the hell deep in Aphelion's depths—and the formal tone was a joke.

After a moment, Victoria allowed the joke to pass and asked, "such formality from one of the people who saved my life?"

Eleni's eyes flicked sideways. Lelantos was no longer watching her. His attention seemed to be fixed on the mug of coffee and half-eaten tart in front of him. Helena, however, fixed her with a pair of piercing blue eyes whose color seemed to be intensified by the blues in her robe. Her expression hovered somewhere between amused and interested, and Eleni wondered how much the cybernetic Titan knew about Victoria's actual past.

Eleni looked back to Victoria. She knew about Helena from the news and from what little about Project Titan had been declassified already, but seeing her in person proved the most pervasive of the rumors true. Face-to-face, she was a very unnerving person.

To Victoria, she said, "I was not sure you would remember me."

"Of course I do," she replied. "I think about that team frequently. I assume, because you're here, that you got the transfer you requested?"

"Sort of," Eleni admitted. "I'm technically still assigned to Project Titan, which is how I got in here in the first place. Rather than get a transfer from job to job, I just took a different task as part of the Project. Officially, I'm here as support staff for the six of you, but practically, I'm a squadron commander aboard the *Justice*."

Victoria put a hand on Eleni's shoulder, heavy but companionable. She smiled. "Congratulations."

Eleni beamed, feeling a sensation of satisfaction radiating out from the point of contact between Victoria's hand and her shoulder. "Thank you, Spatharios."

"What did I say about formality?" Victoria asked, then laughed. "I have a name, Eleni. You're welcome to use it."

She swallowed a sudden lump of convoluted emotion in her throat, then nodded. "Of course. Victoria."

"Come, sit with us. Do you have the time?"

"I'm not on duty right now, and..."

From the far side of the table, Helena smiled, enigmatic, and almost predatory. "We have four chairs and only three people to sit in them. Join us."

"Yes," Lelantos added. He smiled, lips thin but genuine. "I'd very much like to hear more about the woman who saved our captain's life."

Eleni laughed as the tension in their meeting suddenly vanished. It was Lelantos, of all people, who made her feel welcome. Helena continued to unnerve her and she still felt unable to quite measure up to Victoria, but it was Lelantos's unassuming smile that put her at ease.

She reached for the chair. "I can't very well refuse all three of you, can I?"

Victoria sat a moment later and addressed the other two Titans. "Eleni was part of the team who..." She paused, briefly, as a strange expression crossed her face. Her lips smiled, but her eyes fell. Most people would never have noticed, but Eleni had been around Victoria before. She knew Lelantos and Helena were perceptive, and noticed it as well, but neither pursued the issue.

After that brief hesitation, Victoria continued her story. "...saved my life when a test early on in my training went wrong..."

Chapter 2

First Lord Rivka, Hexarch of Kipos, sat back in the plush leather chair in her personal study, in her palace, on her planet, and sighed. Prosgeiosi was nice enough, but the gleaming metal and glass never quite lived up to the coziness of things that were properly hers. Unlike many of her compatriots in the Council, Rivka had ordered a new palace constructed, one which sprawled across the side of a mountain whose foothills sank into a deep, wooded valley.

She stayed busy as it was. Being Hexarch of Kipos was already a full-time commitment. Objectively, Rivka knew she could delegate more than she was, and she did exactly that when the work became truly difficult to deal with. Still, she preferred to stay busy, and when the day-to-day work of being a Hexarch left her some free time, she often filled it with the sort of black market operations that brought her to the Second Lords in the first place.

Those connections had been especially useful lately. Since problems with Ouroboros blew several large holes in her security force—both from injury and those guilty of treason and conspiracy—replacing the lost personnel had been at the top of her list. She could circumvent many of the usual steps in the vetting process. Since she already knew these people, selecting those personnel she trusted was much easier than it might otherwise have been.

Still, the additional work that came from a normal trip to Prosgeiosi meant her Kiposian work took a back seat. Given the—and Rivka again searched her mind for the right term to describe what happened, because the official term of "incident" seemed too sanitized—nature of events during her stay at the capital, work piled up worse than usual.

Despite that, she stayed on Prosgeiosi for three days after the Titans left. They rode at the head of an army made up of militaries from each of the six Hexarch's holdings. Obviously, Enyalios supplied the majority of the troops, while Aegesander provided the battlecruisers that would fly escort. The crews, however, came from everywhere. All told, they sent nearly twenty times the force she used to defend *her* blood-soaked planet five years before.

Time was short, she knew that. Somehow, that thought was a comfort. If the Titans had to venture to the outer rim, the trip would have taken many times longer than it already would. Yes, she continued, if their assessments were off, the mastigas *would* land on Dasos, but there was little she could do about that anymore.

In a strange way, that was freeing.

What was decidedly *not* freeing, and in fact sent her pulse rate through the roof with a surge of adrenaline every time her thoughts ventured his way, was that Second Lord Lelantos was out there. She spent five years training him, turning a bitter, angry man into a cool, calm weapon. She then aimed her dearest friend at the mastigas and let him loose.

Rivka feared for his safety. Enough of the chronodrug had been synthesized to allow him near-unlimited use for well over a year and no part of his training had been neglected.

None of that mattered in the face of her fears, though. Intellectually, she understood the risks the mission entailed. He would be, perhaps already was, facing an enemy very few humans had stood up against and

22

lived. In that way, the two of them shared an understanding that she felt was lost on the other Hexarchs.

"How *could* they know what it's like to stand up to the mastigas?" she asked aloud. It was the latest in a string of partial thoughts and ideas that came to mind.

Frustrated with her walls' lack of answer, she pushed herself out of the leather chair and began to pace the small room.

"Diomedes faced the mastigas, or he tried to," she muttered. "He sent me instead. Did he really kill himself because he was ashamed, or was he so afraid that I would fail that he wanted to do the deed himself rather than wait for them to come for him?"

She eyed the stack of inactive holodisks on her desk, hardcopies of reports and work she still had to deal with. Fortunately, she finished everything relating to her visit to Prosgeiosi before leaving. Assuming more work did not find its way to her desk, which almost always happened, she had "only" a week's worth of late nights ahead of her. A more realistic estimate would put it at two, or even three, weeks.

Much to her chagrin, Rivka could not do all her own work all the time. Like the other Hexarchs, she had people to read and summarize most of their reports for them. They filtered and sorted the endless stacks of messages and minor things, often handling the less important tasks before they even crossed her desk. At least, that was how things *should* have gone in her brief absence.

Thanks to Ouroboros, Rivka spent some time without that support. It was bad enough that their damned organization snaked its way into her security team, compromising it and leaving her without guards when she needed them most. She could deal with attacks on her safety; it was the disruption of her secretarial staff that posed the real problems.

Their attempt on her life failed anyway. Thanks to Lelantos, the terrorist snipers failed to kill her, failed to kill Aegesander. In the rush, she had not even been aware they took shots at him, but he later confirmed they knew he was there as well, and that she was not their only target that day.

She frowned as a dark cloud passed across her thoughts. Ouroboros might not have killed her, but they did something worse. Their snipers killed her informant, her *friend*, Calliope.

Fixing the problems Ouroboros caused with her support personnel occupied most of her time before leaving the capital. Even with her connections, the list of people she trusted *that* much was quite short. Most of them already worked directly on Project Titan, leaving her pool of potential applicants even smaller.

Then, the day after the Titans returned from Faros, Lelantos came to her with an idea. His brother, Ilias, served in Hyperion's personal guard for years. It took more concessions than she was honestly willing to make—one of which was naming her new stadium after Hyperion himself—but Pteryga's Hexarch finally agreed to the transfer. Technically, Ilias was free to switch allegiances whenever he wanted, such was the collective bargaining power of the Second Lords, but it would have been quite impolite not to ask Hyperion first.

Thanks to his time working for Hyperion, Ilias also had a list of trusted personnel, some of which he already brought with him. Between the two of them, filling the remaining openings with reassignments from Project Titan was rather easy.

The stack of hardcopies on her desk, at least, had nothing to do with Project Titan *or* Security personnel.

She pushed a few of the stacks around until they sat where she wanted them, even going so far as to transfer disks from one stack to another at what appeared to be random. The seeming chaos of her desk belied the order she imposed upon it. The odds of anyone else deciphering her system were low, but she knew where everything important had been set. It was all arranged such that she could tackle the most important things first, then work her way down to the things she really ought to delegate.

She sank into her chair, reveling in its comfort. Prosgeiosi had finer furniture, but this chair had been *hers* for decades now. The leather was precisely molded to her hips and spine, and sitting down in it was akin to coming home.

A sigh escaped her lips, momentary but it helped her re-center. She laughed at the stacks waiting for her. Some things, she thought, never changed. "At least I can deal with all of this, now that the Titans are on their way."

Rivka picked up the first disk and summoned its internal holo. The data matched the label, and a report on how an unexpected change in weather patterns delayed the construction projects she began in her planetary capital before leaving for Prosgeiosi. The stadium was easy, but the unexpected rains had flooded one of the lower levels of the new theater, and the record also contained a request for funding to build and install a pump in case it happened again.

Logical and to the point, so Rivka signed the request without giving it much thought.

"It's all so mundane," she muttered, setting the disk down. "How long until I get one of these that says, 'the mastigas are defeated?'"

The click that followed her words made her blood freeze. Rivka was supposed to be alone, at least in her office. The door would have chimed, even if someone with keyless entry, like Ilias, came to talk to her. The same held for the windows, although given that her office was at the top of a tower, the odds of someone coming through a window to visit her were fairly low.

Her mind raced as she tried to figure out exactly who would be trying to kill her. It was a logical jump. No one with good intentions would be anywhere near her so-called inner sanctum. That only left someone with ill intentions. That list had grown since Ouroboros, but remained short, and her brain already started running down her options.

While she did that, long-practiced routine took her to the wall next to the tall, mechanical clock. She pressed against the wood-grain panel there. It unlatched and swung open, revealing a locked vault. Normally, weapons other than the sort of pistol nearly everyone carried would be sealed away in a safe with multiple locks, usually biometric. When designing this office, she had taken a cue from Diomedes's chambers. Her predecessor had been paranoid enough to install a lock that automatically scanned the space in front of it and unlocked depending on the results of that scan. As the panel in front of her unlocked without having to be touched, she felt a swell of thankfulness for her decision to appropriate that idea.

Reading her spiking adrenaline levels, the door to the vault behind the faux panel vanished into the wall beside it with a pressurized thunk. She reached in and withdrew a compact rifle, checked the magazine, chamber, and safety, and brought it to her shoulder.

Less than thirty seconds had passed since the unexpected noise. A voice in the back of her head told her she was simply being paranoid, but it was not that long ago that terrorist snipers tried to put a bullet in her skull.

The other Hexarchs had changed somewhat during that whole incident as well. Rivka had not spoken to anyone about it, and in fact still was still unconvinced that she was not simply making it up. Aegesander was trying to ingratiate himself with Hyperion again, pushing Eurybia away in the process. While it was not exactly a long time, Enyalios had not entertained once since returning to Katarraktes. Tritogenes not only had not left Prosgeiosi, but he was actually showing up to things on time.

Objectively, she supposed she should not be surprised. They were likely as relieved as she was, *and* as lost for what to do now that their largest joint project in decades was complete. On top of that, the mastigas ship was moving toward Dasos and had already killed thousands of people. The toll continued, because the whole incident with Ouroboros hit on top of everything else.

Still, something *else* was off, and if the circumstances around First Lord Diomedes's suicide had taught her anything, it was that paranoid was simply another word for prepared. Rivka did not believe in coincidences, and for something to make noise right as she mentioned the mastigas was not random.

Rivka scanned the room. Until meeting Lelantos, she had prided herself at being a good shot. She maintained that opinion afterward, with the slight modification that the skill Lelantos developed went far beyond "good." Of course, anyone in her office would be at a range so short that missing would be rather difficult.

She saw nothing. Other than having knocked over the tallest of the stacks of hardcopy in her rush to get to the gun safe, nothing was disturbed. She checked the suite's door; it too was locked. A quick sweep of the rest of her office told her that nothing else had been disturbed.

Satisfied that whatever happened was, at least, not an immediate threat, she reactivated the weapon's safety and returned it to the vault. The door slid closed as she stepped away, and she shut the concealing panel back, hiding it from view once again.

The noise still bothered her, and she continued to search. After several minutes, and several apparently complete passes around the area, she was about ready to attribute it to a random piece of machinery creaking when her eyes settled on a plain steel box sitting on the top shelf of her armoire.

She went back to the hulking piece of furniture and peered inside. It held her most expensive, and thus most formal, clothing and jewelry, and usually she kept it closed. As she moved around, searching, she had opened it, glanced inside, and went on.

The metal case on the top shelf, one of the only things sitting on that shelf in fact, was something she had not touched in several years.

Carefully, she reached up and withdrew the box First Lord Diomedes left her in his Will. It had been locked then, with no apparent key to open it, only a message that it would open when its contents were needed.

Rivka eased the lid open. She expected the metal hinges to squeak or protest, but they were not even the slightest bit stiff. Despite not having moved in at least half a decade, the lid opened as easily as it must have always done. The outside of the box was featureless, without a single word or image to even signify who owned it.

The case was too large to easily balance on one hand, so she took it to her desk and set it in the only available clear spot. Inside the box was, perhaps, the last thing she expected to find. She withdrew a stack of paper, set it aside, and searched the box for any hidden compartments.

She found nothing, and so turned back to the paper. It felt strange in her hands. As a Hexarch, she had seen paper before. She had even seen and read books printed on real paper—a treat few other than the most successful Second Lords could afford. What she had not expected to find in a sealed, keyless lockbox was a stack of loose paper covered not in printed text but in actual hand-written notes.

Before she even started to read, she wondered what secrets she now held. It made sense—paper was untraceable, and if the messages had been written by hand, then no computer record of those words ever existed. She stared at the text, never having known that Diomedes studied, let alone practiced, calligraphy.

Then, she started to read, and her eyes grew wider with every line. By the end of the first hand-written page, her heart raced faster and harder than it ever had. That page ended with a list of names: Hyperion, Stephania, Aegesander, Ophion, Diomedes, Meriones.

Diomedes's flowing script opened that page with, "Our sins are many." First Lord Hyperion talked about "our sins" during the Titan's sendoff. His choice of words had been no coincidence. As she continued to read, a knot formed in the pit of her stomach and she learned exactly what those sins were.

She ended up reading the entire stack of paper three times, start to end, before getting up from her chair. Papers in hand, she searched for another lockbox in which to store them, one whose lock she alone would be able to open.

Several more minutes passed, and she failed to find anything, and so she hid the paper in one of the deep pockets inside her robe and called for Second Lord Ilias.

He arrived in minutes, buzzing through her door as instructed. Concern flicked across his face as he took in Rivka's expression. She knew she was failing at concealing her emotions, but right then did not care.

"Second Lord Ilias, bring me a tamper-proof lockbox with a retinal key, please, and have a ship prepped. I may be away for some time, so please attend to any urgent business that comes up in my absence."

"Yes, First Lord. May I ask what troubles you?"

"You may not."

"As you say, First Lord. Where should I tell your flight crew you will be going?"

She eyed him for a moment, fighting the urge to commandeer her own liner and kick her flight crew out, at least for this one trip. She could; she had that right, but if she could not trust the people she kept around her, then she was already fighting a losing battle. Ouroboros did their best to shatter that trust, and she would not let that continue. "Pteryga," she said, "I need to speak with First Lord Hyperion in person."

***

Second Lord Ilias left the top level of Rivka's personal tower with a confused and somewhat annoyed frown on his face. For approximately the next thirty seconds, he could allow his displeasure to show without having to worry about anyone else seeing it. He was the only person, other than Rivka herself, with access to the security feed for the top floor, and Ilias did not particularly care if she knew how he felt.

Granted, with the way she was acting, Ilias very much doubted Rivka was looking at the security feed at that moment. Something spooked her, and that was the source of Ilias's unease. In their brief time working together so far, Ilias felt he had a reasonable grasp on Rivka's personality. Others thought her soft and easy to push in one direction or the other, but very few saw the iron behind her smile or the long game she played. Ilias saw through to the steely core of her personality as soon as they met, which was probably why Lelantos recommended him to the Hexarch in the first place.

Lelantos also told him Rivka had some sort of information network in place that her security staff did not have access to. Despite being the younger brother by some fifteen years, few things passed by Lelantos without his notice. That was even more true now than it had been before Project Titan, before the chronodrug put his mind at ease.

He stepped into the lift and composed his emotions. It went down two floors, passing the armored story of the tower which housed First Lord Rivka's personal servers and security hardlines. Data fed into those computers from a variety of places, but they were the only systems— other than anything she personally brought in like the black market connector he officially knew nothing about—that could access her suite.

The next floor was occupied by the facility Ilias referred to as his "office," even though only a small part of it actually belonged to him, and that much came from his predecessor. He considered abandoning the entire floor upon taking over as her personal guard; they were *still* finding traces of Ouroboros's tampering. Any other location would have lengthened his response time when his Hexarch needed something, and so he stayed.

More importantly, though Rivka was the only one who knew this part, Ilias found the puzzle somewhat *fun*. Rooting out all of the secrets and trash left by the Ouroboros operatives who infiltrated her previous security staff gave him something to do. In fact, even now, he routinely came in an hour early every day just to search in more detail for something he might have missed.

His office, the actual office rather than the floor in general, had nothing he needed for the moment. Ilias was sure he would have to come back before leaving the planet—because Rivka was *not* leaving him here, no matter what she said—but for the moment, he had other things to deal with.

First, he thought, the pressing.

He turned to a well-groomed Second Lord. She had a spray of black and green tentacles creeping up over her jawline from the collar of her robe, but otherwise had done nothing notable with her makeup.

"Good morning, Melaina."

She smiled as he approached. "What news from the top?"

"The First Lord is going to Pteryga," he said, plainly. He might have to conceal some of his emotions here in order to put on a more professional face, but this work space was not public and he had no need to couch things in flowery niceties.

"Did she say why?"

"No." She frowned at his answer, eliciting a small laugh from Ilias. "That was my reaction as well."

"I assume you need me to vet a shuttle crew?"

Ilias nodded. "If she won't tell *me* what she's doing, these need to be people who understand discretion. Use Raven's List if you need to."

"Raven's List" was a personal project of Ilias's containing a list of people whom, in his words, he "trusted enough to give a pistol and close his eyes."

Melaina's name was on that list, and she knew what it meant. She nodded. If anything changed in her expression, it was a minor hardening around the edges of her eyes. "Understood, Security Chief."

From the next desk over, another Second Lord spoke up. A single piece of brass clockwork dominated the right side of his face, painted with exquisite detail and shading. He never did anything else, no matter what the occasion, but Ilias could not fault the practiced intricacy of the design.

"This is about Ouroboros?" he asked. His face remained fixed on the single-sided holo floating above his desk, but his eyes were raised in a questioning gesture toward where Ilias stood. The rest of the question, the unspoken part, hovered in the air between them.

Ilias chuckled quietly, then allowed that to turn into a proper laugh for a moment. "Not as far as I know."

"Sure?"

Ilias shrugged. "If it was, I'm sure the First Lord would have dealt with it herself without me."

"Just let me know."

"Of course," he replied, then started to walk away. He got a step before turning and going directly to the second man's desk. "Isocrates?"

This time he looked up from his desk, attention firmly held by the sudden shift in Ilias's tone. "Sir?"

A low wall separated Isocrates's desk from the area arbitrarily deemed "the walkway." Ilias laid his elbows against the top, leaning in to create a momentary illusion of privacy. A quick gesture summoned a pair of tall, one-way holos on either side. The room was small enough that the others could overhear their conversation, and everyone knew it. That was part of the point of the room's entire existence. The gesture was a formal indication, without taking the time to actually say it, that he did not want anyone *officially* eavesdropping on his conversation.

"I'm going to get right to be point."

"Of course."

"You know why you were chosen for this office, right?"

He nodded.

"When my brother brought the First Lord into that safe house, where did you go?"

"Sir?"

"Lelantos told me there were two of you in that room, and that he ordered you out."

Isocrates nodded. "When we realized what was going on, we joined in the crowd control effort, and later the rescue."

"And it was after midnight when you were done?"

Another nod. "My team was still operating when the Titans assaulted the Ouroboros facility."

Ilias reached into his robe. Anyone else would have stiffened at the gesture, wondering what sort of item Ilias would withdraw, and whether it would be a weapon or not. Isocrates, however, simply sat with his hands on the armrests of his chair and waited. He came from Rivka's lists and his past was, to put it lightly, colorful. Even an unexpected weapon would not cause him real alarm.

Ilias passed over a holodrive. "Here."

Isocrates raised an eyebrow. "Sir?"

"First Lord Tritogenes forwarded this to me. It was apparently compiled by his adviser, a 'Second Lord Philip.'"

"I assume that's not his real name."

Ilias shrugged. "No one I know matches that name, anyway, but it's immaterial. Tritogenes can keep his secrets. The point is that this is apparently a record of *every face* present in the Molyvos marketplace that day. Can you guess what your job is now?"

Isocrates nodded, extending a hand. "I'll get it done, sir."

"Excellent. Oh, and Second Lord?"

"Sir?"

"Quietly. This Ouroboros business is officially over. We broke them when the Titans assaulted Faros."

Isocrates nodded again, slipping the holodrive into an internal pocket in his own robe. "Understood."

Ilias straightened and dismissed the one-way holos. Now, he thought, on to the Mundane.

"Where is Kyriaki?" he asked, scanning the room.

"She's on armory duty today," came the reply from the back corner, nearest the door helpfully labeled, "ARMORY."

Ilias nodded. That was actually good news, because the next thing after talking to Kyriaki was to deal with some requisition requests for the

First Lord's trip. Even he had to go through official channels for some things.

At the armory door, Ilias tapped the password into the dim, gray holo projected there. It accepted the code, vanished, and then the retinal scanner activated. Annoying, he thought, but there were far fewer ways to bypass a retinal scanner than there were a simple passcode.

The heavy door slid into the wall on silent bearings, admitting him into the armory. If he had any doubt that it was Second Lord Kyriaki's shift in the armory, the sudden chill in the air confirmed it. Kipos might have been among the cooler planets in the binary, but it still had climate, and Second Lord Kyriaki came from a city far above the planet's arctic circle.

The room was not "cold" per se, but it was most definitely ten degrees cooler than the rest of the floor, a feat achievable thanks to the thickly armored walls.

Her voice came from somewhere in the back of the armory, behind a rack of weapons and amid the high-pitched tinking of tools. "Good morning, Chief."

"It's the middle of the afternoon."

"For you, maybe. I've only been awake for two hours."

"You're going to have to get used to palace time eventually."

"Not if I can help it," she replied. "Sir. Anyway, what can I do for you?"

"Two things, actually. Both related."

Kyriaki came around the rack of weapons, wiping her hands on a once-white apron covering the front of her blue Second Lord's robe. "I assume one of them is a requisition."

He nodded. "You assume right."

She summoned a holo, deliberately colored ice-blue in reference to the climate of her home city. "Go ahead."

"The Hexarch is heading to Pteryga in," he made a show of checking the time on his own holo, "about an hour. I need at personal weapons for myself and a few others."

"Give me a few minutes and I'll put it in. Go ahead and get what you need."

Ilias laughed. "I'm not carrying them downstairs myself."

She smiled. "Of course. I'll have them ready for pickup, then."

"Thank you."

"What was the other thing, sir?"

"Like I said, I'm going to Pteryga with her. You're in charge of the tower while we're away."

"Sir?"

"You heard me, Second Lord. Try not to freeze the others."

***

First Lord Rivka nodded with satisfaction as Ilias pointed out which shuttle they would be taking. She wore the same robe she had been wearing when they last spoke and did not appear to have packed anything extra beyond the barest necessities. Ilias approved a minimalist cargo manifest that had already been forwarded and loaded, but the thing that stood out most was the small briefcase she carried.

Despite providing her with that case, Ilias had no idea what she actually put in it. Given the strength of the latches and locks, he knew it had to be important, but that was the extent of his participation.

He did not like that.

At least, he thought, he had been able to secure reasonable transport offworld. Nestled amid the various craft was a sleek, sporty shuttle. At least, so it appeared from the outside. This particular ship once belonged to First Lord Diomedes. Few of the former First Lord's ships *looked* like they were as heavily protected as they were, and this shuttle was no exception. Ilias knew where the cannons and missiles were hidden, and even then he found it hard to spot them.

Still, he appreciated the symbolism of the polished, refined exterior that fooled the eyes into forgetting how deadly it actually was. It was, he reflected, like his Hexarch in that regard.

The engines, too, had been extensively upgraded. Not only could they put out enough thrust to push the ship's artificial gravity to—perhaps even past—its limits, it could be started and ready for takeoff in mere *minutes.*

Plus, continued Ilias's mental appraisal, if nothing else, the turquoise-hued hull concealed one of the more comfortable ships he had ever seen.

Now that they were out in the public eye, he had a part to play. Even though this was the palace's landing area, it was still a public venue. Whether by design or oversight, Rivka herself had no private place to land. Ilias was not sure he liked that, but there was little he could do unless she could be convinced to place a landing pad on the top of the tower.

And that, he thought with a smile and amusement that carefully did not reach his face, was not going to happen.

He bowed respectfully, more for the eyes of anyone nearby than for the First Lord herself, but Rivka barely acknowledged him.

Now, he really wished they were not in public so that his face could properly react to the thoughts in his brain. Rivka loved ceremony. Even amid the destruction when Ouroboros bombed Aegesander's stadium, she projected the sort of persona that people expected to see from a Hexarch.

For her to miss an opportunity to make a show of things meant that, whatever they were, her reasons for going to see Hyperion in person were still weighing heavily on her.

"Hopefully, it meets with your satisfaction, First Lord," he said, stepping forward to stand even with her. "It was the nicest I could manage on such a short notice."

"It will be sufficient. Thank you, Second Lord Ilias."

"First Lord," he began. "If I may..."

36

"You may not."

"You said that earlier," he replied. "First Lord."

"Ilias," Rivka said. "Second Lord. Please. You *cannot* ask me again."

He allowed himself to smile, just a little bit. "Because you'll tell me?"

Rivka shook her head. The small muscles in her jaw worked for a moment before she replied. "No. Because I will *fire* you, Ilias."

"Rivka, I..." He started to argue, then thought better of it. This was the Rivka from the stadium disaster, not the Rivka he saw on a daily basis. "As you say, First Lord. May I..."

She eyed him, steel and fury, for a moment before nodding almost imperceptibly.

"May I ask why?"

"I can't answer that."

"I can respect that."

"You misunderstand me, Ilias. I can't tell you because I don't yet know."

"The case?"

She nodded again. "I can't show you what's in it, because I don't know what it means, not truly, not until I speak to Hyperion. Just," she paused and finally smiled. Her eyes never changed, hard and determined, but the rest of her face rose and brightened for a moment. "You have to trust me on this."

He bowed stiffly, from the hips, but as he straightened, Ilias allowed himself to smile. His face was aimed at her, so that no one else would see the mischievous gleam in his eye. "As you say, First Lord.

She eyed him, waiting.

His grin vanished, replaced in a moment with cool professionalism. "The reverse is also true. If you say the material in that case is for Hyperion's eyes only, then it is for him alone. I will not look nor attempt to open it." His eyebrows rose. "However."

Rivka raised an eyebrow. Whether automatic or in reflection of his gesture, Ilias was not sure. "However?"

"Will the information contained in that case jeopardize your safety or the safety or anyone else?"

Rivka waited a long moment before replying. Ilias watched her eyes dance around, tracing out thoughts and potential conversation paths. He suspected she was trying to figure out the best way to answer without getting drawn into another attempt to determine the contents of the case.

More to the point, he realized as her eyes traveled across his robe and bounced to the ships parked flanking her shuttle, Rivka was likely sizing up the answer to that question even as she debated with herself whether or not to answer it in the first place.

Finally, she took a breath and said, "it shouldn't."

"Should is not a very comforting qualifier, First Lord."

"It isn't, no, but that's all I can tell you."

He nodded. "That's why we're going to see Hyperion."

Another lengthy pause, this one focused on him more than their surroundings. "Yes."

Despite his promise not to pry further, Second Lord Ilias's job was still to protect her, and his mind continued to race as they approached the shuttle. They passed the ship's security with little trouble, settling into their cabins with only minor words passing between themselves and the ship's crew.

His mind was too active to permit him to engage any more than that, even when the pilot, a man Ilias worked with before, tried to talk to him.

If Rivka was going to see another Hexarch rather than deal with it directly, and was doing so in person, it meant the problem was significant. It likely predated her own position as Hexarch. That she was going to see Hyperion specifically, rather than someone she worked with more frequently like Tritogenes, implied that whatever it was also came before his time as well. That likely included Enyalios.

That left the Council's three seniors, Hyperion chief among them. Rivka and Hyperion worked together before, so it was not strange for her to contact him, but he so rarely held actual audience in his palace that this upcoming meeting tripped a great many of Second Lord Ilias's mental warning sirens.

She also could have gone to see Aegesander, but had not. He was older, but had become rather withdrawn since the Ouroboros incident. Privately, thoughts he only ever voiced to Rivka directly, Ilias thought Aegesander had been shaken by the attack on "his" suburb. He felt the danger and threat presented by Ouroboros haunted Aegesander, as evidenced by the change in his personality over the last few days.

The problem, he realized, is that there was so much he did not know. Hyperion had been a Hexarch for nearly a century and in that time had done a great many things. Diomedes rose to the Hexarchate of Kipos before Hyperion did and reigned for nearly a century himself. Any one of them could have left behind something unsavory about which Rivka now demanded answers.

Ilias's thoughts continued like that for two full hours after boarding the ship, interrupted and put to a halt only when the craft's flight crew announced that it was time for dinner.

When he left his small cabin, he found the only-slightly larger dining area full of people. The pilot, not needed as the ship hurtled through interplanetary space between worlds, sat opposite First Lord Rivka herself. Two women, both from a short list who qualified both as guards and as general technicians, flanked them.

To Ilias's surprise, Rivka was smiling and laughing. She seemed intent on some story the pilot was telling, though Ilias only caught the tail end of it as he stepped into the ship's common area and the punchline seemed to have something to do with a naked Second Lord losing his blue robe in the ocean.

"Ilias!" Rivka called, waving him over. "Come, eat."

"You're feeling better, First Lord."

She smiled again, giving him the same familiar gleam he was used to seeing. "I am, yes. I took some time to myself, but now that we're underway, I feel like a lot of the weight has been lifted off my shoulders."

He watched her intently as the small crew maneuvered around and made room for him at the table. One of the guards-slash-technicians reached behind her and produced a place of food and a canned drink from an alcove in the wall. She placed it at the newly empty spot.

As Ilias sat, he realized something that simultaneously gave him a swell of pride and sent a cold shiver through his stomach.

Rivka, he realized, was not acting. She actually was feeling better after that short passage of time. She still possessed the information that spurred this sudden trip to Pteryga, and it still hung like a shadow over her. She was not putting aside her worry or ignoring it only to let it crush her later.

He opened his can and drank, watching his Hexarch, his charge, for a moment more. No, Ilias realized, all of that worry and concern and *terror* remained. But through it all, First Lord Rivka was still smiling.

Chapter 3

"Mastigas ship location confirmed," crackled the voice on Victoria's intercom. She sat in the tight confines of her assault shuttle which, along with shuttles housing the other five Titans, was clamped to the underside of the *Hammer of Ares*.

She had been sitting in that spot, waiting for that exact announcement, for two hours now. The ship contained her gear and just enough water and air to last for the trip to and from the mastigas ship. Sheathed in First Lord Enyalios's most advanced armor and with just enough internal space to house the engine and stealth systems, the tiny shuttles did not exactly offer much in the way of comfort.

Once they launched, the ships ought to be stealthy enough for even the most advanced Technocrat systems to have difficulty tracking them. With no hard data on the mastigas ship's capabilities, it was as good as they could manage.

Victoria hoped it would be enough.

Already, the six of them were arranged close to their final orientation. Her ship sat at the front of the formation with the other four smallest shuttles forming a square. At the center, Daniel's ship dwarfed the others. The Aegis, in excess of five times more massive than any human occupant, was equally larger than the ships "flown" by the other Titans.

Victoria looked over her shoulder, somehow expecting to see the larger ship directly behind her. Instead, a bank of glittering indicator lights greeted her. Those lights, all a cool amber at the moment, offered the only semblance of control she had over her ship. In reality, very little she did could affect the ship; all of that was being handled from the comfort of the *Hammer of Ares*.

Ahead of them, the engine flares from the battlecruisers that were to escort them close to the mastigas warship stretched across her vision. Directly ahead, the huge troop carrier *Justice* lurked at the center of their formation.

Though long, their flight was hardly to be absent of work, however. Victoria was already setting up a strategy game from her holo to keep the other Titans busy and their minds awake.

The voice of the carrier's flight controller continued, "requesting manual system's check."

Victoria pushed the hologame to the side for a few minutes and ran through the checklist of things she had to do to prep the craft for launch. Over the last two days, the six of them had been drilled over and over again on what they needed to know about their shuttles. It should have been a three-week training program, but with the chaos surrounding Ouroboros and the mastigas battleship's assault trajectory, their training sequence had been cut somewhat short. Fortunately, the trip was also short, and and the sequence had become second nature.

"Second Lord Titan Helena, system check complete." Helena finished the entire check as Victoria herself was barely past the first item.

As the minutes rolled by, Daniel reported in second, followed by Panatakis. Victoria reached the end of her checklist and double-checked the final indicator less than thirty seconds later. Korakti and Lelantos confirmed their readiness nearly simultaneously afterward.

The flight controller said, "all ships confirmed. Central control active. Prepare for detach in sixty."

A small shudder ran through the ship as the gravity of the carrier dropped away, leaving her in the meager gravity of her shuttle. Purpose built for the mission at hand, the ship maintained the bare minimum for life support and stealth. Artificial gravity was not exactly considered a "luxury item" per se, but the generators had been stripped of all but the minimum required to ensure proper cardiac function.

Victoria laced her fingers together in her lap. The designers had thoughtfully left her what she had been told was a normal control setup for a ship of that size, but the sticks and buttons were disabled as long as the *Hammer* had control.

Thirty seconds ticked by as she coasted on the momentum imparted by the speed of the massive carrier. Like operation of the ship itself, this was a sequence that had been drilled into her mind over and over. Thirty seconds passed—she counted them with practiced precision—before the shuttle's thrusters lit off.

Acceleration pushed her backward. The cushion of the specially-designed chair was filled with little pockets of gel that molded and conformed to her body as the force of gravity abruptly shifted direction and drove itself into her chest like a hammer.

Their training had included harsher g-forces than she currently experienced, g-forces endured without the aid of the acceleration chair's dampening effect. Like everything else, that training had been severely truncated. The preparation did little more than let her know what to expect, and she fought to stay awake and keep the edges of her vision from graying as the ship rocketed forward.

She should have had a flight suit. Pilots of craft that were regularly subjected to the sorts of forces she was under now, typically racers or stunt-fliers, would have had a pressure suit to force the blood out of their extremities and back into their brains.

The six Titans had no such pressure suits. They were bulky and hard to move in outside the cockpit. With no real data on the interior of the mastigas ship, none of them knew what they would be getting into once they reached their destination. For all anyone knew, every square meter of the ship would be crawling with mastigas that would ambush them the moment they stepped out of their ships. In that sort of environment, a flight suit would be more of a liability than a help.

So, they did without, and Victoria resisted the urge to grit her teeth against the immense weight threatening to pancake her ribcage. Except for Daniel, already ensconced in his combat armor, each of them would be experiencing the same thing. That thought brought some comfort, albeit rather slight.

Then, as quickly as it came, the crushing weight stopped. The blood rushed, pounding, back into her head as inertia threw her against the seat's restraints in exactly the opposite direction.

"All ships report," ordered the flight controller.

Barely three seconds passed before she heard another click and, "Titan Helena reporting all systems green."

"Titan Victoria reporting." She spoke through teeth gritted in pain, but she would not be the last to reply. "All systems showing green."

Victoria sat there, panting, for several moments as the others gave nearly identical reports. Her forehead was dotted with little bits of sweat, so intense had been her exertion against the g-forces threatening to crush her body. Then, as everything returned to normal and her head quit pounding, she let out the last of the tense breath she had been holding while her shuttle accelerated.

It would happen again, she knew, but the final burn would hopefully be less intense than this one had been. The exact nature and timing of the maneuver would depend on the mastigas ship's defenses. The heavier they were, the faster their six shuttles and the large transport full of soldiers would have to come in.

"*Justice* reporting in," came the voice of the transport's captain. Its acceleration had been less intense than that of the tiny shuttles, and it now dropped behind them. "Burn successful, CIC. We are on target. Expect arrival in approximately six-point-two-five hours from now."

Following the troop transport, their escort ships reported in. As they did, Victoria tried not to think of the thousands of people aboard those ships. Their job would be to draw the fire of the mastigas ship and keep attention on themselves rather than the "more important" ships containing the Titans and soldiers.

"All ships' status confirmed," their flight controller replied once the long string of replies ended. "We will update you as we close with the mastigas ship. All forces: go with the suns."

"Go with the suns," Victoria found herself replying automatically, despite knowing that no one would hear her with her microphone turned off.

Silence fell, and her mind focused on the people around her. As the minutes ticked by, she found them to be harder and harder to ignore. The danger to Victoria herself was concern enough, but it was eclipsed by the overwhelming feelings directed at the people around her. Not just the Titans, but the entire complement of the *Justice*. It was the danger to them that hung over her like a guillotine.

To put her nerves at ease, she shifted around in her seat to a more comfortable position in which to ride out the ballistic part of her journey and called up her holo. Despite planning the training simulation, she found little desire to begin it now. Instead, she told herself she would read—if she was going into certain death, Victoria would at least do it with a slightly shorter to-read list.

A picture of herself with Pallasophia greeted her first, the last thing she looked at before locking herself in the cramped confines of the shuttle. A fond smile crossed her lips as she dismissed the picture. It resumed its place off to one side of her main menu. Amid red text—the same red deliberately chosen to match her first memories—she navigated to the program that held her electronic library, found a book, and started to read.

For the next hour, nothing passed the armored window of her cockpit but the stars. Those cold lights were so far away that they seemed to not be moving at all, which created a sense of frustrating stillness. She knew the ship was moving, but every one of her senses told her the exact opposite.

An hour and a half after the end of their initial burn, she saw it. The mastigas ship hung in space, a dot barely the size of her thumbnail. She raised a hand, blotting it out for a moment, feeling a surge of power as she did so.

Victoria looked down at the holographic display floating above her lap. She marked her place in the book she had been reading and shut down the application, replacing it instead with the tactical feed from the carrier, relayed through the *Justice*. It showed the relative positions of the six shuttles, the massive troop transport, and their dozen escorts.

What the display did not show, at first, was the mastigas ship. She had to adjust the scale to include the distant behemoth. It hung nine-hundred and fifty thousand kilometers away, somewhere between four and eight hours of travel before they reached it, depending on the speed at which the shuttles would approach.

At one end of the enormous, three kilometer ship, the engines burned with a baleful blue glow. When they first came within a million kilometers, that flare stretched across the sky like a comet. It faded over the next half hour as the ship turned toward them, coming to meet them with the inevitability of stone.

Even with their best sensor resolution, the three-kilometer ship was too distant to make out any detail. It just sat there, a gray shape longer than it was wide, waiting on their approach. She had seen it up close, or at least images taken from a very long way away with very good cameras, and had a general idea of what it would look like as they drew closer.

The mastigas ship's three kilometer length was end-to-end only. Its width was a fraction of that size. From top to bottom, it was even thinner, scarcely more than twenty-five meters in places, though scans seemed to indicate that the interior of the ship in those areas was perhaps two or three decks flanked top and bottom by several meters of solid armor and defensive weaponry.

At the engine end loomed a large pyramid some hundred meters above the rest of the ship at the peak. That pyramid housed some of the strongest energy emissions detected from the ship, and everyone involved in planning the mission agreed that it was likely that there the mastigas housed their control systems. Even if they were wrong about that, it was close to the engines, and if the only thing they accomplished was destroying them, the mastigas would pose far less of a threat.

Her intercom clicked on, a message from flight control. The first part was redundant, but she supposed it would come in handy if any other others were sleeping. The rest, however, gave her chills. "The mastigas ship has changed course and is headed toward our ships. Be advised: this is inconsistent with previous behavior. We will not abort the mission. Expect an updated trajectory in five minutes with a new burn to follow."

Exactly on schedule, her holographic display updated. Her new course would take her shuttle to where it would intercept the mastigas ship's path far ahead of its current location. From there, the display noted a second burn to bring them back on target for an intercept with the actual ship itself.

The escort ships, she noticed, would be following a radically different pattern. Their courses, outlined in blue relative to the green of the shuttles and the yellow of the troop transport, spiraled around the massive ship, constantly intercepting the paths of the shuttles to provide as much cover fire as they could once they drew closer.

The transport was vastly larger than even the armed escort ships. Unlike them, it could not maneuver as easily, and its new heading lacked the nuance of the shuttle's paths. The yellow line that represented its course simply curved straight for the mastigas ship. Victoria suspected it would be coming in under constant thrust until the last possible moment, but odds were good that she and the other Titans would be doing something similar.

Data indicated a small-craft launch area at the base of the pyramid. That was their primary goal. If that failed, the escort ships were to blow open a section of the hull and allow the Titans and the *Justice* to enter that way. Concentrated missile fire with bleeding-edge guidance systems ought to be able to penetrate even the battleship's thick armor.

Her electronics shut down automatically for the new burn. The first few seconds were relatively light. The shuttle pivoted swiftly on every one of its axes at once. Those few seconds of wheeling stars gave her more of a sensation of movement than anything else so far.

Gravity and motion disappeared for six long seconds as the computers confirmed the new heading. Then the engines lit off again, subjecting her to the worst acceleration thus far, and Victoria struggled to retain consciousness against the gray hand of the gods that had taken hold of her ribs. The thought or even reflex of breathing was the last thing on her mind as everything before her eyes turned gray.

When she opened her eyes again, she had a vague recollection of a feeling of floating and fuzziness, but otherwise she was motionless. The stars outside were static, or they seemed that way, at least. She first checked her ribs to make sure the intense g-forces had not broken any of them.

One by one, she confirmed that her ribs and sternum were indeed still whole. She then turned to the second item on her new to-do list and reactivated her computer. Two minutes had passed, though she had no idea how much of that time had been spent under acceleration and how much passed with her simply listing there, unaware of the waking world.

Third on her to-do list, she keyed the intercom. Her tongue felt swollen, but she was able to manage a relatively clear, "Titan Victoria reporting all systems green. I must have passed out during the burn."

"You and most of the others," flight control replied. "Green status confirmed. Thank you, Titan."

Last on her list, she reconnected to the tactical display, wondering how much she had missed. Each of the ships was on target, a good sign of a successful burn.

More important, at least for the moment, was the status of their escort ships. Some time ago, they had passed into missile range and began bombarding the mastigas ship with long-range firepower. Many dozens of missiles streaked away from their escort ships, rendered as faint blue lines with a single white dot to mark the current position of the missile. They could fire more at once easily, but the goal was to maintain a constant state of attack to distract the ship more than it was to destroy it—previous missions and larger ships had tried and failed at that approach and they would not waste their time trying again.

The first missile volley had not yet reached the mastigas ship, but the escorts were already launching the second. From the look of the display, they would likely be able to launch a third volley before the first one struck its target.

The display also now included a countdown timer. Before the last burn, the ships at their previous speed would have taken four hours to reach the mastigas. Now, especially with the ship coming toward them as well, the time was down under two hours. The option to accelerate again was still there, but all that would depend on how heavy the mastigas ship's defenses were.

Looking at the display again, a blossom of faint red lines erupted from the huge ship. There were more than she cared to try and count just then, certainly more missiles were headed their way than they were firing at their enemy.

Victoria had been promised that the shuttles would be too small and stealthy to easily target. If the mastigas saw her at all, she was a tiny target compared to the larger attack ships. Combined with the escort ship's distraction and defenses, she knew intellectually that she had very little to fear from the cloud of missiles headed her way.

That knowledge did nothing to stop the cold pit in her stomach as she, despite her desire not to, counted thirteen sets of ten missiles coming from the mastigas.

Out the window, the flares of the missiles' drives radiated away from the ships that had launched them. Two clusters of blue streaks led back to the Technocrat ships while flares like the spokes of a wheel pointed back at the mastigas ship.

All she had to do now was wait, and she suspected it would be the hardest two hours of her life.

***

Victoria's ship had just made its last course correction when her intercom crackled to life. The previous burn had not been quite as intense as the one before it, and she had managed to retain her grip on consciousness through it all. Despite that, it still took her a moment to come completely to her senses and realize exactly what the buzzing noise at the edge of her awareness actually was.

She flipped the switch that would open the communications channel without checking to see who it was. She assumed it would be flight control; no one else should have had access to the comm system. So, when the voice that came across her radio was not flight control, she sat up a fraction straighter, despite the protestations of her pounding head.

"Spatharios Victoria, this is Second Lord Helena."

"Helena?" Victoria asked, clearing the last of the g-force-induced haze from her brain. "I thought only the carrier could broadcast."

"It was a simple matter to alter the lock on the system," she replied. "I apologize if my message comes as a surprise so soon after our last acceleration period, but there is news I believe you must hear."

"Why me?"

"You are our commander, are you not?" Before Victoria could reply, Helena continued, "in any case, I will convey the same message to the other four momentarily."

"What is it?"

"For the past several hours, I have been listening to the radio chatter aboard the carrier and the troop ship. There's not been very much of interest. Truthfully, I tapped into their comm system because I was bored and wanted to listen to something."

"Why is this important?" Victoria asked, hoping she that did not sound quite as short as it felt.

"My apologies, Spatharios. I believe there is information not currently being shared with us that we all should know."

"Patch it through, then."

"One moment."

Her comm went dead. Not only did the channel to Helena's ship go silent, her entire comm system shut itself off. The indicator light on her system analysis board showed the angry red light of a deactivated system.

A minute passed and she found the single, unchanging red light on her console more riveting than the byplay of missiles and drive flares outside her window.

She started to worry. If Helena had been wrong about her ability to hotwire her systems from a distance, then Victoria was now left completely out of touch with everyone else. More important, if her communications were shut down, she had no idea what that meant for any future maneuvering burns they would have to do. At best, she would have no warning for her engines activating. Worse, though, was the thought that her engines might not activate at all, leaving her with no choice but to try and break the locks on her own systems and manually pilot the shuttle to its destination.

And Victoria had no idea how to do that.

A small window flickered into existence amid her holographic control panel. A line of text above two simple buttons read, "Manual Control of Communications System Active. Confirm?"

Victoria touched the projection reading "yes" and the window disappeared. A few more seconds passed before the angry red "deactivated" light turned green again. This time when it reappeared, the plain light came on with a small triangular symbol in the center, signifying manual control of the system.

The hotwired system came on with slightly less clarity than it had before, and Victoria wondered what Helena had actually done to unlock control of the system. It buzzed and popped for several moments like an antique analogue radio.

When the the radio signal finally cleared itself, the captain of the *Hammer of Ares* itself was speaking. That channel had been reserved for the captains of the various ships and Victoria wondered, again, how Helena managed to access it, let alone allow everyone to listen in.

"...ay again, *Justice*. Our sensors aren't seeing what you're seeing."

Victoria marveled at the apparent lack of formality between the two captains. They were both Second Lords, but it seemed to her that they still ought to be discussing things with more propriety. Of course, she thought as she considered the behavior of the soldiers she met when Pallasophia came to bring her out of the labyrinth, perhaps that was simply how equally-ranked military officers spoke to one another.

Her attempts as understanding the captain's tone almost distracted her from the troop ship's reply. It came back equally informal, colored with confusion and barely-controlled alarm.

"Three points on the mastigas ship just lit up, sir. Each spot is putting out more thermal and electromagnetic radiation than the rest of the ship combined, engines included."

"Can you identify what's causing the energy spike?"

"Negative. Two spikes are situated on opposite ends of the bow face of the ship, and the third atop that pyramid. The signature doesn't match anything we have on file."

"One moment, *Justice*, while we patch into your sensor feed."

"Affirmative."

The line went silent. After the first minute with neither ship speaking, Victoria started to navigate around her controls. The settings that enabled remote control of her shuttle by the carrier's flight control were well labeled. She made sure to stay far away from them, not wanting to risk even a stray movement altering the state of the controls.

The more she dug, the more she discovered that had been modified by whatever it was Helena had done to her system. More than the communications system had been placed under manual control. In fact, as she looked through menu after menu, it seemed that every system had been unlocked. Most of them remained under remote control, but she could deactivate that at any moment. What interested her most, however, was the discovery that she was now able to control what information she saw about the battle around her.

She toggled the display to show her the maximum available sensor information, and waited. Rather than appearing solely in the little control area above her knees, a handful of holoprojectors scattered around the cockpit hummed to life. They covered the windows with projected data that matched the ships and events she was seeing outside. Another display activated, this one above and slightly further away from her than the main controls, that showed the entire area. It showed much the same information as she had been seeing, only now the display was fully-three dimensional and could be rotated to show different perspectives on the battlefield.

The synthesized data that made up the map in front of her was interesting in its own right. However, there was very little she could actually do with it. It showed the positions of the Technocrat attack force and the mastigas ship, all of which were separated by much less distance than they had been when she first brought up that information hours ago.

What actually interested her was the augmented view through her windows. Each of their ships had been overlaid with key information about it. She knew, or had known before such information became secondary to things pertaining to her own ship, the names of every ship out there. Now, not just their names, but information about their energy and ammunition reserves populated the tags.

Currently, her shuttle was on one side of their formation. The others were too small and too far away to see with her unaided eyes, but the overlay pointed them out as little bullet-shaped icons. Helena was directly to her right and closest, with Panatakis opposite her. Lelantos and Daniel were above her, currently following an angular trajectory that would put them on their final approach paths as they drew closer. Korakti's ship was out of view, indicated by a little arrow labeled with her name at the bottom of her window.

To her left, the mammoth silhouette of the *Justice* cruised on its silent path. Spiraling around all seven ships were their escorts. The information overlaid on her windows told her that the four escorts in her view had taken their share of damage—with a gesture, she could pull up even more information on each ship, including what sort of damage it had taken and where, and the current status of any or all of its systems—but none of them were in real danger.

Victoria decided to see exactly how much control she now had over her systems, communication especially. She paged through the menu, trying to recall the single lesson they all had been given on the use of the system. Much like thruster control, their radios were supposed to be controlled from the carrier and what little instruction they had been given focused on how to reestablish that connection. Failing that, they had been taught how to operate the navigation systems, but the communications had been glossed over out of a need for completion more than an actual desire to teach any of them how to use it.

Fortunately, it was not a complicated system. With the radio controls active, everything was grouped according to what audience the message should have. She navigated through to select an individual ship, then Helena's shuttle.

A moment passed while the computers, likely still running through whatever bypass Helena put in place, connected the two ships. A little light came on in the holographic display next to the words "channel established."

"Helena?"

The reply was full of static, but it was easy enough to hear the other Titan's voice. Despite the slight distortion, she thought she detected a bit of amusement in the Second Lord's voice. "Titan Victoria. I see you devised the secret to controlling your systems."

"I did, yes. How did you manage to undo the locks on everything?"

A pause, then, "it was fairly easy. I would not bore you with the technical details. Suffice it to say that security that is sufficient for a normal person is still no match for my skill. It was, however, tougher to crack these systems than those Ouroboros put in place."

"You couldn't have hacked the system to have better signal clarity?" Victoria asked, grinning with amusement.

"These shuttles were not designed to allow easy communication, especially with one another. The static is an artifact of hardware limitations, not software."

"I was joking, Helena."

Another pause, then, "I understand now. You're feeling tense, I suppose?"

"Right now, 'bored' is more like it. I knew we would be sitting in these shuttles for hours, but that doesn't make it any more enjoyable."

"How have you been passing the time?"

"Reading," Victoria replied. She was about to say more when the sounds from Helena's shuttle abruptly shifted to the right side of her cockpit. The conversation passing between the carrier and the troop transport came from the left-side speakers.

"*Hammer of Ares*, this is the *Justice*. Those energy readings we were getting before just spiked again. Tell me you have something on the analysis."

"Negative, *Justice*."

"Dark take it, these sensors are brand new," cursed the *Justice*'s captain. He apologized a moment later. "Sorry, sir."

The mission commander replied from the *Hammer of Ares*. He seemed unperturbed by the *Justice*'s outburst. "Our analysis is incomplete, but at present it seems to confirm yours. Your initials scans were thorough and, we're afraid to say, told us exactly nothing."

"Orders?"

"You're far past the point where aborting the mission would be easy or safe, *Justice*. Continue under previous orders."

"Sir?"

A moment passed, then, "I'll be instructing the battlecruisers to begin single-point bombardment."

"Understood."

The conversation between the two large ships cut out and the background noises from Helena's ship returned to both sets of speakers.

"Do you have any idea what they're detecting?" Victoria asked.

"I do not," Helena replied. "Much like our communication systems, these ships have very limited sensor range. With time, I might be able to narrow the focus to 'scan' the ship, but that is a process that would take more time than we have left."

"Can you guess?"

"Guess?" Helena echoed. "I do not 'guess.'"

"You did well enough during the Ouroboros incident coming up with alternate explanations and ideas."

"There is a difference between expounding upon given data and finding alternate explanations for it. I have no data, thus I have nothing to expound upon."

"What do..."

Victoria never finished her question because the next moment she found herself unable to tear her eyes away from the sight in front of her. Now that they were fairly close, the mastigas ship had swelled to take up most of her view. In reality, it looked even less inviting than the computer generated model she had seen during training.

The front of the ship faced her now, a sort of squashed triangle or pentagon many times wider than it was tall. Strange red lights shimmered on the flat face of the ship, giving the entire surface the ominous glow of a distant wildfire.

Overhead, augmented by the data flowing across the window as the ships moved, several of their escort ships were trading missile volleys with launchers situated near the middle of the mastigas ship.

All of that paled in comparison to the thing that actually caught her attention. Three points of light, exactly where the troop ship reported the strange energy bursts, had appeared on the mastigas ship. True to the report, two of them were on opposite ends of the wide, flat front face, and the third glowed like a distant beacon atop the pyramid.

Unconsciously, Victoria found herself straining against her seat restraints in an attempt to lean forward for a better view. Even if she could have moved, the gesture was meaningless given the vast distance separating her from the mastigas ship.

A moment passed in tense silence. Absently, some part of her brain noticed that she was still connected to Helena's ship. She could hear the woman's breathing, but no words passed between them.

As the hair on the back of her neck started to stick up, Victoria wondered if Helena was as glad just to have the illusion of physical company as she was.

The light atop the pyramid flared brighter for a moment before a long red line sprang into being between it and the tag labeled *Phobos*.

The battlecruiser at the other end of the bright line crumbled and then exploded in a matter of moments.

Victoria's heart hammered in her chest. She had never seen a weapon like that, nor had it been anywhere in their briefing material. Nothing in any of the material she had ever seen concerning the mastigas or their ship held records of a weapon like the one that destroyed an escort battlecruiser in a matter of seconds.

Her hands wrapped around the useless controls as a single thought raced through her mind. The *Hammer of Ares*'s captain was right: there was no turning back anymore.

Chapter 4

The comm system erupted with a dozen voices, all scrambling to be heard.

"The *Phobos* has been destroyed!"

"...matter of seconds!"

"What do we..."

"...ot to retre..."

"Orders? Orders, damn it!"

The bustle only intensified when the two lights, the two *weapons*, mounted on the bow of the massive ship flared and then fired. The indicators for the *Pyros* and the *Abraxas* disappeared from her window.

Victoria mentally blotted out the shouting voices, focusing instead on her sensors. Helena said they might be able to narrow the sweep to get a better picture of what she was looking at. The radar itself was nothing but static and distortion. That made it obvious exactly how much energy those weapons were putting out. It also meant that any plan she might have been about to form regarding scanning the ship was dead before it could even be put in motion.

A voice cut through the din. Victoria wondered how the captain did it—her voice was easily twice as loud as any of the others. It rang and echoed inside Victoria's cockpit. "This is the *Deimos*," the voice barked. "All cruisers target those weapons. Our first priority is still to protect the Titans, but if you can get a firing solution on them, unload everything you have on those three energy sources."

"The *Deimos* is correct," added the deep voice of the *Hammer of Ares*'s captain. Victoria marveled at how he could sound so calm and collected considering what was going on. The *Diemos*'s captain had not sounded afraid, but angry. In contrast, the captain of their carrier, while he did not sound relaxed, sounded much less moved by the carnage.

Perhaps, she thought, he was too far removed. Though, for Victoria, a distance like that would make it all the *more* painful. More likely, he was simply good at his job.

A quick adjustment to her radar display cleaned up the information tremendously at the expense of a loss of overall data by patching through the escort ships' systems. The signal from the *Diemos* was strongest, which probably explained how the captain was able to cut through everyone else.

Victoria's stomach dropped as the weapon at the top of the pyramid started to glow again. She could see the *Diemos* front of her and slightly off to the upper right. It was rolling rapidly along its long axis, shifting out of place as quickly as it could without sacrificing forward momentum. She knew it would be the next target. The message it broadcast had required so much extra energy that it would have been, for a few moments, the easiest target for whatever tracking system the mastigas had.

Despite knowing it was coming, Victoria could not tear her eyes away from the *Diemos* even as the red light lanced into it like it had the *Phobos*. Its evasive maneuvering helped, but as the ship spun to one side with a string of explosions ripping apart one flank, she knew it had only prolonged the inevitable for a few moments longer.

The bright blue trail of a missile slammed into the gaping wound in the *Diemos*'s side. For a heart-stopping moment, Victoria thought that maybe this particular missile out of all the hundreds that had been traded thus far might be a dud. Her brain entertained the idea that, for one reason or another, this missile might not explode.

That moment ended with a flash of light that burned an afterimage into her retinas and the "*Diemos*" indicator vanished from her screen.

By now, the front of the mastigas ship was past her view. Some part of her brain recognized that that was a good thing. She and anyone even with her was safe from the two weapons at the front of the ship. The third still maintained a full field of fire, but the slight pressure against her chest told her that their flight controller had turned on her engines to bring the shuttles closer to the surface of the ship. Low enough, and they might be able to escape the wrath of that weapon.

Her radio cracked to life again. "This is the *Justice*. We are going to maximum thrust. Recommend the shuttles do the same. All battlecruisers target Point Iota on the mastigas ship."

"Message confirmed, *Justice*," replied their flight controller.

The big troop transport surged ahead of her shuttle as the pyramid fired again. This time it held a sustained burst that it swept across the stars like a sword. Victoria's stomach sank as two explosions answered and two more name tags, the *Konabos* and the *Aethon*, vanished from existence.

A moment passed and the red beam lanced out at her ship, close enough to fry her sensors and temporarily blind her with its sunlike brightness.

She hammered the communications key, heedless of whether or not her message was going out to all the ships around them or just the Titans. "All shuttles report."

One by one, they all answered her and she breathed a bone-deep sigh of relief. The shuttles maneuvered through a series of harsh turns as space around them erupted into hellfire. The explosions from the mastigas's missiles spread out as the shuttles put as much distance between themselves as their speed allowed.

Victoria's stomach tried to rip its way past her lungs as the shuttle spun and abruptly shifted direction. For a heart-stopping moment, she was frozen in space. The ship had made a complete one-eighty along its short axis and the *Justice* dominated her view. Below, the battleship's hull continued to flow past, backwards now.

That lasted all of a moment before her ship jerked sideways again, riding on a wave of nuclear fire.

The explosion rocked her little ship, and a number of systems indicator lights in the cockpit went red. It also turned her ship through another half circle, bringing its axis of thrust back in line with its forward direction. Off to the right, the indicator for Lelantos's shuttle streaked ahead of her.

Her ship rolled, bringing Daniel's large shuttle into view. That sight buoyed her for a moment, but then her eyes snap-focused on the long streamer of light pointed at his shuttle like a laser.

"Daniel!" she screamed.

Victoria slammed the communication switch, but the indicator light burned a steady red. It taunted her, sitting there and leering its silence.

"Close your eyes, my friend," she whispered. Victoria was unable to take her own advice.

No wreckage remained of Daniel's shuttle when the hateful glare of nuclear fire subsided.

Victoria had no idea how much time passed while she sat there, too numb to scream or curse. Finally, her comm indicator light turned from red to amber.

"...ent... Sel... uide him," muttered Lelantos, apparently unaware he was still speaking to the rest of the team on an open mic.

The light turned green and Panatakis's voice came across clearly. "What are your orders?"

Another one of the red beams lanced past her ship and, this time, Victoria cursed.

"Spatharios," Helena said. Her voice cut through the red haze in Victoria's mind. "Give us orders."

"We finish the mission," she replied. Victoria knew her voice was cold. None of the fury she felt reached her lips, or perhaps all of it did. Perhaps the icy certainty that frosted her every word was in fact the result of the unutterable rage building deep within her.

***

Sixty percent of their assault force had been decimated and the Titans were not yet to their target. An hour ago, the *Balios* had not been the only one of their battlecruisers following its original path toward the mastigas warship.

Thirty minutes ago, the *Abraxas* had guarded their lower-right flank and the *Phobos* their upper-left.

Just five minutes ago, the *Balios* had been joined by the *Boreas*, the only other one of their battlecruisers headed for Point Iota to survive. The other two, the *Skylla* and the *Phlogeus* were elsewhere, defending the *Justice* from the massive ship's frontal cannons.

"Mastigas targeting active!"

The announcement tore Second Lord Dafni's attention away from the ship's primary holodisplay long enough to acknowledge it. Her mind went to work even as her eyes settled back on the projection of their positions relative to the juggernaut they were sent to stop.

"Target?" she asked. Her voice was quiet, barely louder than the hum of machinery around her, but it carried well enough. No one else on the bridge had spoken an unnecessary word since the destruction of the *Phobos*.

"It's targeting the *Justice*."

"And the bow cannons?"

"Hard to determine through all the interference, but telemetry from the *Skylla* indicates those are also targeting the *Justice*."

"Understood. Target the pyramid's peak."

"Sir, our orders are..."

"Dark take our orders!" Dafni snapped. "Those are *your* orders."

"Captain?" Second Lord Phoibe asked. It was the first thing she said some time. Her eyes never left her own holo, but a copy of her workspace appeared alongside Dafni's own. The targeting data showed a series of targets beginning with the peak of the pyramid and following a straight line to the *Justice*.

"Explain."

"We have no data on that weapon, but it appears to be some sort of directed energy emitter. A laser, but impossibly more powerful. I believe enough energy and radiation in its path may affect the next blast."

Second Lord Dafni nodded. "Do it."

The bridge fell silent for several minutes as she uploaded the targeting data and fired a full volley into the path of the mastigas superweapon. The point of the pyramid began to glow again, impossibly bright now that they were close, and moments later, the now-horribly-familiar red lance speared outward.

This time, however, the beam fizzled and twisted. Each time it passed through the remnants of one of the *Balios*'s nuclear warheads, it grew fainter and more dispersed. When the twisted, pale shadow impacted the *Justice*, it did little more than blacken a section of the transport's armor.

The *Balios*'s bridge erupted in cheers for several seconds. Even Captain Dafni felt herself getting swept up in things, which was the moment she put an end to the celebrations. They had lost too many ships to take their eyes off the battle for even a second.

The other bridge officers, to their credit, did not grumble. Rather, they knew the same Damoclean sword hung over their heads, and they acknowledged her orders without protest.

"Time until optimal range to Point Iota?"

"Ninety seconds from..." Second Lord Klytie replied. A moment passed, and she added, "now."

Dafni nodded. "Estimated recharge time on the superweapon?"

"Four minutes and," another pause, "ten seconds."

Dafni nodded. She carefully kept any trace of her thoughts from her face. That would give them roughly two and a half minutes until the mastigas ship fired again. Once they opened fire on Point Iota, she knew her survival odds were exactly fifty percent.

The next shot would either destroy the *Boreas* or it would destroy her.

"Once we're in range," she began, speaking slowly and with careful control over her words and tone, "I want all weapons to target Point Iota."

"Understood."

Point Iota had been chosen because what little data they had on the battleship seemed to indicate a thin spot in its armor. She shared the prevailing theory that it was some sort of shuttle bay or small craft hanger that had been added before the raid on Kipos five years before. It was better armored, but less defended by missile tubes than the so-called "main" launch bay that had been the Titans' original target.

She allowed herself to frown at the display, eyes riveted on Point Iota. She had not been on Kipos at the time, but her parents lived in an outer colony called Kythira when the mastigas arrived thirty years ago.

She and one of her fathers survived the attack, crammed into a tiny shuttle with five times too many people as they limped along to Prosgeiosi. Her other parents and one older sibling were not so lucky.

"Target point reached," Second Lord Klytie announced. "Nav, begin strafing maneuvers."

"Understood."

The ship turned, allowing it to accelerate perpendicular to its previous path. It also began rotating, allowing a constant stream of missiles to be fired from the flank of the ship closest to the mastigas.

Stopping on a dime was, of course, impossible in deep space, but their current path would make a series of long, looping circles around the mastigas. With luck, the *Boreas* would take a similar path, dumping as many missiles into Point Iota as they could.

She watched the holographic representation of her ship as it circled the much larger mastigas battleship. The lines indicating her missiles lengthened as it began the first loop, but they were so close that nearly seventy-five percent reached the battleship's hull. Of those, a full fifty percent stayed on course and impacted Point Iota directly.

A minute passed, and curiosity struck.

"Status of our point defenses?" Dafni asked.

"Few missiles are targeting us right now, Captain. Most are aimed at the *Justice* and the remaining Titans."

Her heart sank at that turn of phrase: *remaining* Titans. If they were dead, what hope did her little battlecruiser have?

The report continued. "But we're achieving one-hundred percent coverage. At present, the only danger is..."

Second Lord Klytie interrupted. "The peak cannon is charging, Captain."

Dafni nodded. "Status of Point Iota's armor?"

"Uncertain at this point, Captain. The *Boreas* has opened fire as well, but interference is preventing a clear image of the target area. Blast analysis indicates that the area is still intact, however."

She nodded again, regarded the plot for a moment longer as the *Balios* looped back around. In moments, they would be once again at optimal distance.

Second Lord Dafni rose. What she had to say felt like it should be delivered from her feet, not from a chair.

"When we come around again, I want to target Point Iota with everything we have, including the point defense cannons. I am aware that such an action will leave us defenseless, but our job is not to preserve our own lives, but to ensure the Titans and the *Justice* reach their target."

The responses came back immediately. They were quiet, but she could not detect a single note of fear in any of them.

"As you say, Captain."

She remained standing as the first mastigas missile impacted the *Balios*. The ship shuddered, but continued firing. After the second impact, the missiles beating her ship apart became too numerous to count.

Dafni watched the status indicators for her ship dwindle. Engine efficiency, firing rate, armor, all of it drained away to nearly zero as she watched.

When she spoke, her voice cracked. No one acknowledged it. "Status of Point Iota's armor?"

"It's breaking up, Captain," replied Second Lord Klytie. Her voice was nothing but steel, anger and fury distilled into a few words. "We did it."

"We did it," someone echoed.

"The weapon is targeting us."

"I know."

"Ten seconds."

"Thank you, Klytie. It's been an hon—"

***

Victoria looked at her display, cold and helpless. Only three of the battlecruisers still survived. The other seven had been destroyed either directly assaulting the mastigas battleship or in defense of the Titans and the *Justice*. At that latter task, they still failed. Daniel was dead, atoms scattered to the interstellar wind, mingling even now with the ashes of thousands of other human souls.

The only bright spot was that the odds of the rest of them reaching their target were much higher now. The entire task group had now circled the massive ship, coming at it from behind where the nightmare weapons on the bow end could not reach.

Not long now and the mastigas would die.

On her holo, Point Iota loomed just a short ways out. The assault from the *Balios*—no, she corrected herself, the *sacrifice* by the *Balios*—finally put a substantial crack in the mastigas ship's armor. It was small, too small to enter yet, but the opening had been created. Further damage from the surviving battlecruisers would only open it wider.

Victoria's comm system crackled to life, buzzing and humming with the interference generated by Helena's modifications.

"Spatharios," began Dasos's Titan. Her voice came across clearer than the others, leading Victoria to suppose Helena was routing their communication through her shuttle now.

"I'm here," she replied. Victoria realized her voice was weak, tired, but she could do nothing about it. True, it was the job of those battlecruisers to see them safely to their destination, but for so many of them to die while she sat there helpless was a bitter wound.

It went against everything she told herself she stood for, and Victoria swore she would avenge every single life lost on her behalf.

"Spatharios," Helena repeated. "It has come to my attention that our proximity to the mastigas warship, combined with the intense electromagnetic flux generated by its beam weapon, have resulted in an eighty-two-point-three-one-percent increase in signal transmission times to and from the *Hammer of Ares*."

Victoria nodded. Helena's matter-of-fact tone helped bring her to a more stable mental point, and Victoria latched onto that to steady herself. She could grieve later, she told herself, but for now they had work to do.

"That was expected," she replied. The despair was gone now, banished behind the veneer of responsibility, but the chill remained.

"Expectations did not exceed a seventeen-point-two-five percent drop due to the ship itself. The beam weapon is making automated communication with the *Hammer of Ares* slow at best, and many signals are being double-sent due to the interference."

"What do you propose?"

"With your permission, Spatharios, I will assume direct control of our shuttles. Point Iota approaches, and our orders are clear. Cutting down the signal lag could save our lives in the event the mastigas ship fires upon us directly or interference grows worse."

"Do it."

"Understood. I will inform you when the process is complete."

Silence fell as the conversation ended and the static died.

The top of the battleship's pyramid began to glow again. Victoria knew space was empty and no sound could be transmitted, but they were now so close to that damnable weapon that she truly thought she could hear the vibration as it powered up again.

From so close, the flare was blinding. She only saw it as a scratch of light across her vision. The first thing she could see was the holo just above her lap, and relief flooded her system as Victoria realized none of their ships had been destroyed.

Then she looked up, and the *Justice* was on fire.

Flames from escaping atmosphere licked at the edges of a long gouge on the ship's dorsal surface. Missiles streaked toward it, only to be intercepted by the *Boreas* as it swooped to physically interpose itself between the *Justice* and the mastigas battleship.

The light flared again, this time directing its single-purpose destruction at this new target. It impacted the *Boreas* dead center on the battlecruiser's bow. The thick armor there held the ravening energy at bay longer than any other ship she had yet seen, but even it proved to be no match for the impossibly powerful weapon.

Before her eyes, the *Boreas* disintegrated as a shockwave ripped it apart from bow to stern.

***

The weapon fired again, obliterating the *Skylla*.

Second Lord Evimeria had not resumed her position in the Captain's chair in some time. The crew was used to her pacing, looking over their shoulders, and talking to them as they all worked. The *Phlogeus* was the first of the battlecruisers to be built, and its bridge crew had trained together since the very beginning of Project Titan.

Those days had been simpler. That thought once again surfaced, refusing to go away. Show up, run simulations, and go home. At the time, she thought it was going to be the best job in the military, potentially even a stepping stone to a Hexarchate when Hyperion or Aegesander grew too old to rule.

In those days, the hardest thing about her job was that none of them could speak to anyone about it. For years, she was involved in a "top secret training program," but even that much information was pushing the limits of how much she could disclose.

Now, nine of her few good friends had been killed by a weapon none of them knew existed. She wanted to blame the Hexarchs or the military or any one of a list of people who should have known this was coming. She could not—none of them knew about the beam weapon. She had examined the sensor logs from the *Tartarus*'s battle group in detail.

Tension pervaded the bridge. Early on, in those simpler times, her crew gave her a hard time about her inability to stay in one place for very long.

"Captain," they told her, "the carpet on these ships is expensive. Try not to wear it out, because you know they'll bill us instead."

She laughed. They all had.

Now, none of them spoke, and Lochagos Evimeria stood rooted in one place. She wanted to move, to reassure them individually, and the absence of something that had once been so commonplace was affecting the others as well. Despite that desire, she could no more force her feet to move than she could destroy the mastigas battleship with her bare hands.

It did not, however, stop her from doing her job. "Status of the *Justice*?"

"They've sustained heavy damage, but are still operational. Their projected course will put them intersecting Point Iota in seven minutes."

She nodded, thinking. Just a few minutes more and at least the *Phlogeus* would survive. When she saw her fellow captains again, she would buy them all drinks. Lady Selene's divine hospitality could not possibly hold a candle to hers.

"Captain, the mastigas weapon is powering up again."

Her heart thundered in her chest. "That's too soon."

"After it fired on the *Justice*, the next activation came twenty-five percent faster at an apparent loss of accuracy."

She nodded. It took that warship two shots to destroy the *Skylla*, during which time the *Justice* finally crossed the point of no-return.

"Target?"

Silence fell for a moment before a small voice, devoid of fear and full of anger, replied. "They're targeting us, Captain."

Inwardly, she cursed violently. On the outside, however, Evimeria remained as calm as she could manage. Her hands clenched into white-knuckled fists at her sides, but otherwise she contained everything inside.

There would be time to be afraid when their mission was over, she told herself.

Aloud, she asked, "status of Point Iota?"

"The armor is cracked and broken, but the opening is not large enough for the *Justice*."

Evimeria nodded. "Understood."

"Orders, Captain?"

She laughed, letting out some of the tension.

"Captain?"

"You know," she began. "I hoped this job would lead to a promotion to First Lord one day. I would have loved to sail Pteryga's oceans as its Hexarch." She trailed off for a moment. "There's one more thing I think I've always wanted to say, but didn't realize it until this moment."

No one spoke, but all eyes on the bridge were fixed on her.

"Navigation, target Point Iota."

"As you say, Captain."

71

"Helm, go to maximum power. Give me ramming speed!"

***

The *Phlogeus* slammed into the base of the mastigas ship's pyramid and the fireball that vomited outward was studded with debris of indeterminate origin.

Unlike the first ships to be destroyed, she felt nothing at the loss of the *Phlogeus*. The horror and sorrow of the battle was simply too much, and Victoria watched the flames fade with numb distance. The only thing that tingled in the depth of her soul was a distant sense of triumph when the breach in the mastiga ship's hull yawned wide, big enough for the five of them who survived to land alongside the *Justice* and finally put an end to the mastigas.

Without the coverage of the battlecruisers' defenses, missiles started impacting the *Justice* directly. That had been expected and the ship had been built with armor that could stand up to anything the Technocrat military could throw at it.

In fact, between the overlapping layers of defense from the battlecruisers and the developments in armor spurred by Project Titan, they should not have lost a single ship.

No one planned for the mastigas superweapon. No one planned for the Technocracy's best armor to crumple like foil as that weapon picked them off one by one.

Her comm came to life with the clarity of the battle group's official systems. "This is the *Justice*. We are making our final approach. Beginning assault procedures. We have sealed the hull breach from the weapon, and missile damage thus far is minimal."

Victoria wondered how her voice still sounded so calm when her ship was burning around her.

The reply from the *Hammer of Ares* was dead and flat. It sounded like Victoria felt, cold and empty. "Roger, *Justice*. If the suns' light reaches you in there, may it carry you to victory."

"May the su—"

72

The captain of the *Justice* never finished her blessing. The weapon fired again, this time angled down so far that it hit the mastigas ship itself. In between the peak of the pyramid and the spot of hull that now glowed a faint cherry red, the *Justice* burned.

Unlike the smaller ships, the *Justice* survived this second blast from the weapon. It streamed burning atmosphere from a hole that ran cleanly through from the top to the bottom of the ship, and it listed to one side slightly as the sudden change in mass threw off its thrusters.

Victoria's comm system beeped once, indicating an incoming message. The flags on it indicated that it originated from the *Justice* itself, and Second Lord Eleni in particular.

She opened it.

The first part of the message was a picture, the one Eleni took that day aboard the *Hammer of Ares* when she met Victoria for lunch. All of them, even Helena, were smiling. It warmed her soul a bit, but the chill persisted, and Victoria wondered if anything would ever make her spirit feel warm again.

The rest was a simple text message.

"I wish there was more I could do," it read. "I'm sorry, Victoria."

The impossible weapon fired again, tracking from bow to stern along what remained of the *Justice*. A series of explosions blew the ship apart, leaving nothing but shattered wreckage on a ballistic course for the side of the pyramid.

Victoria screamed. "NO!"

"All remaining ships, abort!" thundered the voice of the *Hammer of Ares*'s captain. She felt the inertia pinning her to her seat shift slightly.

Faster than she could think, Victoria opened her communication menu. She threw holoprojections around the cockpit as though they were real objects until she uncovered the menu she needed. Helena's ship was at the top, and slammed her fist through the holoprojection. "Helena!"

"Yes." If Victoria could have felt anything in that moment other than the urgent, soul-tearing desire to *act*, she might have been unnerved by the sound of Helena's voice. The other Titan actually sounded afraid.

An indicator appeared off to the side of Victoria's holo. It burned yellow, then red, and finally green. A heartbeat later, lights appeared at the base of the previously-nonfunctional manual controls.

Victoria gripped them like swords, guiding her ship around to point directly toward Point Iota, where wreckage from the *Justice* and the *Phlogeus* continued to rain down like hellfire.

"All Titans, this is Victoria. Your controls are unlocked. Take your ships and follow me! We are going to finish this!"

She dismissed her holos. The mastigas ship was too close now for anything other than the most rudimentary cointrol setup to matter. A single display showed her destination and the best course, and that was all.

Victoria pushed the throttle control as far forward as possible and acceleration pinned her to her seat. As her vision started to dim, she hoped the shuttle was as resilient as it was supposed to be.

The gray bulk of the mastigas pyramid filled her vision and she tried very hard not to think of the hundred-thousand people aboard the Justice.

She failed.

***

Victoria remembered darkness punctured by the screams of the damned. When she came to, the ruined hulk of her shuttle seemed to have entombed her. Blackness sat close around her, and with the ship too damaged to function, turning on the exterior lights was not an option.

As soon as the thought of her ship being too damaged crossed her mind—overlayed in her mind with the crimson flare of the Justice's last moments—she realized that she could feel a direction that was definitely "down." That was good. That meant she was inside the mastigas ship, close to where she should be.

It could also mean that she was dead and hell was a lot like the inside of her ruined shuttle.

She looked around for anything that might still be functioning, but in the darkness, even her own hands proved impossible to see. Victoria struggled blindly against whatever force held her in her seat for a moment before her brain finished waking up.

Cursing the restraints, despite knowing that they probably saved her life, she undid the clasp and wiggled out of the tough material. She did not have far she could go. Without power, the canopy of her cockpit remained sealed. Without the computer active, she had no way to access the emergency backup power.

That, of course, assumed that her backup batteries were intact.

A minute passed and she forced herself to stay calm. One breath in, one breath out. Another breath came slower, and she held this one. She ticked off three seconds in her mind before slowly releasing the air in her lungs through pursed lips.

Her pulse refused to slow, despite the feeling that her negative emotions were bleeding away. If anything, it quickened, hammering loud in her ears. She forced herself to think, to examine the situation with an objective eye.

Her head swam, leaving her wondering if it had been doing that the whole time. She lifted an arm to support her head, dragging it through thick, hot air. Her fingers caught in what little hair she had, slipped, and she jerked her head upright.

Victoria opened her mouth. She was going to ask, not that it would do any good with a dead ship computer, what the symptoms of acceleration sickness were. Her tongue felt swollen in her mouth, too thick and sluggish to form words. It felt like the rest of her head, heavy and fuzzy and refusing to work right.

Something beeped at the edge of her mind. It beeped again, louder and more insistent this time. She waved a hand to shoo it away like a bug, when she realized the beeping was coming in time with an orange light above her wrist.

Her training kicked in, but it felt like it was kicking in somewhere else. Somewhere far away from where she now sat, she remembered that she set her holo's alerts to orange.

Victoria swatted at the alert, too incoherent to verbally ask the thing what it wanted. It read the alert aloud, and something in the words made her pulse quicken. Her brain remained unsure what it had just heard, but something in the dim recesses on her mind picked out the words that meant she was in danger.

"Re," she slurred. "Re...pea-pea-pea. T. Th. Ts. Repeat. T. T-t-t-t."

The programming in her computer seemed to comprehend her current mental state, and when it spoke again, the voice was loud and slow. "Atmospheric oxygen below critical levels. Blood oxygen below critical levels."

"Ca. Can. C-a-an we f-f-f-fix. It?"

"Recommend immediately moving to an area with higher oxygen concentration."

At that moment, Victoria did not have the energy or ability to concentrate enough to roll her eyes at the obviousness of the suggestion. With the computer's voice to focus on, she found she could shake off some of the cobwebs and focus a little better.

"Light-t," she commanded, only slurring slightly.

Her computer obeyed, illuminating the cockpit. The light confirmed the suspicions she held before the lack of oxygen started turning her thoughts to tar. Everything was inactive, even the status lights that would have showed the red of broken systems were dark.

"Can-n-n-n. Can I sh. Sh. Shhhh. Shoot. The window?"

"Negative. The canopy is composed of a high-strength aluminum alloy that..."

Victoria no longer had the energy to tell the computer that she did not need to know what the material was. As the low oxygen warning grew more rapid, it also grew quieter again. In a few moments, she could not hear it at all.

She took a deep breath, warm and strangely comfortable, before darkness came to her mind once again.

Chapter 5

"It's true. All of it."

First Lord Hyperion's voice was full of resignation. He had been angry at first, though it was obvious that his anger was not directed at Rivka. Hyperion himself was not known for his temper; in fact, he was most known for the exact opposite. Having been a Hexarch longer than Rivka had been alive, the mask he placed over his emotions was almost never out of place. She had seen his feathers ruffled only once in memory. So when that mask had slipped, the realization—that what she brought him might be true—hit her like a punch in the gut.

To hear Hyperion admit it drove that feeling home a second time. He was not angry anymore, not even at the information she brought him. Despite that, his mask was still missing, showing the complex emotions surging across his weathered features more plainly than she had ever seen them.

When she first showed him the contents of First Lord Diomedes's case, Hyperion's blue eyes had lit up like fire, but he never looked directly at her. Instead, the person he seemed to hate more than anyone else alive was himself.

After a few moments, he muttered. "Damn Diomedes." Then, stronger, "damn him."

"I am sorry, First Lord. Had I known that the information he left me would trouble you so..."

Hyperion cut her off with a sharp wave of his hand. "You did the right thing, Rivka."

"I apologize, First Lord. I should not have read it."

The noise Hyperion made might, charitably, have been called a laugh. "'Should not have read it?'" he echoed. "What should you have done, then, with an unmarked, locked case left to you and you alone by First Lord Diomedes's Will?"

She had no answer for that, and the two of them sat in silence for several minutes while Hyperion idly shuffled the stack of untraceable paper taken from Diomedes's case. Rivka took that time to look around the other Hexarch's office again.

They were alone, which was in itself unusual. She had never met with anyone else, not even another Hexarch, without at least one guard present. Those guards were always unobtrusive, often waiting around a corner or hidden in the crowd, but someone was always there. If nothing else, having a third party observing any discussion avoided dicey legal issues where one person might claim promises that were never made.

Not only were they alone, but Hyperion had actually locked the door once he fully understood what she was bringing him. No one, neither guard nor assistant could come into his office until they were done. He had already confirmed the worst of her fears simply by agreeing to read the documents. In some ways, the existence of those notes and records was more terrifying than what they actually said.

The first time she read them, she wondered if they might not have been some sort of elaborate blackmail kept by Diomedes in case he needed to get one of the other Hexarchs to do work for him. That thought alone was perhaps worse than the truth of the matter, because that would have shattered her image of the man she admired so much.

Yet, knowing every word of it was true somehow made it worse precisely because it did *not* shatter her image of the deceased First Lord. In life, she knew Diomedes to be a man of strong convictions and a caring soul. He never subverted any of his morals, never did anything, so far as she knew at the time, to harm the people of Kipos or the Technocracy at large.

The contents of the box now resting on Hyperion's desk did help to explain the paranoia that always seemed to follow Diomedes, though. She never judged him on it—the gun safe that responded to levels of stress hormones in her office was proof enough that it would have been hypocrisy to do so—but now she thought she understood it.

For the moment, though, she wanted to focus on anything but that nondescript gray box.

Hyperion's office showed the collections and detritus of a career spanning well over a century. He had spent most of that time in possession of this very office, and it showed. A handful of awards given to "Second Lord Hyperion" hung on the walls for things he had done before she was even born. Plaques for his service as Hexarch shared dates with her teenage life seventy years before.

The weight of his accomplishments made her feel uneasy because they now sat here as equals. She felt a wall between them, though, erected in the exact spot occupied by Diomedes's records. That was the difference now; Hyperion's name—worse, *Diomedes's* name—was on that document and hers was not.

She watched Hyperion for a moment. His attention was on the paper in front of him, rereading it for what must have been the third time. She could not blame him, she supposed. He likely had not thought of the things and events described there in decades.

Or, perhaps, she thought as she searched his face, Hyperion thought of those events daily. That would certainly explain his emotions when she first presented the box to him.

Watching his bright blue eyes scan across the paper, she realized finally that it had not been anger that broke his mask, but fear. Fear that someone else now knew his secrets had given way to anger, but for a few fleeting moments, First Lord Hyperion, the senior Hexarch who had held power longer than she had been alive, was for the briefest of moments *afraid of her.*

"First Lord," she said, finally, then dropped all pretense of speaking formally. Rivka had to remind herself that she was speaking to a colleague and not a superior. "Hyperion. I didn't know."

He looked up and met her eyes. She thought he looked sad, which was another expression she never expected to see on his imperious features. "Now you do," he replied quietly.

"What are we going to do about it?"

His firm reply came quicker than she expected. "Nothing."

"Nothing?" she asked, shocked.

He nodded once. "Nothing."

"Why?"

"What would you do?" he demanded, or tried to. The resignation was still there in his voice, and the demand came out more like an exasperated request for any ideas other than the ones he had thrown out years ago.

"Don't people deserve to know?" she pleaded.

"Deserve to know what, exactly? How close we came to extinction?"

"Yes!"

"Why? What good will it do? I want you to think about this before you answer me, Rivka. What good will it do to tell people what we did long ago?"

"People deserve the truth."

He laughed again, this time with only slightly less bitterness than before. "They do, don't they? You know, that's exactly what Meriones told me twenty-six years ago. Does that date sound familiar?"

81

"I know First Lord Enyalios was elevated twenty-five years ago after Meriones's de—no." She stopped in the middle of the word. "You didn't."

"I didn't, no. I can promise you that. I suspect I know who did, but there was little I could do about it then."

"Why not?" she demanded. "If someone was ki—"

"Don't finish that thought out loud," he warned. "You're a Hexarch. You ought to know you can't just throw accusations like that around without ample proof. Whoever did it, if there even was an 'it' that was done, was careful to cover their tracks perfectly."

Rivka's heart-rate spiked and she instinctively looked at the door—the locked door. "Hyperion..."

"I agreed with Meriones," he said in his best calming tones. "At least I agreed with his motives. I asked him the same question twenty-six years ago, and do you know what he told me?"

"No?"

"He told me that people had a fundamental right to information."

"He was right," Rivka said. Her voice was firm and her reply came out perhaps more strongly than she intended.

"I know about your work as a Second Lord, Rivka. Your real work."

"Then you know..."

"I know," he said, emphasizing it with a hand gesture that indicated he did not want to go down that conversational path.

She nodded, accepting his decision. Talking frankly with the Council's senior member about her former, and not-so-former, information-brokering activities, especially the legal gray areas in which they operated, would not be productive.

It did, however, impress her in retrospect that, despite it all, she knew nothing about the contents of Diomedes's case. Never in all her meetings in her garden back on Kipos did anyone give any indication that the things she now knew about the Hexarchs who came before her might have been true.

Hyperion spread his hands in front of him. "Keeping this information secret has prevented people from panicking. What do you think would have happened if they knew, I mean really knew, why First Lord Diomedes killed himself?"

"Riots," she replied softly.

"Riots," he agreed. "Or worse."

"Why?"

"Why would people riot?"

She shook her head, clearing the fog that settled there under the deluge of information and confessions. "No. Why did you do it?"

Hyperion was silent for a moment. His features—his snowy white hair and beard, and his blue eyes—seemed to drop yet another layer of guards that she never realized he still held up. Hyperion seemed to relax, and the sharp edges of his image softened. A smile came and went across his face, never touching his eyes, as he struggled not to put a cap on his emotions once again, but with whether he even should.

His eyes flicked to the stack of paper on his desk and, rather than answer, he straightened it and placed it back in the box. He locked it and passed it across the desk where Rivka silently took it and laid it in her lap.

She spent most of her life visualizing First Lord Hyperion as this grand leader of the Technocrat people. She remembered him standing with Ophion in the Council chambers and thinking, as a girl, how much they looked like kings in their purple robes.

In those days, Hyperion had been more a force of nature than a man, or at least she saw him that way. If Ophion was a statue of obsidian, Hyperion had been hewn from marble. Strong, and with just the right amount of passion, Hyperion was a shining example of what a Hexarch *should be.*

Decades had passed, and the gods had taken Ophion in his one-hundred and forty-fourth year. Hyperion was younger now than Ophion had been on his death bed, but two and a half decades had passed since then. Many more decades passed since Rivka's childhood memories and the day she decided *she* would stand up there with them. Even in those days, Hyperion always wore the same six rubies in his beard.

The man across the desk from her was not that man. The Hyperion she now spoke to looked more like a kindly old man, more like a grandfather, than a king. His once brilliant eyes were sad, glittering with barely-suppressed sadness and fear rather than charisma. In his eyes, Rivka saw a distant past that she was only now learning about.

He spoke quietly. "At the time, we didn't feel like we had a choice. First Lord Stephania came up with the plan and Ophion helped her with it. I came in early as well, full of youthful vigor and eagerness."

He looked at her, eyes that she once felt could bore through steel showed a watery sadness instead. "We were going to save our people. Instead, our sins almost cost us everything."

"Was it worth it?"

Hyperion's gaze never wavered. A lesser person would have broken eye contact. Rivka had seen it plenty of times, especially during her work as "Lady Whipcord." People who espoused strong convictions or postured as though they were in charge of the meeting would crumble as soon as she picked at that one spot at which to stare. Everyone had a spot like that—everyone except First Lord Hyperion, it seemed.

Finally, he answered. "We believed so at the time."

"And now, knowing what you know of your great endeavor?"

His reply was quiet, a single word. "No."

Rivka sank back into her chair, feeling deflated. She looked down at the case in her lap, wondering once again if opening it was the right decision. When she looked up again, Hyperion was still watching her. His expression was pinched, lined with care.

Wordlessly, Hyperion reached up to his face. For a moment, Rivka thought a particularly difficult itch had settled in underneath his snow-white beard, but when he took his hands away, she realized what was happening.

Hyperion held out a hand, and in that hand glittered six rubies. Rivka never realized how large each of them were, but in Hyperion's hand, it became clear that even one of those six rubies likely cost more than a luxury shuttle.

He prodded at them with one finger of his other hand. After a moment, he arranged them in a rough circle, despite their apparent instability and desire to roll to the center of his palm.

Rivka's eyes went wide as she realized the symbolism of those ostensibly simple jewels he always wore. Six rubies, six stones the color of blood, not for six Hexarchs but for the specific six names on Diomedes's documents.

Hyperion closed his hand, tightly, then his eyes. He heaved a great sigh, the sort that came after a long and painful exertion. When he opened his eyes again, they had regained the luster she was accustomed to seeing, the power and charisma that marked him as the greatest Hexarch of her life.

He turned his hand over and reached the rest of the way across the desk, long arms easily spanning the distance.

Rivka blinked in surprise, but held out her hand in automatic reflex.

Hyperion opened his hand and the six gems fell into her palm.

She closed her hand over the stones and pocketed them. She wanted to ask why, but the sudden lump in her throat would not permit the question. Rivka feared she knew the meaning behind the gift, feared that it was not just because she knew his secrets.

Finally, she swallowed hard and in a voice that was smaller and weaker than she intended it to be, choked out, "why?"

Hyperion's eyes softened, the corners fell, and a ghost of a smile crossed his lips. "Because I may never get another chance."

"What do I do now?"

"Now that you know the truth?"

She nodded.

"Nothing. The problem will take care of itself now."

"Yes," she replied. She paused. "And if it doesn't?"

Hyperion sighed again, sinking back into his chair. "Then Meriones was right all along, and the people should know what we did."

"That's not a price I want to pay."

"I thought you wanted to tell everyone."

"You said you know what I used to do for a living. I know things that *no one* should know. Hyperion..." She paused, collected her thoughts. "I don't like it, but I understand."

He nodded. "Thank you, Rivka. Now, please leave me. I want to be alone for a while."

"Of course," she said, rising and tucking the case under her arm. "Thank you for your honesty."

She got halfway to the door before Hyperion spoke again. "Rivka?"

She stopped, turned. "Yes?"

"Whatever you do. Whomever you tell now. There is one request I would ask of you."

"What is it?"

The heavy imperiousness she had come to expect from him returned. "Do not tell Tritogenes. It would destroy him."

Her eyes narrowed, a glare so reflexive and automatic that it broke through her control before she even knew the sudden rage was there. Her voice held none of it, but she knew her emotions were obvious on her face. "As it did me?"

"You are far stronger than he is, Rivka. Would you wish that pain on him?"

She closed her eyes and sighed, echoing Hyperion's wordless sentiment from moments before. Then, aloud, she said, "I'm not going to betray your trust, Hyperion."

"Then there is one last thing."

"Yes?"

"Diomedes was my dear friend. He could not have chosen a better successor than you. I am proud of the Hexarch you've become."

That lump in her throat returned and rather than reply, she simply nodded. She stood there a moment longer, letting Hyperion see the naked emotion on her face. Pride welled up inside her as well, threatening to erupt as tears, before she turned back to the door.

***

Rivka reasoned that First Lord Hyperion's request made sense in context. Tritogenes was himself on Pteryga, after all. He arrived a few days before she did, ostensibly to celebrate the success of Project Titan. That made sense as well; the Titans, and she tried not to think of Lelantos, her friend, should be nearing the mastigas ship even as she shut the door to Hyperion's office behind her. Most likely, he was also here to negotiate some sort of business deal. With Project Titan winding down, the six of them would have an entirely new set of contracts to negotiate.

He could not, technically, stop her from telling anyone what she knew. Hexarchs only held the power to order other members of the Council around in matters that affected their own corporate holdings. Even then, the orders often came as firm requests or business sanctions. Now that she knew, and even sympathized somewhat with, Hyperion's reasons for keeping everything secret, a voice at the back of her mind told her to continue keeping the secret. She suspected Hyperion had his own reasons for not wanting Tritogenes to know, more than the potential mental anguish he would suffer. Much like how her image of First Lord Diomedes had been altered, warped even, by the information he left her, Hyperion did not want to destroy Tritogenes's image of himself or of First Lord Ophion, Tritogenes's original patron.

It was for the greater good, argued her logical side. Hyperion was right. If people knew, they would riot.

On the other hand, the thought that they deserved to know the truth and decide for themselves whether the Council had acted in their best interests or not continued to gnaw at her. Perhaps, she reasoned, she could get Tritogenes's input on the matter without actually telling him what she knew.

Yes, she decided, that would work best. Mind made up, she recorded a short message for him, requesting Tritogenes's presence in Hyperion's "royal courtyard." The reply came back in moments: Tritogenes was already there, a fact which Rivka verified as she rounded the corner of the squat building that housed Hyperion's office.

The plaza was a wide, open space situated at one end of Hyperion's sprawling palace complex. Rather than build upward as she did, Pteryga's palace spread itself across almost a full square kilometer of low buildings and wide skies. This particular plaza, like Hyperion's office, sat on the extreme edge, within a literal stone's throw of the seaside bluff.

Few people milled around, and most of them wore the blue robes of Second Lords. Within a hundred meters of Hyperion's office, that was no real surprise. Anyone here would likely have some important job or other to do—such as carrying around a case full of the most classified information in the last century.

Fortunately, that made Tritogenes easy to spot where he stood against the railing halfway across the plaza, watching the ships at sea.

The sound of that ocean filled her ears as well, drowning out any potential conversations. Rather than go directly to Tritogenes, she turned slightly and avoided the main part of the plaza. With Hyperion's request still echoing in her mind, she went for the waist-high railing at the edge of the area and looked out over it.

She needed a moment to think.

Despite her love for all things green and growing, she often felt an attraction to the ocean. It was fortunate, especially given her mental state at that moment, that Hyperion still occupied the castle that the first generation of Pterygan Hexarchs built.

Rivka inhaled deeply, savoring the smell of the salty air. The ground abruptly ended a meter or so past the fence against which she now leaned. From that point, the ground gave way to a two hundred meter drop that ended at the water. Pteryga's weather was volatile, and the wind had kicked the ocean up into great waves that smashed against the base of the cliffs with mechanical precision.

It might not have been green, she thought as she looked over the blue water, but it was rather nice.

"How did your meeting go?"

Rivka jumped, reflexively clutching the box containing Diomedes's records to her chest. She turned to see Tritogenes standing a few meters away.

"My apologies for startling you, First Lord," he said, formally.

"It's alright," she replied, doing her best to mask her flustered reaction with laughter. She pointed out at the ocean where a black dot flanked by two smaller black dots was crossing the horizon. "I was just focused on watching the ships go by is all."

"I often wonder how Hyperion manages to get anything done when he has the option of just sitting and watching the ocean," Tritogenes mused.

"I asked him that once, actually."

He raised an eyebrow, interested. "Oh? What did he say?"

"The noise helps him think," she replied. "That's why his office has so many windows as well."

"That makes sense."

"Working with him for thirty years off and on and you never thought to ask?"

"Forty." He shrugged. "It never came up in conversation. I talked to Ophion about Limani a lot more. Did you ever meet him?"

She shook her head. "Not personally, no. Not outside of business."

"You would have liked him. He turned the palace into the grandest garden I've ever seen. You'll have to come visit one of these days."

"I'd like to, now that things are going to be calm for a while."

When Tritogenes's eyes flicked to the case still clutched against her chest, Rivka realized that she had gripped it even tighter as she spoke.

Tritogenes indicated Hyperion's office with a sideways nod of his head. "Everything go smoothly in there?"

She laughed nervously, again to cover a sudden feeling of anxiety. Her heart beat faster as she thought of what to say. She wanted to tell him the truth, but she also wanted to maintain the comforting lie.

"Well enough," was her answer.

"I sympathize."

His comment surprised her. "You do?"

Tritogenes nodded. "Hyperion can be a bit, let's say, intimidating."

Rivka smiled. "He can, yes. But I just needed to have a second pair of eyes look at some documents. Make sure all of the information I had was accurate."

"You came all the way to Pteryga for that?" For a moment, he smirked.

"Some of it was fairly sensitive," she said, wondering how far she could carry the half-truth. "Personal information and the like."

Tritogenes nodded. "That makes sense. You know, of course, Hyperion is going to want to invite you to dinner tonight. The man loves putting on a feast."

"I expected as much."

Tritogenes looked like he was about to say something else when a voice from across the plaza called, "what a surprise to see the two of you here."

They turned, Tritogenes moving faster as the owner of that voice seemed to register in his brain. "First Lord Aegesander. What a.." He almost concealed the momentary stop in his voice. "Pleasant surprise."

The other First Lord nodded once, crisply. He was older than Hyperion by twenty years. Rivka herself was twenty years older than Tritogenes, but they still looked fairly close in age. Aegesander looked as old as Hyperion did, but in a totally different way. Hyperion's wide face and features had an imperious cast to them, to be sure, but when he smiled it was clear that the feeling of power he radiated came as much from his bearing as anything. Aegesander, by contrast, was thin-faced and hawkish, and radiated an entirely different type of authority.

He approached them at a modest pace, placing Rivka between himself and Tritogenes, before speaking. "I came to speak to First Lord Hyperion."

"With respect, First Lord." Tritogenes spoke with such perfect formality that, from where Rivka was standing between the two men, it almost seemed to be an insult. "I have my doubts that First Lord Hyperion would be willing to see you, especially without an appointment."

"He will see me," Aegesander replied, equally formally. "I am confident of it. I have need to speak to him of matters concerning Project Titan. I informed him of my arrival when my ship came into orbit around Pteryga."

"It will have to be later," Rivka said. "I just left his office and he told me he was going to be busy the rest of the day."

Aegesander regarded her for a moment, but said nothing. The expression that crossed his face, if it could even be called an expression, was one of annoyance.

"Coincidentally," interjected Tritogenes, "that subject is also what brought myself and First Lord Rivka here."

"Is it? And what does our Council's *newest* member think of Project Titan's success?"

"I am concerned," she began, "as, I feel, we all are, about the safety of our Titans and about the toll this Project and the mission has taken on us all."

A smile crept across Aegesander's lips. "How true. Something else weighs on you, girl."

She bristled. She was a bare five years younger than First Lord Eurybia, whom Aegesander often worked closely with and whom he never, at least in her hearing, addressed with such disrespect.

Rivka managed to keep her temper, but dropped the formal tenses from her reply. "Lelantos is my friend, Aegesander. I'm worried I sent him to die."

Annoyance passed across his face, gone in a moment. "We all did our best. I trust you know that. For my part, I feel Second Lord Helena is exactly where she needs to be."

Over her shoulder, still speaking with mechanically perfect formality, Tritogenes said, "if you wish to meet with First Lord Hyperion, perhaps First Lord Rivka or I could speak to him ahead of your arrival and ensure he is willing to receive you. She did, as you now know, just meet with him."

Now, Aegesander glared. Rivka knew Hyperion refused to meet with Aegesander in private, and had so refused for decades, but had never known why. Now, with the case she still held tight containing information that bore both their names, she thought she understood.

"I can go speak to him, if you so desire," she said. She was unsure, in that moment, exactly which of them she was addressing.

Aegesander turned his glare on her. Anger turned in inquisitiveness after a moment. "What did you say you were here to discuss with the First Lord?"

"Details of Project Titan," she replied. "I had some records which contained personal information that I felt he needed to see before I disposed of them."

"I see," he replied. Aegesander's eyes were a cold brown as he studied her face.

His gaze flicked down to the case under her arm, then immediately back to her face. She realized too late, exactly as had happened with Tritogenes, that she instinctively held it tighter for a moment. Her control was slipping, betrayed by her racing heart and veins that carried more adrenaline than blood. His eyes came back to meet her own, then to the case, and back again, growing wider with each passing beat of her thundering heart.

In that moment, she felt exactly like the new-minted Hexarch she struggled for the last five years against being. Aegesander, with only slightly less experience than Hyperion himself and a career longer than her life, stared her down with eight decades of authority. Worse than his simple imperious presence, however, was the feeling that he not actually trying to intimidate her. He was simply doing it, intent or no.

She blinked and looked at him again. His expression changed slightly and he simply said, "I see."

His voice was different now. That short comment had been delivered with a mixture of scorn, fear, and anger that was altogether different from the way in which he had been addressing her before.

As he turned on his heels, she realized what just happened. First Lord Aegesander had read her like a book, and he now knew why she had come to Pteryga.

"First Lord?" Tritogenes called.

Aegesander ignored him. Instead, he headed directly for the door to Hyperion's office. He went in without knocking or otherwise announcing his presence. Hyperion's guards, in the building opposite his office, would not stop a fellow Hexarch from entering. Aegesander's widely-acknowledged "ban" was never official, and without a direct order from Hyperion, they had no power to stop him.

Rivka watched the building in silence. With each passing second, the cold pit in her stomach threatened to envelop and freeze her racing heart. Her pulse beat faster and faster, hammering in her ears and eyes and lips.

"We should join them," Tritogenes said. His voice had a hard slant to it that suggested he was not talking about a friendly meeting. He knew about the animosity between the two senior Hexarchs perhaps better than she did. "I'm sure there's something you forgot to ask him, or perhaps left in his office."

She nodded once and felt her feet turn toward Hyperion's office. She took one step, then two, before a shadow passed over Hyperion's window.

A thin silhouette, too small to be Hyperion, slammed into the window. A moment later a much larger shape joined it in a tangle of limbs. Faster than she could react, the larger shadow reared an arm back and drove it into the smaller shadow, which again was thrown against the window.

Tritogenes's knees softened, a heartbeat away from running toward the building, and Rivka grabbed his arm. She wrapped fingers around his arm so tight she knew she had to be hurting him.

"What?"

Rivka pulled him backward. "No!"

"We have to help!"

The smaller silhouette pushed the larger one away, the curtain fluttered, and the world went sideways. Rivka's chest tightened. Fighting the sudden dizziness, she spared one last look at Hyperion's office and then turned back to her fellow Hexarch.

Still holding Tritogenes's arm in her iron grip, Rivka turned for the nearest of the plaza's exits. She took one step, yelling what she hoped was not a pointless order given too late.

"TRITOGENES, RUN!"

His facial expression was confusion, but his reflexes understood what Rivka was trying to do even as his brain struggled to comprehend why. He took a step, then another, and was running a step behind her by the third.

Despite herself, Rivka screamed when she heard the gunshot.

Chapter 6

Victoria awoke to the feeling of hands on her face and neck. She jumped, body reacting to the stimuli before her eyes were even open. Her right hand closed around the wrist attached to the hand touching her throat while her left brushed the other hand aside and struck out for where she assumed a face should be.

"Victoria, stop." The voice was familiar, and as the fog finally cleared from her brain, she realized her blind punch had come within a handsbreadth of Helena's face.

She relaxed, pulling her fist back and releasing her hold on Helena's arm. "Sorry," she mumbled. Her tongue still felt too large for her mouth, and talking around it was a chore. "What happened?"

Helena stood upright, extending a hand. Only then did Victoria realize she was on her back. She scrambled to a sitting position, then took Helena's offer of help. As she came to her feet, unsteady at first, Helena answered. "Your ship was damaged when you crashed. Something you hit tore out your power core."

Bits and pieces came back to her. She remembered hammering on the inside of her canopy, which was followed by a flash of a memory of her struggling with the flight stick as her systems abruptly shut off.

She remembered the burning feeling in her lungs as darkness swallowed her. Without sight, that memory came in a rapid fire sequence with other, similar memories from past lives in the labyrinth. The memory of the seconds before she passed out in her cockpit were overlayed with a remembrance of another life drowning, of choking to death on lungs filled with fluid.

Each time a death came from oxygen starvation, the same sensation preceded it, warmth and comfort.

She was millions of kilometers away from Aphelion, and even if there could have been a hundred-and-first at that point, Victoria did not exactly relish the idea of being one in an ever increasing string of remembered deaths.

That was a burden she would not share.

Aloud, she asked, "how bad was it?"

"Your heart stopped," Helena replied. "Between the first aid kit and a generous donation of antichrono from Lelantos, you seem to be back with us."

"Antichrono?" Victoria asked, still feeling the effects of nearly suffocating to death.

From her right, a voice replied, "yes. It's the other half of the awareness drug."

Victoria turned to see Lelantos reattaching a series of small tubes to the collar he wore around his neck. A long, bloody gash ran across his forehead, but the quick heal smeared across it seemed to have stopped the bleeding. "What's in it?"

He laughed. "A long list of chemicals, most of which have names this big." Tubes reattached, he held out both hands in front of him, about a meter apart. "The important one right then was adrenaline. In me, it's used to flush out the chronodrug quicker. In you, it jump-started your heart quite nicely."

"Thank you," she said. She stood a step, balance slowly returning.

"Thank me by not needing any more of it," Lelantos replied. His smile failed to completely cover the automatic defensive twitch in his muscles. Victoria supposed she could not blame him—if he overused the antidote drug, coming down from the chronodrug would likely be much harder.

Victoria shook her head. Some of the fuzziness remained, but most had cleared. "How long was I out?"

"Your ship impacted first," Helena said. A pause, then, "that was close to an hour ago."

"No wonder my balance is all over the place," Victoria muttered.

"I calculated your relative location from my own crash site," Helena continued. "You were closest, and so I came here first."

"Thank you for that. If you hadn't, I don't really want to think about where I'd be right now."

"Still in the ship," Helena said. A moment passed before she seemed to realize that Victoria was making a joke, albeit a grim one, and she added, "better off than the rest of us, I imagine."

"Where are we?"

Helena summoned a holographic image of the mastigas ship. She zoomed in on a green dot near the base of the pyramid. "Here," she said. "The impact of the *Phlogeus* opened a wide hole in the mastigas ship's hull, but much of it is now either closed off by debris or sealed by internal pressure doors."

"And here?"

"Have you noticed the chill?"

Victoria smiled, lips thin and grim. "I thought that was just part of almost dying."

"Atmosphere is leaking from this area at a rate faster than is advisable for sustained survivability. Decompression is only being delayed due to," she paused as a shudder ran through the area and loose debris rained down from the ceiling, "debris from the *Phlogeus* itself."

"And the others?"

Helena looked down at the dark floor under their feet for a moment. When she looked up, the best description that Victoria could come up with for the expression on her face was shame. "I don't know."

"It's alright. We'll find them."

"No," Helena said. "Well, yes. You're correct. We will find them." She placed extra emphasis on "will," then added, "but you don't understand. My training should have prepared me to hack into this ship's systems, and yet I cannot."

"How did First Lord Aegesander know what to expect from the mastigas computers?"

She winced slightly with annoyed frustration. "He didn't, but I was trained to break every conceivable type of encryption. Aegesander's own computers were no match. But this..." She made a wide, helpless gesture with both arms, "I don't know what's wrong."

Victoria nodded. "Keep trying."

"I will," she replied. Helena's face took on a faraway look for a moment before she seemed to realize that Victoria was still watching her and she returned her overt attention to their surroundings.

Now that Victoria's brain had been properly re-oxygenated, she looked around. The three of them stood in a large open room, perhaps ten meters to the ceiling. A few, irregularly placed dim lights glowed overhead, giving just enough light for the humans to see.

Looking around, she started to understand some of the destruction the mastigas inflicted on the lower levels of the Aphelion facility. Even before the chill of space started eating away at the room's heat, it had been cool here. Some of the lights had doubtless been destroyed, but it had always been dim. Even now, despite the slowly escaping air, the atmosphere was damp and moist around her.

She gestured to Lelantos. "Come on. Help me unload whatever I can salvage of my gear from my shuttle."

He nodded, sparing a glance back at Helena while she worked. She had a holographic display floating in front of her face streaming data as almost pure code, but she seemed to be interacting with it very little. Her hands, for the most part, stayed by her side as the data moved and shifted in front of her face.

Before turning back to her crashed shuttle, Victoria wondered how much of that was actually useful for her and how much was a display for their benefit. Having lived with her, even for a short time, Victoria knew that a manual interface was low on the list of things Helena needed.

She double-stepped, nearly tripping over feet that were not quite connected yet, to catch up with Lelantos. "So. Who found who?" she asked. She needed to make conversation. The more Victoria spoke, the faster her brain seemed to recover.

"I found Helena, actually. It's easy to pinpoint sounds when everything is slow, and I recognized her footsteps."

Victoria was surprised. She thought she was perceptive, but the idea of telling someone's identity from several rooms away just by the sound of their stride was impressive. "She walks that distinctively?"

He nodded. "You all do, in your ways. You take long steps, but very light ones. A slow, heel-toe rhythm. Daniel takes—took—big steps too, but heavy ones, like he wore boots all his life. You'd be surprised what you can pick up when someone only takes one step every eleven seconds."

"Are you on right now?"

He shook his head. "No. I don't know how long we're going to be here and I want to conserve it as much as I can. If I need it, I can go from taking a dose to full effect in just a few seconds, your time."

They reached the ship, and Victoria finally had a chance to examine it. The cockpit itself was practically missing. The canopy lay to one side, next to what appeared to be a pair of large pipes. Much of the canopy had been shattered before what remained was cut free.

Looking back along the ship, Victoria saw the damage Helena mentioned. The entire front had been smashed in, crumpled and shredded. The nose held most of the little craft's sensors, and they probably went out as soon as she hit the the first piece of debris.

That explained why the ship never picked up on the lack of oxygen in the cockpit, she thought.

Victoria gestured to the pipes. "Your doing?"

He nodded. "I wish Korakti or Daniel had found you first, to be honest. Neither Helena nor I are very strong, though she did surprise me."

Victoria felt a chill in her stomach and her throat lurched as she tried to say the fallen Titan's name. A deep, shuddering breath, and she said, "Daniel is..."

Lelantos nodded once, closing his eyes. "I know. I saw. Daniel..." He paused for a moment before looking into Victoria's eyes, almost asking permission before finishing his thought aloud. She nodded, and a ghostly smile crossed his thin features. "He would have appreciated the light show."

She smiled, thin and hollow. "Yeah. I think he would have. Anyway, thanks again."

A little smile crossed Lelantos's face. "Like I said, if you want to thank me, don't make me save you again."

Victoria laughed. "I'll do my best."

Further along the shuttle, the hull had been ripped open. The cavity that was supposed to house most of the equipment, including the power core and backup life support, was empty. It looked like it had been shredded by the hand of a giant, clawing and tearing until the ship stopped functioning.

Inside the back end of the ship, wires and hoses hung limp. Some of them, she knew, were the air hoses for the cockpit. She supposed that

100

when the life support was ripped out by the crash, the ship used what little power it had to seal the armored cockpit against any air loss.

Amusement crossed her face at that thought, dark though it was. If the systems had failed just a little sooner, those connections might have stayed open, allowing air from the mastigas ship into the cockpit. Instead, the ship functioned exactly as it was supposed to, and it nearly killed her.

Fortunately, the meager storage locker built into the inside of the shuttle was as armored as everything else. With Lelantos's help, including the generous application of his cutting torch, the two of them made it in.

The crash had thrown the contents around, but even the supplies she brought with her had been secured against the rigors of combat. A little violent deceleration and repeated impact damage was not enough to break anything, even the comparably delicate computer equipment.

She said a small prayer, thanking whomever was listening for small miracles.

Most of the gear was in a variety of bags and satchels that could be strapped to her combat uniform. It all went into the storage space instead of already being strapped to her to save room in the cockpit itself.

Two set of pouches went around each of her thighs and another one around her hips. A large backpack with straps that crossed her upper chest and waist held important things like food and water, while smaller pouches on her front side held deadlier supplies such as spare magazines for her weapons.

She strapped her mastigas knives to her calves, finding an odd pleasure in that act. The other gear and weapons were important, probably more so than her knives, but those two little weapons represented something to her. Symbolically, they reminded her that she had bested Aphelion's labyrinth, surviving everything it could throw at her.

Along with her mastigas knives, the baton she took from the gigas, itself also more of a symbol than a useful weapon, hung from her waist by the same strap of black mastigas fabric she originally made for it.

"Tell me something," Helena said, approaching. "We crashed over an hour ago now, so why..." She enlarged the hologram she was examining. It showed their position as green dot. Scores of red dots surrounded them, but none closer than two hundred meters in any direction. "Have the mastigas not attacked?"

"Maybe they're waiting?" Lelantos offered.

Victoria shook her head. "No, the mastigas attack in the dark, sudden, and with no warning. They should have been on us as soon as the ship sealed the breaches we made."

"I agree," Helena said.

The room shuddered again as the hellish scream of twisted and tortured metal ripped through the air. A moment passed, silence fell, and another shudder ran through the floor beneath them. A breeze stirred the air, one that did not stop.

"That may have something to do with it," Lelantos added.

Helena frowned. Her implants had been smeared with grease and dirt. "Perhaps," she said. "Still, their behavior is unexpected."

Victoria did not want to be dismissive, but the longer they stayed in the room they were in, the more the chill started to prick at her. She was not sure if the air was actually getting thinner or not, but her brain certainly thought it was. "Whatever the reason, they're giving us the time to regroup. They'll regret it, but let's not waste any more time."

Helena dismissed the hologram. "I suspect they are planning a trap for us."

"I know they are," Victoria replied. "But I'd prefer to be trapped with as many of us in one place as possible rather than all separated. Any luck finding the others?"

"No," Helena replied, frustrated. A moment passed and her face brightened. "I correct that statement. Panatakis is trying to patch into the mastigas sensors just as I am. I have found his location, but..." Her face fell.

"Helena?"

"We cannot communicate beyond simple data packets. He is having more trouble than I with the ship's systems. I have a vague read on his location and..." Her eyebrows drew together for a moment. "Blue screen it all, I can no longer sense his location."

"Take us close," Victoria ordered.

Helena pointed as an angry look—one not directed at anyone present—flashed across her face. "That way. I will furnish you with the maps."

Victoria's wrist computer beeped, indicating acceptance of the file from Helena. She overlayed a two-dimensional version of the map on her helmet's visor. It was controlled by her eye movements, allowing her to scroll or dim the map as needed.

Victoria adjusted the sling on her rifle. It was the same weapon she used against Ouroboros during their mission to Prosgeiosi's second moon. Unlike her weapons from their first battle, or the one with which she escaped Aphelion, this one had been crafted specifically for her by the binary's finest gunsmiths.

Like her other weapons, the short rifle was a symbol for her. More than an asset in a fight, it reminded Victoria that she was, indeed, the soldier she had been designed to be. Her thoughts continued: if she was going to fulfill that goal, she would become a paragon.

She supposed, objectively, that relying on so many symbols might hurt her in the long run, but that had not stopped her yet. Knowing the weapons she carried had seen her through multiple life-or-death skirmishes helped give her confidence.

If Helena's map was correct, confidence might just be the only weapon in her arsenal that stood a chance against the odds.

She gestured to the far end of the room. "Let's go."

***

Lelantos was rather fond of the mastigas ship's climate. The cool, damp air reminded him of the deep forested valleys around Rivka's palace on Kipos. The smells were all wrong, of course, but there was nothing he could do about that.

What the smells were, however, was familiar. The atmosphere might have lacked the harsher elements, but he recognized it all the same. Even without the scents of blood and death to remind him, he picked out familiar aromas. Even if the air lacked the thick, oily black smoke it held the first time he smelled the mastigas, it still stank of them.

He reasoned the mastigas had to be intelligent in some capacity. They spoke to one another, wore clothes, and used technology. Their motives might have been alien, but at least that one thing was clear enough. If they could think, they could understand fear, suffering. If Lelantos could bring to them even some of the terror and destruction the mastigas brought to Kipos five years ago, he would consider the mission a success.

He never gave form to the thoughts at home, but now that he was there, surrounded by the metal of the warship that set his planet ablaze, a thought percolated through Titan Lelantos's mind. Survival, he reckoned, was secondary. His primary mission was to *eradicate* the mastigas, every last one of them, no matter what it took.

Realizing his face had gotten rather pinched and had fallen into an angry sort of frown, he pushed those thoughts aside. Passion had its place, he reminded himself, but that place was not on the battlefield. He could hate the mastigas once their job was finished, but until then, he could not afford such indulgences.

Victoria led by nearly three meters. Behind him, Helena watched their rear. Nothing was there but the wreckage of Victoria's destroyed shuttle, but that could change at any moment. Victoria was the only other one of them to fight the mastigas on their own terms, and the both of them knew exactly how much the mastigas seemed to enjoy surprise attacks from above.

Spurred by that thought, he raised his head and scanned the ceiling. The crash destroyed many of the lights there, plunging the room into worse darkness than usual.

Lelantos cursed. The chronodrug only made things seem slower, letting him take that extra time to perceive things and make the correct decision before others could react. It did not actually slow down time, and no greater number of photons reached his eyes than anyone else's.

Without more light, the longer ranges on his rifle would be useless, and he took the few moments they seemed to have to reconfigure the modular weapon into something that would operate better at shorter ranges.

Helena and Victoria did not seem bothered by the darkness, which was yet another reason he wanted the Spatharios to lead. She actually seemed to *like* the light level as it was.

In her black suit, with her weapon holos deactivated, Victoria was almost invisible in the darkness. When they attacked the Ouroboros facility on Faros, they tried to use darkness to cover their escape, but Victoria strode ahead, seemingly unfazed. That image continued to resonate with him.

Tritogenes might have been a fool, he thought, indulging in a sentiment he would have kept hidden around Rivka, but he took his security seriously and Ouroboros had been completely unprepared for the human storm that was Victoria. Lelantos was glad Victoria survived the mastigas outbreak at her training facility—he valued her as a leader and a friend.

Behind him, Helena cursed. *That*, Lelantos thought, was not normal.

Victoria seemed to realize it as well, because she stopped, signaling them to stop as well, and turned. With all of their personal gear working properly again, her voice came through his helmet's comm system. The speakers there "projected" it in the right direction and her voice did not have the unsettling unidirectional quality that mass-produced military systems often produced. "Is everything alright?"

105

"No," Helena replied. She sounded annoyed, which coming from her normally cool persona was almost worse than if she actually sounded angry. "I have lost all sensor data for the surrounding area."

"Damaged components?" Victoria asked, coming to form a triangle with him and Helena rather than the rough line they had been in before.

"Perhaps, though I doubt it. I was only able to access a rudimentary thermal sensor and apply known mastigas body temperatures to the readout in order to pinpoint their approximate locations."

"And now?"

Helena pushed her holo to the center of their group. It expanded, still showing their own locations and a map of the room around them, but everything else was empty. Corridors branched and twisted away from them, but they no longer held the mass of moving red dots that they did before.

"Orders, Spatharios?"

Victoria picked up the holo and rotated it, zooming out to show the entire battleship. She pointed to their location, which had been rendered in Helena's wireframe map as a jagged mass of destruction. "Point Iota was believed to be the largest of the mastigas's small craft launch bays, yet it's empty."

Helena rotated the map. "Point Kappa was the other, and a backup location for our assault."

"It's probable that the mastigas moved their ships," Victoria said, gesturing upward. Lelantos followed her motions, but only saw vague outlines of machinery. He wondered again exactly how good her eyes were. "That's going to make Point Kappa one of the most well-defended points on this ship."

Helena highlighted the bow of the ship in red, and parts of it twisted and exploded into stylized bits of holographic light. Little triangles floating away from the bow represented debris. "Our escorts rendered the bow cannons inoperative, but I have no data on how quickly they could be brought online again."

Victoria zoomed the view until only the pyramid was visible. She highlighted the superweapon at the peak of the pyramid. "Then we go here."

"That's going to be heavily defended, possibly moreso than Point Kappa," Lelantos said, careful to control his intonation so that it came across as an observation rather than a protest or complaint.

"It's a smaller area," Victoria said. "There are only five of us left. We'll get overwhelmed at Point Kappa, but here..." She tapped the peak of the pyramid with one finger. "We ought to be able to fight on more even terms."

"I have no objections," Helena said.

"Nor do I."

Victoria nodded. "Good. Then the first thing we need to do is locate Panatakis and Korakti. Helena, consider that task more important than breaking into the mastigas sensor suit at large."

"Understood, Spatharios."

"Now, we need to..."

She never finished that thought, because the mastigas ambush Lelantos had been expecting finally arrived. One hand raised his rifle to his shoulder while the other reached up and activated the device around his neck that dispensed the chronodrug into his bloodstream.

Cold fire flooded through his veins and his limbs grew heavy. The effect began deep in his core before spreading out like the bloom of strong liquor. On either side, Helena and Victoria raised their weapons as well, moving exponentially slower with each passing moment.

Victoria fired first, long before he could react. Those moments while the chronodrug took effect were, for him, several minutes of intense disorientation. None of his muscles moved correctly and the world around him shifted and contorted seemingly at random as his senses grew accustomed to the drug again.

Fortunately, that period of disorientation only lasted a short time, even from his perspective.

The nearest mastigas fell in slow motion now, blood spurting from a tight trio of brilliant red spots on its chest.

Helena fired, downing another of the ones closer to them in a similar fashion.

Lelantos took several steps backward even as Victoria moved closer to their attackers and scanned the area. For the moment, the masitgas were confined to the one area, but that meant nothing given the size of the room.

He took a few seconds, his seconds, to count the mastigas. Leaving aside the ones Victoria and Helena already killed, fourteen fonias now scattered in random directions. The small mastigas were rarely armed with guns, seeming instead to prefer coming in close with knives. Lelantos did not want to come within arm's reach of even one of those greedy monsters, let alone more than one.

These were no different. Their knives flashed in the darkness, dull but still metallic, as they caught fragments of light from overhead. The knives were easier to focus on than the mastigas themselves, and Lelantos watched for his opening.

To his left, one of the fonias pulled away from the others.

He peered down his weapon's scope, watching as the fonias took a step. Ordinarily, they were fast, hard to hit. Dim awareness of the sounds around him told him that Victoria and Helena were firing more shots than they had targets, implying a frustrating lack of hits.

Well, he thought as the fonias took another step several of his seconds later, he did not miss.

The bullet landed exactly where he wanted it to, and the fonias's head vanished in a splatter of brilliant crimson.

He counted again. Ten of them remained, but they were not attacking. Rather, the fonias spread out in a circle, weaving and evading. Even at a normal pace of time, those fonias would take a full minute to reach the three of them.

Lelantos pivoted and shot another of the fonias as it broke away from the others and ran for Victoria's back. The shift in her posture told him she realized it was there about the same time he did, but when it fell and tumbled to the deck, Victoria turned back to the ones in front of her.

He told himself that Victoria and Helena could handle the fonias. That would have been true even if the mastigas were not acting so strangely. With nine remaining—eight as Victoria landed a burst of gunfire on the lower torso of another one—the two Titans alone should have little trouble.

A glance upward told a different story, however, or at least it hinted at one. The shadows there still proved too deep and dark for him to really see what was going on, but he did not need the ability parse fine detail to tell that things overhead were moving.

Worse, those things were directly overhead.

"Move!" he yelled. His voice rang out for two full minutes from his perspective, a bellow with every ounce of energy he had. The microphone in his helmet would modulate the actual volume to something that was not deafening, but the urgency should still be there.

Helena leaned and pivoted, exhibiting spectacular muscle control by not falling during the maneuver, and in a single step sprang into a run. She angled toward him, raised her rifle, and shot past him.

Lelantos turned on his own heels even as Victoria threw herself to the side. The fonias in front of him fell to the deck, blood spraying from two widely-spaced holes in its torso.

Seven, he counted.

Lelantos raised his rifle even as the floor shook underfoot. He held his aim as his arms, and thus the rifle, bounced around. The shaking only lasted a few seconds, even from his perspective, and Lelantos quickly re-centered his aim and put a bullet through the nearest fonias's neck.

Six.

Behind him, he heard the unmistakable roar of a gigas. He knew Victoria had killed gigas before, even without a proper weapon, but that was a fight no one wanted to go into alone. He watched those giant monstrosities tear too many people apart to ignore them for long.

As though sensing his thoughts, Helena said, "help her. I will handle these."

Lelantos nodded and pivoted on his heels again. Four gigas stood in the spot where Helena and Victoria had been moments before. Two of them held massive semi-circular shields, and the third one carried something that might charitably have been called an ax if it was an order of magnitude smaller. The fourth and final one held a gun that he would have recognized as being "something bad" even if he had not seen that type of double-barreled autocannon during the attack on Kipos.

Victoria's attention was torn between the gigas and the fonias around them still. Lelantos spared a moment to look for the sophont. Those gigas, he reasoned, were acting too intelligently for there not to be one of those four-armed things nearby.

One gigas turned, ready to slam its shield into the deck. He had seen this formation before, like so many other things about this ship, this exact formation occurred more than once on Kipos. If they finished, those four gigas would dominate the entire area without even having to move.

He aimed low, thankful for all the benefits of the chronodrug, and put a bullet through the nearest knee of the closer of the two shield-carriers. That gigas howled and dropped the shield, turning toward him with rage in its posture. It bent low and bellowed, ready to charge him even with only one leg.

Victoria darted toward the cluster of gigas and Lelantos laughed. Even in his own ears, the sound was strange, because no logical course of action ended with a sane human running toward a cluster of gigas. Then again, he thought, it was possible that none of them were completely sane anymore.

She vanished into a flurry of movement as the three gigas all turned toward her, suddenly stumbling and off balance as their carefully laid plan began to fall apart.

110

The chronodrug let him see all that happening even as the closest gigas ran towards him. It took a step, stumbled, scrabbled at the deck, and then launched itself forward with its arms. On three working limbs, it propelled itself at a speed that quickly became alarming even to Lelantos's slowed senses.

He stepped back and dropped the center of the scope just below the gigas's helmet. He remembered Victoria's tales of the gigas she trained against having weakened helmets, but these looked like the same ones they wore when the mastigas burned Kipos. At best, even his bullets would only crack that material—and he would *not* get another shot.

So, instead, the bullet tore into the gigas's collarbone, ripping through its internal organs and coming to rest somewhere in its torso.

Lelantos did not stop to see whether the gigas died, but turned to the side and ran.

More footsteps echoed around the room as another wave of fonias sprang out of the shadows, prompting Lelantos to wonder exactly how long the mastigas had been prepping this particular ambush. Not for the first time, he cursed that damned superweapon and the destruction it caused, because they *should* have been starting this assault with the backing of thousands of Technocrat troops.

Instead...

His thought process came to a screeching halt as a voice like old machinery roared. "Die now, humans!"

Lelantos did not often feel fear. Even before the chronodrug, "afraid" was not an experience he commonly had. His brain simply was not wired that way, and even as a child he had very little concept of personal safety. Since the chronodrug slowed things down and allowed Lelantos to out-think and out maneuver many dangers that might otherwise threaten him, he felt those moments of fear less and less.

That sound, however, tore open something deep in his soul and exposed it to a rush of ice. Worse than the gigas, worse even than a new wave of fonias, three new mastigas slinked out of the shadows some thirty meters past where Helena killed the last of "her" fonias.

The two taller mastigas, four armed demons carrying spears and rifles both, flanked a much shorter four-armed creature. The sophont pointed and the elites raised their weapons, opening fire immediately.

Lelantos dropped to the floor, a long plummet that lasted a full half minute, but the bullets did not land anywhere near him. He rolled as soon as his perception-slowed muscles would let him and saw one of the gigas attacking Victoria crumple to the deck.

She sprang out from behind it, running as fast as she could, as the elites continued to fire. She jumped, then dove into a long somersault, then came back to her feet again.

"Fall back!" she yelled.

Lelantos did not have to be told twice. He came to his feet as quickly as possible, scrabbling with his hands as he rose. For the moment, his rifle hung from its sling, all but forgotten against his shoulder.

Ahead, the shadows moved, too slight and too quick for anyone without his senses to perceive. He could not tell what lurked there, only that something waited for them with nightmare claws and teeth.

"To the right!" he yelled, already moving that way.

Helena's voice came across his helmet speakers, but in the rush of the moment, he could not tell where she was. She should have been to his right, but her voice seemed to come from all around him, piercing his fear-muddled senses.

She spoke with a cool monotone, precise and clear. She was running too, she had to be, but only the barest hint of exertion made it into her voice.

"Seven meters ahead and two to the right, there is a hatch in the floor at the base of the wall. I believe I can access and open it if I am given twelve seconds."

Victoria's voice, by contrast, roared in his ears. "We don't have twelve seconds! We need another way out of here."

Lelantos's blood ran cold at the thought and his mouth threatened not to give voice to the idea, but he forced himself to speak. Much like hate, there would be time for fear later. Once they were all safely hidden away from the mastigas, he could take the time to wallow in those emotions, but not now.

Not now.

"Toward the elites. The others came from overhead, but the elites came from the ground. There's got to be a door behind them."

"We can't fight them."

"No," Helena's cool, calm voice said. "But I possess several flashbang grenades. One moment, yes. I have the optimal angle. Count to three, cover your eyes, count two more, and then run."

One.

Lelantos did as instructed, skirting the wall and running as fast as he could. With three of them to target, the elite's shots all went wild. Their bullets tore up the floor in chunks and splintered against the wall, and Lelantos knew what would happen if even one of those shots hit them.

Two.

He raised his rifle. The sights bobbed uncontrollably as he ran. Even his precision and control under the chronodrug was no match for the instability created by a running human body. Still, the elites were large and growing closer by the moment. They were easy targets and his shot had no trouble finding something to hit.

Three.

He dropped, rolling hard onto his right shoulder, turning his face away and covering it with his left arm. Brilliant white light still lanced into his eyes as Helena's flashbang went off, filling the air with burning magnesium.

One.

The flash persisted. The elites and sophonts yelled in anger and pain as burning magnesium powder blinded them.

He wanted to rise and shoot at them, but even blinded, the elites were too dangerous. They could pinpoint his location with sound and smell. Even if they lacked the precision that eyes provided, their automatic weapons would make short work of anyone standing still near them.

Mastigas healed quickly. He knew this, and even damage to the eyes would not last long, but it would last long enough. They would see these three again.

Two.

Now, he rose as the magnesium flare faded. Helena was ahead now, once again placing him in the middle. A look over his shoulder told him Victoria was only a few paces behind. Lelantos ran, feet pounding against the deck precisely every seven seconds.

"Will find you, we! No place to hide, there is. Kill you all, we!"

Lelantos ignored the bellowing sophont, trusting Helena to take them *away* from this sudden nightmare.

Chapter 7

The two Hexarchs had barely made it out of Hyperion's garden when the palace's intercom blazed to life the first time. Now, they huddled in a small storage room, trying to make sense of what just happened. Neither of them were able to articulate any reason why Aegesander would want to actually kill Hyperion, and Tritogenes waffled between confusion and rage with every passing moment.

He had looked at her, and asked how Rivka could be so calm. She had no idea. In fact, she was sure she radiated as much anger and fear as Tritogenes did. She was unsure how he took "calm" from that, but perhaps in his current state, anything sort of nigh-murderous rage seemed calm and collected.

If she was being honest with herself, she had a good idea why Aegesander might have wanted to kill Hyperion. In fact, given the pain on his face when he confirmed that the information in the Diomedes's documents was true, Aegesander's motive was clear enough.

She made a promise, and now that promise was to one recently dead. She could not tell Tritogenes her suspicions, no matter how they ate at her. Hyperion's rubies felt like weights in her pocket.

Every noise sent her heart racing. Despite what Tritogenes seemed to think, she was anything but calm. Yet that knowledge failed to bother her. It had been her paranoia, moments that dissolved for a few fearful seconds into an anxiety attack, that got them both moving. For all she knew, Aegesander was behind them, just out of sight, following to finish what he started with Hyperion.

If their positions were reversed, Hyperion might have shot Aegesander. That idea brought no comfort. If Hyperion was going to kill to keep his secret, he would not have let her leave his office. She still had no idea what Aegesander had seen on her face in that moment, but she knew she had somehow given everything away.

The intercom roared to life again, forced to the same maximum emergency volume that was intended for use during disasters. Fortunately, the chemical-scented supply closet that now concealed two of the six most powerful humans in the binary had no speaker overhead. The announcement *still* reverberated through everything, rattling things on the shelves and grating in their ears.

"This is First Lord Aegesander, Hexarch of Dasos. Terrorists opposing action against the mastigas have struck Pteryga."

"Bullshit," Tritogenes swore through gritted teeth. He was careful to keep his voice down. The storage room had no window, and only by carefully watching the patterns of light under the door itself could they know if someone was outside.

She shushed him. No one stood waiting on them in the hallway, at least not that she could hear, but that knowledge did very little for her nerves. Also, simply because no one stood close enough to cast a shadow on the door did not mean no one was searching for them right that very moment.

After a suitably dramatic pause, Aegesander's voice continued over the intercom. "As you know, much of First Lord Hyperion's personal army was sent to fight the mastigas along with our brave Titans. In light of that, and in light of the danger of any further terrorist incidents, I have conferred with First Lord Hyperion and we have decided that my forces will place the Blue Spire, and by extension all of Pteryga, under guard."

Tritogenes grunted. "There goes our easy exit."

She almost shushed him again, but Aegesander continued speaking, overriding anything she was going to say.

"Please cooperate with my forces during this time of uncertainty. They are here for your protection. If you see something unusual, please do not hesitate to report it."

"Unusual like two Hexarchs hiding in a broom closet?" Tritogenes whispered with what sounded like an attempt to defuse the tension he was feeling.

Rivka frowned. Her voice grated, and she knew it, but there was little she could do. Despite her best efforts, Rivka could not quite keep her anxieties under control and they sat in a lump in her throat. "Most likely, his 'forces' have orders to engage on sight."

Tritogenes's eyes went wide. She suspected she just verbally confirmed whatever fears were percolating in his head. "You don't think he'd have his guards shoot us, do you?"

Rivka shook his head. "I doubt it."

He breathed a momentary sigh of relief. "Thank Selene."

"I think he would have them apprehend us so he can do it himself."

"*Wonderful.* Can he do that?"

"With enough guns?" she asked. "Yes. We need to get off this planet. If we move now, we ought to be able to get to our ships before Aegesander locks the place down."

"We *need* to stick together," Tritogenes argued. "If Aegesander really did come here to kill Hyperion, he likely already had troops in place, ready to go."

"Agreed."

"I didn't come prepared for a fight," Tritogenes said. "I assumed that Pteryga would be one of the places where I wouldn't have to watch my back all day."

117

"Normally, you would have been right."

"Normally," Tritogenes said, "First Lord Aegesander would not have been allowed on planet, for exactly this reason."

Rivka grit her teeth. She sent her guard detail away, explicitly away rather than just into low-profile positions. She wanted to curse her own stupidity and arrogance, but Tritogenes was right. Hyperion's palace was one of the few places where that *should* have been just fine. "I brought weapons, but they're in my ship."

"They won't do us any good there," Tritogenes said. He seemed to be struggling to keep his frustrations under control. "Why did you bring them and leave them where they won't do any good?"

"Like you said, I thought I'd never need them on Pteryga."

"If we can get to your ship, we might as well just take it off planet."

She nodded. "Exactly."

Tritogenes thought for a moment. "How capable are your crews?"

"Ordinarily?"

"There's that word that's giving us so much trouble right now. Yes, ordinarily."

"On any normal day, we would be fine. Diomedes taught me well, I suppose."

"But?" Tritogenes asked, picking up on the unspoken thread.

"But," she continued, "We're back to the same crashed problem. This is Hyperion's palace, or," and the words caught in her throat, "it was."

"And they're not *at* the ship right now, are they?"

She shook her head. "They're not. I'm sure they're going to be heading back now, but if it's going to be hard for *us* to get to the ship, they're going to have more trouble."

Tritogenes was silent for a moment before raising a fist. He made like he was going to punch the wall of the supply closet, to let out at least some of his frustrations, but stopped and took a deep breath. Through gritted teeth, he rasped, "why?"

She tapped the case nestled under her arm. "This."

Tritogenes eyed it for a moment. "Whatever is in that made Aegesander kill Hyperion."

"It means you're on his list, too."

In the dark of the closet, Tritogenes's face paled. That lasted only a moment, before his expression twisted into a wry grin. "You're not telling me anything I don't already know."

Despite the tension, for just a moment Rivka felt her spine unknot and she was reminded why everyone trusted Tritogenes—at least everyone except First Lord Aegesander. His smile was infectious.

"I remember the confirmation hearings for your elevation," she said. "I thought the Council would never agree."

He quirked an eyebrow. "Jealous?"

Rivka scoffed, shrugged, then laughed very quietly. "I always wanted this job, to be honest. Diomedes thought I would be good at it, and gave it to me. I didn't have the sense to say no."

"What about now?"

"Now," she hesitated. That was a much more complex question, especially given the events of the last half-hour. "I don't regret accepting the job he left me. Today is probably going to go down as one of my least favorite days, but... Tritogenes, we're Hexarchs so that we can do right by our people."

He nodded, lips set in a firm line. "We have to get away from here, somewhere where we can tell everyone the truth."

Rivka's stomach clenched at that thought, and her mind immediately went back to her conversation with Hyperion. She felt a subtle hardness settle on her expression, but nothing else externally changed. Tritogenes, thankfully, was looking elsewhere at that moment.

Some secrets needed to be told, she reasoned, just like some needed to stay buried. Fortunately, "Lady Whipcord" was used to making that sort of decision.

Another firm nod and her mind was made up. "Let's get out of here. Do you have a plan?"

"Part of one."

She nodded. "Think as we move, then."

"Wait." Tritogenes held up a hand, presumably to stop her on her way to the door. The closet was so small that the gesture was useless; she could not leave until he did.

"What?"

"Give me a second. I worked for Hyperion for years, and I *know* there are alternate paths everywhere. If we're going to the spaceport, I just need a second to refresh my memories."

"And you're sure it's not changed?"

He smiled, damnably infectious. Rivka felt her tension ebb. "This palace hasn't changed, not really, in longer than Hyperion's been alive."

He continued after a moment's wait, presumably in case she had anything to add. "If we can get off planet, if I can get a message to Second Lord Pallasophia, she should be able to help. Barring that, First Lord Enyalios would be able to take us to safety, but I would rather not ask for his help."

"Why not? I thought you were friends."

"We are, and he would help, but Pallasophia could get us off planet quietly. Enyalios would be much more likely to start a shootout with Aegesander's troops."

"I would like to avoid that."

"Agreed."

"Are you armed right now?" she asked, trying to bring the conversation back to their immediate needs. Future needs, even near future ones, could wait until they were out of the storage closet.

He nodded, following her train of thought and, from the expression of his face, her reasoning easily. "Nothing fancy, but if we need to shoot our way out of here..."

She snorted derisively. "'If.'"

"Yes," Tritogenes said. "If. We're going to try to just walk out first. Barring that, we sneak out. If that fails, then I call Pallasophia and we shoot our way out."

"She needs to know now. Even if we don't have to use her, she needs to know so she can plan."

Tritogenes nodded. He forced a smile, then, "she'd probably shoot me herself if I didn't tell her what was going on."

Rivka, despite her overwhelming sense of terror and impending doom, smiled. She appreciated the relationship Tritogenes and his Project Director had. It reminded her of herself and Diomedes.

"Are you ready now?" Rivka tried to keep the exasperation and tension out of her voice, and was fairly sure she succeeded.

Tritogenes nodded. He withdrew a small pistol from his robe, checked it, and returned it to its hiding place. Despite having done it once already since the two of the locked themselves in the storage room, Rivka did the same.

Satisfied, she moved the small gun to a hidden holster in her sleeve. She stood and held out a hand to Tritogenes. It felt strange, almost conspiratorial, but she supposed that had become the order of the day.

Tritogenes accepted the hand up. "Let's go."

"I'll lead."

"Let me lead. You need to keep that case out of sight if we can."

"We're going to my ship."

"I know where your ship is, Rivka. Please don't argue with me on this. If that," he jabbed a finger at the box under her arm, "is why Aegesander killed Hyperion, we can't take any chances."

"But."

"No." His voice was firm, but not the sort of cold iron or immobile stone that she often expected from a Hexarch. No, when Tritogenes gave an order, he did so with the assuredness of an opera star who *knew* that no one would countermand it.

Rivka stood there for a moment, fighting down anger. Aegesander killed a fellow Hexarch because of the contents of that case, and now Tritogenes was trying to tell her how best to manage the very thing that started it all.

Yet, he was right. With a sigh just loud enough for his benefit, she said, "alright. Lead the way."

Tritogenes moved to the door of the storage room and pressed his ear against the cool metal, listening. He backed away, shaking his head.

"People?" Rivka asked. She dropped her voice even quieter than it had been moments before.

"I hear footsteps," Tritogenes replied, voice barely above a whisper now.

"Military?"

"Can't tell."

"Are they marching?"

"I can't tell!" he hissed.

Rivka nodded and crept toward the door as well. She set the case gently on the floor and carefully, slowly, flattened herself to the ground. She turned her head, bringing one eye as close to the floor as she could and straining to see anything.

After spending ten minutes in a dark room, the hallway outside was almost painfully bright. Despite that, the silhouettes of booted feet were obvious enough. The mere presence of boots told her that whoever was out there was likely military, but beyond that it told her nothing. Frustratingly, boots alone did not tell her anything about the allegiance of the people wearing them.

Finally, the boots moved on. Rivka waited several minutes before moving, just in case they turned back or others were following. She stood and reached for the door handle.

"Wait!" Tritogenes hissed.

"What?"

He took a step closer and made several swipes at her robe. "The floor's dusty in here. If someone sees a Hexarch covered in dust, they might get suspicious."

"Good catch," she said, and helped him dust the front of her robe.

Finally satisfied that they were both presentably clean, she unlatched the door and eased it open. Her pounding heart reminded her that this was the most dangerous part. If someone saw them emerging from the storage room, there would be problems. The best thing she could hope for under the circumstances would be a sex scandal.

"All clear," she whispered.

Tritogenes emerged from the storage room a moment later, looking smug and adjusting the belt of his robe. She wondered if he had had the same thought she did and had come to the same conclusion. It certainly seemed that way, and he was playing his part for any audience they might have had.

Fortunately for both of their dignities, no one was around.

They turned and silently made their way toward the nearby spaceport. It would be crawling with Aegesander's troops, but they were Hexarchs, and Tritogenes expressed doubt that even Aegesander would be foolish enough to blockade the port.

Rivka wanted to say, "granted, he did kill Hyperion," but she felt like giving voice to that sentiment now that they were out in public would be bad. She had no way of knowing whether or not Aegesander already set up listening devices.

In his place, that would have been the first thing she did.

They saw no one in the halls around their erstwhile hiding spot. That did not engender very much confidence on Rivka's end of things. She was about to suggest a change of plans when Tritogenes abruptly turned right and ducked into what appeared at first glance to be a conference room.

"I don't like how quiet things are," he said by way of explanation.

"I was just thinking that," Rivka said, then explained her thought process, emphasizing that, were she in Aegesander's shoes, she would have been tracking them as soon as possible. She ended by saying, ordering almost, "call Pallasophia."

He nodded and brought up the communication system on his personal holo. Before her meeting with Hyperion, Tritogenes said that his Operations Director might have been out at Aphelion. If she was working at his secret Project Titan facility, the time lag on the communications would be deadly.

Fortunately, she picked up quickly and the transmission seemed only to have about seven seconds of delay. That was good, that meant she was on Limani and could get there quickly.

Rivka stayed silent as Tritogenes explained what happened, both with Aegesander's announcement and what happened after. Rivka struggled to listen to the sorts of coded phrases that he would have to employ to include the information that Aegesander shot Hyperion, but she had not spent enough time around the other Hexarch to put together that sort of mental toolkit on him yet.

"When can you get here?" he asked.

The silence of communication lag turned into the silence of reluctance. "I can't."

"What? Why not?" Tritogenes's voice sounded more confused than angry, like he could not have imagined Pallasophia not being able to help.

"If my estimate of the timetable is right, we got a similar 'for your protection' message shortly after you did. Whatever's going on is big, and it's bad. The 'terrorists,'" Rivka could practically see the air-quotes, "aren't just on Pteryga. I'm afraid they're everywhere, Tritogenes. I'll get you out if I can, but Limani's under some intense, and well-armed, scrutiny right now. There's whispers that this is Ouroboros."

"I understand," he said. "Be safe."

Rivka found the concern in his voice touching. "Be safe," went beyond something simple and rote, invoking their twin suns or the grace of Lady Selene. "Be safe," told her that he did, in fact, care for his people.

Not only that, it told her that Tritogenes was worried.

"You too. I'll be in touch soon."

Footsteps echoed in the hall outside, cutting off anything either of them were about to say. Tritogenes dismissed his holo.

"We have company," Rivka said.

"I think you're right," Tritogenes said.

"I think I am, too." Rivka replied. Her pistol was in her hand a moment later, springing from its hidden holster in her sleeve. Tritogenes took a moment longer, but armed him himself quickly enough.

"Move to the far side of the room," he whispered.

"Why? We need to be near the door."

"We're past that. Can't you tell how close those footsteps are?"

She listened, but Tritogenes apparently possessed a level of spatial awareness she lacked. Rivka shook her head.

"They're close," he said, then gestured to the table. "And Hyperion invested in bullet-proof material for damn near everything after Ophion's death."

"I thought Ophion died of natural causes."

"You thought."

Her eyes involuntarily flicked to the case, secure in the hand that was not holding her gun. "Do you know?"

"Know what?" he asked, eyes fixated on the door.

"What Hyperion and Ophion did?"

"I assume you're referring to what's in your case? The information that Aegesander's going to try and kill us over?"

She nodded, then her brain caught up and reminded her that Tritogenes had his back to her. "Yes."

"Ophion told me once that he, Hyperion, and the others had gotten their hands dirty a long time ago, but he asked me not to pry. So I didn't."

125

"You trusted him."

"Ophion was a good man, just like Hyperion. Now hush. They're almost here."

She nodded, adjusting her sleeves so that the long, purple fabric obscured her hands. In front of her, Tritogenes settled for simply holding the pistol behind his back.

A pair of black-uniformed soldiers, all bearing the blue stripes of Second Lords, rounded the corner. They carried military rifles, though their posture was fairly relaxed. They bore no insignia other than their rank stripes, not even military ranks or positions.

"First Lord Tritogenes, First Lord Rivka. We have orders from First Lord Aegesander to escort you to him," announced the apparent leader.

Rivka arched an eyebrow. "For 'questioning?'"

"The First Lord did not say."

"And if we refuse?" Tritogenes asked. His voice was all sweetness and politeness, the very picture of Hexarch propriety.

"Our orders were very clear."

Rivka noticed a change in the two soldiers' positions. Their knees and shoulders softened by exactly the same amount as their hands tightened.

"We are Hexarchs. You cannot hold us against our will."

"Our orders, sir, were very clear," the lead solider repeated.

All Tritogenes said was, "Rivka."

She brought her pistol up. Tritogenes stood slightly to her right, meaning the target on the left belonged to her. She felt a pang of conscience—these two men were only doing their job. It was the man who gave the order who ought to be under her muzzle just then, but she could do nothing about that particular injustice.

She squeezed the trigger twice. The light rounds from her pistol would not have done much against the armor she suspected was hidden under those uniforms, but they never encountered that level of

126

protection. Instead, the bullets both hit home in the middle of the man's neck.

He toppled, first to his knees and then to the floor in a fall so well executed he might have been faking if not for the blood.

Tritogenes was not as good a shot, especially as he was already backing away, toward the bullet-resistant table. He fired several rounds into the other soldier's chest ineffectually.

At least, Rivka thought, her theory about their armor was right.

The second soldier had his rifle raised and aimed by the time the first one hit the floor. Rivka decided. She acted. Cover could wait. She pivoted and fired, three shots. One hit the rifle itself, the second the soldier's body armor, and the third turned his support hand into pulp.

Tritogenes fired again, tracking four shots from the armored center of mass to the poor man's head. He, too, fell to the floor in a puddle of blood.

"I didn't want it to come to that," Tritogenes muttered. His hands were shaking.

"Are you alright?" Rivka asked.

"I'm fine. I will be fine, anyway, once we're off this planet. What the hell is Aegesander doing?"

"Protecting his secret," she snarled.

"Whatever it is, it's been secret for longer than I've been a Hexarch. It could have stayed secret for all I cared. Why," he paused, turned toward her. His gun, whether intentional or not, was pointed at her right thigh. "You brought this here."

Rivka held up her hands, realizing after a moment that the gesture aimed her gun squarely at Tritogenes's chest. "I didn't know. Diomedes left me the information and I came here to see Hyperion because I had to know if it was true or not."

"Is it?" Tritogenes growled. "Did Hyperion die for the truth?"

Rivka nodded slowly. "It's true."

"He told you that?"

"Yes."

Tension seemed to flow out of Tritogenes's shoulders. "Then I trust that you tried to do the right thing. Now let's get the hell off this planet."

"Where to? I suspect Kipos is crawling with 'terrorists' as well."

He did not need any time to think. "Aphelion," Tritogenes replied without hesitation.

"Call Enyalios. I think we need his help after all."

"Agreed."

***

"I fucking *knew* Tritogenes was involved with those Ouroboros bastards somehow."

"Seriously, Efthymia?"

She shifted on her stool, adjusting the rifle slung across her back. Second Lord Efthymia leaned closer, letting her shoulders convey the emotions that her masked and helmeted face could not. She shook her head, then crossed her arms first, then one leg over the over. "Seriously what?"

"You don't think there's something else going on here?"

"Why? Do you? Because the First Lord would be interested to hear your thoughts, I'm sure."

Second Lord Sara sank back. For the moment, she was glad both of them were suited up. Efthymia had been her squadmate for over a decade, but recent months had brought out a side of the woman that Sara would not have expected.

First Lord Aegesander always treated them well, and Sara would never deny that, but ever since Ouroboros first attacked his stadium, some of his more loyal personnel started seeing threats in every shadow. Sara prided herself on being more pragmatic, on not jumping at every little thing, but that was before someone shot First Lord Hyperion dead.

That *someone* was First Lord Tritogenes, according to the information that she had available. The Ouroboros link was just

128

conjecture, but it was conjecture that was spreading *fast* among Aegesander's personnel.

"Aegesander," she began, then stopped. "The First Lord has never lied to us. Why would he start now?"

Efthymia nodded. "Why, indeed."

"That was an actual question."

She leaned closer. "Was it?

"You know what I mean. Look, you know I don't like Tritogenes. He's needlessly antagonistic, especially towards the First Lord. But for him to kill Hyperion..."

"And yet..." Efthymia said, spreading her hands in a gesture that was simultaneously superior and resigned. "He did."

Sara pushed away from the wall she had been leaning again. "But *why?*"

"Does it matter why?" Efthymia demanded. "Tritogenes *killed* a Hexarch."

"And Rivka? What's her part in this?"

Efthymia shook her head. "Those two have always been too close. The only other person Tritogenes would have gone to with this plan would have been First Lord Enyalios, but *he* is too smart for this kind of crashed nonsense."

Sara fell back against the wall once more, looking upward into the lights overhead rather than at her squadmate. She was aware her voice was thin, pulled tight and stressed, but at the moment she did not care. "I just want to know *why*."

"Why what?" Efthymia asked, bringing the conversation back to where it was a few moments before.

"I was thinking out loud before. Aegesander has no reason to lie to us. You know that."

Efthymia nodded firmly. "I do."

"So why," Sara continued, "would Tritogenes do this now? Ouroboros was defeated when the Titans attacked Faros. Hells, the

Titans are probably attacking the mastigas as we speak. So," she paused, "why now?"

Efthymia shook her head. "I don't know. Listen. I just," she stopped, visibly gathered her thoughts, and went on. "Maybe Hyperion blackmailed *him*?"

"You think Tritogenes didn't start it? But you hate him."

"Just because I hate him doesn't mean I think he's stupid. He and Hyperion used to work together before Tritogenes went to work for Ophion—Selene rest his soul. Maybe, just maybe, Hyperion was the one who..."

A holographic alert appeared in the air between them, interrupting their conversation. Both women fell silent as the text, automatically generated by Hyperion's "Palace Monitoring System," sprang into focus. The projection tracked Sara's eyes as she shifted around, pushing away from the wall in order to present a more professional air—even if that air was only to herself and Efthymia.

"Targets Alpha and Beta have been acquired," the message began. That was followed by a complex series of coordinates that corresponded to their current location.

Sara frowned. "Isn't that where Dekaneas Myron's squad was stationed?"

Efthymia was already turned away, muttering something subvocal into her helmet's microphone. While she spoke, Sara instructed their system to synthesize the data into a detailed map, or at least as detailed as they could make it.

The text alert vanished, replaced with a wireframe map of the palace. Each hallway was dotted with infotags that she could access if need be, but for the moment, Second Lord Sara contented herself with simply watching the two rogue Hexarchs as they made their way through the palace's twisting halls.

The question she still had no answer for again came to her mind: why?

"Myron's squad has been appraised of their location and he's spreading out in groups of two to better canvas the area."

"So now what?"

Efthymia rolled out one of the room's unused chairs and propped her feet up on it. With a gesture, she cloned the main display, bringing a miniature version of it closer to where she sat. Small gestures let her pan and zoom, and Sara watched for a moment as she tracked a path through the halls.

"They're going for the spaceport," Efthymia announced.

Sara reached a similar conclusion. The only way the Hexarchs could get off planet, at least without a long overland trek where Aegesander's airships could catch them, was the palace's spaceport. The difficult thing, at least on the part of herself and Aegesander's other troops, was their shuttles awaited them there. If the rogue Hexarchs could get to the spaceport before Aegesander's regular troops, then devil knew what would happen.

"Now," Efthymia replied. "*We* are on overwatch. Have a seat, Sara. We're not going anywhere as long as we have access to this kind of data."

"I'll stand."

"Tense?"

At the mention of the word, a knot tightened between her shoulder blades. In Efthymia's defense, however, Sara suspected that sudden tension came more from watching Tritogenes and Rivka as they ducked into a side room. Two of Myron's troops were close by, and Sara tried not to come to the obvious conclusion.

Sara exhaled, unaware that she had been holding her breath. "They're not going to..."

"I'd bet otherwise."

"I'm not betting on this, Efthymia. It's wrong."

"Look at it this way. Tritogenes and Rivka are running, right?"

"Yes. Hyperion is dead."

"And if they *didn't* kill him, why are they running?"

131

"Because," she started. Sara wanted to say that they were running because they were afraid of the person who did kill Hyperion, whoever that was. They were afraid of what this mystery killer would do to them in turn.

But that was not the simplest explanation. The simplest explanation, the one that did not require yet another roots-deep conspiracy, was that Tritogenes and Rivka were as guilty as Aegesander's report said they were.

She never finished that statement. On the holo, data tags indicating gunfire sprang up. Moments later, first one and then both of Myon's soldiers vanished from the map.

"Gods between," Sara swore.

Efthymia shot to her feet. She said nothing at first, but flashed through her own holo menus until she reached the communication interface. First Lord Aegesander's name was at the top, and she nearly punched the hard-light projection.

It connected in moments. Aegesander's voice sounded thin and strained, probably afraid that Hyperion's fate would become his as well. "Yes, Second Lord?"

"Tritogenes and Rivka just shot two of our people."

The comm channel was silent for a long moment before Aegesander replied. "I was afraid of that. Whatever their motivations, those two are dangerous. I'm sending more personnel to reinforce the patrols."

"First Lord?" Efthymia began.

Sara's heart sank, but if she wanted to interrupt, that time was now past. She said nothing, instead pressed her back against the wall as though just a little more willpower would push her through its cold stone.

"Yes?"

"I believe they are headed to the spaceport."

Aegesander hummed. "That's logical. Thank you, Second Lord. I'll have one of the support ships in orbit land another transport to keep an eye on things."

"As you say, First Lord. Have our orders changed?"

This time, he did not hesitate. Despite that, Sara felt like the heartbeat between Efthymia's question and Aegesander's reply took far too long. This was wrong, she tried to say. She knew what Aegesander was going to say. He was no fool, and the now-rogue Hexarchs left them with precious few options.

Sara pressed herself tighter against the wall, mouthing Aegesander's reply even as he said it.

"Shoot on sight," ordered the First Lord.

Efthymia cut the transmission and sat back. Even with the mask and helmet, her posture radiated pride.

Sara, for her part, felt sick. "How did it come to this?"

Efthymia turned back to her personal holo, focused on the rogue Hexarchs' positions. It seemed like she had no answer. Sara was not sure she would have wanted it if she had one to offer, anyway.

Chapter 8

Second Lord Panatakis stood still, waiting in the middle of a long corridor, watching the sounds around him. Thousands of pairs of feet moved, shuffling, but every time he moved to either avoid or approach them, they moved with him.

If he moved away from the largest concentration of what he could only assume to be mastigas, the colors of their movements still drifted down the hall. After everything settled, the colors had the same shade, the same change over distance. When he went the other direction, toward the brownish-red of their footsteps, they retreated.

Maneuvering as he had been for over an hour had gotten him nowhere useful. He lacked Helena's ability to hack into any computer system via her implants. They could talk to one another, provided they were close enough, and he could see through the strange digital sea of her mind, but he could not perform the same tricks she could.

If he had direct access to a computer, he was still a fairly proficient hacker. Helena had taught him a lot about how to manipulate computer systems to get them to do exactly what he wanted them to do. The problem with that was the corridor he now found himself in had one terminal, which quickly locked him out.

He cursed, muttering under his breath in an angry red cloud. The six of them were supposed to land, or crash as it happened, together.

Panatakis tried not to think of Daniel's ship—the last he saw of the armored Titan was the trail of a missile after that damnable screaming weapon began destroying their escorts. If they really were "one down," to say nothing of the loss of the *Justice*, then things were going to be even worse than they expected.

Still, they had a job to do, and he swore an oath to do it. It might have been a private oath, one that no one else except perhaps Helena knew about because she had been in his mind, but it was an oath nonetheless. Either the mastigas threat would end or he would die upon this sunless hulk of a ship.

He wandered on, watching for the sounds of the mastigas skittering in the halls around him. He wanted to yell, to shout, to force them to come out and face him head on. Despite that, he knew pursuing them like that was a bad idea. Combat, especially outnumbered like he surely was, was not his specialty.

As Panatakis traversed the mapless corridors, he put his mind to the thing he was good at: tactical analysis. The mastigas outnumbered the six of them probably thousands to one, if not tens or even hundreds of thousands.

"So why are they not swarming us?" he asked aloud. "Don't they know why we're here?"

He turned a corner, watching the dark red sounds fade away as the mastigas continued to keep their distance. He grew frustrated.

Panatakis stopped, listening. The mastigas stopped as well, still seeming to wait upon his movements. That was growing more and more unnerving by the minute. He knew they were out there, and he knew they knew where he was. They had to, otherwise they could not be keeping pace with him as well as they were.

He started to run, but stopped three steps in when the shade of the mastigas's movements grew lighter. He listened again, taking a few tentative steps. The color of their sound stayed dim, dark red.

Panatakis ran again, exactly seven steps and then stopped. The mastigas's footsteps grew closer, then faded away as he started walking again.

Continuing his experiment, he ran a third time, this time for longer. The mastigas again drew closer, scrabbling what looked like only a few corridors away.

Panatakis stopped, watching the colors change as the mastigas tailing him adjusted their own speed and positioning.

In a flash, it hit him. The mastigas were not simply waiting out of reach, they were taunting him. He suspected similar groups were doing the same thing to the other Titans.

"Wherever the crash they are," he muttered, again thinking aloud.

He stopped, thinking, trying to put together everything he suspected about the mastigas movements. If they were reacting to his movements, not just his position but the actual type of movements he was making, then there had to be a way to out-think them.

They were still no match for a trained Titan of the Technocracy, he thought to himself. The smugness came through even in his thoughts, but he made no effort to hide what he was feeling. No one was here to judge him as he indulged in a momentary rush of emotion. The surge of confidence felt *good*.

He looked around, watching the dim red wisps of noise carried on the dank air. He whistled a simple tune, watching the bright blue notes sail through the air like mist.

The mastigas color-noise dimmed; they were pulling away.

"So," he muttered. "They attack when I run and pull away when I, what, make them think I'm..." A smile spread over his face as elation struck. "Running sounds reckless, so they come closer, thinking I'm afraid of them. If I sound like I'm not afraid of them, like I'm not going to make a reckless mistake, they keep away. Fascinating."

From far away, words came, carried on a dim, blue-green fog. "I heard a whistle. Where are you?"

His heart sped up. That was not the voice of a mastigas. Victoria had shocked the lot of them—save, perhaps, Lelantos—when she played the tapes from her training where the mastigas spoke to her. None of the published information about them indicated they could do that.

That left only one thing. Well, he thought, technically it left four or five things.

He whistled again, this time a simpler tune.

The voice replied, slightly closer now. "Blue screen it, I know mastigas don't whistle! Where are you?"

Panatakis turned in the direction of the voice. It was close enough to identify at this point. Voices came through his ears as well as his eyes. He had simply never found a way to visualize speech that satisfied him, and so speech went back to where biology put it in the first place. Speech had too many subtle tones, things that helped identify the speaker and what their emotions were, to change that part of his brain.

"Korakti!" he called, moving in the direction her voice came from.

"Panatakis?"

"I'm fairly close by. Can you follow my voice?"

Laughter answered him. "Not as well as you can follow mine!"

"Keep talking. I'll come to you."

He literally tuned out what she was actually saying at that point, instead following the visual trail of her voice. As he rounded a second corner, however, the dim red of the mastigas started to brighten.

He cursed, quietly but vehemently. If they were monitoring him, they would be monitoring Korakti as well. Whatever their game, they were moving rapidly now. Panatakis could not be sure if they were trying to separate them or trap them together. Either way, he had to get to Korakti before the mastigas found either of them.

137

Panatakis relayed, loudly, what he suspected of the mastigas's plan. If the mastigas were listening, he hoped telling them that he knew what they were planning would help. Of course, it was just as likely to make things worse, but he needed to do *something* to disrupt their movement patterns. So he chose that particular gauntlet to throw down.

Whatever the ultimate result, his announcement resulted in a temporary halt to their movement. It only lasted a few seconds, but those were seconds in which he got closer to his fellow Titan while the mastigas remained where they were.

Korakti's voice was louder now, but the mastigas were on the move again as well. They were close enough that the sound of their massed footsteps threatened to overwhelm any noise she was making.

"Talk louder!" he shouted. The mastigas were close, and he broke into a run.

The color of her voice brightened significantly as Panatakis rounded a corner. Korakti stood about a dozen meters away, hands clasped in front of her. As Panatakis re-tuned his senses, he realized that she was reciting poetry.

Before their training, that would not have been something he expected to hear coming from the broad-shouldered woman. Now, it was a welcome relief. If nothing else, finding her meant that at least two of them survived.

"Have you seen any of the others?" she asked.

Panatakis shook his head. "I was able to pass a few words to Helena earlier, I think, then we lost contact. Since then, just you. And I've heard a whole lot of mastigas."

She stepped forward and wrapped her strong arms around his shoulders. It was an odd gesture, spontaneous, and one that would have gotten them no end of strange looks on Prosgeiosi.

Panatakis was glad to be away from that capital world and its extreme aversion toward physical contact. None of the planets were terribly different from one another, but Kokkinos was known as one of the friendlier worlds in the system. His world did not frown on public displays of affection quite as hard as the other planets.

He tried to push thoughts of home from his mind. He would see Kokkinos again, one way or another.

Korakti stepped away, muttering a sheepish apology about propriety.

He brushed it off with a simple, "it's alright," then, "we have more important things to consider right now."

"How close are they, can you tell?"

Panatakis replied with a thin smile. "I was never able to fine tune specific frequencies to distance." The smile vanished and he added, "but they are close."

Korakti nodded. Her blue-black robes swirled as she drew her weapons. A few symbols, including the six symbols they all designed for their team, had been stitched in black thread. The images were almost invisible against the dark fabric, but they were there. Panatakis heard more than saw them—they hovered as spots of silence amid the quiet soprano aria of her robe.

He never understood why she preferred to fight in a robe. They were fine for social functions, but for combat they seemed impractical. Her explanation of obscuring her motions only went so far, but he supposed that the others would see a swirling mass of blue and black rather than a song whose tone changed as she moved.

Under all those robes, he knew, she carried the same burden of gear and weaponry that he did. Equipment, weapons, spare ammunition, and even food and water weighed her down the same as any of them. In Panatakis's mind, that only made her decision to wear a robe all the more unusual.

Yet Second Lord Korakti had proved her combat skill, even beating Victoria in hand-to-hand combat a few times during their brief trip aboard the *Hammer of Ares*, robe or no.

In her left hand, she carried a sword with a wickedly curved blade. A cage of bars protected her hand. The mastigas used swords from time to time, especially the larger ones, but it was unusual to see such an elegant weapon employed amid so much military gear.

The sword did match her robes, he thought.

Her other hand held what he once believed to be an oversized pistol. The large-framed weapon looked like it should have been the sort of high-caliber pistol no rational soldier would carry because of the low ammunition capacity, difficulty of maintenance, and general inaccuracy and unreliability. The weapon Korakti held was actually of a much smaller caliber, and the bulky gun possessed an intricate magazine system and an array of targeting and stabilization features.

That was a good thing, he thought as he unlimbered his own weapon. Unlike Korakti and her flare for the dramatic, Panatakis had chosen a weapons with a much more utilitarian apperance. The heavy rifle had more than its share of tricks that ran the gamut from normal stabilizers and targeting assists to a grenade launcher attached to the underside.

If his instincts were correct and the noises he was seeing were coming from massed hordes very close to them, then his decision to bring along the explosive launcher would prove to be a good one. Even if he only encountered a few mastigas, the grenades would come in handy.

As Second Lord Daniel put it one day, "against the mastigas, overkill was only part of the job."

He smiled at that memory, choosing to focus on it rather than the tide of green eyed monsters bearing down on him.

Panatakis shifted his grip on his weapon, moving his forward hand back slightly to operate the grenade launcher. Let Korakti be the one to worry about precision shooting—he had explosives.

He tuned his senses, slipping away from the colorful world he preferred and into what he dubbed, "battle mode." The human brain could process motion better without color interfering, and so he shut down that part of his eyes.

The world plunged into black and white, but every detail of every little motion made it to his brain now. Sight and sound mingled together, both feeding the same data to their respective processing centers. His mind interpreted each differently, but they came together in a whole that was, in its stark way, beautiful.

Sound registered in his eyes as patches of brighter motion: the louder the sound, the brighter the light. Meanwhile, motion came to his ears as simple tones whose pitch defined location while volume matched distance.

Panatakis lacked Lelantos's precision sense of time, but his implants could still overlay useful information across his vision. In addition to ammunition reserves, he had also started a counter when he first found Korakti. Sixty-two seconds had passed since the two of them reunited, and four more seconds passed before the first mastigas rounded the corner.

Korakti, with her faster reflexes, took aim and fired. Panatakis trusted her precision, but still the feeling of someone behind him firing over his shoulder made him flinch. The bullet struck the little mikros square between its three eyes, toppling it.

"We need to get to cover!" Korakti barked.

"I haven't seen any!"

"Then we move!"

"Which way?"

She pointed the way the mikros came from. "The way they don't want us to go."

Panatakis nodded, allowing Korakti to shoulder past. Several more mikros and a pair of fonias scrabbled around the corner at that moment. The mikros carried small pistols and the fonias both wielded their characteristic knives.

Each of their footsteps was a bright flash on the floor. Korakti leveled her pistol, taking aim at the nearest target—one of the fonias. It made sense from her perspective. The almost-man-sized mastigas were fast and deadly in close quarters.

141

What she did not see, what Panatakis *did* see because of his altered senses, were the little flashes of noise from one of the mikros's guns. A normal human could not have heard the machine noises of the pistol's mechanism, but to his eyes they were bright spots amid the cold, dim gun.

He reacted instinctively, hoping he could move faster than the mastigas. Panatakis shifted his grip as Korakti fired. Her shot took the nearest fonias in the head. It collapsed and rolled, coming to a stop a meter later. The second fonias vaulted over its dead twin, seeming to gain speed.

Finally, his hand found the trigger loop and he squeezed the trigger. The weapon spat out three rounds. Two of them missed, but one bullet from the burst seemed to be a little luckier. It hit his target in the shoulder.

The mikros screamed, more in rage than in pain, as its arm went limp. Its gun clattered to the floor in a flash of bright purple and the creature itself turned and fled.

Korakti shifted her aim and downed the fleeing mastigas before it could move more than a few steps. Panatakis fired again, holding down the trigger and sweeping the gun across the small group.

Three bursts of fire later, and two more shots by Korakti's precision pistol, and the mastigas were all dead.

Korakti's laugh of victory came as loud as boisterous as anything she did.

Panatakis panted. Adrenaline made up for the lack of actual physical exertion, sending his heart rate skyrocketing and threatening to take his knees out from under him. Like Daniel and Victoria, he fought captive mastigas as part of his training. Facing them in combat, real combat, was altogether a different matter as far as his nerves were concerned.

"Come on!" Korakti called, already two steps ahead.

"I need a moment to listen for more of them!"

"We don't have a moment," she argued, still moving. Panatakis followed, more concerned with staying with his fellow Titan, if he was truthful, than pinpointing the mastigas. Korakti continued, saying, "we need to keep moving. We move, we increase our chances of finding the others."

"Point," he conceded.

They turned a corner, finding an empty hallway. "Can you do that telepathy thing with Helena?"

"No," he answered. He found it difficult to keep up with the tall woman's long strides and so kept his response to the minimum.

"Because?" Her tone indicated she expected more of a reply.

"Because I can't find her again. The mastigas systems locked me out before we could share enough data to make a map. For anything like that, we need to be close."

"How short range is your telepathy?"

He resisted the urge to correct her terminology, because their connection was fundamentally no different from a wireless comm. On the other hand, now was not the time for pedantry. "It gets unreliable past about ten meters."

"Shit," she cursed, then, "apologies."

"You're not saying anything I've not been thinking since I climbed out of my shuttle."

Heavy footsteps bounced dim light off the walls around them. Panatakis quickly reactivated his color vision, hoping to use the actual hue of the noise to identify the source.

The effort proved to be in vain when the bellow of a gigas filled his vision with angry red haze.

Korakti stopped. "Damn all these hallways. I can't tell..."

Panatakis interrupted her, pointing behind them. "That way."

She resumed her fast pace, not quite running, moving away from the direction he pointed. "Then we keep moving."

Noise ahead of them reflected light on the walls.

"There's more ahead!" Panatakis announced.

"Gigas?"

"Doesn't sound like it."

Korakti turned her shoulders slightly, bringing her sword in front of her body without slowing or altering her pace any. "We're not stopping."

"I wasn't planning to."

The noise from the gigas behind them was closer now, as was the noise from the mastigas ahead of them. With his senses, he could see past the next curves of twisting hallway. Nothing branched off of it, at least nothing between them and the mastigas.

Panatakis slowed. "Take the gigas."

"We need to keep moving."

He shook his head. "We need to fight them on our terms. If we run headlong into that," he pointed ahead of them, "then they dictate where we fight that." Now he pointed the other way, toward the thunder of the running gigas.

Korakti came to a halt, stopping immediately with the grace of a lifelong martial artist. She looked from end to end of the long, curving hallway, made eye contact with Panatakis, and nodded. She pivoted on her heels, raising both her sword and pistol.

He did likewise, facing the opposite direction and shifting his hands back to the trigger for the weapon's grenade launcher.

The mastigas rounded the corner as one coordinated unit. Seven mikros ran behind a dozen fonias. The knife-wielders scrabbled against the metal floor, skidding some as they changed directions. The mikros came slightly slower, but even they had to rely on their short, stubby secondary arms for balance. The fonias surged forward, knives raised, as the mikros came to their feet again.

Panatakis's heart thundered. Flashes from the gigas's footsteps echoed on the walls around him, but he dared not take his attention away from the horde in front of him. Behind his back, a roar, then scrabbling of feet and claws echoed by gunfire and the sounds of steel on steel. In his face, the decision to address the closer threat or the more well-armed threat.

This time, the decision was easier. The grenade launcher attached to the underside of his rifle fired projectiles slightly larger than his thumb. It held six of them at a time, and he loaded several different ones into the tube magazine.

Panatakis worked the release lever, dropping the first grenade to the floor, unfired. It would detonate if armed, which it had not been. In such close quarters, it was liable to do more harm than good. Second in the tube, however, was a smoke bomb, which he had much more use for. The grenade launcher coughed, kicking against the padded shoulder of his uniform jacket as it shot the projectile down the corridor. It started spewing smoke immediately upon leaving the barrel, giving the grenade a short, erratic trajectory. It fell several meters short of the mastigas, filling the intervening space with smoke in a matter of seconds.

He took full advantage of those few seconds, adjusting his grip again and firing burst after burst into what should have been a gray haze. For the mastigas, as their repeated misses attested, the hallway had become exactly that. Panatakis, however, could hear through the smoke just fine and his eyes showed him the sounds of the mastigas moving as clearly as if there had been no smoke.

Without a sophont to direct them or their sight to rely on, the mastigas milled about in random directions. The fonias stalked in mostly the right direction, but the mikros, so dependent on their trinocular vision, stood very still, aiming and waiting for the smoke to clear.

Unfortunately for both types of mastigas, Panatakis was able to pick them off fairly easily. He fought the urge to simply fire another grenade into the smoke and take care of the problem that way, but he did have a limited number of the things. With no way of knowing how long they were going to be aboard the ship, especially without the support of the personnel aboard the *Justice*, he wanted to conserve the grenades as much as he could.

Bullets, however, were much smaller and lighter than the explosives, and he carried significantly more of them. And so, round after round, he emptied the magazine of his rifle into the confused mass of mastigas.

"Problem so—"

He was about to say "solved," but as he turned, he saw Korakti's gigas problem had become much worse in the handful of seconds it had taken him to eliminate the confused mass of enemies on his side of the hall.

The positive to the situation was the simple joy of watching Korakti fight. Her flamboyant personality showed through in her fighting style. Swirl-patterned fabric, sword, and pistol all danced together in pirouettes and twirls, dealing death and dismemberment with every movement.

She really was an artist, he thought.

Despite her skill, there remained a problem. What started out, he thought, as one gigas had become three of the towering monsters accompanied by another dozen fonias. A mikros rode on the shoulders of each gigas, pointing and barking orders.

Panatakis's blood ran cold. Not simply because the mikros seemed to be directing the fight from atop their giant mounts, nor because of the number of enemies Korakti faced. If either of those things had truly given him pause, the three dead and seven wounded fonias would have put his mind at ease.

No, what froze his blood was the fact that he understood the mastigas. The orders they were giving were simple, directions left or right, forward and backward, attack, defend, and so on. They did not seem to possess any groundbreaking tactical skill. The problem was that the mikros were speaking Lexeis Archeio. It might have been an ostensibly dead language among Technocrats, but it was still used in certain religious rituals and older, scientific texts.

Mastigas should not know a dead Technocrat language.

A moment longer, and he saw yet another problem. Past the fonias and the gigas, just in sight on their side of the long curve in the hallway, stood a sophont. The tall, three eyed monster held its long arms behind its back like a director watching a play unfold. Its short arms were clasped in front of its chest like a gleeful child. It said nothing, simply watching the fight unfold and rubbing its hands together.

Panatakis wanted to fire a grenade at the sophont. A high explosive could go right over the heads of the gigas, even as tall as they were, and be dropped right at the feet of the most intelligent of the mastigas varieties. Two or three seconds of travel and then a single moment and the mastigas attacking Korakti would lose most of their intelligence.

Yet, the gigas were tall. If his aim was off by even the tiniest amount, his grenade could impact one of them or the ceiling above their heads. The explosion would take out the entire group of mastigas as easily as the sophont.

It would also take Korakti out.

Panatakis nodded, more to confirm his plan with himself than anything, and moved his hand to his rifle's normal trigger. He aimed, high above her head, at the chest of one of the mikros.

The first round hit the gigas in the ear, and subsequently struck the mikros on its shoulders in the hip. The second round hit the mikros in the shoulder, leaving the last round to spall uselessly against the ceiling.

"Fall back!" he called. "There's a sophont!"

"I know!" she grunted in return. Her reply came in bits and pieces, two or three words at a time in between movements. "I can't get a clear shot on it because these mikros keep moving the gigas around, and I can't kill them because the fonias keep trying to jump me."

He instantly reassessed that tactical situation. She was right. The gigas should have been using the fonias as distraction to keep her occupied so that they could line up the killing blow. That was standard behavior for this sort of group; footage from the assault on Kipos showed that clearly enough.

Panatakis asked himself why this was different. The gigas were clearly protecting the sophont, but not only were they not taking

147

advantage of Korakti's fight with the fonias, they were not attacking her at all. The fonias seemed unaware of that fact as they repeatedly attempted to drive her toward the trio of gigas. At times, the gigas seemed to maneuver independently of the mikros's orders, almost like they were moving into position to attack Korakti themselves, but they always slunk back after a snapped order from the mikros.

"Help would be appreciated," Korakti said. Her words came out in a staccato rhythm, enunciated between attacks.

"Push the fonias apart and I'll do what I can."

Korakti grunted, whether in acknowledgment or in frustration, he could not be sure. Either way, she did seem to adjust her tactics slightly, employing larger attacks and sweeps with her sword that kept the horde of knife-armed mastigas at bay.

He fired a burst at the fringes of the fonias swarm. Two of the bullets hit their target, and impossibly red blood fountained out from the fonias's back. It splattered on the wall and on the gigas behind it.

Movement at the far end of the hall caught his attention. The sophont still had its long arms behind its back, standing hunched now. Its short arms reached out, trying to grasp some invisible object in out of reach. It also slowly, very slowly, stepped forward again.

He maneuvered, trying to get a clear shot. Every time he took a step to the left or right, one of the gigas would move to block it. Neither they nor the mikros looked back, but invariably, they always moved with perfect precision, interposing their nigh-indestructible bulk between his weapons and the comparatively fragile sophont.

His eyes ran back to the gigas. Something was different now. They all still moved to obscure the sophont from his line of sight, but the third one had adopted a much more aggressive posture. It had moved much closer to Korakti than the other two.

A moment later, it clicked in his head that that gigas bore the mikros he shot seconds before. The little mastigas teetered atop its mount, its bright red blood soaking black fabric.

148

He raised his rifle, firing another two bursts. The first impacted the gigas square in the chest. The giant grunted, knocked back a step by the force of the bullets, but did not go down. It took much more punishment to penetrate the dense muscle of those towering giants. The gigas had not been his target, however, and as the muzzle of his weapon climbed with recoil, the second burst knocked the mikros from its shoulders.

The mikros fell to the floor with a wet thump, dead before it impacted.

The sophont took another step.

The two gigas still carrying mikros on their shoulders stood ramrod straight for half a second, then turned on their heels with the sort of military precision he had only seen in recordings from Kipos. They leaned forward and bellowed incoherent rage at the sophont, causing it to back up several steps.

"What the blue screened..." Korakti mumbled. She pirouetted between two fonias, laying long slices across both of them with her sword. A deep back bend and a yoga-like stretch of her arm brought her pistol on target and she put a bullet through the skull of a third.

The third gigas, the one without a mikros, lumbered toward her. Korakti's attention had been so focused on the immediate threat that it looked like she tuned out the presence of the gigas. Now that at least one of them was more than a biological wall, she still failed to take notice of it.

The sudden change in the gigas surprised even Panatakis. It took him a moment to react, and in that moment, the gigas had taken one too many steps. Yelling was useless at that point; the gigas had its arm raised overhead. It was empty-handed, but even without a weapon, the massive creature could easily crush a human.

His aim was not as good as Korakti's. If their places had been switched, he would have trusted implicitly that her shots would fly true. Panatakis had no such trust in his own abilities. Neither did he have any other option.

He aimed, waiting as long as possible to make sure his aim was as true as he could make it, and squeezed the trigger. Three more bullets impacted the gigas's torso, missing the other Titan by a wide margin.

Panatakis breathed a sigh of relief, but the damage to the gigas was still minimal, relative to its bulk. He started to squeeze the trigger again, but quickly jerked the weapon upwards when Korakti made a move for the gigas.

She lunged forward, sword arm outstretched. Almost reflexively, her pistol hand darted to the side and put a round between the eyes of a nearby fonias. Another step and she went low, raising her sword overhead.

The gigas did not have time to react before her sword bit into the inside of its thigh. Strong and tough as they were, they were still mortal. Anything died quickly with its femoral artery spurting inhumanly-bright blood everywhere.

It stumbled, then fell. Panatakis had only a few moments to appreciate the artistry and efficiency of her kill before a fonias jumped her from behind.

Korakti wrestled with the little mastigas for a moment, managing to throw it off of her shoulder and into one in front of her. The interruption in her rhythm allowed the fonias to close closer, forcing the Titan on the defensive. No longer was the horde spread out, kept away by her sword swings, but the fonias now seemed to climb over one another, eager to get at the human in their midst.

Panatakis did not have time to think. He ran forward, shifting his grip on the long rifle so that he could use it as a bludgeoning weapon. The fonias were simply too close to his comrade to risk shooting anymore.

"No!" she shouted. Her cheek had been split and parts of her robe hung in tatters where the enveloping fabric caught and deflected the fonias's knives. "The gigas!"

The tones of command in her voice his a primal nerve in his brain, and he obeyed. He skidded to a halt, stumbling over his feet with none

150

of Korakti's grace. Now, much closer to the fight, his aim would be better. Korakti, for good or ill, was also moving around less, allowing him a clearer field of fire against the gigas.

Panatakis raised his rifle, taking aim at the pair of giants. Thoughts ran through his mind like lightning. He killed the mikros riding the third one and the gigas immediately went on the offensive.

Something was not right.

He maneuvered to try and put the sophont under his sights again. With only two gigas left, the wide hallway was less easily blocked by their bulk. The sophont itself was on the move, and the gigas seemed confused, distracted. They did not seem to know whether to pay attention to Panatakis, to Korakti and her fight, or to the sophont rapidly gaining on them.

One settled on the sophont, turning and bellowing. The sophont ignored the unspoken threat this time, continuing to stride forward. As it drew closer, the gigas seemed less and less hostile towards it. As the distance closed, the giant slowly turned toward Korakti.

The second gigas, further away from the sophont, reared back and punched the first one in the back. The first gigas turned away from Korakti, now wholly focused on the one that had attacked it.

That also opened his sightlines to the sophont. It stood off to one side, away from the fighting and far removed from Korakti. Panatakis poured four three-round bursts into the large-headed mastigas. The hail of bullets knocked it backwards and onto the floor. It continued to twitch for several moments before falling still. As it did, the two mikros seemed to regain control over their erstwhile mounts, forcing them away from the mass of fonias.

Panatakis turned his attention back to Korakti's fight. He did not see her.

"Korakti!" he shouted. Again, "Korakti!"

A shouted curse from the midst of the fonias swarm answered him. The curse was accompanied by a gunshot and one of the mastigas fell.

For half a second, he caught sight of Korakti, bloody and on one knee. Few of the fonias remained, but with every passing second, their attacks grew bolder as hers grew slower.

In the corner of his eye, the two gigas lumbered away. One paused to grab the sophont by the leg, dragging it behind them as they retreated.

Panatakis rushed the few remaining fonias, swatting one away with the butt of his rifle. He pivoted, raised the rifle again, and smashed a second one in the face. It fell backward, scrabbling at the faceplate of its helmet.

That left three fonias. Korakti lashed out with her sword, catching one in the stomach with a thrust. It let out a gurgle and reached for her wrists. Before she had been wounded, Korakti would have been able to pull the sword free and defend herself against the mastigas next to her.

Before she had been wounded, her reactions would have been faster. She jerked the sword free, but the dying mastigas had held firm for a moment too long. On her far side, where Panatakis could not reach, the last fonias raised its knives.

Korakti raised her pistol, or she started to. The fonias plunged one knife into her forearm. The muscles spasmed and she dropped the pistol. It plunged its other knife into the the crook between her neck and shoulder.

Panatakis slammed his rifle into the nearest mastigas, one of the only two left, and lunged forward. The butt of his rifle crushed the last mastigas's helmet, knocking it off its feet and sending it at least a meter through the air.

As he looked down, Panatakis realized they both had been too slow to react. The damage had been done. The jagged wound at the base of her neck spurted arterial blood.

He wanted to fall on his knees and scream and cry, but several of the mastigas around him were starting to come to their feet again. Bleeding and unsteady from the impact of his rifle butt, they were nonetheless still alive and armed.

With no need to worry about friendly fire, Panatakis emptied his magazine into the surviving mastigas, firing until nothing moved.

Then, with all the mastigas dead, he fell to his knees, screamed, and cried.

Chapter 9

Tritogenes fumed, at least on the inside. He was careful, very careful, to keep it off of his face. His mentor was dead, shot in what he could only imagine to be cold blood by one of the five people in the entire binary he should have been able to trust.

Not only that, but that same man, that Hexarch who should have been a paragon of virtue, sent armed men to capture or kill him. "Should have been" and "actually were" were rarely the same thing, especially when it came to the world of politics. Hexarchs often bartered and traded in areas so gray that notions of right and wrong were left at the door. However, to kill another Hexarch was unthinkable.

No, he thought, anger was a perfectly reasonable reaction to what had happened. What anger would not help, however, was the news he was hearing from Katarraktes. He had not really wanted to call in help from First Lord Enyalios. Though he was a good friend, the other Hexarch's idea of "extraction" would likely involve bombers and assault troops. But with Limani under the same "terrorist threat" as Pteryga, and Pallasophia unable to come to his aid with something a touch more subtle, he had made the call to Enyalios.

Yet, according to Enyalios, "Katarraktes is under some sort of terrorist warning. Ouroboros, they said."

Tritogenes cursed in his head. Pteryga, Limani, Katarraktes were all under lockdown by Aegesander's forces. Limani bothered him most, but his immediate problem was Pteryga. He had to get off of Hyperion's world, or the world that belonged to First Lord Hyperion up until the "terrorist attack" an hour and a half ago. He suspected every planet in the system except Dasos, and possibly Kokkinos, had found themselves under simultaneous thread from "Ouroboros," the crashed snake they all thought was dead.

Only Tritogenes, Rivka, and now Enyalios knew the alleged "terrorist" was one of their own. Unfortunately for their chances of easily leaving Pteryga without another firefight, Aegesander's troops also "knew" the terrorist was a Hexarch, but they had been grossly mislead as to which of their number it was.

The little holographic image of Enyalios floating above Tritogenes's forearm looked like he was torn between wanting to vomit and wanting to kill everything and everyone in sight, and knowing he could not do either of those things. First Lord Enyalios had seen Tritogenes lose his temper before—in fact, he had been the cause of that very thing happening more than once in the past—but for the moment, Tritogenes had no one to be angry *at*.

"Aegesander's troops hit the high orbitals about an hour ago," Enyalios continued. The look of anger remained on his face, but his voice was level and controlled.

Tritogenes held up a hand. "Wait. The high orbitals? Does that mean Aegesander's troops haven't landed?"

The hologram of Enyalios shook his head. "No," he replied. "Something smelled wrong when he arrived. None of his accusations made any sense, so I had his ships quarantined."

Tritogenes raised an eyebrow. "Quarantined?"

"Yes. I denied them landing permits on account of 'suspicious data packages' in their transmissions. That, of course, sent the captains into a frenzy. Ten minutes later, they came back with a message that, according to First Lord Aegesander, they had clear orders to land and deal with the Ouroboros threat."

"Very clear orders," Tritogenes muttered.

"Hmm?"

"That was what the soldiers he sent to capture Rivka and me said. They said that about six seconds before trying to put a pair of bullets in our heads, anyway."

"What the blue-screened hell is he up to?"

"He killed Hyperion," Tritogenes said. His tone was flat, anger hiding under a mask of steel calm. Words that he did not dare give voice to when talking to Pallasophia came easily now that Aegesander's troops were shooting at them.

"I am aware," Enyalios replied. He paused for a moment. Even on the hologram, the fact that his internal monologue was conflicted came across clearly. Finally, he admitted, "I'm not surprised it happened."

"What?" Tritogenes demanded. "Why not?"

"Several years ago, shortly after the start of Project Titan, Hyperion and I had a very long conversation about the past. I had suspected some things for a while based on things First Lord Meriones said to me."

"About what?"

At Tritogenes's side, Rivka tensed, but said nothing.

Enyalios shook his head firmly, twice in each direction. "That's not important right now. What's important is that I can't send a force to extract you."

"You own the largest military-industrial company in the binary," Tritogenes protested.

"Yes, and for the last half-decade, I've spent most of that company's funds building assault cruisers for Project Titan. What's left is currently sitting in my high orbitals with missiles locked on Aegesander's ships."

Tritogenes laughed, a bleak sound that was aimed more at the absurdity of their situation than anything actually amusing. "That bad?"

"His captains did not take well to being told they could not land. I lost two patrol boats before I could get the rest of the fleet into position."

Tritogenes was aghast. "He fired on you?"

"Said that pair of ships had been 'subverted by the Ouroboros terrorists.'"

"Good Lovelace," he muttered.

"That was about my reaction," Enyalios replied. The hologram grinned. "But with a lot worse swearing."

"Is there anything you can do?"

"I can probably detach a frigate to come pick you up, but most of my troops are aboard the *Justice*. Well, right now, they should be aboard the mastigas battleship. The troops that aren't otherwise engaged are stationed at my own spaceports in case Aegesander's captains get jumpy. Either way, I don't have the manpower to mount an invasion of Pteryga."

"I understand," Tritogenes replied.

"I'm sorry, my friend."

"I know."

Enyalios nodded. "I'll update you when I know more."

"Thank you," Tritogenes replied, then, "my friend."

"Go with the suns, Tritogenes."

He returned the formal parting words, then cut the transmission. He looked around the little room in which he and First Lord Rivka had spent the last ten minutes. It was fairly sparse, but had enough of Hyperion's bullet-resistant furniture to fashion crude bulwarks in case they needed them.

Their shuttles still waited at Hyperion's private spaceport. The only advantage that now gave them was that they did not have to leave the Blue Spire to get to their ships. If Aegesander truly controlled the planet now, or at least the area around Hyperion's capitol, then moving out in the open would be a poor choice.

The disadvantage, of course, was that Aegesander's troops landed there as well. They would likely be concentrated at the spaceport itself, which made them their primary problem. Even if they could duck every single guard, if they stumbled at that last hurdle, it would ultimately not matter.

He shook his head. He was thinking too many steps in advance again. It would do them no good to worry about the spaceport itself if they failed to reach it in the first place.

Their next move was simply to leave the room.

Rivka stood a few meters away, keeping watch at the door. While he spoke to Enyalios, she stripped off her robe, claiming "convention be damned." Tritogenes was surprised at how much armor she managed to hide under that voluminous, purple garment, but it was what it was.

Now, she wore little else other than a form-fitting layer of black fabric studded with impact absorbing gel pads and rigid plates. Rivka had supplemented it with pieces of armor from the soldiers Aegesander sent after them, but there was little she could do to improve the kit she already wore.

Tritogenes initially objected, but she pointed out two reasons for it. First, she argued, they could move and fight easier without the robes. Second, she asked him a question.

"What marks us as Hexarchs in the eyes of the general public?"

He was about to say something about the work they did or identifiable faces, but then realized where she was going with her question. He replied, "the purple."

"Exactly. So we lose the robes and we gain maybe a few seconds where Aegesander's guards don't think, 'Hexarch.'"

Her reasoning made sense, and he quickly stripped off his robe as well. Unlike his more paranoid companion, Tritogenes did not wear a full suit of combat armor under his robe. None of the soldiers sent after them were precisely his size either, but he made do as much as he could by scavenging their armor, gear, and clothing.

That, more than anything, had told Enyalios immediately that something was wrong when Tritogenes contacted him.

Now, the two of them made an almost comical sight dressed as two different movie cliches. He wore a stolen uniform in the wrong size and Rivka looked like some fetish version of a soldier, all tight clothes and random patches of bare skin.

The most important parts of their objectively-ridiculous outfits were the weapons. They survived one encounter with their holdout pistols, but the long arms carried by Aegesander's soldiers would serve them much better going forward.

They certainly were better pointed away from him and Rivka, he thought.

Tritogenes stood, once against adjusting the ill-fitting, stolen uniform. It was cinched in key places with strips of fabric which kept most of the loose material from getting in his way, but Tritogenes would never be mistaken for a soldier.

"Is the hallway clear?"

Rivka leaned back into the room slightly, turning her head just enough so that she could see Tritogenes out of the corner of one eye while keeping most of her gaze fixed on the hallway. "As far as I can tell."

"No bad feelings about anything?"

"I've had a bad feeling about all of this since I left my office on Kipos.

"That's fair. Are you ready to move?"

She nodded.

"Good."

"I'll lead," she said. "I'm the better shot."

Tritogenes had no objections this time. She was right, after all. He nodded and Rivka darted into the hall. She swept her rifle to the left, then headed to the right. He followed a second later, alternating between watching where they were going and watching the halls behind them.

One of his tasks before contacting Enyalios had been to break down the firewalls in the rifles' systems. That had been easy enough—his Hexarch access codes might not have worked on the weapons, but a "toolkit" that had been a gift from Second Lord Philip before he left Limani the last time broke the their security in moments.

The harder part had been disabling the tracking software without taking the entire interface offline, but in the end the weapons connected themselves to their personal gear as readily as if they had been issued to the two Hexarchs in the first place.

Along with tracking, the weapons contained their own communication systems, ostensibly to relay information on ammunition supply, fire rate, and all sorts of other information that a high-ranking battlefield analyst would need.

If anyone was going to analyze their progress in that much detail, he thought, it would likely be because he made a fatal mistake somewhere. So the communication software had been disabled along with the basic tracking routines. Even if he had wanted to analyze his fight later, it was not worth the risk of communicating his position to whatever command center Aegesander had set up.

The tracking software offered one advantage, however. It connected to a server which, theoretically, held maps of the area around the soldier carrying the weapon. With some tweaking, and several tools from Philip's kit, the two of them got the map feature reactivated while leaving the actual tracking software non-functional. The map had to be manually manipulated and lacked the typical "you are here" icon, but it painted a clear picture of the route between the two fugitive Hexarchs and their destination.

Tritogenes brought up that map, adjusting the projection to mirror their current location. He looked away from the glowing image after a few moments. "Turn right."

"That will take us away from the spaceport."

"I'm aware. There's also a very large room about two hundred meters down the hall if we go left."

"What is it?"

He frowned at the hologram. "According to the map, it's a dining hall."

"Are you sure there are troops there? We go this way and, if my memory's right, it will add ten minutes to our walk."

"Closer to twenty. We're going in everything but a straight line. Harder to follow that way."

"And the dining hall?"

"It's the sort of place I'd stage an ambush if I were him," Tritogenes admitted.

"That would explain why we've not seen anyone else," she muttered.

Tritogenes nodded. "He's not stupid. After those two failed to bring us in, Aegesander probably moved everyone he could spare to the palace's chokepoints."

"I didn't think," she said, stopped, then, "ok, yes, I've been thinking about how stupid he is to pull this sort of thing."

"Unfortunately for us," he said, then interjected, "two doors down and then left," followed by, "'evil' and 'bad at tactics' aren't the same thing."

She followed his directions, coming to a closed door. He indicated it with a jerk of one thumb and a sideways nod of his head. "Maintenance passage."

"Can you get it open?"

Tritogenes scrolled his holographic map in several directions before looking at the door again. Rather than answer, he tried the handle—locked. He manipulated the map again for a moment before slinging the rifle over his back. The map, projected by the gun rather than his personal holo, went with it.

He knelt and examined the lock. During his tenure as House Master in First Lord Ophion's opera house, Tritogenes had seen plenty of locked doors. In fact, the skill of opening such doors had come in handy more than once when an actor or member of the crew got locked out of, or in, someplace they needed to be.

That experience ultimately proved useless as the lock thwarted every trick he had. Rivka patrolled back and forth, tracing out a five meter path each direction, while he worked. After the third attempt failed, she stopped and nudged his shoulder.

"Find another route," she ordered.

"I could break it down."

"You break it down and every one of Aegesander's soldiers on this floor is going to hear and come after us."

"Point," he admitted. He pulled himself up using the stubborn door's handle as a lever and dusted off his too-big uniform. He brought his rifle, and with it the map, back around in front of his chest. A few moments of manipulation and he pointed over his shoulder. "That way, then left."

"We came from that way," she reminded him.

"I know," he replied. His eyes were fixed on the glowing gray-white projection as he moved it around. He enlarged an area, then swiped a finger through it to highlight a path in green. Another swipe and he highlighted a second path in blue, then a third in red. "See this?"

"The red one goes to that dining hall," she said. "The place you're worried is going to be an ambush. The blue," she peered, "that looks like where we just were."

Tritogenes nodded. A gesture erased those two lines and brightened the green path. "This is the way we're going to go now, provided we don't..."

"Don't say it."

He fell silent. A moment passed before he continued. "Anyway, the green path is shorter than the blue one by a good five minutes, but it goes much closer to this room than I would have liked."

A wave of his hand highlighted an entire, high-ceilinged room in red.

"I don't recognize that room."

162

"Most people don't," he said. "It's a server control room."

Rivka looked thoughtful for a few seconds before saying, "and if he has control of the broadcast, then he likely has troops there."

"More than that. I said 'control room' for a reason. That room is where most of the actual broadcasting is done."

"So, Aegesander might be in there."

"It's a possibility."

"Good." A hard look shadowed her eyes. It failed to touch anything else on her face, and it was gone in a moment, but it lingered in her eyes long enough for Tritogenes to recognize it.

"You're not going planning on confronting him, are you?"

"He killed Hyperion."

"He's dangerous."

Her voice came out an angry hiss. "He killed Hyperion!"

Tritogenes growled. "Don't you think I know that? Hyperion was my mentor, my friend! But he's probably surrounded by armed guards, and just because we trained Titans does not mean we *are* Titans. You go after him right now and you'll die."

Anger boiled across Rivka's face. She looked on the verge of reminding him, again, of Aegesander's crime, but thought better of it. She exhaled, deflated. "You made your point."

"Thank you."

She scoffed. "If it's a public showdown he wants, he's going to be waiting at the spaceport anyway."

Before Tritogenes could say anything, Rivka drug her finger through the holomap, adding another line. The system automatically gave it a green color to replace the previous one. Her path diverged from Tritogenes's several turns before they got near the server room.

"Bad idea," Tritogenes said. He panned the map and highlighted another room in red. Rivka's path went right by the door. Unlike the others he had objected to, this particular room was small, scarcely larger than an office. "Security checkpoint," he called it.

He drew another line. The map gave this one an orange hue. It branched from Rivka's path, but dropped down several floors in a staircase before going in a nearly unbroken line for the underside of the spaceport.

Rivka moved the map back some. The line intersected a hallway that connected to the locked door that had thwarted them. "Maintenance tunnel?"

"A different one, but yes. This way is much longer than either of the other two paths, but we should be fairly well hidden as we move."

"That will give us time to make a plan for the port itself, too."

Tritogenes nodded slowly. "Yes," he said. He was not looking forward to that part of things. "It will."

***

The end of the maintenance tunnel stood before them, smeared with the same dusty grease that had covered everything so far. Beyond it was the stairwell that would take them back up seven levels to the spaceport. Neither of them wanted to guess what they would find at that point, so they made plans for every conceivable outcome.

Tritogenes wished that a few more of those outcomes ended with both of them getting away safely, but the only thing that realistically would improve their chances anymore was luck.

Rivka, still leading, tried the door. She gave an audible sigh of relief as another piece of good luck found them. The door opened easily enough, gliding on silent hinges. It was likely lubricated by the same grease that had been smeared on the handle itself.

Tritogenes held up a hand. "Wait. We need to change first. If the spaceport isn't under Aegesander's control, a pair of Hexarchs might be able to talk their way through better than two action movie cliches."

"If we can't," Rivka argued, "I don't want my last moments to be staring up at the sky or down at the ground because I tripped over my own hem."

Tritogenes started to argue, then thought better of it. After all, it had been him to caution that the spaceport would likely be under Aegesander's control in the first place. More important than that, however, was the simple fact that if it had been possible for a pair of Hexarchs to talk their way out of the corner they had been backed into, they would have done it with those two soldiers.

It failed then, he reminded himself. There was no reason to think it would work now. As much as he did not want to go that particular route, shooting their way through was the most likely path.

He was not a commando; he was an opera singer who happened to have a talent for managing human resources. Despite that, he was still here, feeling like he was playing dress-up in his older brother's uniform. The weapon in his hands was real enough, though, and he knew the odds of not having to use it were dropping by the minute.

The stairwell gradually became cleaner as they climbed toward the port level. Each floor had a landing with a windowed door; those they skirted past in comical crouches. With no way of knowing what was on the other side without looking through, and not wanting to look through the little window in case one of Aegesander's soldiers was looking back, they did everything they could do sneak past, out of sight of the window.

It was, Tritogenes reflected, a poor way for a Hexarch to end his day.

At the top of the stairs was another door. It, too, had a window, but this time the door was their destination rather than an obstacle to be avoided. Until they had a finalized plan, however, they kept out of sight of this last window as well.

Crouched under the window, backs pressed tight against the door to bring them as far out of sight as possible, the two Hexarchs took a minute to catch their breath. They had not exactly sprinted up the stairs, and they both were in decent shape, but climbing down seven flights of stairs, trekking down a half-kilometer tunnel, and then climbing another seven flights of stairs back up was more physical exertion than either of them were used to on a regular basis.

While they rested, they communicated with crude hand signals and soundless, mouthed words. It took time, but eventually they had a semblance of a plan. Conditions on the other side of the door were still unknown, and neither of them particularly wanted to risk making any noise that might be overheard.

Rivka gave one final sign, then motioned for the door. She, the better shot, shuffled around so that she would be closest to the door when it opened. Remaining crouched, she motioned for Tritogenes to take his position.

He moved, crouching, until he was away from the door. Between his backpack and rifle, pressing himself against the wall next to the door was a bit of a challenge, but he managed. He stood, slowly reaching out for the handle.

They made eye contact, and Rivka shifted around slightly. She went from crouching with both feet on the floor to kneeling. She braced her rifle against her shoulder, aiming up slightly at what would be the center of mass of someone standing on the other side.

Tritogenes wrapped his fingers around the door handle, willing his heartbeat to slow down. They had been lucky so far. Between their fast, stealthy movements and a streak of good luck, the two Hexarchs had not had any trouble after that first incident.

Either that, or they were walking into a trap.

It was too late to worry about that, he reminded himself. Whether or not the bodies of those specific soldiers had been found was immaterial; the entire palace was on high alert and Aegesander's troops were looking for him.

He wondered if the overall lack of military presence was because most of Aegesander's forces were busy containing Hyperion's palace guards. That thought brought some measure of comfort, but ultimately did very little for his mood.

The feeling of comfort was, in its way, less rational than any worry. If Hyperion's soldiers were resisting, then there was a chance

166

Aegesander's coup would fail. That Aegesander still held the palace either meant Hyperion's guards bought his story and would be helping or they were already contained.

Coup. Tritogenes rolled that word around in his mind. They discussed it in the tunnel, away from Aegesander's prying eyes and ears. It was the only thing that explained his actions completely. Whatever his reasons, Aegesander had to be making a bid to eliminate the other Hexarchs.

He again wondered what sort of blackout-insane plan Aegesander cooked up. Rivka was more concerned with what he was doing, especially what he was doing here and now. That was good. Those were the thoughts that would get them offplanet alive. Tritogenes himself, however, found his thoughts continually going back to the "why" of everything.

He was going to have a long talk with First Lord Aegesander when this was all said and done. Stripping a Hexarch of their rank was an exceedingly rare punishment, but it had been done before. Tritogenes thought it was high time it happened again. Then, a social pariah, Aegesander would be thrown in prison and, if Tritogenes had anything to say about it, never released.

He tightened his grip on his rifle, thinking that fate would be what happened if Aegesander was lucky.

Tritogenes worked the handle as slowly as he could, trying to eliminate even the barely-audible click of the latch disengaging. He mostly succeeded, and now the door remained closed only because he was pressing it against the frame.

He made eye contact with Rivka again. She nodded, and he flung open the door.

Rivka rose with a lunge, rushing into the room with a confidence that, they hoped, would surprise anyone waiting on the other side. When she did not immediately open fire, Tritogenes turned the corner, shouldering his way through the now closing door.

He swept the room with the muzzle of his gun, looking for anything or anyone out of place. The room had two doors other than the one they came through. One led back into the palace proper and the other to the open tarmac of the spaceport's landing area. These doors were for staff to use, not guests, and none of them were fancy. The walls were conspicuously bare of any decoration.

More important, it was empty. He shot a hand backward to catch the door and ease it back into place with as little noise as possible.

One more down, he thought. He quickly followed up with a mental reminder that the door they just came through led to a very small room that would not be a good place to stage an ambush.

He gestured toward the next door with his free hand and Rivka nodded. They repeated the exercise from the top of the stairwell. She knelt in front of the door, weapon ready, while Tritogenes positioned himself next to the door with his hand on the handle.

Rivka nodded again, prompting a repetition of the second part of the plan. The door swung open on silent hinges and she lunged through. Previously, he gave her a moment to sweep the room herself. They had known the space would be small and that they would have gotten in one another's way if they tried to shove through together.

The spaceport's landing pad was much, much larger. Despite being the "private" landing area for the relatively small number of people who lived or worked in Hyperion's palace, its size rivaled most commercial ports.

That, Tritogenes thought as he pivoted around the doorframe, could be a good thing or it could be a very, very bad thing.

He pulled his rifle tighter against his shoulder, raising it and already fitting the front and back sights together in his eye. He took aim, gun as level as his admittedly limited training could manage, and swept the tarmac. When nothing moved and no one tried to shoot him, he swept the area again, then made a third visual sweep without squinting down his weapon's sights.

Ahead of him, Rivka had lowered her rifle as well. Her voice shook the same way it had in the moments before Hyperion was shot. Wherever her sense for danger came from, he suspected Rivka was to be trusted when she said, "I don't like this."

"I don't either."

Tritogenes looked around again, turning in a full circle so that he could inspect the outer wall of the palace itself. Nothing was out of place, even to his theatrically-trained eyes. Most of the windows overhead were shut, as were all of the doors on their level. A handful of new shuttles had landed since he arrived, likely bringing Aegesander and his personal guards, but even they were quiet. Heat haze rose from two of the larger ones, but their hatches remained shut.

They moved slowly toward Rivka's shuttle. Of the two of them, she had been able to land closer to the palace, and to the door they came through. Rivka advanced in a half-crouch, moving with enough military precision that her objectively ridiculous fetish-soldier outfit almost looked appropriate. Tritogenes stood more upright, watching the area around them without the hindrance of a rifle sight.

"You don't think he played us?" Rivka hissed. They were halfway to her shuttle. "Do you?"

"Tricked us into thinking he killed Hyperion so that he could implicate us in, what, exactly?"

"I don't know," she admitted. "Ouroboros, maybe. I'm thinking out loud. It helps."

"What's bothering me the most is the complete lack of ground crew," Tritogenes said as they passed an empty workstation. From a cursory glance, it was a simple monitoring station, but it should have had at least two, if not four or five, people working at it.

"You think it's a trap, too?"

"I know it's a trap," he replied, firm. He shifted into formal tenses. "But we have no choice but to hope we escape before it can be sprung."

"Tritogenes," Rivka said. She spoke slowly, like she was reluctant to say the words. Something in her tone, an urgency he had not heard from her before, caught his attention and they stopped for a moment. "There's something you need to know. It's about why I came here in the first place."

"Whatever it is, it can wait until we're aboard your ship."

"I don't know if it can. I don't want to break my promise to Hyperion, but..."

"Then don't."

The hesitancy was gone, but the urgent feeling remained. "You need to know, Tritogenes. All of the Hexarchs need to know."

He sighed. "If it's that important to you, then I'll listen."

"Thank y—"

"Once we're aboard your ship."

She nodded quickly, swallowing hard. "Alright."

Behind them, the click of a door opening interrupted the next thing Tritogenes was going to say. The noise was quiet, perhaps even quieter than he had managed to be opening the maintenance access door.

"I should not have said that," he muttered. He turned so quickly it might as well have been a pirouette, then raising his rifle as the main door to the palace itself opened.

Rivka turned as well, but stopped halfway through. She suddenly sounded wary. "Tritogenes..."

He glanced behind him. She was looking to their right, the direction that had been their left before turning to face the palace. Her rifle, if she ever lowered it in the first place, was level, aimed at something even he had not yet noticed.

The door to the palace was open now, drawing his attention back to it. Without looking back again, he quietly asked, "what is it?"

"Two of the ships over there just opened. Troops. I'm assuming they're Aegesander's."

"Get ready to run for it."

"Yes."

Tritogenes peered down his rifle sights at the open, empty doors to the palace. Each one stood two stories high, inlaid with blue enamel and gold in designs durable enough to withstand the wind and weather. Now, they looked foreboding, giant shutters on a dark hallway.

From the depths of the entrance hall came the sound of applause. Each clap was loud, then a long pause, then another. This was not the pleased applause of a satiated audience, but the slow, mocking clap of an angry patron.

First Lord Aegesander's voice called from the darkness. He spoke with the same slow, measured rhythm of his clapping. "Rivka and Tritogenes. You know, I never thought you would make it this far before we could talk."

Aegesander, resplendent in his Hexarch's purple, walked out of the shadows of the palace. His squinted, but carefully did not raise a hand to shelter his eyes against the sudden brightness of the outside world. He was flanked by two groups of four soldiers.

Resisting the urge to look away, Tritogenes quietly asked, "how many do you have?"

"Six from each ship."

The math was easy enough. Twelve soldiers from the ships, eight with Aegesander. The two of them could not take out twenty armed, well-trained troops. Victoria could do it, he thought, but Victoria was hundreds of millions of kilometers away, fighting to save the very civilization Aegesander seemed determined to destroy.

Aegesander laughed, a carefully controlled breach of propriety. It was devoid of the feeling of mockery that everything else he had done in the last few moments had. For a few moments, he actually seemed genuinely amused by the situation. "Using the maintenance tunnels, hiding your robes. I have to admit, Tritogenes, that those were strokes of genius."

The guards at Aegesander's sides still held their weapons down, seemingly oblivious to the fact that Tritogenes had their Hexarch under his sights.

"You killed First Lord Hyperion."

Aegesander looked alarmed. "Why, Tritogenes. Why would you think something like that?"

"We heard the gunshot," Rivka replied. She growled her words, abandoning all pretenses at Hexarch formality.

A look Tritogenes could not identify crossed his face before an expression of profound sadness crossed his features. Aegesander heaved a sigh and, gesturing with his arms as if to emphasize his point, replied, "First Lord Hyperion's death was tragic, but it was not my fault. He had become a danger to the Technocracy, Tritogenes. You must understand that."

"Is that why you sent soldiers to kill us?"

Aegesander spoke slowly, enunciating every word with care and dignity. Tritogenes knew this was being recorded for broadcast. Aegesander had to say things the right way if people were going to believe his version of the story. "I send guards to escort you to me so that we could talk, my friend. It was never my intent for this to turn violent. So, please Tritogenes, Rivka, come with me. We can discuss this like the Hexarchs we are. There has been enough blood shed today."

Tritogenes watched him. Years of working in a theater gave him the ability to tell acting from truth, another skill he had found fairly useful in his career as Hexarch. It soured his stomach to realize that, as far as his own perception was concerned, every word Aegesander said was true. Acting affronted at his accusation had been exactly that, an act, but now he seemed to be telling the truth.

Yet, "why the quip about not expecting us to get this far?" he demanded.

Aegesander spread his hands. "What else was I to say? I expected to meet you somewhere pleasant, or at least to catch up to you inside so that we could sit and talk. I would rather not squint into the setting suns while we have this conversation."

Tritogenes had not lowered his rifle. "We're having it now."

"Unfortunately so."

"So, if you want to talk, why the soldiers?"

"You did kill the last two I sent," he said. Then, somehow without scorn, he added, "my friend. Before we begin, I would ask you why. Those men were sent to *protect* you."

Tritogenes ignored the question. It was a lie and he knew it, and any answer he could give to that question would be caught on recording and twisted. Instead, he tried to put the proverbial cross-hairs back where they belonged. "Why did you kill Hyperion?"

Aegesander's posture shifted, dropping some of the pretense. He came more upright before replying. "As I said, Hyperion had become a danger to the Technocracy. Come back inside, Tritogenes, and we can talk about it. It's not too late to sever yourself from him. Come with me and we will make all of this right."

"Why blame us?"

Aegesaner shook his head slowly, sadly. "A mistake on the part of my security personnel. Their error has been rectified and Hyperion's death laid at the feet of the Ouroboros. No one outside this conversation needs to know what Hyperion did. Let him die with dignity, Tritogenes. Now, come back inside and let us talk."

Tritogenes froze at that. Perhaps, he thought, Aegesander was not recording this at all. Plausible deniability—the phrase came into his head unbidden. Aegesander need not worry if the encounter worked out in his favor. If not, the twenty rifles pointed at Tritogenes and Rivka served as his insurance policy.

"Not a chance," Rivka growled. "You killed him because of what he told me."

Aegesander nodded once, slowly. "I am sorry, First Lord Rivka, but some knowledge is too dangerous. Come with me, give me the case, and all of this will be forgotten. I will speak at Hyperion's funeral and make sure everyone knew him as he was when we were young—vibrant, strong, noble. He will be missed."

"No," Rivka said. She moved toward the shuttle again.

"We can put an end to this. Just give me the case and come with me. Do not put yourselves on the wrong side of this."

Rivka took another step, as did Tritogenes. He walked backward, still aiming his rifle as best he could at Aegesander.

Aegesander raised a hand, a calm, slow gesture, and twenty rifles zeroed on their position. He sighed, and—damn it all—his words sounded to Tritogenes's ears like he actually regretted them. "Kipos will mourn the loss of your beneficent hand, I am sure."

Tritogenes's hand tightened on his rifle. "You'd kill her too?"

"I do not want to, but sometimes sacrifices must be made."

"I'm not going with you," Tritogenes said. He heaped scorn on his next words, saying, "First Lord."

"I am sorry, Tritogenes. Truly. I did not want any of this to happen. I did not want it then, and I do not want it now."

"Liar!" Rivka hissed. Tritogenes had never heard such venom in her voice before.

"So that's it, is it?" Tritogenes asked. "You killed Hyperion, and you'll kill us now, because the information First Lord Rivka uncovered implicates you in a way you don't like."

"It implicates us all," he replied. It shocked Tritogenes to realize that Aegesander still was not faking his remorse. "Hyperion would have told the worlds of our sins. Now First Lord Rivka would do the same, and I will do whatever must be done to prevent that."

"Rivka," Tritogenes said. A distant part of his brain was shocked by how calm he sounded. "Run."

She rose from the crouch she had settled into, and looked him in the eyes. "Don't, Tritogenes."

He smiled, or tried to. "I'll be right behind you."

"Tritogenes." His name came out of her mouth as a warning, begging him not to do whatever it was she thought he was going to do.

"The only way either of you will leave this planet is with me," Aegesander snapped. The remorse was gone, replaced with anger.

Tritogenes tried to smile again, succeeding this time. "Don't argue with a Hexarch, Rivka."

She came around to where they could look face-to-face again and stared at him for several seconds. Tritogenes felt strange under her stare, like she was dissecting him and his motives. She almost said something, then decided against it. Her jaw muscles worked, clenching and unclenching before she finally nodded once.

"Run," he ordered.

She did, and the moment her second step hit the ground, Tritogenes opened fire. He had three magazines left. If he was lucky, that would be more than enough ammunition to end things, and then it would be his word and Rivka's testimony against Aegesander's reputation.

Behind his back, he heard her footsteps on his left and right. She ran in a zig-zag pattern, minimizing her chance of being shot as much as possible as Aegesander's soldiers opened fire. They were confused for the first few seconds. Tritogenes's first burst dropped one of the soldiers next to Aegesander and the others simply reacted to the threat.

Bullets hit the ground at his feet, the ground between where he stood and where Rivka now ran, the walls a hundred meters away, and even the ships themselves. His heart hammered in his chest at the subconscious realization of what any one of those hundred rounds would have done to him if their aim had been just a bit better.

Tritogenes started backpedaling, shooting as he went. He got three steps, shooting another of Aegesander's guards. That was good in itself— it meant fewer bullets coming his way, but he had been aiming for the Hexarch who now rapidly slunk back through the palace doors.

The doors started to close and Tritogenes almost ran after him. His brain caught up with his reactions, however, and he sped up in the opposite direction. He fired several more times, dropped his weapon's empty magazine to the ground, and fumbled for a new one.

As his shaking fingers tried to manipulate the metal box into the receiver of his rifle, he heard the door to Rivka's shuttle open. A thud followed, likely she had jumped and climbed into the ship rather than wait for the stairs to fully extend.

Rivka was smart, he thought. She would start the launch procedures as soon as she was inside. Now, he just had to get this crashing magazine into his rifle, and...

He never finished that thought. All semblance of rational thought had been immediately replaced by a white-hot spear through his chest.

His arm went slack and the loaded magazine clattered to the ground. Another bullet struck the meaty part of his thigh, far away from anything fatal but painful and damaging enough that he tripped over the suddenly malfunctioning limb and fell to the ground.

"Tritogenes!" Rivka's voice cut through the red haze in his head.

He fumbled for the magazine again. His right lung was rapidly collapsing and that shoulder refused to work right, but the rest of his arm did, and he finally got the thing in its proper place.

"Go!" he yelled.

"Not without y—"

"Go!"

Tritogenes drug himself to his feet, swaying back and forth. That slight motion saved him as bullets whizzed past on either side. Aegesander's troops were advancing now, marching in lockstep, firing in sequence, and if the shuttle stayed on the ground for much longer, it would never launch.

He spared a look back over his shoulder, praying to every god he could think of that he survived long enough to throw off some sort of cocky parting line. He smiled and this time it came easily.

"Find Pallasophia," he called. His voice was weaker than it should have been, and the collapsing lung gurgled, but he was still loud enough.

"Tell Victoria what happened here. Go save our worlds, Rivka. Tell Limani," he coughed and pink foam dribbled from his chin. "Tell my people I love them."

He turned, and as he did, he flicked the selector switch on his rifle to fully automatic. Straining against the recoil of the weapon, he tracked it back and forth across the advancing line of Aegesander's troops.

Four more fell before the next bullet hit his right arm. Without a second hand to control the weapon, it climbed high as reflex made him clamp down on the trigger with his left hand.

Another bullet tore through his stomach and Tritogenes fell to his knees. His pistol, the same one he started the fight with, was holstered at his left hip. That side of his body still worked, and he drew that little gun.

He managed three shots before more bullets tore through him. He was beyond pain at that point, and instead simply felt the pressure and then the cold.

Tritogenes slumped to his back, falling into something wet. Strange, he thought, he never remembered there being a pool there.

His eyes started to fade as the ground rumbled. Straining with what little remained of his strength, Tritogenes managed to move his head slightly. A black ring turned the sky into a vignette of blue, but that vignette was pierced by a single object: a shuttle rising on a plume of white.

Tritogenes felt warm, even content, as everything went silent and black.

Chapter 10

"What can you tell me about this wall?" Victoria asked, removing her helmet's faceplate to get a better look. "Other than the fact that its existence is a pain in the code."

The wall in question was a featureless gray facade, not quite vertical. The angle was noticeable only from up close. It leaned toward them, looming and distorting perceptions.

The short, twisting hallways they had been traveling down for the better part of the day held nothing like it. In fact, though they had seen plenty of branching corridors, there had been no doors or anything else to break up the monotony.

Strangely enough, they also had not seen any mastigas, despite the shared feeling that the three of them were being watched. Panatakis also remained out of reach of Helena's implants. That, more than anything else about their environs, seemed to distress her.

Now, their path was abruptly cut off by the slanted wall in front of them. It seemed to cut through the floor, ceiling, and walls rather than being part of them. Under Victoria's hand, the metal felt different as well, somehow cleaner and rougher than everything else. It showed fewer signs of age as well—the floor and walls bore wear marks and the accumulated damage of years of feet.

The slanted wall, on the other hand, was almost fastidiously clean.

Helena touched it, closing her eyes for a moment. The first thing she said confirmed Victoria's suspicions. "The material composition is different from everything surrounding it. Both are too new to precisely date, but I believe whatever this wall is connected to was built after the ship itself."

"The pyramid?" Lelantos asked.

Helena nodded. "Most likely. The slope matches the slope of the pyramid as we saw it from the outside."

Victoria turned away from it, crossing her arms over her chest. "How do we get through it?"

"I doubt we can get through it," Helena answered. "The alloys are much too strong for the tools we still have. Perhaps something aboard the *Justice* could have..."

"We can't let ourselves drown in what might have been," Victoria interrupted.

Lelantos nodded. "I fought for Kipos when the mastigas invaded five years ago. If we dwell on regrets we might as well give up now."

"I do not," Helena started, then stopped herself. She visibly collected her thoughts before continuing. "I mourn the loss of the people aboard the *Justice*, but most of all I mourn our failure, my failure, to see this coming."

"See what coming, exactly?" Victoria asked.

Helena rapped on the metal wall with her knuckles. The silvery-blue metal on the back of her hand, tracing her bones like an exoskeleton, rang with a loud, sharp sound. "This."

"The pyramid?" Lelantos asked.

Victoria corrected him. "The superweapon."

"Titan Victoria is correct. While none of us could have predicted the existence of a directed-energy weapon, we should have had plans in place in the event the mastigas deployed a weapon we did not foresee."

"We can't..."

Helena interrupted him, showing more emotion than Victoria had seen from her. For a moment, her face showed nothing but anger. "We could! There are things we ought to have done, I see them all so clearly now. Different formations we could have used, different ships, even a different vector of approach. It's all so obvious!

"But we did not! We approached in a straight line, helpless and sheltered by our escorts. Now there are only five of us left. Five, when there should be one hundred and one thousand, four hundred and six!"

Lelantos recoiled slightly, but Victoria had been watching Helena instead. She never looked directly at Lelantos. Her anger was not directed at him, but neither was it directed at herself. She took a moment, several in fact, to fully examine things. Helena's eyes darted around, almost settling on her, then on Lelantos, but finally seemed to look into the distance at something impossibly far away on the other side of the strange, slanted wall.

"Helena," she said. Victoria hoped she was phrasing things the right way. "Who do you blame?"

Helena started to open her mouth, but it shut with an audible click of teeth.

"Helena?"

"I do not blame Tritogenes," she replied. Her voice was strained like every muscle from her shoulders to her jaws was held tight.

"I didn't ask who you didn't blame," Victoria said.

Helena's jaw muscles tightened still further as her head swiveled to face Lelantos. Her words came out slowly, like she had to force every syllable. She looked at Lelantos, then closed her eyes tight. "I do not blame First Lord Rivka."

"Are you alright?" Lelantos asked. He spoke with the quick, even cadence he took on when under the effects of the chronodrug. He confessed to the others once that he used it at times as a sort of lie detector, slowing down everything else to the point that even little movements were obvious. At that pace, his mind moved faster than even his own body.

Victoria noticed that Helena had the beginnings of tears in the corners of her eyes. Alongside the tightness in her mother muscles, they looked like tears of pain rather than anything else.

"Helena?" she asked again. Victoria instinctively reached out a hand to comfort the other Titan.

"Tritogenes would not have known," she ground out.

Victoria almost asked her who would, but stopped before the first syllable was out of her mouth. She stood there, mouth agape for a moment before finally managing to speak. "Are you saying that Aegesa—"

Helena twirled around, pivoting on her feet with mechanical grace. She crossed the small distance between herself and Victoria in a moment, eyes wide with repressed pain. One of her hands grabbed Victoria's collar and the other clamped firmly over her mouth.

Another step and Helena pinned the much larger Titan against the wall. Victoria knew she was the stronger of the two, or she thought she was, but the sudden ferocity of Helena's movements surprised her.

"Do not," she growled, "finish that sentence."

Victoria stared into her wide, blue eyes for a long minute. The other Titan hovered there, mere centimeters away, until Victoria nodded. She then released her hand and slowly stepped away.

"What in the hell was that?"

Helena took another step backward. Her eyes glittered as anger, sadness, and pain all welled up at once. "I am sorry."

"'Sorry?'" Victoria demanded. "That won't cut it. What was that?"

181

Helena's jaw clenched again. "I can't tell you," she said, again forcing her words out.

Lelantos stepped forward, taking Victoria's hand. He led her away, moving with chrono-induced fluidity. "A word?"

Victoria followed, keeping her eyes on Helena. The other woman turned away, some mixture of shame and anger on her face. Victoria could not tell at whom it was directed. Once they were out of both eyesight and, she assumed, earshot of where Helena stood, Lelantos stopped.

He spoke quietly, slowly. He did not seem to have purged the chronodrug from his system yet. "I believe there is more to Titan Helena's problems that it seems."

Victoria nodded. She tried to speak as quickly as possible, to limit the amount of time Lelantos would have to stand there, from his perception, and listen to her drone words out at one-sixtieth speed. "What do you mean?"

"Her implants," he drawled. Victoria was again reminded that the taciturn Titan sounded fully drunk when under the effects of chrono. "I fear First Lord Aegesander may have done something to them to prevent her from saying certain things or engaging with certain topics."

"So when I mentioned Aegesander..."

Lelantos interrupted. She could not blame him, objectively. His mind likely sat there for three minutes while she said Aegesander's name. "She was in pain, trying to speak. When you said his name, she reacted."

"Violently."

Lelantos nodded. "There was something more. Two movements. She first made a violent attack, then she covered your mouth." He tapped the metal collar around his thin neck that was the primary dispenser of the chronodrug. "I saw it. Two movements."

"You think the attack was not voluntary," Victoria said. It was not a question.

"Yes."

"And silencing me was, what, her way of stopping the reflex?"

"It appeared so. I watched her muscles war with themselves. She wanted to choke, but instead she silenced. Before you could say his name."

"And she can't tell me that because that would trigger the same reflex."

Lelantos nodded. "She wants to tell, but cannot. She is..." He stopped for a moment, a long pause even for him. "Sad."

"Keep an eye on her," Victoria ordered, "but don't start mistrusting her."

"I won't."

"And don't run out of chrono."

Lelantos smiled, lips a thin red line. "I will not."

Victoria turned, took a step back in the direction where they left Second Lord Helena and said in a loud voice, "but you're right. We need to find a way around the pyramid wall."

Helena turned as they approached. The sadness Lelantos mentioned was written plain on her face. Likely, Victoria thought, she knew exactly why the two of them had needed to talk, but found herself unable to ask about it.

As far as Victoria was concerned, that single act of control was more terrible than anything Tritogenes had done to her by leaving her alone in the labyrinth. Risk of death was nothing compared to loss of autonomy.

She added another entry on her list of things to address upon returning to Prosgeiosi. Was it not enough, she asked herself, that Aegesander tried to kill Helena once? Anything she had to say to Tritogenes paled in comparison to the rage that now smoldered, directed fully at the Hexarch of Dasos.

She turned that rage into a different instinct: protection. She stepped closer, placed both hands gently on Helena's shoulders. The other Titan looked wary, afraid a slip of Victoria's tongue might trigger another programmed reaction, but she stood still.

183

Victoria closed her eyes for a moment, longer than a blink. When she opened them again, a smile crept across her face. She said nothing, knowing Helena could read her emotions as plainly as if they had been written in a book. Words were extraneous just then.

Victoria stepped away.

Helena took the moment to compose herself, and gestured to the floor. Her voice betrayed none of the anger or hurt she showed before. "I analyzed the materials here while you were away. I believe our equipment is suitable to cut through it."

"Won't that attract the mastigas?" Victoria asked.

Helena nodded. "Perhaps, but I believe we are near the bottom of the pyramid wall. The weapon may be atop it, but this structure is newer than the rest of the ship, and I believe there is likely to be something below of importance."

"The engines," Lelantos supplied.

Helena's eyes tightened as her lips thinned. "No," was the only word she could manage. She struggled for a moment before changing the subject slightly. "You are correct, however. Even without sufficient numbers to truly destroy the ship from within, we three ought to be able to sabotage the engines and postpone its arrival at my planet."

Lelantos's voice was still distorted by the chrono when he said, "then let's do it."

Cutting through the floor took mere minutes. The three of them worked together to cut a hole a meter wide, then Lelantos dropped through. With his enhanced perception, he was the logical choice to go first. When he announced that it was clear, Victoria and Helena fed the gear through and then dropped down themselves.

The hall below them was empty in both directions. It was also pitch dark. Victoria's heart hammered in her chest for a moment as flashes from Aphelion's labyrinth, and the lives of death she remembered from those dark halls, came back into her mind.

She pushed the worst of them away. This might not have been Aphelion, but it was still a hell the mastigas made for themselves. Some of her memories might help here, but most were nothing but pain and death. Those could not be allowed to slow her down.

Ahead, the slanted wall was a touch further away now, but down in the tunnel it was as dirty as everything else. In fact, she realized as they clicked on weapon lights, everything around them was comparably filthy.

Unlike the levels above them, this hall was full of the sort of things Victoria expected on a ship. The ceiling was higher, covered in exposed pipes and conduit. Computer terminals and equipment were everywhere they looked.

It also looked completely unused, at least in recent history. A thick layer of dust and what Victoria hoped was some sort of shipboard grease covered everything in sight.

Helena smiled, actually looking happy. "If those terminals still function, I ought to be able to patch into the ship's systems."

"Aren't you worried about where we are?" Lelantos asked.

"Not yet," she replied.

"We're in a maintenance access tunnel," Victoria replied. She pointed, trying to stop her outstretched finger from trembling as her pulse thundered once again through her veins and adrenaline threatened to steal away all fine motor control.

Helena turned. "How...?"

She fell silent as she saw where Victoria was pointing. The wall opposite them had been painted with green lettering. In Lexeis Archeio, it read, "MAINTENANCE ACCESS DELTA." Below that, in smaller text, "No unauthorized personnel."

"I was unaware you read Lexeis Archeio," Helena said. A moment ticked by in which her eyes grew wide, almost frightened. She clutched the side of her head with one hand. Her face showed pain again. Her voice was tight, demanding, but she was talking to herself, not to them. "Why is it written in Lexeis Archeio?"

"Use those terminals," Victoria ordered. "Break into the mastigas's system any way you can. We'll find out."

Helena nodded. "I will share anything I find. And Victoria?"

"Yes?"

"I will," she stopped as her jaw threatened to seize. "I will find a way to tell you everything."

***

As they went, the three Titans discovered and more and evidence that, at one point in the past, the dark and disused hallways where they now moved had been heavily used. The equipment was not decorative, not that the mastigas would have had any use for it if it was, but much of it had been severed from the rest of the ship.

Helena stepped away from the fourth terminal they came across, shaking her head in the negative. "Nothing," she reported.

"Does this one work at all?" Lelantos asked.

Helena nodded and gestured to the dull, flickering holo projected above the terminal itself. "The machine's internal systems are functioning, but it has no connection to the rest of the ship."

"Is there a way you can break whatever firewall is there?" Victoria asked. She took a step toward the terminal as though proximity would help her understand better.

"The lack of communication is not due to a firewall," Helena said. "I believe the physical connections between these systems and the rest of the ship have been severed."

Lelantos passed them, moving with the unnatural grace of the chronodrug. Days must have passed for him already, but the only outward sign of his mental state was what appeared to be bored disinterest on his face.

He knelt next to the terminal where it protruded from the wall. He held up a hand, then paused and turned that bored expression toward Victoria and Helena. "You may wish to cover your eyes."

Victoria did as instructed, using her forearm so that she could still see directly in front of her feet, just in case something other than the three humans lurked in those disused corridors. It would have been no surprise at all to learn the mastigas battleship was haunted or somehow infested with degenerate, feral versions of the mastigas, and *that* was why these areas were sealed off.

Light strobed from Lelantos's holo, sudden and fast. Despite covering most of her vision, the bright flashes left eerily-colored afterimages on her eyes. Victoria shook her head to clear them, but they simply floated around at the bottom of her vision.

She approached and knelt next to Lelantos as he pried at a section of the wall next to the terminal with his knife. Victoria drew one of her own and slipped the thick mastigas blade into the gap he created. Her knife flexed under the strain, but the section of wall popped free after a few seconds.

Lelantos reached into the wall and withdrew a bundle of wires. They had all been cut, but roughly and to different lengths. A crude tie held them all together, but little else about them seemed useful. Like everything else around them, they were covered in greasy dust.

He let the wires flop sideways. They fell halfway to the floor, supporting one another thanks to the tie that wrapped them.

Victoria gestured to the wires, then to Helena as Lelantos reached into the wall again. "Can you do anything with these?"

Helena shook her head. "Nothing."

"Hah!" Lelantos exclaimed. The noise was short, sharp, more like a sudden exhalation than anything. Victoria realized it was automatic, not a noise he made for their benefit. Leaning away from the wall, he produced the end of a similar bundle, one than ran upward rather than towards the defunct terminal.

"That," Helena said, "I can work with." She frowned. "I hope."

She sat on the floor next to the cut bundle of wires and examined them. Victoria could not tell what exactly she was looking for, but after a moment Helena nodded in satisfaction and withdrew her holocomputer's core unit. Opening a panel on the side, she inserted the entire tangle of wires and a holoprojection appeared in the air behind her.

Most of the projection was meaningless data at first, but it quickly resolved itself into a map of the ship. The holo rotated, zoomed, and moved around, likely under Helena's mental control, until three dots representing the three of them sat in the center.

Red swarmed above them, moving through the halls and tunnels of the massive battleship like blood cells. Helena frowned, closed her eyes, and the map skewed sideways until another friendly-colored dot appeared some distance away.

"Panatakis?"

Helena nodded.

"Where's Korakti?"

The map panned and scrolled more, twisting and spinning as Helena sifted through the data.

"I cannot locate Titan Korakti. However there are one hundred... there are many mastigas directly above us. And, here," the map expanded to include the entire pyramid, "appears to be their focal point."

Victoria studied the map, trying to follow the paths of the mastigas more than anything.

"Look quickly!" Helena snapped. "They know I'm here. I estimate no more than seven-point-zero-two..."

The map vanished before she could finish announcing the result of her calculation.

"It sounds like we need to go back upward," Lelantos observed as Helena removed the now-useless tangle of wires from her holocomputer and slipped it back into her pocket.

"Yes," she agreed, "but we must move forward somewhat before doing so. I do not think the map projection showed sufficient detail, but the pyramid appears to be a concentric object, and I believe our theories about its creation are accurate. Spatharios," she said, turning to face Victoria. "I would like your permission to formulate a plan?"

"Of course," Victoria said.

"I believe we should not go to the engines. We will be unable to stop this ship. That area is very cramped, and the mastigas will be familiar with it in ways we are not. I do not like this suggestion, but it is going to be in our best interest to remain near open areas."

"They'll swarm us."

Helena nodded. "Yes, but they will be unable to utilize side passages or come at us from twisted and dark passages."

Victoria nodded. "So we take a chance at being outnumbered or we risk being ambushed."

"I believe the dangers posed by an ambush to be far greater, but look." She summoned a copy of the ship map and wiped away the dots representing the mastigas. Another gesture and the layers of the pyramid illuminated themselves with different colors. The outermost armor glowed red, the layer inside that orange. The wall they circumvented by dropping into the disused corridor was now yellow, and another wall a little ways in glowered greenly at them. At the center of it all was a great blue pyramid full of twisting passages.

Lelantos pointed at the peak of the blue pyramid, where a tower-like structure connected it to the outer shell. "That's going to be the control room for the superweapon."

Helena nodded. "Before I lost connection, I was able to trace a series of power conduits that ran through that area, and I believe you are correct."

"Then that's our destination," Victoria said.

Helena gestured and the holo vanished. "I agree."

"And Panatakis?"

An expression of longing and pain crossed Helena's face, but when she shook her head, it vanished. "He is strong."

Victoria nodded. "Then we keep looking for the best way up. Inside the inner pyramid?"

"I believe that to be the best course of action. If I could reach Panatakis and Korakti," Helena said, then stopped herself. "No. He is strong and he will reach the same conclusions. We will meet with him again."

Victoria gestured down the dark hall. "Lead the way."

***

A half hour passed in silence broken only by momentary stops as Helena summoned, studied, and dismissed her copy of the holomap of the mastigas ship. That happened twice before she finally said, "this passage has allowed us to bypass some of the more heavily populated areas of the middle pyramid. We are close to an uninhabited location where I believe we should..."

Before she could say anything else, a series of heavy footfalls passed overhead. They thundered through the thin floor and Victoria snapped a hand out, palm down. The three Titans fell silent as the footsteps turned into a semi-rhythmic tapping. Half a second later, they switched off their weapon and suit lights.

From inside their helmets, Helena's voice spoke. Her throat muscles worked, but no sound came out of her lips. Not for the first time, Victoria was pleased about the existence of the implants she had that could turn subvocal signals into intelligible words.

"They're looking for us," her voice whispered.

Victoria nodded, but had no ability to reply. She lifted her faceplate and mouthed, hoping Helena was looking in the right direction. "Plan?"

"Silence," was Helena's reply.

Far down the hall, back the way they came, a speck of light appeared in the ceiling. Something obscured most of the light for a moment, then vanished, letting the hole pour light in.

Overhead, the heavy footsteps they heard before thundered again, moving away and back down the corridor.

Once again, something obscured the light coming from the hole in the ceiling, only this time it completely blocked it for several moments. A grunt of effort carried down the hall, followed by the high-pitched snap of breaking metal, and something crashed to the floor on their level.

"It would appear they know we're here," Helena's voice provided.

Victoria thought the announcement was rather unneeded, but continued to maintain vocal silence. She sidled closer to Helena and picked up the other woman's hands. In the dark, she pressed a series of signals directly into Helena's palm, which the cyborg Titan rendered into orders.

"Lelantos, to the rear. Victoria, to the front. Helena, find an alternate passage."

"Can you tell what it is?" Lelantos hissed.

A roar and a thunder of feet answered him. The sound was higher-pitched than the spoken-earthquake of the gigas, but no less chthonic. Victoria recognized that sound, one that continued to haunt her dreams.

"It's an elite," she said, no longer bothering with any pretense of stealth. It knew where they were and attempts to hide only took time they no longer had.

"Orders, Spatharios?" Lelantos asked. "I've never actually had to kill one of these."

She grit her teeth, synthesizing her own experience with that of a dozen dead predecessors. "Target its arms first. The skull is thick and it has redundant organs in its chest."

"As you say."

"What are you going to do?" Helena asked.

She growled, resonating deep in her throat. "I've killed one before."

"You need a plan."

The elite bellowed again, much closer. This time, after the echoing roar, it spoke to them. "Not welcome, invaders! Sent to kill, I!"

191

"Sent? By whom?" Victoria demanded, trying to make her voice as loud as the elite's. To the other Titans, she whispered, "get ready to turn your lights on. It's got three eyes. Blind it!"

"One!" replied the elite. It roared again, much closer now. "Wishes your death, One!"

"Now!" Victoria shouted, flicking on the light attached to her carbine.

Behind her, Lelantos turned his on as well. He fired first and the bullet struck the elite in the center of the stomach, as close to center of mass as he could likely manage with no real time to aim.

The impact of Lelanto's shot turned the elite's bellow of range and confusion into a sudden scream of pain. It still came onward, running now.

In the uneven light, Victoria realized the towering monster was nearly unarmed. It carried a single sword in its lower left hand, but otherwise had no weapons at the ready. If it was sent after them, surely it would have been given more weapons than a simple sword.

Something was wrong, but with the elite still charging them, Victoria had no time to figure out exactly what it was.

She backpedaled, firing burst after burst into the elite. She tracked lower with each shot, light going wild with her attempts to keep the elite illuminated and under her sights. Most of her shots went wild, and after the third step backward, she held her ground.

Lelantos fired again. His light remained much more stable and his second shot hit the elite in the lower-left elbow. No amount of toughness or armor could properly protect the soft interior of the elbow joint, and the elite's lower left arm flopped at its side in a spray of glittering red.

The sword clattered to the floor, and the mastigas monster slowed only a tiny amount in order to drop lower and reach for the fallen weapon with its upper left arm.

Still Victoria did not back up. She had killed one of these before, though that knowledge did little to still the adrenaline rushing through her body and screaming at her to *RUN*. She stood there, not even firing as the elite took a step, then another, then raised its upper left arm to strike with the sword. Both right arms reached forward to grab her.

Victoria dropped lower and lunged forward and to her right, toward the elite's upraised sword. She pivoted to the left, squeezing her weapon's trigger. Its right arms were closer than the sword, forward to grab her and hold her helpless while it stabbed again and again with the sword in its upper left.

The guiding voice in her brain, the bellow of ninety-nine dead, screamed at her that if she was not going to run, she had to drop to the floor *that instant* if she wanted to live. One misstep, and the immense mastigas facing her would kill her.

Without checking to see what, if any, damage she did to the elite's right arms, she dropped, twisting, and landed on the flat, strong part of her shoulders. The sword passed by overhead.

Lelantos fired again. The elite did not drop the sword, but it screamed in rage and pain once again. Her attack seemed to have had the desired effect, however, as the elite no longer rushed toward them.

"I have a way!" Helena's voice announced over their helmet comms. Her statement was punctuated a second later by a three-round burst from her rifle. It struck the elite in the torso, but if the towering monster noticed, it gave no sign.

On the ground, Victoria twisted violently and lashed out with her feet against the side of the elite's nearer knee. An attack like that coming from human muscles would never actually harm it, at least not without repetition, but it had the intended result nonetheless as the towering mastigas stumbled and lurched forward. She did not have to hurt it if she could unbalance it.

Victoria sprang to her feet as Lelantos fired again. This time she saw the impact, and a spray of red rendered the elite's lower-right arm useless.

She aimed upward and fired twice into the creature's upper left armpit. Its entire arm, somehow still clutching the sword, dropped

193

heavily, unable to support its own weight anymore. Victoria twisted on one foot, throwing the other foot to the side, and avoided the elite's arm as it fell.

Lelantos fired again, this time hitting the monster in the throat. Helena added another trio of bullets, tracking them along the elite's inner thigh. Impossibly red arterial blood answered both shots.

Victoria raised her own weapon and shot directly into the base of the monster's skull from the rear. She shot a second time before it toppled finally.

She stepped around it, fighting the ingrained urge to strip it of anything useful that helped keep her alive during the early days deep in Aphelion. To Helena, she said, "you said you found a path?"

She nodded. "Yes. And I believe it should lead us to Panatakis as well."

"Let's go."

***

Bullets cracked overhead, splintering against the wall behind the three Titans. The mastigas did not approach any closer, but whenever one of them would move closer to the edge of the wall providing their only shelter, the mastigas would answer with a hail of bullets.

The only things behind them were the inner wall of the middle pyramid and the hatch that led to the lower corridor. Nothing pursued them down there after they killed the elite, but none of them wanted to chance it, even with the blockade ahead.

Helena stepped furthest away from the edge, trading places with Victoria. She summoned the map, attempting to pinpoint their location. Without an active feed from the ship's computers, it was difficult, but she and Lelantos quickly narrowed things down to a very short list of possibilities.

The hail of gunfire stopped. Victoria wanted to come around the edge and shoot, take out as many as she could before they started shooting again, and then return to safety. The sounds of their footsteps came in disturbing, march-like unison every time they stopped shooting.

So far, the pattern had not changed. A hail of gunfire, then three steps closer, then another hail of gunfire. Since their arrival, it repeated itself four times. She knew the mastigas were very close now, and their options were getting fewer by the second.

Based on her assumptions from the first and only time she was able to look down the hall, Victoria estimated that they had two more firing cycles before the mastigas would be close enough to round the corner themselves.

She hissed through clenched teeth, wishing their tactics made sense. It was like the crashed green eyes, at least this group of them, were trying to herd them in different directions rather than actually kill them.

"There's no other way," Helena said. She spoke with her actual voice rather than the subvocal implant, which Victoria preferred. Her real voice was warmer than the synthesized version coming from the implant.

The mastigas opened fire again, and Victoria cursed, realizing she had edged closer to the corner than she intended and some of the gunfire sprayed debris onto her shoulder as the bullets ripped through the corner itself. "Gods between!"

She took a breath, composed herself, and then asked, "what do you mean, there's no other way?"

"Unless Lelantos and I are wrong..."

"Which we are not."

Helena continued as though she had not been interrupted. "There are no side passages between where we now stand and that group of mastigas. Either we return to the lower level and go another way or we fight them."

"Blue screen it," Victoria said. "I *want* to fight them, but we're not in a good place right now. We go back."

"As you say, Spatharios," she replied, with drawing another flash grenade. Helena opened a holo menu on the side of the bomb and altered

195

a few parameters, explaining that it was now on a thirty second timer and that afterward, it would be motion activated.

She set the grenade on the ground and the three Titans quickly backpedaled to the hatch in the floor.

Lelantos dropped first, but Victoria put a hand on Helena's shoulder to stop her for a moment.

"I thought this was the only way forward?"

"It wasn't the only way forward," she replied, "only the best one."

"It would seem the mastigas agreed."

Despite the tinted faceplate, Victoria was close enough to see Helena's expression change. She frowned, angry. "Yes," she replied. "It would appear we remain at their mercy."

"So why don't they just kill us?"

Helena laughed, once. "You really would like to fight them head-on, wouldn't you?"

Victoria hesitated, then admitted, "yes. I would. I want... No, I *need* a chance to avenge the people who never made it to this ship with us."

Helena reached out and placed a hand on Victoria's shoulder. Her grip was soft, reassuring. "That time will come. I am sure of it."

Victoria looked over her shoulder. The flashbang had not gone off yet, but the mastigas could not be far away now. "And when they follow us?"

"I do not believe they will. Some, like that elite, may pursue us again, but I believe this group simply wanted to stop our progress."

Victoria frowned inside her helmet. "They're herding us."

"It would appear so."

"To where?"

"I cannot say. But for now, we must find another way to the pyramid."

"And to Panatakis."

Her smile came through in her voice. "Yes. Now hurry!"

Chapter 11

Second Lord Pallasophia, former Project Titan Operations Director, was not a fan of being shot at.

When Aegesander's troops initially landed on Limani, claiming a resurgence of the Ouroboros threat, she had been suspicious. All the same, the Second Lord had no reason to doubt their story. If there was to be a terrorist attack, planning to strike when the vast majority of the combined militaries of the Technocracy were away would be a smart move.

It even made sense that First Lord Aegesander would be the one to organize the bulk of the resistance against this new version of Ouroboros. The Titans were away, and First Lord Enyalios's larger and better equipped military made up the majority of the attack force. Aegesander had the second largest military, which had been kept in reserve just in case something happened while Enyalios's forces were away.

At that time, that made sense. Hyperion had objected, but even Tritogenes agreed with Aegesander's plan. So the Hexarch put his military into a patrol pattern that, in theory, would allow him to respond quickly to any incident at any one of their seven planets.

That is, until the news broke of a terrorist attack on Pteryga and First Lord Aegesander landed soldiers on Hyperion's planet. His troops made haste to garrison the other planets as quickly as they could, though reports trickling in gave her the impression that he failed to take control of Katarraktes.

With First Lord Tritogenes somewhere on Pteryga amid all the fighting, and with Pallasophia herself busy arranging a trip Aphelion to start the shut-down procedure, Aegesander's troops found Limani's palace an easy objective. The bulk of his forces landed directly at the palace spaceport, garrisoning it within an hour without the rest of the planet being any wiser.

Like so much else relating to his plan, a plan whose long-term goals were rapidly becoming more and more apparent, at the time she thought little of it. If Pteryga had truly been attacked, then she ought to welcome the reinforcement to Limani's defenses.

The feeling of relief lasted all of thirty minutes before Tritogenes contacted her. The conversation turned the entire situation on its head. After learning what really happened to First Lord Hyperion, Aegesander's soldiers were no longer a welcome augmentation to her police force—they were an invading army.

That would have been bad enough on its own, but ten minutes after she gave the order for Tritogenes's own police to "politely escort" Aegesander's troops off the planet, things went, as they do, from bad to worse.

The very first confrontation between Limani's military and Aegesander's soldiers turned into a shooting match inside of five minutes. They delivered her "request," which the occupation force ignored. When the police insisted, Aegesander's troops opened fire.

Of course, to the bystanders unlucky enough to be nearby, the story was that her massively outgunned and outnumbered police were all secret Ouroboros agents working with the terrorists who attacked Pteryga.

The soldiers came for her next, and so she ran.

Theoretically, Tritogenes was supposed to check in with her every hour. It was far from normal procedure, but nothing about the situation was normal. Still, if he had been caught up in the same sort of unpleasantness that she had, Pallasophia supposed she could forgive him being late updating her.

All of which brought her back to the present and the bullets blowing chunks of sheetrock out of the wall behind her. She supposed she envied Tritogenes right then. The Blue Spire was built to withstand any siege and Hyperion was careful with his defenses. Limani was significantly less urban than Hyperion's planet and Aegesander's soldiers were tearing through the palace's thin walls with ease.

That was going to be first on her list of things to change as soon as this was over, she thought. With a grimace, she remembered Tritogenes poking fun at Hyperion, Enyalios, and then-First Lord Diomedes for the precautions they took with defending their respective homes. Secret weapons caches, armored walls, and more that she still did not know about dotted the homes of those other Hexarchs. All Tritogenes did was indulge his love of theater and build a series of secret tunnels.

Their paranoia would have been welcome right about then.

The one thing in the room that was bullet-resistant was the table, a gift from First Lord Hyperion. It now sat on its side, acting as an impromptu barricade. She huddled behind it, cradling a shotgun in her arms. It was not her first choice, but it had been the first long gun she came across with the palace armory on lockdown. It had served her well so far, not that she particularly wanted to dwell on that part of events.

"On the authority of First Lord Tritogenes, Hexarch of Limani, I order you to stand down!"

It had not worked the first few times, but she wanted to avoid any further shooting if at all possible.

"I'm sorry, Second Lord," one of the three soldiers waiting on the opposite side of her barricade replied. Her emphasis on her rank dripped

199

with condescension. "But we have orders to deal with the Ouroboros threat here and I'm afraid you've been implicated in the plot to kill First Lord Hyperion."

She froze. The fact that Aegesander's guards would speak so openly about Hyperion's death told her two things. First, that word was already spreading about what happened on Pteryga and Aegesander was either unable or unwilling to suppress the truth. Second, it told her that whatever plan Aegesander had, it had been in motion for some time.

It was entirely possible that the guard was telling the truth, at least as far as Aegesander's official record of things would indicate. She had no doubt that, should she be shot, he would have ostensibly legitimate information linking her to what remained of the Ouroboros organization. When they took the fall for for Hyperion's murder, so would she.

That also meant that Tritogenes was likely implicated as well. That thought, more than her own safety, spurred her on.

The revelation was an unwelcome one, coming as it did when she was in imminent risk of death. She suppose she loved Tritogenes, probably in much the same way as he himself loved First Lord Ophion and even First Lord Hyperion. He had been mentor and friend to her for years and the idea that one of his fellow Hexarchs would frame him for such a heinous crime made her blood boil.

Still, it was worth a try, she thought. Deadly force or not, these people were simply doing the job they had been ordered to do by a man they thought they could trust. Aloud, she shouted, "I had nothing to do with what happened on Pteryga. I've been here for weeks!"

"Maybe so, but your boss spent the last four days there."

"Tritogenes would never harm First Lord Hyperion."

"Of course you'd say that," the soldier continued. "You'd have to be stupid to confess right now."

"I don't have anything to confess to," she growled.

Pallasophia heard footsteps moving back and forth. One of the soldiers, probably the one she was talking to, was pacing. "You know, I met First Lord Hyperion once. It was years ago now, when I first joined the military. I hadn't sworn myself to any one Hexarch yet, and so I got picked by lottery to be in his honor guard."

Pallasophia remained silent, wondering where this story was going.

The footsteps stopped. "That was fifteen years ago. First Lord Hyperion was unfailingly kind to me."

"He was a good man."

A gunshot split the air, slamming into the table she was braced against hard enough to make the entire thing shake.

"You'd say that, wouldn't you?" the soldier demanded. Her voice was on the verge of yelling, rage and grief mixed together.

"I say it because it's true. Whatever happened to First Lord Hyperion was tragic and..."

Another bullet hit the table. It was resistant to being shot, but only so far. It would eventually fail if Aegesander's troops continued shooting it.

The soldier growled. "I ought to just lob a grenade over that Styx-dipped table and be done with you."

"What's your name?"

"What?" she snapped.

"Your name," Pallasophia repeated. "What is it?"

"Third Lord Chara," she replied. A moment later, "why?"

"My name is Pallasophia."

There was silence on the other side of the barricade for a moment, then, "I know who you are, Second Lord."

"Not Second Lord," she said. "Just Pallasophia."

"What's your point?" she demanded. "*Pallasophia.*"

"I met Hyperion too. Several times. It was my pleasure to call him a friend."

"Then you..." She stopped, then roared with frustration. "Silence! Whether you killed him, had him killed, or were simply involved in the

201

plot, First Lord Hyperion is dead. A Hexarch of our people is dead and you were involved!"

"I wasn't."

"Then explain what your Hexarch was doing there."

Pallasophia gritted her teeth. She wanted to yell back, but it would do no good. Instead, she kept her voice as neutral as she could, only failing at that particular effort by a small margin. "He was visiting a friend."

"If he didn't do it, why did he run?"

Pallasophia sat in silence, putting more of the pieces together. She wondered how much information Aegesander was actually forwarding to the teams on the other planets. She responded after only a few moments of thought. "I imagine he wanted to put distance between himself and whoever killed First Lord Hyperion."

"Or because he had to escape before someone else found out what he did."

"He didn't," she started to argue, then stopped. After a deep, theoretically calming breath which did not do what it was supposed to do, she said, "I don't know what else to tell you other than you're violating First Lord Tritogenes's authority as a Hexarch simply by being here. Just," she took another deep breath. "Just leave and we will get all of this unpleasantness sorted out as soon as I can reestablish contact with my Hexarch."

The soldier, Chara, growled. "Your Hexarch is a traitor."

She ground her teeth together. For a moment, Pallasophia wished she and Third Lord Chara were alone. With three of Aegesander's soldiers on the other side of the table, she and her ornamental shotgun stood very little chance.

If she could simply be alone with the angry soldier, perhaps Pallasophia could calm her down. If that failed, she thought with angry reluctance, killing one woman with a shotgun was easier than killing three.

One last, desperate argument remained before her options narrowed to a small set of choices, all of them violent and none of them particularly good for her chances of survival.

"Third Lord Chara," she snapped. "On my personal authority a Second Lord, a Lochagos of the Technocrat military, I order you to retreat."

Silence answered her, then laughter. "Your rank doesn't mean shit!" She did not recognize the voice.

Third Lord Chara snapped something under her breath, loud enough for Pallasophia to hear the noise but not loud enough to understand what she said. Then, "Sotiris is right, you know, even though he lacks..." She cleared her throat. "Tact. Still, we're only leaving this room one of two ways: with you willingly, or with your corpse. I can be very patient. Second Lord. Lochagos."

Pallasophia cursed, rather vehemently and colorfully. The gunfire had stopped, a fact for which her ringing ears were grateful. Spitting out rock dust from the wall had gotten old after the first few shots ripped through what should have been a nice-looking fresco. After her hastily converted barricade stopped their next two shots, the soldiers seemed to treat the tabletop as being bulletproof, rather than highly resistant, and focused their shots above it.

If that was all it took for them to stop shooting and let her think, though, she would take what she could get.

Five minutes passed. During that time, all she heard from the other side was the occasional unintelligible grumble and the shuffle of three pairs of feet.

After another five minutes, she heard Third Lord Chara laugh. "You know how I said I was patient, Pallasophia?" She paused. "I lied. Sotiris. Grenade."

"With pleasure, Third Lord."

Pallasophia cursed again, torn between two options. She could rise and shoot now, hoping she could not only identify Sotiris but kill him before he could throw his grenade before being shot herself. Her other option was to hope that these soldiers were not as well trained as they seemed, that he threw the grenade early, and than she could throw it back before it killed her instead.

Neither option seemed pleasant, though the second afforded her a slightly better chance of survival. If she rose and fired, she most certainly would be shot. If she survived this fight, even a graze would show her down fatally if more soldiers came after her.

Throwing the grenade back at least allowed her some illusion of agency over her own death.

She steeled herself, ready to spring in whatever direction she had to to grab and throw the grenade back. Seconds ticked by and it never came, leaving Pallasophia to wonder if they were simply baiting her, preferring to shoot her rather than waste an explosive on a single person.

A sound like a sharp burst of air caught her attention. The sound of the unseen soldiers moving around in an apparent panic interested her far more than whatever made the puff of air.

"What the?" Chara demanded. "Sotiris. I want you to actually throw that blue-screening grenade. Now!"

A single thought flashed through Pallasophia's mind. Whatever was happening on the other side of her barricade was bad for the soldiers who were trying to kill her. That did not explicitly mean it was good for her, but she was willing to at least entertain the notion.

The threat of the grenade still remained, but now it seemed the soldiers were in disarray. With a deep breath, she repeated a silent mantra in her head as she rose to her knees and pivoted to face her attackers: *one chance.*

Still using the table as cover for everything from her ribs down, she pointed the shotgun at one of two armed figures.

The realization that there should have been three people facing her, and that the third one lay on the floor, bleeding and writing in agony, shocked her into inaction for just a moment too long. The figure to her right, a large hulking shape of a man, held a small object aloft, ready to throw.

He never finished the movement as another soft puff of air accompanied the clamor of Pallasophia's own gunshot. She dropped behind the barricade again, counting the seconds until the grenade would explode.

Halfway there, a small sphere of metal hit the floor next to her. She reacted, moving without thinking, and grabbed it. With no time to aim, she simply lobbed it overhead and dropped even further. She covered her head with her hands, curling into a fetal position.

The blast was deafening, but the pressure wave was the real killer. Even behind her cover, sheltered from the bulk of the explosion, the concussive front hit her like a hammer.

Pallasophia fought to get the air back into her lungs, then pushed herself first to a sitting and then to a crouching position. She fought legs and arms that felt like pudding with every movement, but finally managed to come upright.

She dropped the muzzle of her shotgun across the edge of the table, aiming at nothing. Nothing was all that remained. Third Lord Chara was gone, though the smear of scorched blood and entrails on the wall to her left told her everything she needed to know.

Pallasophia panted. Her heart had been hammering hard and fast for so long that she forgot what it felt like for it to slow. Her chest felt empty without the constant thunder, but she was glad her adrenaline was finally subsiding.

It meant she was safe.

She took several long moments to breathe, still aiming the shotgun at the empty room. The world-shattering thunderclap from the grenade still rang in her ears, blocking out even the rush of her own blood.

A high, small voice spoke to her. It sounded like it was shouting, but with the ringing in her ears, it was hard to tell. "Second Lord Pallasophia?"

"Who the *fuck* is out there?" she demanded. "Show yourself!"

A small girl, one whose eyes barely came up to Pallasophia's shoulder, stepped around the corner. She wore no robe. Instead, she had dressed in a black bodysuit, one that Pallasophia thought oddly reminiscent of the one Victoria made for herself during her time locked in the basement levels of Aphelion. The girl had short hair, like Pallasophia herself, but beyond her unadorned hair and black clothes, one thing drew the Second Lord's attention.

The girl held a rather large rifle in her arms. It was a lightweight weapon, stripped of most of the protective bulk usually found in military hardware. An expensive sight was fixed to the top as well as a large suppressor to the end of the barrel.

Pallasophia also could not shake the feeling that she had seen this girl before. "Who are you?" she demanded. She might have been shouting too, but ears continued to ring.

"Sixth Lord Alexis," the girl replied. Pallasophia could barely hear her, but her quiet voice forced her to be still, to relax, and to pay attention to something other than the thunder of her own heart.

Why this girl had stuck in her memory, Pallasophia could not say. She was the little girl who spoke to Victoria on the train back on Prosgeiosi, offering the Titan a necklace she weaved herself. They exchanged only a few words. The girl, Alexis, had worn her hair long then, braided to match the symbols on her Sixth Lord's robes. She was here on Limani for a marksmanship tournament.

To see her, probably no more than twelve or thirteen, standing there in a copy of Victoria's black suit and sporting the same haircut Pallasophia wore was strange. An entirely different person stood there, one who probably killed two of First Lord Aegesander's soldiers to save her life.

Pallasophia asked if she had indeed shot the first soldier.

"Yes, Second Lord," Alexis replied. "I shot the man with the grenade too."

"Why are you here?"

"I was on the planet for a tournament, Second Lord. I had a meeting with Tritogenes today, or rather the winner of the tournament had a meeting with him, but I won, so I suppose that would have been me."

Despite the gore and carnage, Pallasophia smiled. The girl was nervous, and somehow *that* brought a tiny ray of warmth into her soul just then. "But why here?" she asked, gesturing to the room around them.

"I saw those soldiers attacking the palace guards and herding people around. I knew it couldn't be right, then I overheard them talking about you, so I went back to my suite, the suite where I'm staying right now, I mean, and got my rifle. I..." She paused, looking down at the ground. "I thought it was the right thing to do.

"I want to be mad at you," Pallasophia admitted. "You're too young to get mixed up in this."

"But if I hadn't, you'd be dead!"

She smiled. "I know. It was still a gamble."

"I'm from Kipos, Second Lord. This is, well... We talk about the need for people like me to help out in bad situations."

Pallasophia raised an eyebrow. "You're militia?"

Alexis giggled a bit. "Like I said, I'm from Kipos. We all are."

"How did you know you could trust me?"

"You work directly for First Lord Tritogenes. When I heard what First Lord Tritogenes had been accused of, I knew it had to be wrong." Her hand tightened on the grip for her rifle for just a moment, barely a heartbeat of time. It was enough; Pallasophia saw her tension and fear clear as day. "It *is* wrong, isn't it?"

"It's wrong, yes. Tritogenes, my Hexarch, did not kill First Lord Hyperion."

"I knew he would not do something so heinous."

"He didn't. Trust me."

Alexis seemed to relax. Her shoulders drooped slightly, and she leaned on the rifle for support. "That's good. I never thought he did. I want to help you, Second Lord."

"Call me Pallasophia."

"I can't, Second Lord. It would not be proper etiquette."

"The dark take etiquette right now," Pallasophia replied. "We have bigger concerns."

Alexis nodded, seemingly unfazed by Pallasophia's sudden change in tone. "Alright," she said, then repeated, "I want to help."

Pallasophia tried to smile. "From the looks of things, you already have."

"Thank you, Seco—Pallasophia. Where do we go now?"

"Somewhere safer than this," she replied. "I need to get in touch with Limani's police force and try and coordinate things so that maybe I can free my planet. So that we can free my planet."

Alexis nodded vigorously. Pallasophia could see tremors in her arms and legs, but whether they were from exhaustion, nerves, or simple adrenaline, she could not say. Whatever the case, she remembered the little girl from the tram rather vividly now. Seeing her transformed into a fighter was both a welcome sight, and a troubling one.

Children her age should not be involved in this, Pallasophia thought to herself. The girl had proven herself a good shot, and the fact that she landed the shots she did without revealing herself to Aegesander's soldiers spoke volumes about the control she had over her nerves.

And, Pallasophia's thoughts continued, she volunteered. She could not crush the girl's spirit by turning her away now, especially not after how she helped.

No, she thought, "helped" was not what she did. The fighter standing in front of her saved her life. She just happened to *look* like a little girl.

"Come on," Pallasophia said. "We need to move quickly. There's a safe room not far from here. It's where I was headed when those three started chasing me."

"I'm with you, no matter what happens," Alexis replied. "Pallasophia."

***

Third Lord Mihalis, formerly of the Technocrat navy, had survived the destruction of his ship at the hands of the mastigas. He survived being kidnapped and relocated to one of Prosgeiosi's twin moons by Ouroboros, and then survived the firefight while the Titans rescued him and the other survivors.

Then, just that morning, he woke up to the news that First Lord Tritogenes had been accused not only of killing First Lord Hyperion, but also was implicated in various parts of the Ouroboros conspiracy. The official word from Dasos was that Aegesander's people uncovered ties linking Tritogenes to the funding and directing of their activities.

To the credit of most people on Limani, they did not believe the official story. However, with Aegesander's troops on planet for "security," there was little they could do. Limani was not Kipos, after all, and the general populace did not possess the kind of weapons they needed to successfully resist.

Like them, Mihalis did not believe the story coming out of Dasos. Tritogenes was a good man and a good leader, and he would not have attacked First Lord Hyperion. More important, Tritogenes would not have been involved with Ouroboros at all.

Mihalis at first had hesitated, waiting for Tritogenes to clear his own name, but when that never happened, he decided waiting to be arrested and secreted away *again* was not as appealing a way to spend his afternoon as it might have seemed.

Thankful he let his paranoia get the better of him after coming back from Faros, Mihalis dropped the last spare magazine for his nearly brand-new rifle into a pocket. He wished he had something better to wear than his robe, but his replacement military uniform, the one he never got to wear, was under lock and key along with the rest of the planetary armaments. Tying up the hem of his robe would work well enough.

Catching a glimpse of himself reflected in the mirror of the rented palace suite, he laughed. His robe ballooned around his knees where the voluminous fabric spilled out around the ties, but at least it was nowhere near his feet.

"What I really need," he said, "is armor."

With armor locked away alongside Limani's military weaponry, he did not want to think about the best way to get any sort of protective gear for himself.

His suite had a balcony and he stepped out onto that first, leaving the door open. The ground was not far below, but further than he would have considered a fun jump. The balcony, like all the other ones in the square hotel, looked out over an open courtyard.

Mihalis selected this hotel, despite its cost, because it was actually part of Tritogenes's palace. Until the attack on Hyperion, things had been calming down, and Mihalis was going to use that as an excuse to actually *meet* Tritogenes, rather than interacting with him as a recent refugee and then escaped prisoner.

He could not remember her name, but he would recognize Tritogenes's second-in-command by sight. Her face was almost as public as his was, especially thanks to her role in Project Titan and no-longer-secret relationship with Limani's Titan, Victoria. If he could find her, things would be much better.

A pair of soldiers stood opposite him, turned away. They were interacting with someone inside one of the hotel rooms. From the other side of the courtyard, Mihalis could hear nothing of their conversation, only gestures.

The soldiers shut the door back and Mihalis ducked back into his suite, heart hammering in his chest. Standing out there with a rifle slung across his chest might not have been the best idea, he told himself. His hammering pulse seemed to agree.

Still, when he worked up the courage to look back outside, the soldiers were still there, another door further down. This time the conversation seemed to be getting heated, and one of the soldiers stepped through the door while the other watched. A few moments passed, moments where Mihalis imagined a struggle, before a pair of gunshots went off in quick succession.

The second soldier darted into the room, rifle raised to his shoulder as Mihalis jumped the railing of his second-story balcony. He acted without thinking, moving before fully rationalizing his way out of it. Fortunately, he was fairly stout and his reflexes were good. The short drop was barely an inconvenience for a few seconds.

Two more gunshots came from across the courtyard and Mihalis sped up. When those shots were answered by a burst of automatic fire, he realized nothing he could do from that distance would help.

What would help, however, was his original plan. The entrance to the courtyard was to his right and if he ran, he could probably make it before the surviving soldier exited the other suite.

"She's got to be in the palace proper," he muttered, already running. "I just have to find her."

***

Pallasophia ducked behind the maskeshift barricade, dropped a magazine from her stolen rifle, and slipped a fresh one into place. She was thankful, at least, for the pristine way in which Aegesander's troops seemed to maintain their weaponry. Suffering a jam right then would not have put her in a very good mood.

What passed for a barricade was a pile of debris from where an earlier firefight by now-unknown Limanian citizens and Aegesander's troops demolished the facade the building that served as their backdrop. Attached to the building, the facade had been a rather flimsy applique of marble and ceramic tile, but on the ground it provided a waist high pile of surprisingly bullet-resistant material. Decorative marble debris was no sandbag, and every shot caused the entire pile to shift. Pallasophia knew it would only be a matter of time before something punched through it—and into her.

For the moment, she had no other choice. The debris gave her an excellent field of view and, as long as she kept her head down, was protective enough for the moment.

Having Alexis a floor up, inside the building, providing cover with her competition rifle was a help as well. Designed for tournaments, it fired small, lightweight bullets that were explicitly intended for target shooting. They worked well enough in the first engagement, against targets that were not moving very much, but the small rounds did very little unless they hit a vital spot.

Fortunately, Sixth Lord—and that was something Pallasophia would fix as soon as possible—Alexis was, in fact, a champion marksman and nearly every shot she made hit something vital.

Pallasophia tried not to think about what that was doing to the girl's mental state.

In the short term, however, she wished Alexis was able to line up her shots a little bit faster. Every time there was a break in their defensive shooting, Aegesander's troops moved closer. For the moment, they remained a ways away and down the street, out of grenade range, which was one of the few things Pallasophia was happy about right then.

Alexis fired again, and return gunfire pocked the side of the building.

Pallasophia counted to five, waited for the gunfire to stop, then rose above the barricade again. Her weapon had no scope, which made shooting at the ranges they were at difficult, but at least the rifle sported a holo-sight that adjusted itself for range and wind automatically.

In her head, she could practically hear Strategos Glaukos's voice chastising her for everything she was doing wrong with her form and her tactics. Her own mental voice supplied the counter arguments, mostly that she had no other choice.

She pictured Glaukos laughing, boisterous and loud, and wished he was on Limani instead of still working security at Aphelion.

Wind chose that moment to kick up and the targeting dot slid to the side a few millimeters. That was enough change to throw off

Pallasophia's aim, but she did manage to get a clear count of the enemy soldiers and their positions.

Positions could change, but they had not gotten much closer lately. Instead, they seemed to be sticking to a cafe a few hundred meters down the palace street that had brick half-walls around its patio.

Four of Aegesander's soldiers lay dead or dying in the street, and Pallasophia knew several more had already been drug to safety.

A scream echoed from their end of the street, one of the "dead" had only been unconscious. She chanced a peek over the top of her barricade. One of the bodies in the street was indeed moving around now, calling out for his squadmates.

Seven soldiers remained huddled in the cafe's patio, moving back and forth. She could see the tops of their helmets as they moved, occasionally bobbing up above the brick, but that would do her no good. Unlike Pallasophia, the attacking troops had functional armor.

One of the enemy soldiers bobbed closer to the edge, and Pallasophia's heart sank.

"Don't do it," she mouthed.

He dashed out into the street, keeping low and going for his fallen squadmate.

Pallasophia rose, feeling cold inside.

Two of the enemy soldiers rose from their positions behind the cafe's brick wall.

Overhead, Alexis fired and one of the defending soldiers slumped forward.

Pallasophia cursed and laid her targeting dot over the soldier trying to drag his fallen squadmate, then sank back behind her barricade. Those soldiers might have been their enemies, but that one was trying to *save* a life, not take one. There were certain lines she would not cross, no matter how bad the situation looked.

From a practical standpoint, she thought with a grimace, now that the enemy squad had a wounded man to take care of, they would be slower to move and less prone to offense.

For that to work, however, she had to move quickly. Leave this squad behind. Let their injured keep them rooted in place. Throwing a glance upward, she ordered, "Alexis! Out the back door!"

The girl did not reply verbally, but the silenced end of her gun barrel vanished from sight. Pallasophia fired an indiscriminate burst overtop of the barricade, then came to her feet in a low crouch and darted into the building.

Just a little further, she told herself.

***

Mihalis saw Pallasophia, accompanied by a small figure he did not recognize, dart across an alley. He searched his brain for the best way to get to them safely.

The first option, calling out, would be the best way to get her attention without any risk to himself. It would also alert any of Aegesander's troops in the area to their location. While he was sure those same troops would find them soon anyway—they seemed to devote more attention to him after he used an entire magazine in his first firefight—the longer it took, the better.

Second, he could chase after them. That posed significant risks because they were already being chased and a "shoot first, ask questions later" mentality would not be unexpected in their position. Truth be told, he probably would do, or at least think about doing, the same thing. His reflexes were not suited for urban combat where things came faster and closer than they did from the bridge of a warship. He shot his way through the Ouroboros base on instinct and fear-adrenaline, not skill.

Third, he could sneak toward them, but that posed the same problems.

Finally, he settled on trying to get ahead of them and surrendering. Even though they were on the same side, humans did not come with convenient IFF transponders like warships did, and they needed some sign that he was not an enemy. That sign also needed to be something Pallasophia could interpret in under a second, and kneeling with his hands in the air was the best way he could think of to do that.

He made his way through the twisting streets of Tritogenes's palace, trying to keep a rough idea of where Pallasophia and her child-like companion were, but lost them after several minutes of pursuit.

Mihalis stopped and tried to curse, but the exertion left him unable to do anything but drop into a crouch and try to breathe deeply. He leaned backward against the facade of a building to catch his breath and stayed there for about a minute before gunfire from somewhere ahead shocked his body into movement again.

He followed the sounds of combat, trying to stay close to the dark places near the buildings. Fortunately, that proved easy enough as the slowly setting suns cast long shadows. It took ten minutes, but he eventually found not only Pallasophia, but another stroke of luck.

She and, he assumed, her companion had been pinned down in the front of a nearby building. They made it inside, but were now returning fire from the front windows. Three sets of gunshots came from that building, but many more outside it answered.

The stroke of luck came from the position of Aegesander's soldiers. At least four were directly ahead, attention fixed on Pallasophia's position. He looked around for a rear guard and did not see one. That only served to make him nervous.

Earlier, Mihalis "liberated" two grenades from one of Aegesander's soldiers during his first actual engagement and his hand strayed to them for a moment, but he stopped. He had seen people killed by explosions during the mastigas attack on his ship and the thought of doing that to someone else made his hands shake.

But these people were attacking his *home*. That was all the motivation he needed, and Mihalis plucked the grenade from his belt, armed it, and threw it as hard as he could.

215

The soldiers were nearly fifty meters away and the grenade landed far short. It rolled several meters, but not close enough to matter. When it exploded, none of the enemy soldiers were within the blast radius, and all of them now knew he was there. They rose slightly, looking around for him in every direction.

"Bad decision," he said, whipping his head back and forth to look for shelter.

Nothing was obvious, and his only directions were backward and forward. His destination was ahead, so Mihalis raised his rifle back to his shoulder and stepped forward.

He got three paces before they saw him, turned. He fired without aiming, pocking the dirt between him and the soldier ahead first, then fired again higher. He had to keep his aim low to avoid hitting Pallasophia across the street, but that...

Was apparently no longer a problem, he realized. Two soldiers fell in the same moment, shot from Pallasophia's position across the street, then two more at they tried to turn to engage her again.

He waited, listening for more gunfire, but the soldiers directly ahead seemed to be the only ones. Carefully, he advanced, taking his rifle sling off his shoulder as he went. He kept it in his hand, ready just in case there were more of Aegesander's troops waiting, but the muzzle was pointed down and to the side.

Mihalis stepped out into the light, looked left and right, and raised his hands overhead.

"Declare yourself!" demanded the voice of an old man from Pallasophia's makeshift bunker.

He replied with military precision the sequence that had been drilled into him. "Third Lord Mihalis, previously in service to Second Lord Anaxagoras aboard the cruiser *Phlegethon*, captained by Second Lord Cepheus, himself in service to First Lord Tritogenes."

"And now?"

"I, um." Mihalis fumbled for words. This was not routine. "I'm here to help Second Lord Pallasophia. I want to be of service to First Lord Tritogenes."

"Approach, Second Lord Mihalis. The door will be unlocked."

He did, crossing the street quickly and slipping through the door. Pallasophia, flanked by an old man and a young girl, waited for him. A gash smeared with quick heal crossed her face, likely the result of a knife rather than a bullet. The girl was dirty and looked like she was too tired to be properly afraid of the situation anymore, but otherwise was unharmed.

The old man, who now approached and introduced himself as, "Second Lord Emilios," was much cleaner. "This was my house," he said, gesturing to the bullet-pocked room around them.

"You came here to help, Mihalis?" Pallasophia asked. Her voice, despite the outward damage and fatigue, was as clear as he ever heard it in a broadcast.

He nodded. "Yes, Second Lord."

"Good. Half an hour ago, I sent a squad to retake an armory to the north of here." She opened a holo menu and transferred a token to Mihalis. "They'll recognize you with this. Go help them."

He bowed low. "As you say, Second Lord."

Chapter 12

First Lord Rivka slumped against the wall. The case with Diomedes's, and by extension Hyperion's and Aegesander's, confession lay in the corner where she had thrown it the day before. She did not want to think about its contents or even acknowledge their existence at that moment. She had enough contemplation over what that little bit of knowledge cost not just her, but everyone.

She watched Tritogenes fall, fighting to get her to safety. Whatever he did during Project Titan, whatever ghosts had haunted him prior to coming to Pteryga were wiped out in that moment. Aegesander likely would have killed them both if they agreed to "talk" with him, but Tritogenes had robbed him of that, choosing the time and place himself.

Of course, she recorded everything from the ship. How much use it would be remained to be seen. Aegesander's murder confession happened before she came aboard, before she could activate the cameras and microphones. What she had was footage of twenty of First Lord Aegesander's troops gunning down a lone Technocrat Hexarch.

Rivka had no idea where her security team was, or their condition. They would survive, she knew it. Lelantos would be devastated if what happened to Tritogenes happened to his brother, and Rivka could not allow that. She tried to console herself with the knowledge that his team probably tried to reach her, then went into hiding when her shuttle escaped.

Yet, she thought, if they had been captured...

Rivka failed to muster anything at that thought beyond an empty ache. She could do nothing for them now, just like she was unable to do anything for Tritogenes.

She was alive, at least. That counted for something, and her escape had been even more narrow than they expected. Rivka meant to get past the orbital blockade at high speed and then shut down every nonessential system, rendering her little ship virtually undetectable, until Enyalios's cruiser arrived to pick her up.

What happened instead was that several of Aegesander's ships opened fire on her without warning. She had accelerated as hard as the little craft could, pushing its gravity control past its limit. With the force of five standard gravities pressing on her chest, she thought she might have been going fast enough to escape unharmed.

One of the blockade ships landed a lucky hit on her engines, destroying the main thruster array and all but one maneuvering thruster. She thanked every god real or legendary she could think of that the missile missed anything more important. Without artificial gravity, she would have been instantly liquefied in her seat, and a loss of life support would have meant slow suffocation.

She closed her eyes again, thinking of Tritogenes despite every effort not to. Rivka wondered if she would have done the same thing in his place. Perhaps she would have still run, leaving them both to die as soldiers disabled the shuttle before it could launch.

On the other hand, she asked herself how much difference it really made. Tritogenes and Hyperion were dead and it was her fault.

She brought the case to Pteryga. She could have read it, locked it, and never spoken of it again. If she had, Tritogenes would still be alive.

Aegesander came to Hyperion's planet for a reason. He might still have killed his fellow Hexarch, no matter what Rivka did. Maybe that had been his entire reason for being there in the first place.

Hyperion's death was tragic, but she could not help but to dwell on the idea that had she not been there, at least one more Hexarch might still be alive.

She leaned back, banging her head into the bulkhead and staring up at the ceiling. She ran out of tears some time ago. When they dried up, they left behind a void where little more than idle thoughts flitted through her mind.

She screamed. "Damn it!" Her voice was hoarse and felt even drier than her eyes. She pounded a fist on the floor, repeating, "Damn it! Damn it! Damn it!" until it, too, ached.

Rivka sighed, cradling her hand. Everything was going wrong and the knowledge that she had, objectively, done the right thing helped little. Hyperion told her as much himself. She knew, in her mind, that he was right. That did not help very much.

Dwelling on the things in Diomedes's letter would have driven her insane. Perhaps, in time, she would have become like Aegesander. Perhaps she, too, would have come for her fellow Hexarchs with guns and steel, killing them for the crime of simply knowing a secret.

She eyed the case again. Or, she thought, perhaps she would have turned into Diomedes. His confession, his sin, was shared by them all. Eventually it became too much for him to bear.

Yet Hyperion had told her she did the right thing, bringing that information to him. She trusted Hyperion; they all did, even Aegesander in his own way. Perhaps that was why Aegesander went for Hyperion first. He knew how the long-serving Hexarch would react, exactly what he would do and say, and so Aegesander would be "forced" to kill him.

Anger bubbled up in her gut. It was the second time she felt any emotion other than bitter pain and sorrow since shutting the door on Tritogenes's bleeding corpse, and the second time that emotion had been

220

rage. Aegesander admitted to killing Hyperion and admitted his goal was to kill her as well, and Tritogenes if he got in the way.

She remembered his face, clear as crystal despite the anger and hate fogging everything else. He looked sad, not angry.

"What if that bastard was telling the truth?" Her voice came out weak, thin, and dry. "Oh, gods between, what if he was telling the truth and Hyperion really was dangerous and it had nothing to do with..." She waved a hand at the box containing Diomedes's confession. "That."

Rivka rose, pacing the small cabin.

"No," she said. Then, stronger, "No! No way in hell was he telling the truth. But if he was, and I got Tritogenes killed for no reason..."

Rivka turned and slammed both open palms into the bulkhead. She screamed a primal scream of frustration and anger, long and loud. When it was over, her throat hurt and she tasted blood.

"I did the right thing!"

She slammed her hands against the bulkhead again, balled them into fists, and slammed them against the unfeeling metal.

She repeated herself, voice growing quiet and weak. "I did the right thing!"

Slowly, she leaned her head against the wall between her hands, panting and staring down at the floor. Her pulse raced, and she willed it back to normal as best as she could. Long moments of slow breathing finally pushed away the feeling of vertigo, but the void remained.

Again, she slumped to the floor, ending another of the cycles that had been repeating themselves every so often since barely escaping Pteryga.

"Darkness take it all," she growled. She finally understood Diomedes.

Aegesander would kill to keep his secrets. That was fine, she thought, because she would die to unmask them.

The ship fell silent for several hours. After the first hour, she drug herself off the floor again, breaking out of her routine of emptiness-rage-emptiness long enough to reheat some of the survival rations stored in the shuttle's cramped kitchen.

Food made her feel better, but she barely tasted any of it. Afterward, she would have been hard pressed to recall what, exactly, she ate.

Another hour passed before one of the few working parts of the ship's controls flashed from amber to blue. Her heart rate immediately sped up again; blue meant an omnidirectional transmission. She told the computer to let it play without formally accepting it and giving away her position.

"...the *Lefkada* under command of Second Lord Lochagos Antonius. We were sent on an Grade Omega priority assignment on First Lord Hexarch Enyalios's orders to find, retrieve, and safeguard First Lord Hexarch Tritogenes and First Lord Hexarch Rivka."

The voice was a deep bass, resonating even through the little speakers in her cabin. He continued speaking a moment later.

"To all ships under the command of First Lord Hexarch Aegesander, do not open fire on us. We are prepared to answer force with force if necessary."

She checked the passive sensors as the captain of the *Lefkada* continued to speak. The ship was several hundred thousand kilometers away, much closer to her than she was to Aegesander's ships after her time drifting.

"Computer," she grated in her tired voice, "hail the *Lefkada*."

"Hailing," replied the incongruously soothing voice. "Open."

"*Lefkada*, this is First Lord Rivka. My shuttle has been drifting for two days with no engine power. You will have to come to me, I fear."

A minute passed as the transmission crossed several light seconds, the reply was dictated, and it too crossed that vast distance. "Understood, First Lord. Is First Lord Tritogenes with you as well?"

Rivka's stomach tightened as an iron fist clamped down on it. Her mouth refused to answer for a full minute before she said, "no, Lochagos Antonius. First Lord Tritogenes did not survive."

In the silence that fell, she realized that she did have some tears left to shed after all.

***

Mihalis caught up with the squad Pallasophia mentioned a few minutes up the road. Their passage through areas of the palace still controlled by Aegesander's troops slowed their progress, allowing him to make up the difference in time easily enough. Better, at least for the few minutes where he needed to move unimpeded, the invading soldiers were starting to congregate at choke points and important locations rather than simply patrolling the streets.

Of course, he reminded himself, that meant they were likely to encounter a much larger group ahead, but that was something to be dealt with in the future.

In the present, he had bigger issues to worry about, such as linking up with a squad he had never met without benefit of any sort of communication technology. Mihalis supposed he admired the foresight to hijack the palace's communication framework, but that meant the only way to talk to anyone else was a direct data connection, and those were unreliable outside of distances where it was easier to just talk a little louder.

More to the point, he had to link up with that squad without them shooting him, which was his current concern.

The squad was just ahead, likely dealing with injuries sustained from their most recent firefight. That shootout had been the primary reason they were so easy to find. Mihalis had their route thanks to Pallasophia and all he had to do was follow the sound of gunshots until he caught up with them.

Unfortunately, that meant they were going to be jumpy, and so rather than approach closely, he cut down a side alley and stepped onto the main road a dozen meters ahead of them with his hands raised.

Thirteen rifles aimed at him within moments, but no one fired. Near the center, one of the people, probably the leader, held her rifle with one

223

hand. The other was in an upraised fist, signaling to the rest of her squad to wait.

Mihalis took the moment to survey the group ahead of him. Two, including the ostensible leader, wore the torn and dirty remnants of Tritogenes's palace guard uniforms. The others wore a random mixture of clothes, robes and workwear both, in a variety of colors. The militia members, if they had even been that organized before Aegesander's assault began, carried a mix of weaponry as random as their clothing. Some had high-end military hardware, whether their own or looted from enemy soldiers, while others had hunting rifles or even target weapons.

Before the apparent leader could ask, Mihalis offered an explanation for his presence, saying, "Pallasophia sent me."

The two palace guards conferred with one another while the militia members continued watching him through the sights and scopes of their various weapons.

Finally, the reply from the apparent leader came. "Prove it."

"She gave me a pass token. Let me send it over."

"Do it."

Mihalis slowly lowered his arms and summoned his holo interface. The token was easy enough to find, which was good. He was not fond of standing in front of the business end of a squad's worth of weaponry, and so anything that made the process go faster was a pleasant surprise. He picked up the holographic token from its place in his workspace and passed a copy across.

It took a moment. Not only was the token a fairly large object, but he suspected the palace guards had their personal systems on heavy lockdown to prevent Aegesander's troops from tracking them. Finally, the woman who spoke to him raised a hand and opened her own holo, which presumably displayed the token.

It was too small to see from as far away as he stood, and Mihalis fervently hoped nothing happened to it as he passed it across. Direct transfer like that should be fairly reliable, but his luck with electronics was not exactly the best when the situation was calm. With Aegesander's forces running interference programs, he had no real way to tell if it worked until she motioned to the rest of the squad.

A quick palm-down gesture and everyone facing him lowered their weapons. "Come on over," she said.

Mihalis did, still keeping his hands in plain view. They might have acknowledged that he was not an enemy, but given how tense things were right then, hiding his hands or fiddling with his weapon was a good way for one of the more nervous militia members to hit a point where their nerves overcame their good sense and they shot him anyway.

Up close, the squad looked even more motley than it had from a distance. Only a few actually looked comfortable with their weapons. The rest kept idly touching them as they shifted about, apparently unwilling to accept the fact that, at least for the time being, those weapons belonged to them now.

Mihalis was a bridge officer, or he had been before the *Phlegethon*'s destruction. That meant he had to pass a certain minimum fitness level, but that level was far lower than anyone who saw direct combat would have been expected to meet. He might have been strong and with decent stamina, but the makeshift militia staring him down, by and large, did not even meet those lax standards.

Of course, he reminded himself, none of them expected to be suddenly thrust into a warzone that morning either. In light of that, they were doing quite well.

Expressions on their faces ranged across a variety of emotions. Some of them looked angry, others tired. Most of them had a hollow, haunted look to their faces, and Mihalis again reminded himself that these were not soldiers. None of them expected to wake up, be given a weapon, and be expected to kill in defense of their homes.

Nor, he realized as his eyes drifted downward for the first time, did they expect to have to watch their friends and neighbors be gunned down.

The two palace guards were a different story. Their matching white uniforms were just as torn, dirty, and bloody as everyone else's clothing, but the difference was in their posture and expressions. These two might "only" have been guards, but they still trained for this type situation. In fact, unlike a field soldier or a Marine, these two guards trained for *exactly* this situation, and it showed in their expressions.

The guards' emotions were harder to get a read on. He thought they looked angry at first, but as he got closer, Mihalis realized that instead they simply had closed off their emotions from the outside world for the time being. Angry, sad, afraid—the might have been feeling anything at that moment and none of it came to the surface. Despite everything going to hell around them, those two, at least, maintained something very close to perfect propriety.

He hoped he could emulate their example.

The leader gestured to herself, then to the other guard. "Third Lord Mihalis? I'm Lochias Nymphadora. This is Lochias Diocles."

He nodded greetings, but none of them moved to shake hands. That particular nicety could be forgone given the situation, and with no ship and no crew, his status as a naval officer was dubious.

Nymphadora introduced the militia members one by one in a flurry so quick that Mihalis only caught a few of the names—Demostrate, Yiannis, and Stamatia. The others entered his brain but never made it into memory. He hoped he would have time later to remedy that, but there were more pressing matters at the moment.

"Pallasophia said you were headed toward one of the palace armories?"

Nymphadora nodded. "You're navy, right?"

"Yes. I was aboard the *Phlegethon* when the mastigas attacked."

"I thought I recognized your face." She cracked the smallest of smiles. "It wasn't too long ago that Ouroboros kidnapped you and stole you away to the moon, was it?"

"No," he said, grinning. "It wasn't."

"Well, you survived *that*, so let's hope you're good luck."

"I like to think I am."

"Good, good. Are you ready to move?"

He nodded. "Where is this armory?"

Nymphadora pointed. "That way, on the other side of a bunch of Aegesander's soldiers. So if you're ready, let's go. You're watching our rear."

"As you say, Lochias," he replied. As the group advanced in ragtag fashion, he slowed a bit to let them pass, then took up his new position at the rear. At least, he thought, looking over his shoulder was practically second nature now.

***

Second Lord Ilias motioned for what remained of his team to take up their positions. Two people dropped to the ground to his right and one to his left. All things considered, he thought, those were good survival numbers given the sudden shift in allegiance from Aegesander's "security" forces.

Earlier that day, he had been angry. Not only was his Hexarch in danger, nor only was his brother's friend in danger, but that danger came at the worst time possible. Rivka gave him and his team the day off to enjoy Pteryga. Free time, true free time, was a vanishingly rare thing given his occupation and so, bowing under the weight of Rivka's insistent orders, he took some personal time.

Of course, Ilias thought at the time, that was when Aegesander chose to make his move. Rivka and Tritogenes were in the palace, virtually defenseless, and then he sprang the trap. Rivka's first and only message to him had been quick, vague. Aegesander's people did not, at that point, have control over the palace's communication system, but she had no way of knowing that. In light of that uncertainty, she included as little information as possible.

Little more than a note, it ordered him out of the palace, told him she and Tritogenes would get off planet any way they could, and instructed him to go to ground.

The first part of that had been more difficult than expected, because it was his bad luck to already be in the palace. The day's shopping and entertainments were done and he was on his way back to speak with Rivka and possibly see if she would tell him finally what her meeting with Hyperion had been about. Aegesander's troops had other ideas, and now only he and two others remained out of the personnel she brought with her.

Fortunately, he knew Rivka and Tritogenes made their escape. From outside the palace walls, he watched her shuttle lift off. Even if he had not recognized it, the gunfire pinging the outer hull would have been enough of a giveaway to guess what was going on.

A few hours later, another shuttle lifted off, this one without being accompanied by gunfire. He assumed First Lord Aegesander was aboard, but that part of things was no longer his problem.

It was not his place to guess why First Lord Aegesander attacked the palace under the guise of security. The official word was that First Lord Hyperion was dead, Ouroboros was involved, and that was that. Unofficially, it seemed Aegesander's troops believed Tritogenes and Rivka were somehow also involved in whatever plot was going on. Granted, in all the chaos, it quickly became impossible to tell the official story from the rumors. Being unsure bothered him, but he could ignore it until later..

Ilias had his own Hexarch to worry about. He obeyed the first of Rivka's two orders well enough. He did not want to be anywhere near Pteryga's palace as long as it was crawling with Aegesander's soldiers. The second order, however, he chose to ignore. Rivka's safety came before his own and it was his duty to link up with her as soon as possible.

"I make seven guards," Ilias said, taking the binoculars away from his face.

"Seven as well."

"Seven."

"Agreed."

"Zenais, you're the best marksman we've got. Take the first and fifth ones."

"Acknowledged."

"Eudora, numbers two and six."

"Yes."

"Valentina, three and seven."

"Understood."

"I've got number four. As soon as they're down, convert your weapons and make a run for it. Understood?"

"What if there are others?"

"We hope there aren't. If there are, we deal with them on the way in. But if we take too much time on our approach, there *will* be others."

"What's our destination?"

He lifted the binoculars again, counting the spaceport's guards. There were still seven. Satisfied, Ilias turned his attention to the ships parked there. Unlike the palace's landing pad, this was a public area and whatever they were about to steal belonged to a private citizen of Pteryga. After it was all said and done, Ilias would compensate whoever it was personally if he had to.

He picked four different ships. "They're all going to be locked and our overrides aren't going to work like they would back home. We take whichever one we can get going first. Understood?"

They nodded, nearly in unison.

"Good. Ready?"

Several moments passed as the four of them settled into position. On their stomachs, with the rifle scopes trained on the spaceport, each of them waited with their fingers poised over their weapons' trigger. Ilias adjusted slightly, re-centered his scope over its target and exhaled in a long, slow breath.

"Now."

The four rifles cracked in unison. Three of the guards fell. A moment later, three shots rang out again. Two more of Aegesander's soldiers fell.

Ilias cursed as the remaining two, one wounded and one not, ran for cover. "Zenais! Left!" he snapped.

Ilias chased the soldier on the right with his scope, trying to get a decent line of sight on him. He thought he had one, shot, but his only answer was a puff of dust from the spaceport just centimeters behind the fleeing soldier.

"He's calling for reinforcement," Ilias said. He was surprised at how calm his voice sounded. "Zenais, cover us. Valentina, Eudora, with me."

Ilias rose, ratcheting and adjusting parts of his rifle as he ran. The others followed, performing similar adjustments to their weapons. The modular armaments might have lacked the performance of a purpose-built weapon, but much of the technology that went into Lelantos's weapon made it into theirs as well, and Ilias was a fan of versatility.

The grass underfoot was slick with evening dew, making their footing on the hill treacherous, but within moments Ilias was running too quickly to worry about falling. If he slipped, he would simply tumble the rest of the way.

Behind them, Zenais's rifle cracked the air. The shot impacted the corner of the control console protecting Aegesander's last soldier. To his right, one of the others fired a burst, but Ilias could not see which it was.

They were too far away, running too fast for any such shot to be accurate, but he was not going to chastise anyone just then. Covering fire was covering fire.

A moment passed and Aegesander's soldier rose again. This time, the weapon in his hands was larger, easier to identify from their hundred-meter distance. Ilias raised his own rifle this time, shooting wildly, but none of the shots landed.

The anti-vehicle rocket erupted in a pillar of fire and smoke, streaking for their previous hiding spot. Ilias cursed—of course the spaceport had heavy weapons on hand. The rocket exploded in a spectacular light show whose concussive wave reached them before he even had time to call out.

Ilias, Eudora, and Valentina lost their footing and tumbled as a hammer made out of the atmosphere itself swept them to the ground.

Valentina was on her feet first, sprinting again before Ilias could even clear his head. He came to his feet a second later with Eudora right behind. Less than ten meters remained now, distance any of them could cross in seconds.

Aegesander's last spaceport guard rose again from behind the console that sheltered him from Zenais's bullet, aimed at Valentina with less than six meters between them, and shot her in the chest three times.

This time, Ilias had enough air in his lungs to curse, though he was unaware of what actually came out of his mouth beyond rage. Few meters separated them, close enough that even running did not disrupt his aim very much. That mattered even less when Eudora fired as well.

Ilias had no idea how many bullets actually struck the guard, but he crossed the distance before the man even hit the ground. Ilias smashed his rifle butt into the side of the guard's head as he ran, aiming for the nearest shuttle.

"Dark take the plan!" he shouted. "Help me get this one running!"

***

Second Lord Nymphadora looked around with an expression Mihalis thought was almost proud. Despite his initial reservations about the militia members around him, he had to agree. They lost two assaulting the armory, but pushed on despite that. After suffering much greater losses at their hands, Aegesander's forces pulled away amid shouted insults and threats from the militia.

He could not blame them, though his ingrained military discipline kept him quiet while they jeered. Mihalis thought he would not have come up with anything more impressive than, "that's what happens when you attack someone's home!" anyway.

The armory had been heavily looted already, but enough equipment and ammunition was left for their squad to standardize their weapons to fire the same bullets. That cut down on a lot of extraneous weight some of them were carrying, because they no longer had to haul extra ammunition that would only feed into their hunting rifles.

"Mihalis," Nymphadora said. "May I speak to you outside?"

He nodded, following. She led him out the armory's back door, which led to a simple fire escape. The armory had been built on the side of a hill, which meant the font door was at "ground level," but the back was a story higher. That had been useful at one point, but the vehicle garage below them was empty and the fire escape let nowhere.

During their engagement, night fell, and a cool breeze blew in, bringing with it a perverse mixture of smells. Blood and death, fire and grease, all of the smells of battle came wafting in on a wind made of roses and jasmine. Somewhere, or perhaps everywhere, cicadas filled the air with their shrill cries.

Limani's palace was an awfully idyllic place to have a war, Mihalis thought.

"I'll be quick," Nymphadora said. "We don't have enough officers to hold this armory and manage the militia as well."

Without thinking, he replied, "I'll stay."

"How many of the militia do you need?"

He shook his head. "I'll be fine by myself." A moment passed and he cracked a grin. "Besides, I survived Ouroboros, remember?"

Nymphadora frowned. "It's not a good idea to leave only one person here."

"It's a worse idea to split up your already small squad," he retorted, then added, "Lochias."

"What was your rank aboard the *Phlegethon*?"

"I was a Dekaneas."

She hummed in thought. "You're a Lochias now. I'll send anyone we can spare back here."

He knew his face lit up, but Mihalis did everything he could to keep his voice under control. "How long until you leave?"

"We're leaving now. You're in charge, Lochias Mihalis."

"Thank you," he said. "Ten Thousand guide your steps."

"Suns go with you," she replied, turned, and stepped back inside.

Mihalis waited until the squad filed out and watched them circle the building to the lower side before stepping back inside. He carefully latched the back door, then moved to the front door and latched it as well.

Fortunately, he thought as he collapsed downward into a nearby chair, it was fairly comfortable as far as military buildings went. The chairs had actual cushions.

As the night drew on, he busied himself by performing maintenance checks on the armory's remaining weapons.

Near midnight, a knock came at the front door. He picked up his rifle, switched off the safety, and crossed the small armory. Tapping on the holo controls next to the door to activate the two-way speaker, he asked, "yes?"

"Mihalis, it's me."

His pulse sped up and he opened the eye slit in the door. Her voice had not been faked, and it might have taken him a full minute, but he unlocked the door and opened it. Third Lord—no, he corrected himself as he saw the stripes on her uniform—*Second Lord* Aella stood there in the dark. She was armed, but the rifle was pointed downward.

"Thank the gods you're alive!" he said, stepping back to let her into the armory. "Where have you been?"

Aella laughed. "Well, there's a war out there, you know."

Despite the grim situation, he smiled. "I've noticed. Did Nymphadora send you?"

Aella blinked, then smiled and nodded. "Nymphadora? Yeah. I never got her name, but she said you needed help."

He gestured to the empty armory, then shrugged. "There's not a lot to do here, but I'm grateful for the company."

233

"I'm glad," she said, then stepped fully into the armory. The door shut under its own weight and the mechanism locked automatically.

"It's good to see you're alright," Mihalis said, settling back into his chair.

Aella leaned against the flat side of a nearby weapon rack. Her face fell for a moment, but then she smiled. "You as well. To be honest, I was hoping you were somewhere far away from all this fighting."

Mihalis shrugged. "I would have been, but I was already here in the palace. I wanted a chance to meet First Lord Tritogenes without being kidnapped by Ouroboros right afterward."

Aella laughed, looking away from him. "I imagine that put a damper on your day."

"A bit, yeah."

"So," she began. Aella paused. "What made you take up your weapon?"

"Tritogenes," he said automatically. "And Limani, I suppose, but when I saw what was going on, I couldn't just sit by and watch his planet be invaded."

"Yeah," she said. Her voice was quiet, but it still sounded like agreement, or at least acknowledgment of what he said. "You've seen the broadcasts from Pteryga?"

He nodded. Mihalis felt his face tighten in anger. "I have. Hyperion is dead."

"They say Tritogenes did it."

"They say a lot of things, Aella. I don't believe it for a second."

"Why not?"

He took a deep breath, ready with a hot, angry retort, but stopped. Instead, he took another, slower breath, and simply replied, "because Tritogenes is a good man. I can't believe that he would assassinate a Hexarch."

Aella frowned. "Someone did."

"And that someone is probably working for Ouroboros."

"I thought the Titans stopped them."

Mihalis shook his head, still angry. "I watched hundreds of their people flee that base as the Titans assaulted it. That's the only part of the news I believe. Ouroboros is behind this, you can bet on that."

She nodded. "Yeah. I believe they're behind it as well."

"And Tritogenes had nothing to do with it."

"You know," she said. Aella pushed away from the wall and laid a hand on his shoulder. "I admire your loyalty."

He smiled. "Thanks. Tritogenes was good to my father his entire life."

Aella stepped back, leaned against the weapon rack again. "That's good to know. I've heard he was a kind, talented man."

"He was," Mihalis said, "at least everyone said he was. After the mastigas attack, he took the time to meet with me personally. He could have sent an intermediary, but he came himself. That's the kind of man I want to work for when I become a Second Lord."

Aella was quiet for a moment. Mihalis looked up at her and found her expression baffling. She was lost in thought, but whatever thoughts those were seemed to be sad. He turned back to the table where he currently had a rifle half-disassembled and cleaned.

"You said your father worked for Tritogenes and that's why you went to work for him."

He nodded, tinkering with the rifle's recoil spring. The tension was wrong.

"Mihalis," she said. "I'm sorry."

"What fo—"

A white lance of heat and pain ripped into his lung, interrupting the rest of his question. He fell forward, scattering rifle parts, then fell to the ground.

"You're not the only one loyal to your father, Mihalis."

Breathing hurt, and his lungs felt wet. Mihalis scrabbled to right himself, but none of his limbs seemed to be working right.

"Put me through to First Lord Aegesander," Aella's voice said from somewhere far away. There was a pause—he had no idea how long—before she spoke again. "It's done. Yes. Thank you, father."

Chapter 13

The explosion behind him thundered in the narrow corridor as smoke and debris washed across his back. Panatakis tuned his senses, checking his ears, but all they picked up anymore was an overstimulated whine. Detonating grenade after grenade would do that, he supposed, and the cyborg Titan was quite happy he could literally tune out that specific frequency before it gave him a headache.

What he could not tune out was the strain on his back muscles. He carried his backpack and gear on one shoulder and what remained of Korakti's backpack and gear on the other. Her sword and pistol hung off the back of the bags, out of reach but not forgotten.

If he ever got time to rest, he would try and figure out how her gun worked, but for the time being, grenades were serving his needs well enough. In one of his few strokes of good fortune since leaving the *Hammer of Ares*, he discovered that Korakti brought extra explosives.

She did it at the expense of some of her food stores, but that was immaterial now. Even if she only brought half the advised amount of rations, that meant Panatakis now had that much more food. He did not particularly relish thinking of her death in such utilitarian terms, but it was either that, or let his grief overwhelm him.

More to the point, she would have wanted it that way. He could, and did as he practically looted her body, imagine her saying, "gods between, Kokkinos! Take what you need. It's not like I need it where I'm going!"

Her grenades helped keep his grief away as well, if for no other reason than they were the only thing keeping him alive at that point. Panatakis lost track of how many mastigas he killed, but the count had to be well over a hundred now. Yet they kept coming. There were too many of them to fight normally, with guns, which made lobbing explosives in their general direction his best option.

Behind him, he heard more scrabbling and cursing in Lexeis Archeio. If he ever had time to sit down, eat, and think about anything other than how to survive the next few seconds, he might have been more concerned about an alien menace from beyond their system speaking a semi-dead Technocrat language.

He armed the most recent grenade, threw it hard over his shoulder, and darted down a new corridor to his right. He counted the seconds until it exploded. Thanks to the enhancements in his ears, the overpressure from the concussive blast did not burst his eardrums or shatter the delicate bones in his inner ear. It did, however, knock the breath out of his lungs like a hammer.

Panatakis doubled over, grabbing in vain at a wall devoid of anything to grab. For a few terrifying moments, his lungs refused to work, but then he finally sucked in a deep breath of cold, humid air.

He froze, feeling a chill beyond that of the air in his lungs. Something was different about that air. He tasted it and smelled it, but those senses told him very little. Taste was useful for the pleasure of eating and for finding poisons, not for identifying why the air was different in this room versus the others.

Perhaps it had been this way for a while, and he had been too focused on lobbing explosives to keep the mastigas away to notice. Smell was, after all, his least favorite sense.

238

He listened, using his ears and eyes both, but heard nothing in the wake of his last grenade. He deliberately chose a more powerful explosive, hoping to destroy part of the corridor itself. Without going back to check, he could not know if it worked, but he hoped.

While he thought, Panatakis took a meal ration out of the side pocket of his backpack. The brown-gray bar was as unappealing as it was healthy. It had the uniform texture of ground-up paper, and flavor had certainly been an afterthought. Wet paper that tasted like honey and violets was still wet paper.

On the plus side, the bar had enough nutrition to keep him going for a while longer. This type specifically also contained an absurd amount of stimulants like caffeine, which he needed after the better part of a day and a half wandering the mastigas ship without sleep.

As he chewed, fighting the temptation to wash the mushy bar down with more water than he ought to be drinking at one time, he cycled his senses. Panatakis rarely liked to return things to "normal," but after so many deafening explosions, the machine part of his brain needed time to rest. Piece by piece, the world grew less colorful and things returned to how he had perceived them before Project Titan.

Panatakis looked at the corridor like anyone else would for the first time. The machine parts making his eyes work they way he liked needed to be reset, but the simpler pieces that simply made those organs work again could go for much longer without maintenance. He frowned at the world around him—it was *boring*.

The metal under his feet was a dark gray-green, contrasting only slightly with the lighter gray of the walls and ceiling. Lights were placed fairly overhead, and their dim illumination lent the whole hallway a twilight feel. He supposed anyone but the completely blind could tell that much, but any further detail was out of reach of his damaged eyes.

He heard nothing but his own breathing, which bothered him far more than it should have. He wanted to hear the walls, the lights, to see the sounds of his own movements. Instead, the world felt flat, dull.

He hated it, willing his cybernetic parts to complete their reset faster. He hated being *blind* again.

Still, he had to remain alert, and even without his implants, motion and sound still had their place in the world. He hoisted his rifle, pacing a few meters each way. Not knowing what was beyond his sight, or out of range of his hearing, kept his pulse high.

Worse than actually being blind was the memories it evoked. Losing pieces of his sight as his implants reset themselves called to mind the early days after his injury. Sometimes his eyes worked, sometimes not. One day, he might see color, the next nothing but gray. Now, he saw color and movement, but everything was like a camera whose lens no longer focused.

Panatakis grit his teeth, pushing the memories away. He reached the end of his short patrol pattern and turned. At the far end of the hall, a corridor branched off to the left. His pacing now took him closer to it, and the smell and feel of cool, humid air grew stronger.

Panatakis stopped at the opening in the wall. In the doorway, the floor changed from a dark gray-green to an even darker green-brown. With his senses where he preferred them, he would not have noticed the change unless the new section was textured differently. Beyond the doorway hung darkness and chill. Whatever the source of the cold and humidity, it was in that room.

Without his senses working right, he could not tell anything else about it. His eyes—his boring, *human* eyes—could not penetrate the gloom. His ears, by themselves, were of no use.

Every one of Panatakis's instincts told him not to go in the room. Whatever was there obviously had much better sight in the dark than he did, putting him at a double disadvantage. If his eyes were working right, things would be different. He darted back, away from the doorframe, and planted his back against the wall beside it. With no way of knowing whether or not he had been seen, his only thought was to minimize or eliminate that chance going forward.

A small blue light appeared in the upper-right corner of his vision, a signal from his implants. Such signals were imprinted directly onto his optic nerves, and those parts of his eyes at least worked properly. The notification was jarringly crisp, a clear circle against a fuzzy sea of grays and greens.

He felt a surge of elation. One light meant the basic functions were operational again and he could at least access the computer aspects of the implants. He immediately signaled the implant to overlay a progress meter at the bottom center of his sight, followed by the usual indicators he kept in the periphery of his vision.

A few moments passed as things winked into crisp life, hovering over the muddy real world like holos only he could see. As the final piece of his personal HUD blinked to life, the progress meter at the bottom of the screen hit one-hundred percent, flashed, and disappeared.

Panatakis let out the breath he had been holding since he saw the endless expanse of velvet black. That was all his human eyes could make out from that large, empty room. A few moments more, he reminded himself, and he could take a look and it the right way.

He checked his rifle again, making the movements habitually, then dropped to the floor and crawled just far enough so that his eyes were past the doorframe.

He looked, now using all of his senses and feeding that data through the optic centers of his brain. The room stretched further than he could see or hear. Even sounds faded to blackness before reaching anything that sounded like a wall. Flashes of movement danced around like sparks, sounds blinking here and there like fireflies.

It was still not enough information. The unknown gnawed at him, now worse because he knew the rough size of the room and he knew that something moved out there. More important, he knew that multiple somethings moved out there. With no real way to measure the room, the number of potential threats was, quite literally, incalculable.

Noise came from behind him, sharp peaks of jagged gray-green. The mastigas were starting to clear the hall he destroyed. That left him to choose which of the three unknowns paths he wanted to face.

Further down the corridor, things were black and silent, but the walls and ceiling were where they had always been. Nothing that way appealed to him, especially not the thought of wandering aimlessly down unmarked corridors for another thirty-six hours.

If he was completely honest with himself, which he admitted was rare, what Second Lord Panatakis wanted to do was sleep. It would be so very easy, he reasoned, to just close his eyes and lay still. With his implants, he could shut down his senses at will. If he concentrated, he could even deliberately induce unconsciousness.

It was so very tempting. He had not slept in two days, barely napping in the shuttle. Adrenaline carried him through the hellish hours that followed. Then Korakti had been killed, and his blood was only now starting to slow down again.

Just a few minutes, he thought. His eyes felt heavy and the floor seemed to drop away. Nothing would happen if he stayed where he was a few minutes more.

Sudden silence hit his nerves harder than any noise would have. The mastigas had stopped clawing at the rubble behind him. Ahead, in the impossibly large room, the flashes of noise had stopped. Echoes persisted here and there—nothing he could make use of.

Panatakis pushed himself back, away from the door, and into a sitting position. The heart that, moments ago, wanted to slow and sleep thundered violently in his chest. Reflectively, his eyes darted around, trying to pick up some vestige of sight in the lonely corridor.

He shut his eyes, trying to call to mind the soothing images of his desert home. He had been born on the opposite side of the Kokkinos from First Lord Eurybia's palace, far away from much of anything in fact. Every morning, the suns cast radiant shadows as the angles lined up perfectly and they rose through an arch of red rock.

After receiving his implants, he had gone back home for a few weeks. At the time, he used the cliché of "an enlightening experience" to describe what he saw and heard. The light of the suns sang a chorus on the crags of that arch. The red rock became a bassline playing counterpoint to the billion-voice choir of light. All around him, the wind whipped colors of fire and water as it coursed through the air.

In the same breath that he longed to return to that time, the memories calmed his nerves. Only a few seconds passed since everything around him fell silent.

He looked around again, this time critically examining things with every sense he had. Physically, nothing had changed except for the silence. The silence of the desert calmed him, but the sudden lack of noise here, aboard the mastigas battleship, was troubling. They should have been attacking him, or trying to get through the debris behind him. The huge room ahead of him had to be full of mastigas, but none of them moved.

They had to know he was here. The packs had followed him for hours now, but even they were gone.

Slowly, as slowly as he could manage, he undid the straps of both sets of gear. Unburdened, he climbed to his feet, still listening. He held his heavy rifle with its grenade launcher tight against his chest, and slowly raised it to his shoulder.

Every movement was controlled, slow. He could see the sounds his muscles and clothes made, glowing bright in the silence. None of that light made it more than a meter at most before the dark silence swallowed it.

Panatakis regarded the door for a moment. Standing in it would backlight him and diving through it would cause more noise than he wanted. Either would give away his position. Unfortunately, some compromise had to be made if he was to step through that door at all.

Another idea struck him, one he had not yet considered. The mechanism on his rifle's attached grenade launcher was simple to operate, and he emptied it of high explosive rounds. In a moment, three flashbang grenades sat at the front of the small magazine, a flare behind them, and he re-filled the rest of the tube with high explosives.

Panatakis took another moment to pick up the backpacks full of gear and again strap them on. They made moving, and hiding, more difficult, but they held his food, and that was compromise enough.

With no way to be stealthy, Panatakis reasoned, the next best thing was shock and awe. He rose, readying the weapon and steeling his nerves. The flashbang rounds would fill the room with light and sound, allowing his enhanced senses to get a perfect picture. They would also, he hoped, stun the mastigas on the other side long enough for him to find some sort of cover.

He spun around the corner, into the doorframe, and squeezed the rifle's second trigger. It kicked, sending a solitary streak of light and music into the darkness. It vanished, swallowed by nothing.

In the half second before the flashbang detonated, Panatakis used the sound of the grenade being fired and his own steps to see the area around him. A few meters away stood a protrusion, about rib-high. It sounded solid enough, he hoped, to be a temporary shield from the hell about to be unleashed.

The world erupted into light and sound, and he dove behind what ended up being a workstation. The echoes and sound persisted for several seconds, allowing him to get a clear picture of what he saw and heard.

He was right that the room swarmed with mastigas, but as the moments ticked by and they struggled to decide where to focus their aggression, Panatakis realized why they suddenly lost interest in him back in the corridor.

Illuminated by the fading music, the mastigas were fighting *each other*.

***

The sophont kept its larger hands in the air, raised in the apparently-universal gesture of surrender. Its smaller hands worked underneath its helmet until it removed the sleek, black shell. It knelt, setting the helmet on the ground as it said, "no kill, you."

"That thing should not be speaking," Lelantos hissed. He spoke quickly, forcing the words out around his chronodrug-induced slowness. "I fought the mastigas on Kipos. I lost a sister! None of them ever spoke. None of them showed signs on intelligence."

"It came to us," Victoria said. "Unarmed. We owe it the chance to listen."

"We owe it nothing!"

Three impossibly beautiful green eyes watched their exchange with a mixture of interest and unmasked terror. Its smaller arms were clasped in front of it now. The other, longer arms were out to the sides, deliberately as far from anything that might be a concealed weapon as possible.

"No kill, I. No kill, you?"

"Lelantos?" Victoria asked. "Is it telling the truth?"

"I won't look at it."

Victoria did not like to "pull rank" as it were, preferring to reason her way through problems as she did with Helena and Korakti's interpersonal feud on Faros. At that moment, however, she did not have time for niceties. "Titan Lelantos, as your commander, I order you to examine the sophont and determine if it's being truthful."

He glared, tense and angry, before a deep breath and long, gradual exhalation brought things back under control. "If mastigas tells are anything like human tells, it believes what it's saying."

"What do you want?" Helena's voice was calm, level, every part the cool and collected persona Victoria expected from her. As calm as she sounded, however, Helena kept her rifle aimed at the center of the sophont's chest.

"Want to end fighting, I," it replied.

"I don't believe you," Lelantos growled.

"Truth, is."

"You expect us to trust you?"

The sophont spread its smaller arms in a gesture of, as it appeared to Victoria, attempted reason. "Have not attacked, I. Have allowed, you, to speak, me. Have trust, we?"

Lelantos growled again. His rifle had been converted into its short-range configuration, and now he raised it. The sophont's three eyes fixed on it and it took an involuntary step backward.

With his head, Lelantos indicated Victoria. "I let you come close because she ordered me to."

"To thank you, say I."

"I've spoken to your kind before," Victoria said. "You approached without a weapon. You deserve to be heard."

"Deserve?" it asked, cocking its three-eyed head to one side.

"Deserve," she repeated.

"What mean, you?"

"You showed us respect by asking to talk, and trust by coming unarmed. We owe you the chance to act on that."

It looked confused for a moment. "Then you for many things thank, I."

"Why is it speaking like that?" Lelantos asked.

The sophont eyed him quizzically. "Meaning is how, your?"

Victoria took up the study of Lexeis Archeio early on after leaving the labyrinth, though never did very much with it. Knowledge of reading and writing in the more modern Technocrat dialects was already included in the information First Lord Tritogenes saw fit to implant in her head as part of her pre-birth "training." Lexeis Archeio used the same alphabet and similar words, but the primary difference was grammar.

She started that study when Pallasophia pointed out that the sophont that shot her all those months ago spoke with modern words, but grammar directly from that dead language.

Now that she had a better understanding of the language, it was obvious that Pallasophia had been right all along. The grammar the mastigas in front of them used was identical to the grammar of Lexeis Archeio, which made it identical to the warning signs in the deserted section of the ship.

In her brief access to the ship's database, Helena found no explanation for why the mastigas spoke a dead Technocrat language, or some pidgin version of it at least. She found several useful pieces of information, most important of which at the moment was that everything in the ship's database was written in Lexeis Archeio.

In none of the files or systems was there any indication that the mastigas spoke any other language. Nor was there an explanation for *why*.

She articulated a short summary of those thoughts to Lelantos, who nodded his understanding. "That makes sense," he agreed. For all his anger earlier, he seemed quite calm now. She supposed that was the work of the chronodrug allowing him to process his emotions sixty times faster than anyone else. "But can it say anything without my having to wrap my brain around Archive speak?"

"Can you?" Victoria asked the sophont.

"Speak without," it started, then stopped. One of its smaller arms scratched its hairless head in a disturbingly human-like gesture. The verisimilitude was broken a moment later when it continued that motion, and simultaneously gestured with its two other arms. "Can try, I. I can try."

"Thank you," Victoria said. "Do you have a name?"

"Name?" it asked. It seemed to think for a moment. "Called 63-Echoes-of-Emerald, I."

"That's a mouthful," Victoria muttered.

"Sixty-third sibling, am I. To speak aloud, for efficiency, call me 63-Echoes. For us, much of it smell, is."

"You identify one another by smell?" Helena asked.

"Much communication, smell is," replied 63-Echoes. "Is why I came to you. You..." Another pause. "Smell different, you."

"How old are you?"

"Not very old, I. I remember a planet, fires."

"Kipos." The word dripped from Lelantos's mouth like pitch.

The sophont nodded. "Yes. You smell..." It paused, sniffing the air. "Angry."

"Kipos was my home," he growled.

"I understand. I am..." It stopped speaking. Its mouth continued to move, as though it were trying to articulate something that it simply had no words for. Finally, it spoke slowly, saying, "I am not unhappy when I think that your Kipos should not have burned."

"Not unha—" Lelantos started to speak, but cut himself off. He took a deep breath, then, "you mean you feel regret." At the sophont's confused look, he explained, "it means you wish something didn't happen."

"Yes," it said. "I feel regret. Unfamiliar is, this concept, but feel it, I."

"Why did you attack?" he demanded.

"Could not say no, we. Mastigas are not one people, but ruled by one mind. The smell of revenge was too strong."

"Explain," Helena demanded.

Victoria took a long moment to look at her while the sophont gathered its thoughts. She seemed to be in pain, but was managing it better than she had so far. Tension radiated from her every muscle, but her rifle waited at her side with her hands away from the trigger. Overriding all that, however, was a look of intense interest on her face— Helena was, for lack of a better word, *fascinated*.

The sophont obviously perceived Helena as the greatest threat present. It jumped when she spoke and seemed to wither under her stare.

Victoria wondered what it meant by "smell." Perhaps they could smell hormones, she thought, ending that line of thought when the sophont opened its needle-lined mouth again.

248

"Six, we are. Many want different things, some want even to leave this system completely. Others want fire, blood. It was their smell that controlled us six years ago."

Victoria was about to ask it if her thoughts were correct, but she never got past the first word. The sophont's head exploded, rendering instantly into a fine pink mist and a splatter of bone and brain.

Victoria's first thought was that Helena had snapped again. She wheeled on her fellow Titan, ready to berate her or even to defend herself from another unexplained attack, but Helena's rifle was pointed a completely different direction.

She spun around in time to see Lelantos raise his own weapon with the eerie fluidity his muscles had when under the influence of the chronodrug.

A stench filled the hall, one she had not smelled since the laberynth. The second sophont had not had it, neither had the one that now lay dead at her feet. The first one, the sophont that mocked her as she tried to find her way through the maze of passages surrounding the arena, smelled like what she now smelled.

Some distant, animal part of her brain understood that what she smelled was pure, unbridled hate.

A single sophont, armed and in full armor, stood amid six gigas and uncountable fonias at the far end of the hall. A large pistol with a strange, flared barrel sat in the hands of its larger pair of arms. More fonias erupted out of the side passage from which they came. A mikros rode atop each of the gigas, pointing ahead of them like miniature jockeys

The sophont yelled, voice magnified by its helmet. "Are there, intruders, they! To them bring a killing, we!"

In the moments that followed, several things happened, each timed almost exactly to her hammering pulse.

First, the mastigas lurched into motion. Fonias scrambled over one another, all vying to be the first to bring their terrible knives to bear. Behind and among them, the gigas slowly unlimbered large rifles.

249

Second, Lelantos's chemically-enhanced reactions put a bullet through the skull of one of the gigas. Even those giants were no match for the heavy bullets of his marksman's rifle.

Third, she and Helena fired. Both women shot indiscriminately into the mass of fonias. So many of them filled the hallway that Victoria flicked the selector switch on her short rifle and simply held the trigger down until it stopped firing.

Fourth, as Victoria reloaded, Helena froze in place. She seemed like she was about to fire, but stopped as an expression of surprise and hope passed over her features in the blink of an eye. "Panatakis is near!"

Fifth, a spark of light sprang into existence on the far side of the room. It was bright, but nothing spectacular, rising up like on a column of sparks. The attacking sophont's head swiveled around to look past the door the horde just came though.

The second flash was much brighter. Illumination brighter than a thousand suns dazzled Victoria's eyes, leaving spots in her vision that no amount of blinking would clear. The mastigas fared even worse; the sophont and several of the mikros, all looking in the direction of the flash, screamed. They fell, clutching their heads. Even the other mastigas stumbled, swatting at afterimages only they could see.

Between Helena's announcement and the twin flashbangs, the situation was obvious. She only hoped it was obvious to Lelantos as well, because she did not have time to articulate anything verbally.

As Victoria let loose with another magazine's worth of automatic fire, she hoped Helena could communicate and fight at the same time.

***

The first flashbang illuminated the mastigas and almost forced Panatakis back into the hallway, but before he could move, the mastigas swarm blocked his retreat. He supposed in that moment that charging into the room was the right thing to do, because otherwise the mastigas would have surged into the cramped confines of that hall and likely killed him within moments.

250

The second flashbang allowed him to more properly get his bearings. That one he fired straight up, hoping to reach the ceiling of the expansive room. It did, proving his initial impression correct. The outer walls of the massive room sloped inward, coming to a point so far above his head that even the flashbang barely showed it. Machinery and workstations numbering in the hundreds littered the wide open space between the outer wall and the massive object in the center.

That massive object turned out to be a step pyramid that reached to the apex of the room. Between the outer walls and the pyramid, little mystery remained about his location. Even without knowing where the others were, he now knew where he was. More importantly, he knew the weapon that destroyed the *Justice* was almost within his reach.

Panatakis's feeling of elation quickly vanished when he turned his eyes and ears to the rest of the room. Leaving aside the sheer size of the pyramid and the lack of apparent ways to climb the thing from the outside, a more immediate concern troubled him.

The first flashbang illuminated a group of mastigas near him that were only now coming back to their senses. The second flash showed a far larger horde of mastigas moving on the far side of the room.

Dwarfed by distance, even the towering gigas and elites looked smaller than his hand. With a motion, he could blot out their entire army from his sight. His ears still heard them, probably would have heard them even without the glowing sound-sight of the fading flashbang.

The ones that had been following him before meeting Korakti made very little attempt to be stealthy. After her death, the mastigas pursuing him had abandoned even that effort, running and making enough noise that even a person with normal senses would have had no trouble evading them.

Now this horde, more than he had ever seen in one place, crept slowly. As he listened to the dying echoes of his flashbangs, the mastigas split into two groups. Two sophonts, well over a dozen gigas, an elite, and more fonias than even he could count slunk toward him. Another group, two-thirds that number, went another direction toward a farther exit.

Both surging masses of mastigas stopped for half a second as his flashbang went off. The sudden chill in his blood cut off all other thought, conscious or unconscious. One of the sophonts spoke. Across the vast distance, its words were muddled by the time they reached Panatakis's ears, but the message was clear enough.

The sophont pointed directly at him with one of its long arms. It held something in its hands that the animal part of Panatakis's brain recognized as a weapon long before his conscious thoughts did. He ducked back behind the workstation. Watching with his ears, he saw one of the huge elites, two gigas, and several of the littler mastigas turn and head in his direction.

These were not trying to be stealthy.

Being able to watch them through sound gave him a moment of advantage. Panatakis could see them clearly without having to expose his own head. The elite carried a large rifle in its two lower hands and a pair of long, curved swords in its upper hands. One gigas was armed with a similar rifle and the other with a club easily the size of a human being.

He looked around, but the group of mastigas that came around behind him were gone. He reached out with his senses, trying to pinpoint their location by sound, but he found nothing. Not even the fading echoes of motion remained. If that group was going to attack and kill him, they missed a perfect opportunity to do so while his back was turned.

Instead, they simply *left*.

Panatakis had no time to dwell on the oddities of mastigas behavior. He cycled the action on his grenade launcher, dropping the empty shell from the second flashbang. It hit the floor with a blue-white clatter, illuminating a small patch at his feet for a second.

Amid the dim sound of the shell casing at his feet, another sound came to him. It took a second for him to realize that, no, he was not hearing the sound through his ears. It was hard to make out exactly what it was, but the sound clearly originated inside his own head.

He listened for a moment, trying to focus on the sound. Even without coming through his ears, his brain recognized it as noise. A moment's focus told him that not only was it noise, but it was words.

Someone was speaking to him, or trying to.

He grunted, shutting out that voice for a moment. With every bit of detail he could pick up, he tried to pinpoint the mastigas. They were still on the far side of the room. They approached him more quickly than the rest of the horde moved. None of the mastigas moved very fast as the moment, nor in very straight lines. The after effects of the flashbang would be hampering their movements for another few seconds.

He had until then to identify the voice in his head. He sat still, focusing on the sound of who, or whatever, it was.

"Panatakis!" It called his name in light, feminine tones. Undercurrents of concern, anger, and a mix of a dozen other emotions swirled inside those words. The voice repeated, "Panatakis!"

He had a few more seconds to spare, but whatever message he sent had to be fast. Only one other human being alive could speak directly to his mind like that, and Helena's voice rang out like every cliche choir of angels he read about as a child.

<Panatakis!> she called again.

<Helena!>

<You're alive!>

<I could say the same thing about you.>

<Victoria and Lelantos are with me. Where are you?>

He flashed her an image of the pyramid lit up by the first grenade. The entire conversation happened much faster than words would have. They spoke at the speed of thought, often not even articulating things in words but using pictures, concepts, and feelings to speed things along.

<Are you alone?>

<I am now. Korakti is...>

253

Before he could even process and transmit the idea of loss, Helena replied. <I am sorry, my friend.>

Panatakis cursed, a general feeling of anger and resignation that must have been transmitted clearer than he intended, because Helena's mind picked it up and quite literally obliterated the very idea.

<We have no time, even as fast as our thoughts are. There are mastigas.> She thought at him, using a mixture of images and emotion. The mastigas in the tunnel, dark and terrifying. The sophont, humble, fragile, curious, and very dead. She then transmitted a memory of the first flashbang going off from her perspective, adding, <and this.>

Rather than reply with words, he sent her an image from moments ago: him firing the grenade to see.

Helena replied by looking at the door through which her side of the mastigas horde still poured.

<You're close.>

<It would seem so. Can you come to us?>

He sent two images. The first across was the the sound-picture of the elite and pair of gigas approaching him. Following that he remembered to her the horde filtering through his side of the door she just showed him.

Helena replied with the feeling of adrenaline gripping her heart. The message was clear even before her actual words came across. <Fight!>

He nodded mentally and whistled. That brief noise allowed him to get a general picture of the immediate vicinity. Panatakis took a breath and rose, leveling his rifle at the approaching elite.

He fired the first round, his third and final flashbang, directly at the mastigas. The small group detached to attack him had gotten less than five meters away from the others, close enough that the main horde ought to fall inside the grenade's flash radius.

Compared to a bullet, his grenades were achingly slow. Up against anything that could be thrown by a human being, however, those same grenades were blindingly fast. They could cross the room twice, if not three times, as fast as the strongest thrown ball and with much greater accuracy.

That grenade should have impacted the elite in the dead center of its chest somewhere between three and four seconds after leaving his rifle. A direct impact, rather than simply detonating nearby, would pour most of the energy from the grenade directly into its target. Magnesium and other metals reaching several thousand degrees would instantly burn a hole in the elite's torso large enough to kill even one of those towering monsters.

It did not happen.

The grenade had been in the air for about two seconds when the elite dodged. In mid step, it threw one of its powerful legs to the side, behind the other one, twisting its entire body and bringing its torso out of line with the explosive that should have killed it. The grenade sailed past the elite, past the two gigas, and hit the ground.

The mastigas in front of the grenade flinched. The brilliant flash lit up the room enough that even they were blinded and deafened for a few moments. Despite covering his ears and eyes, Panatakis himself experienced a inhuman feeling of vertigo as every one of his enhanced senses burned and twisted. In moment, he would be fine, but those first few seconds were agony unlike anything he could have imagined before Project Titan.

Many in horde on the far side of the room, standing right where the grenade went off, screamed and fell to the floor. That, at least, would help matters on Helena's end.

Before his senses cleared, he fired another grenade. This one he aimed at a sharp angle upward, not caring where it ended up. The third grenade in the weapon's magazine was a simple flare, and the need for it was long since gone. Three high explosive rounds remained. They would have to be enough; Panatakis doubted he would be able to reload the launcher for some time.

He rose, and that same animal part of his brain that warned him about the sophont's gun thirty seconds before made him turn. He put the advancing group of mastigas to his back and faced the other direction, looking into the depths of the dark room.

The flare he launched had arced up and gone behind his back. It lodged in some piece of electronics three stories up, casting a lurid green glow over the mastigas moving around.

He froze, processing that thought. Like the mastigas approaching Helena's position, these were moving quietly, slowly. Even he had not seen the sounds of their approach. Two elites, six gigas, and another seemingly endless horde of fonias all swarmed around a single sophont, and they were all looking in his direction.

"Gods between us," he muttered as the reality of his situation set in. The mastigas that he thought had been chasing him had simply been shepherding him. He wondered if they were ever as close as they seemed. "I've been ambushed."

Chapter 14

Large parts of Limani's capital city were on fire. The initial skirmishes had been "police actions" as far as Aegesander's official news reports were concerned, but after the first day that pretense had been dropped. This was an invasion, a retaliation for Tritogenes's alleged involvement with Ouroboros and Hyperion's assassination.

The idea of a Hexarch attacking another Hexarch was not exactly unheard of—they all kept standing armies for a reason even before the mastigas attacked—but it was exceedingly rare. To make matters worse, with the bulk of Tritogenes's army in space attacking the mastigas directly, she was left with little more than the local police force, which currently numbered...

"Seven thousand six hundred and eighty-two have checked in across the city."

Pallasophia nodded. A few days before, she would have balked at the idea of getting tactical reports from a twelve-year-old. Then everything had gone to hell with one Hexarch dead and two still missing.

Sixth Lord Alexis, a dainty blond whom Pallasophia probably never would have noticed in a crowd, had quickly proven herself to have not just shooting skill, but analytic skill far beyond what anyone would have expected out of someone so young. She certainly outperformed Pallasophia's own memories of her time as a Sixth Lord three decades previous.

"How many do we have here?" she asked.

"In the palace?"

"Yes."

Alexis's fingers flew across her bright blue holographic interface. Once upon a time, it had been programmed that way because a young girl decided two mornings ago that her holo was going to be robin's egg blue. Now, it stood out as an oddly cheerful piece of normalcy.

"One hundred twenty four," she replied quietly.

That was one less than one quarter of what should have been the palace security force. Those numbers would have been bad enough, but Pallasophia knew that also included local militia forces which, the day before, had numbered over two hundred alone.

The occupation force hit the palace first, ensuring the rest of the planet was cut off from its proper nerve center. Regional capitals fell within hours as his troops "secured" the planet "for their own safety." They even went so far in the last few hours, touched off by her recapture of the palace, as trying to start a rumor that Tritogenes himself had been killed.

"Second Lord," Alexis said. She stood and banished her computer interface with a gesture. At times she looked like a child of twelve, big eyed and frightened by the disaster unfolding around her. This was not one of those times. "May I ask a question?"

She nodded. "You've saved my life more than once now. I think you've earned a few questions."

"Is First Lord Aegesander a traitor?"

The bluntness of her question, to Pallasophia's surprise, shocked her. She had entertained the same thought, certainly, but to hear it spoken aloud was different. Even the quartet of armed soldiers watching the doors and windows of the room they turned into their command center stiffened.

Finally, she replied, "I don't know."

Alexis looked thoughtful, momentarily appearing childlike again. Her eyebrows came together like she was puzzling over a piece of homework, not the fate of a whole planet. "Why not?"

That, again, stopped her in her tracks. "Because," she replied. "I don't know. I can't say why he's done what he's done. Maybe his original story was right and he really did interrupt a terrorist attack on Pteryga."

"But why accuse Tritogenes and Rivka of being a part of it?"

"I," she started, then paused. "If he was telling the truth about the attack, maybe something went wrong."

"Tritogenes wouldn't turn on Hyperion," Alexis stated. She crossed her arms over her chest. "He wouldn't. He loved Hyperion."

"We all did."

"Aegesander didn't."

"What do you mean?"

Alexis shrugged. "Look at me, I'm a kid. Why do you think children have been used as spies for, well, forever? People say things around me they wouldn't say around you. No offense."

"You're probably right. Hyperion hasn't met with Aegesander in private in almost thirty years, shortly after... Sweet Lady Lovelace..."

Pallasophia rose, pacing. A thousand thoughts ran through her mind, all centered around the last thirty years. Words came and went, none of them full sentences or even fully articulated ideas or thoughts. Some of them made it out of her mouth, but most were stopped somewhere between her brain and tongue, further obfuscating what it was she was trying to say.

"Second Lord?" Alexis asked.

"No," she said, barely even aware that Alexis spoke.

"Pallasophia?"

"There's no way," she muttered. "Just... Thirty years? It can't..."

Concern crept into Alexis's voice. "What can't?"

Pallasophia stopped pacing mid stride and turned to Alexis. "I have to call a friend."

Alexis nodded and ceased her questioning, even though her facial expression clearly indicated that she did not understand Pallasophia's sudden and nearly complete mood shift. Even Pallasophia herself did not understand it fully, and in part that was because she did not want to admit she was even thinking the thoughts in her own head.

There was one person other than Pallasophia herself whom Tritogenes always trusted and went to for advice. She paged through her holo's menus. Communication services had been buried deep, unused for some time because Aegesander's soldiers held the communication hub, and finding the person she needed took another few moments.

Eventually, however, a projection of a man who looked strikingly like Tritogenes hovered above her arm. She wondered briefly how they became friends. Perhaps he was an understudy for Tritogenes years before, when the Hexarch had been a simple singer. Perhaps she would ask later.

For the moment, she had something different on her mind. She stepped into the hall. "Good morning, Philip."

He smiled, but his eyes were sad. "It's not quite a good morning, is it?"

"No. No, it isn't."

"What can I do for you?"

Her mind raced as a dozen thoughts all fought to be the first thing to cross her lips. Philip waited calmly for her to put her thoughts in order, a quality that he certainly did not share with his more impatient friend, Tritogenes. "You once told me, warned Tritogenes, that Aegesander would kill to keep his secrets. Don't pry too much into his feud with Hyperion, you said."

Philip nodded. "I remember."

"What did you mean?"

"I meant exactly that."

"Do you think someone," she paused. "Do you think someone looked too closely?"

"First Lord Rivka and First Lord Aegesander both booked unexpected trips to Pteryga shortly before First Lord Hyperion's assassination."

Pallasophia nodded. Philip was a recluse with access to some of the best data sources in the binary. Even Rivka's network could not compete directly with him, though Pallasophia suspected that they cooperated more than they competed.

"Philip?" she asked.

"Yes?"

"What happened to Hyperion thirty years ago?"

Philip frowned. "I think we should speak in person."

Pallasophia's heart stuttered. Even Tritogenes rarely visited Philip in person, and the Hexarch never talked much about the time they spent together. She suspected at one point that they were lovers, but even that would not explain things.

Aloud, however, she kept her composure. "Give me the location and we will be there as soon as possible."

Philip nodded, and his holo vanished, replaced with a location pin on a map of the palace. Pallasophia frowned at it. The location he gave was a floor *below* Tritogenes's server room. She supposed he had a safehouse buried there, or perhaps that room with its access to Tritogenes's servers was how Philip maintained his proverbial ear to the ground.

Whatever the reason for the location, she was glad of it.

She finally turned back to Alexis. "Get your gear."

Alexis nodded, gathering her things. As she worked, Pallasophia felt the girl's eyes on her, watching with confusion. Finally, she asked, "what do you think has happened?"

Pallasophia shook her head even as she tugged on the armored gloves taken from the palace armory. They were black, like the rest of her clothing at present, missing even the blue stripe that would denote her rank. She left her robe there, locked in the now-half-empty armory, because she had no use for it until things calmed down. Alexis still wore the suit of black she fashioned in mimicry of Victoria's.

"I don't want to even say it out loud until I can check some things. Because if I'm right..."

"If you're right, then I'm right," Alexis said solemnly.

"About?"

"What I asked a few minutes ago. About Aegesander."

Pallasophia sighed. The girl was damned perceptive. "Most likely, yes."

"Blue screen it."

Hearing the curse in Alexis's small soprano voice would have been enough to bring a sardonic smile to Pallasophia's lips on any other day. As it was, she simply nodded her agreement. "Pretty much."

With her own gear packed, Alexis busied herself with readying the various computer components they set up in the room. Aegesander's troops, theoretically, had been pushed out of the palace or killed, but neither of them wanted to run the risk that some of them still remained. The gear was spread across six backpacks, one noticeably less full than the other five.

Alexis shouldered the smallest of the packs and picked up her rifle. Pallasophia wanted to ask how she was doing, but every time the conversation strayed that way, Alexis deflected it. Finally, she told herself it was a conversation that could wait until they all were safe. If she forced it before then, she had no idea how Alexis would react. So far, the girl had been running on adrenaline without time to sit and think about what she had done. The brief sleep she managed earlier in the day had been restless, however, and Pallasophia dreaded the moment in which it would all come crashing down on her.

For the moment, though, Alexis bore disaster with as much dignity as Pallasophia would have expected out of someone three times her age.

She removed the magazine from her rifle, checked that it was full, and replaced it. She checked the weapon's action with the smoothness of a movement practiced for years, then asked, "where are we headed, will you tell me that much?"

"There's a server hub under the palace."

"We already checked there. It was clear. I could patch us in from here."

Pallasophia shook her head. "There's apparently something a floor below that one."

"Really? How did I not find it on the map?" Alexis's wide-eyed question was directed at herself more than at Pallasophia, and the Second Lord chose to ignore the implications for the girl's free-time activities. Of course, the girl *was* from Kipos, after all.

"Even I didn't know it was there," she admitted.

"So it's secret."

"It was some private records room Tritogenes kept, I think."

Alexis pantomimed a zipper across her lips, but the twinkle in her eyes was unmistakable. "I won't tell."

Pallasophia laughed. "Good. Because if the information there backs up my theory, you're about to be party to one of the most terrible secrets of the last century."

Alexis's face fell. Suddenly, at least from Pallasophia's perspective, it seemed the idea of accessing a Top Secret server lost its appeal. "Goody," the girl muttered.

***

Limani was not the only planet on fire. Some, like Katarraktes managed to avoid the worst of the bloodbath by stopping Aegesander's forces before they could land. Violence spread across Dasos and Kokkinos, but it was little more than a token show for Aegesander's news outlets. They called it a "mop up effort," doing their best to showcase how much better prepared they were than the other planets—especially

Katarraktes, which they maintained had fallen completely to Ouroboros thanks to First Lord Enyalios's involvement.

Kipos struggled to free itself. Most of the assault—and on Kipos there had been no mistaking the force for anything other than an attack—hit areas of the planet that had yet to recover from the mastigas attack six years prior. Those areas fell like cards to Aegesander's attack as the population and military pulled back into more secure locations.

The attack that hit First Lord Rivka's planet had been different from the others. Even the force blockading Enyalios's forces high above Katarraktes came under an announcement of security. They announced themselves as peacekeepers, there to help ensure the "terrorist attacks" on Pteryga never spread. Ouroboros, they claimed, must be contained. Only later did they change their story, blame First Lord Enyalios, and call themselves an assault force.

The ships and soldiers who attacked Kipos, on the other hand, came in under exactly that banner: Kipos had to be pacified. The entire planet was a risk, they argued. Something on Kipos attracted the mastigas six years ago and now the battleship was on its way back to the inner system. The obvious answer was that something on Kipos drew them in, and Aegesander left his troops with orders to discover what that thing was "by any means necessary."

First Lord Rivka hated to leave her planet behind, but the militia was doing its best already. Her presence could, perhaps, provide a measure of inspiration, but Kipos was strong. They understood the need to fight and would do so without her watching over their shoulders.

There were other places she needed to be.

Fighting enveloped Prosgeiosi, especially in and around Odyssey itself. Highly respected, and often highly skilled, Second Lords in direct service to the Hexarchs fed the proverbial flames—none would risk damaging Odyssey with *real* flames, after all—in an effort to prove *their* Hexarch was the one in the right. The death toll was low, but the capital planet's hospitals would be busy for some time with cuts and stabs, burns, and other minor injuries.

Odyssey was visible from the window of Rivka's shuttle. The dome-shaped city itself was locked up tight. As soon as fighting began, automatic security protocols ten thousand years old activated and locked every access route. That itself had caused no end of damage to the surrounding area as bridges and even buildings attached to the outer hull of the once-mighty starship were immediately severed. Even the top of the ship, left open and used as a landing area for a thousand years had been sealed inside its pearl-like shell. Rubble that had once been people's homes and lives lay strewn around its base.

Even if it was no longer a starship in its own right, Odyssey retained much of the armor it once had. Nothing short of prolonged orbital bombardment could crack its walls and even Aegesander would balk at destroying "the ship that saved mankind."

The capital dome gleamed orange amid the fires in the surrounding towns and cities. Aegesander's forces fought what was once called a "scorched-earth campaign." They made regular public broadcasts asserting the rightness of their cause, urging the citizens to vacate the area, and condemning anyone who resisted their attempts to capture the alleged traitors and conspirators inside Odyssey.

"Ouroboros has taken the city!" claimed the broadcasts, and Rivka hoped and prayed to every god she knew that the populace did not believe him.

Some of her own forces were down there. She had no idea where, because her very presence in the skies of the Technocrat capital world was a secret. A very small handful of people knew she was there. The list began and ended with a man named Strategos Antonius, who captained the ship that rescued her from Pteryga and delivered her to Prosgeiosi before returning to Katarraktes.

Soon, she would add another name to the list. Second Lord Karolina, captain of a ship called the *Eleusis*, was minutes away from becoming the second person to know her Hexarch's whereabouts. The Second Lord did not yet know it, but that would change when Rivka's borrowed shuttle came closer. At the moment, the rudimentary sensors aboard Rivka's shuttle told her that Karolina's ship was currently exchanging short-range cannonfire with a ground-based holdout of Aegesander's soldiers.

Visibly, the *Eleusis* was barely in sight. The cruiser-sized ship was rightfully a space-faring vessel, but it had entered the atmosphere ostensibly to provide support and extraction for Rivka's troops isolated on the surface.

The official story was that the *Eleusis* would evacuate as many of Rivka's people as it could and then take them back to Kipos to reinforce the fighting there. Official news sources claimed Enyalios's forces had nearly pushed Aegesander from the orbitals around Katarraktes. Even Aegesander's own stories backed up that claim—he knew better than to lie on such a scale—but rather maintained that Enyalios had unjustly attacked a peacekeeping mission.

They all knew that once Enyalios broke the blockade, he would descend on Prosgeiosi himself. That was one of the few things that worked in her favor, because most of Aegesander's ships had been diverted to Katarraktes to prevent exactly that from happening. Few of them remained in orbit around the capital.

It took every ounce of rationalizing ability for her not to hate the people her cruiser had engaged. They were, after all, simply following orders and acting with the best information they had. Their Hexarch told them that traitors and terrorists were holed up inside the capital, and so that was what they believed. Rivka struggled not to hold it against them that they were following the orders of a traitor and a murderer.

Aegesander's troops had not committed any war crimes, either. Even on Kipos, they stayed within the letter of the laws of engagement, both written and unwritten. Civilians were given the opportunity to evacuate. Aegesander's troops never attacked housing, sanitation, or anything related to food. They captured and held those areas, of course, and if some of them happened to fall to collateral damage, the invading armies did not seem to care overmuch, but no one stopped to actively commit atrocities.

Subjectively, that made it worse, because she wanted to hate them. Rivka wanted to hate the people who killed Tritogenes and assaulted her planet, but they were just soldiers.

She resisted the urge to summon her holo-computer and replay that footage. The dark knew she had done that enough as it was. The cameras on the outside of her previous shuttle captured it all in the impersonal way security systems recorded everything. It was all clear enough, and no matter how many times she watched it, Rivka could not figure out how it could have gone any better.

She grit her teeth. The cold pit in her stomach had long since been replaced with a fire. Tritogenes knew exactly what he was doing, the objective security footage made that clear enough. She supposed she should be thankful to him for saving her life and sacrificing himself so that she could get to the ship and escape, but she failed.

The only feeling she could reliably conjure up for First Lord Tritogenes was a bitter sort of hatred. Objectively, she knew exactly what was going on. Years of learning to read people—training that failed her in the one second where it was most needed—meant she could read herself too.

Rivka knew exactly what survivor's guilt looked like, and she knew exactly how it felt. She had hated First Lord Diomedes for a time as well. He died and left her with an entire planet to run, smothering his shame with poison. Now Tritogenes had done the same thing, not out of shame and not with poison, but he was dead all the same.

And, once again, it was *her fault*.

The thought of Diomedes brought another flash of anger to the surface. The same thought crossed her brain for what had to be the millionth time in the last few days: if Diomedes had simply destroyed his records instead of bequeathing them to Rivka, things might have turned out differently.

Then again, they might not.

A half-smile crossed her face, part smirk and part grimace. "Survivor's guilt," she reminded herself aloud. She dipped a hand into a pocket on her robe, a black and gray military model provided by the ship that came to rescue her. There, in a small velvet pouch, were Hyperion's six rubies. Now she knew why he never took them off, and she doubted she would, either.

Rivka took a deep breath. "Anyway, don't we have work to do?" she muttered to herself. "Computer, hail the *Eleusis*. Request docking."

"Acknowledged," the computer replied. Unlike her personal shuttle, this ship's computer spoke with the flat personality of off-the-shelf systems. A full minute passed before her computer beeped to indicate a reply. The stilted, metallic voice stated, "the *Eleusis* requests direct communication."

"Confirm," she replied. "Audio only."

Another minute passed, during which she drew nearer to the distant ship. She nudged the shuttle higher, taking it out of the potential reach of most ground-based weapons. Finally, the computer beeped again.

"This is Second Lord Lochias Brontes of the Kiposian gunship *Eleusis*. State your name, rank, and purpose."

Rivka shifted gears in her mind. It felt like pulling a lever, a shift as physical as it was mental. She drew herself up straighter and set her face in an impassive mask. Her voice loosened and grew deeper as she transformed her negative emotions and tension into a sense of solidness. "Inform Second Lord Lochagos Captain Karolina that Persephone Protocol is in effect."

"I don't know who you are, but..."

Rivka cut him off with a snap of, "do it, dark take you!"

The communication line immediate cut off and Rivka prayed that he did as instructed rather than simply ordering her shuttle blown out of the sky. Just in case, "computer," she said, "maximize passive detection sensitivity. If they target us, I want to know."

"Acknowledged," the genderless, emotionless voice replied.

She missed her ship already.

Several minutes passed in which the *Eleusis* did not lock its weapons on her ship. Rivka was about to hail them again when her computer spoke up. "Incoming hail from the *Eleusis.*"

"Put it through."

"This line is secure." She recognized the voice of Second Lord Karolina immediately. "Persephone Protocol is in effect."

Rivka breathed a sigh of relief. One weight, at least, was off her back. "Thank you. No one else knows?"

"No one but me. I'll clear the deck for you, First Lord. When you get here, the two of you..."

Rivka's stomach tightened for a moment, but the angry heat remained. She interrupted the captain, "I am alone."

"Alone, but..."

Her voice was devoid of even the hint of emotion. "I will fill you in when I arrive, Lochagos."

"Understood, First Lord. What are your orders?"

"Continue evacuating my people. Hold the area until First Lord Enyalios's ships arrive. At which point, we will leave Prosgeiosi."

"Understood. Kipos will be thankful for the reinforcements."

"We're not going to Kipos."

"First Lord?"

"We are not going to Kipos," she repeated, speaking through gritted teeth.

The pause at the other end of the conversation stretched on for a full minute before the captain simply replied. "Understood."

The rest of the brief conversation consisted of instructions for her computer that governed how and when it was to surrender control to the

Eleusis's systems. When the line cut, Rivka sat in silence for several minutes as the bulk of the cruiser grew closer.

No, she thought, she was not going to Kipos. Instead, she had a job to finish. There would be *hell* to pay.

***

Pallasophia removed one of her armored gloves and pressed her palm against a panel that glowed with a dim red light next to the door. She held her hand there for a moment before the panel brightened, blinked orange, and then turned a solid green color.

At face level, another dim red light appeared. This one was much smaller and sat next to a little lens. She raised the front visor of her helmet and leaned her face close to that sensor. The light turned first orange and then green as she stood there. Not blinking was the hardest part, and no matter how much time she spent around the retinal scanners in Odyssey, Pallasophia never got used to them.

She took a moment to put her glove back on, but left her visor raised, blinking away the strange itchiness in her eyes.

"Identity entered," a voice from the wall proclaimed. It was a pleasant baritone, different from the usual femininely androgynous alto of computerized systems. "Confirm."

The biometric data was no different than any other high-security or personal area. Her apartment on Prosgeiosi was fingerprint-locked, after all, and she could only gain access to the area surrounding it with a retinal scan. Eye locks were typically Hexarch-level security, and for this particular room, buried under Limani's palace, to have that kind of security was no surprise.

"Pallasophia," she replied, then rattled off the long series of titles that served as the third part of her identification. "Second Lord. Chief of Aphelion Operations. Director of Project Titan Area Six. Lochagos, Sub-Strategos Glaukos."

The computer beeped again. "Please supply verification code."

She nodded, drawing the code out of her memory. She had not used it in years, at least not officially. Only two places required it, and one of them was Aphelion Facility itself. After taking up semi-permanent residence there, she never needed it again.

The only other room with similar security was the server room a level above. Pallasophia wondered what Philip *actually* did in the first place that merited this level of security access.

She wondered if this place had the same sort of defensive measures as the server room. That place had additional locks that could be engaged with different codes, and was even built with a series of progressively more devastating countermeasures should someone attempt to force entry.

The code for the Agamemnon Protocol flashed through her head. First Lord Ophion built this server facility, and that particular element had been part of his original design. She supposed an EMP and a fuel-air-explosive would make short work of whatever secure information was stored there, but even Pallasophia felt it was overkill.

Tritogenes once told her than all Hexarchs were paranoid megalomaniacs, himself included, but she never believed him until he showed her Ophion's server security.

After a moment to double check her own memory, she supplied the code it asked for. "Six-Six-Twelve. Orion. Rho. Interdiction."

"Identify confirmed," the wall replied after a full minute of contemplation. "Confirm identity of second party."

Pallasophia looked down. The guards had all been left in the outer hallway, and only Alexis stood by her side. A combination of terror and curiosity sat on her face, both culminating in a wide eyed look of wonder. The Second Lord remembered growing up on fairy tales of hidden treasure, and she had no doubt that those same stories were going through the girl's mind right then.

By rights, a Sixth Lord should not have been there. Neither should Pallasophia, a mere Second Lord, but Tritogenes made sure she had the proper authorization to go anywhere within his control. Project Titan, he said at the time, was more important than Hexarch-only security systems.

"Sixth Lord Alexis," the girl replied after a moment's hesitation. Pallasophia wondered how bad the temptation to just run away had become.

The door remained silent, and Pallasophia felt the eerie sensation that its mechanical "eye" was watching her now.

"I accept responsibility for Sixth Lord Alexis." she said after a moment. "Protocol Delta-Three. Verification Code: Six-Si—"

The control panel next to the door beeped, interrupting her. The warm baritone said, "accepted."

Her stomach suddenly felt very cold. Machines did not interrupt, especially machines waiting on a verification code. It was possible that it simply accepted her code from before and had taken a moment to process the addition of a second person.

What she felt instead was that the door's security system made a conscious decision to let Alexis in after hearing her declaration of liability. That was a worrying thought.

Another moment passed and the door made a whirring noise that was followed by a series of eight low, resonant thunks. It shifted in its frame and slid into the wall.

The room beyond was, of all things, bathed in a peaceful sapphire blue light. A server rack, visually no different from any other in existence, stood in the corner. The light, at least primarily, came from it. At the center of the small space was a control panel with a holographic interface floating above it. It, too, gave off the same sapphire light and she remembered that that shade of blue had been Ophion's favorite color, something on which she and Tritogenes's predecessor agreed completely.

"Hello, Pallasophia."

She jumped. One hand went to her holstered pistol and the other went out in front of her, ready to fend off who or whatever just spoke to her.

272

The tension radiating from beside and just behind her meant Alexis had done the same thing.

It took a moment for the identity of the voice to fully resonate within her brain. "Philip?"

"I have startled you. I apologize."

The door had been locked, sealed with tighter security than any other place on the planet. Thanks to the last remnants of fighting, no one, not even Philip, could have gotten in ahead of her. Even without the security, the corridor outside only had one exit. For him to already be here, Philip would have had to arrive early enough so that neither she nor any of the soldiers she sent ahead of her noticed.

Pallasophia holstered her pistol, but her eyes continued to sweep the room. It was not very big, and Philip did not seem like the type to hide in the shadows when a friend approached. Yet, it was fairly dark, and she supposed he might simply prefer it that way—Victoria did, after all. She would have loved the light level.

Pallasophia's mind abruptly shifted gears, emotions moving faster than she could control them. Gods between, she swore silently, hoping Victoria was alright.

"Bring her back to me," she said, muttering the words out loud.

"Second Lord?" Alexis asked.

Pallasophia shook her head, forcing her thoughts into a laser focus on the area around them. "It's nothing."

As her eyes adjusted, Pallasophia saw that the only piece of actual furniture was a chair, but it was unoccupied. It looked to be made of some dark wood with deep red cushions. The style immediately spoke of Tritogenes. Rather than sitting at a desk, of which there were none, the chair simply sat in the middle of the room, halfway between server racks and the center console.

"Where are you?"

"I'm sorry," Philip's voice replied. "I wanted to be dramatic."

The image of a head and shoulders appeared in the air, replacing the holographic controls. The holo was of Philip, a young man of perhaps fifty. His hair was plain, and glittered like gold strands had been woven into the brown. One single braid hung from the left side of his face at the temple, reaching down out of frame. His makeup was simple and understated like his hair, dark lips and pale eyes sat as the only pieces of contrast.

Pallasophia had seen pictures of Tritogenes when he was younger, but even in the small holos used for personal communication, Philip looked like the Hexarch. Now, projected near life-size, the resemblance was even more striking. He had a squarer jaw and taller cheekbones perhaps.

"Welcome," he said. "This is where I live."

"Where you..." Pallasophia glanced around, barely aware that she never finished the sentence. She would not have expected Philip to play a joke on her, especially not now, but the single chair had clearly been put there some years ago. Scuff marks on the floor around the feet told that story clearly enough.

Nothing she was seeing was quite registering at the moment, leaving the Second Lord with a strange, detached feeling.

The holo of Philip moved sideways, and when his bust moved away from the holo interface, a torso, arms and legs sprang into existence. He frowned. "Did Tritogenes never tell you?"

"Tell me what? Philip, what sort of game is this?"

He smiled, amused, and shook his head. "This is no game, Pallasophia. I apologize, I thought you knew."

A cold feeling started in her stomach, but that sensation of fear was quickly supplanted by furious curiosity. "Know what?"

Philip shrugged. "My real name is Logosarc. Ophion built me seventy-six years ago. Well..." Philip laughed and the cold feeling in Pallasophia's gut grew worse. "Seventy-six years ago, First Lord Ophion built a computer system to collect information and analyze patterns. His

274

'conspiracy detector,' he called it. I didn't come around for another twenty-two years."

"Sweet Lady Lovelace," Pallasophia whispered. "And you've always looked like Tritogenes?" She simply could not make her brain come up with any better question at that moment.

Philip shook his head, laughing. Even life-size, he looked so very real. She could not wrap her brain around the idea that Philip, Tritogenes's confidant and her friend, was simply *not real.*

"No." Philip shifted, becoming much older. White hair grew long and replaced brown. The cheekbones grew less pronounced and the chin was rapidly covered by a wavy swath of silver-gray hair. The voice changed as well, deepening and growing gravelly. "Ophion preferred a more distinguished visage. This face is the one called 'Logosarc.'"

Logosarc's face returned to the young-Tritogenes version. "I prefer this, if I'm telling the truth. Tritogenes said I looked... friendlier."

"Tritogenes is..." Pallasophia could not bring herself to finish that sentence. The pain was too new, too raw. Even she only found out on the way down to this bunker.

Philip nodded and a look of profound sadness crossed his features. "I know. I'm so very, very sorry. I know how much he meant to you."

"You... you do?"

Philip nodded. His holographic eyes turned away from her and closed. His shoulders slumped. "I feel, if that's what you mean."

"There are rumors that Aegesander was responsible."

"I know," Philip said. He took a deep breath, or made a very convincing approximation of one, and then let it out in anger. His face darkened and pinched together. The expression was very human. "If that man has killed Tritogenes, Pallasophia, you must find out the truth."

"Can't you do something about it? Can't you go after him yourself?" Alexis asked, finding her voice for the first time since Logosarc's appearance.

"Sixth Lord Alexis, is it?"

She nodded, suddenly very, very nervous as the holo turned his eyes on her.

Logosarc laughed. "No. I don't want to 'be let out.' I've read enough stories, fiction of course, about what people do when they're afraid of... something like me. I don't want the first person I ask about souls to panic and have me destroyed."

"You're not lonely?"

Philip knelt. He reached out a hand and rested it on Alexis's shoulder. The hard light making up the hologram was very convincing, even up close. "My dear Alexis, I create worlds within my mind every moment. I could no more be lonely than the stars."

"But the stars are awfully cold."

Logosarc laughed again. "I am cold too, but the stars are many, and I have many worlds," he tapped his forehead, "in here."

"Philip," Pallasophia said, then, "Logosarc. Tritogenes and Rivka went missing within hours of First Lord Hyperion's assassination and a system-wide declaration of martial law by First Lords Aegesander and Eurybia."

His brows narrowed again and he rose back to his feet. "Yes. That much is public now. What did you need 'Ophion's Conspiracy Detector' to uncover, then?"

"Can you plot the deaths of Hexarch Stephania, Ophion, Diomedes, and Meriones in relation to First Lord Aegesander's activities."

"Easily," he replied, then gestured to the chair. "Sit?"

Pallasophia shook her head, but Alexis very nearly jumped at the chance. She assumed at first that the girl was tired, but the expression on her young face as she settled into the velvet-cushioned chair was different. She looked excited, proud, and Pallasophia realized her desire to sit was not because she wanted off her feet.

No, Pallasophia thought with a smile, the girl was excited about sitting in *Tritogenes's chair*.

"Cross reference them with any mastigas activity," Alexis added. Pallasophia nodded, quietly appreciative.

"Momentarily," Philip replied. He closed his eyes for a few seconds before opening them again. A look of concern had settled on his face. Pallasophia found that expression to be profoundly unsettling given who and what Philip seemed to be.

His frown deepened and Philip stepped out of the image, leaving nothing but a man-height shimmer to indicate the holo's location. He returned a moment later, dragging a chair similar to the one in which Alexis now sat. Philip sank into it and crossed his legs at the knee.

From a holographic side table, Philip picked up a piece of paper, reading the information from it. "First Lord Stephania was killed in LY1126. First Lord Aegesander returned from an extended stay on Kokkinos six weeks prior. After her death, he was instrumental in elevating then-Second Lord Eurybia to the Hexarchs."

"Killed?"

Philip nodded. The concerned expression remained, making him look more like the wizened centenarian Logosarc. "Poison in her wine."

"Continue, please."

"The mastigas appeared in LY1151. Despite numerous calls to do something about them from Hyperion, Meriones, and Ophion, First Lords Aegesander, Diomedes, and Eurybia consistently voted against any proposed measures."

Philip paused only long enough to pick up another holographic piece of paper from his side table. "First Lord Meriones and First Lord Ophion died in LY1156 and 1161 respectively. Aegesander sponsored then-Second Lord Enyalios for the Hexarch's seat on Katarraktes personally."

"Where was he when Ophion and Meriones were killed?"

"I have no information to suggest their deaths were anything but natural."

"They were awfully close together," Alexis offered.

"They were," Philip agreed. He plucked another holographic piece of paper from his table and read from it. Pallasophia wondered how much of this was Philip's personal touch and how much was instruction from Tritogenes. "Meriones had just returned from Prosgeiosi when he fell ill. Every medical report claimed First Lord Ophion suffered a heart attack."

"Suspicious."

"I do not make suspicions, Second Lord," Philip asserted. "I, as Logosarc, collate facts. I can tell you that Aegesander immediately began to support Enyalios after Meriones died, and he forcefully supported a woman named Tatiana over Tritogenes."

Pallasophia sighed. The feeling of defeat was palpable. "Then there's no connection."

"I did not say that," Philip argued.

Allied with a twelve-year-old girl, Pallasophia thought, and now I argue with machines. The idea of Philip as her years-long friend continued to override the feeling of existential dread that his existence should have conjured. The holo was also very convincing, lacking even the subtle flickers from dust motes from which most large projectors suffered. Aloud, she asked, "what do you mean?"

"Taken alone, all are isolated incidents. However, when combined with his recent actions, a picture becomes clearer, so to speak. Also, Sixth Lord Alexis asked me to cross-reference with mastigas movements. The only direct connection is in the death of First Lord Diomedes. However, the mastigas battleship made several large positional changes in the months preceding Ophion, Meriones, and Stephania's deaths."

"Do you think the two are related?"

"If it happened once, I would say no. Twice is suspicious, but three times indicates conscious thought."

"Enyalios needs to see this," Pallasophia muttered.

"I can get it there," Alexis offered. Her voice squeaked.

"No," Pallasophia replied. "That's too dangerous."

278

She protested. "But gunfights aren't?"

"Not in the same way. If you go alone, you'll be up against the bulk of Aegesander's military."

"If I may?" Philip interrupted.

"Go ahead," she said to the talking computer.

"First Lord Enyalios has made his public plans to break Katarraktes's blockade and bring forces to Prosgeiosi. Perhaps he could be persuaded to meet you in person?"

"Logosarc is right," Alexis stated.

Pallasophia fought down the urge to argue or point out that she was an adult and a Second Lord and she did not need to be ordered around by a child and a computer. They were, however, both correct.

"Go," Philip/Logosarc implored. "Lock the door behind you. I will be here when you return."

Chapter 15

"Do we have any more information?"

Panatakis nodded. He looked directly at her, eyes focused but sunken and heavy with dark circles. Ever since the four surviving Titans escaped the pyramid room, he had been like that. When questioned on it, Panatakis refused to say anything about it, but the shift in his apparent perception of their survival odds was obvious.

"I've had most of it ready for about three hours," he replied. "Helena and I have been discussing things."

Victoria took a moment to look over her shoulder. Their room was not exactly large, probably no more than ten meters on its longest side, but Helena currently occupied much of one corner. She sat mostly nude—she wore wearing little more than the bandages wrapping three rapidly-healing gunshot wounds—with her legs folded into a lotus position. She used some of her personal share of water to wash her skin and implants as well as her wounds, and the blue-white metal gleamed in the dim light.

Helena's eyes were closed, and had been closed for ten hours. They all knew about the pseudo-telepathy she and Panatakis shared, but the idea of conversing with her while she was deep in meditation, allegedly speeding the healing process of her wounds, struck Victoria as strange.

She turned back to Panatakis as he said, "we wanted to have a complete picture, or as complete as we could form, before broaching the subject. Helena was able to use my memories to form a rough map of the pyramid's interior."

Victoria felt her eyebrows raise. "She can do that?"

"Apparently so. It took some time because she had to work while I was asleep, and sleep has been... elusive."

Victoria nodded. She understood how he felt, at least on that front. Recurring dreams of her memory-selves dying at the hands of the mastigas before she had even been born bled into fantasies of mastigas here and now ending her own life in the exact same fashion.

Most of the time, those memories did not intrude upon her dreams, at least not directly. Here, locked inside the mastigas battleship, she tended to dream of open skies unhindered by walls or domes, but even those dreams turned bloody more often than not.

Victoria had been born into chaos and pain, and exited the arena and the labyrinth covered in so much mastigas blood that, for a time, she thought it would never all come off. Even then, she had precious little time to herself around their missions to deal with the Ouroboros threat. She had only been alive for a very short time, and nearly every waking moment had been filled with violence and danger.

Now, having been sent to the edge of the Technocrats' binary system, personal time was nonexistent. Victoria tried not to dwell on things. For a time, that had been possible. Now that they had a few hours without having to run or fight, she was losing that particular battle.

Korakti had been killed by the mastigas, Daniel as well, and Victoria could not convince herself that they would not have died if she had been able to do more. In her own way, she even felt responsible for the deaths of the men and woman aboard the *Justice* and the cruisers escorting their doomed mission.

Her role in Project Titan would always have been bloody, with life after life being sacrificed to Tritogenes's goal of creating the perfect soldier to protect his people, but it was to have been controlled bloodshed. Then the sophont intervened, slaughtering the personnel tasked with creating her life, and casting her and those who came before into a hell of darkness and blood.

This was supposed to be her chance for revenge and vindication. Thus far, it had gone very wrong.

Panatakis cleared his throat, bringing her back to the present. He fixed his eyes on her. What would have been a normal gesture from anyone else felt strange coming from a person who did not actually use his eyes for sight.

"I thought I was about to die," he confessed, finally. In the dark room that had been their shelter for a full twelve hours, his hunched posture made Panatakis seem much smaller than he really was. "I thought I had been ambushed."

"We all were," Lelantos called from the door. His voice was normal, which after so much time on the chronodrug made every word seem a slow drawl. He was on guard duty at the moment, but had not used any of the chronodrug since they took refuge.

Panatakis shook his head. "No. You three were ambushed. I was," he gestured with one hand. It looked like he was retracing parts of the fight. Given his connection to Helena, it was possible his mind could replay those events exactly as they happened. "I don't know how to put it. I know they herded me into that room, and they obviously didn't want me to rejoin you."

Helena laughed suddenly, more full of mirth and real amusement than she had shown in days. Victoria turned, shuffling around so that she did not have to stand up to move. The cybernetically-enhanced Titan's eyes were open again and she was slowly unfolding her legs from their lotus position.

"The mastigas did not seem very supportive of our desire to rescue you," she said, smiling.

Helena stood up and stretched. She showed very little of the stiffness Victoria would have expected in someone who had not moved in ten hours. She unwound her bandages, starting first with the one that tightly encircled her thigh, and then the wider set of bandages covering the two wounds on her stomach. With the bandages gone, the three bullet wounds had been reduced to angry red tissue, closed and covered with the residue of three generous doses of quick heal.

She rewound the bandages into their own rolls, placing them in a bag marked as potentially hazardous waste. If they had to, they could clean things like that, and so it went back into her pack.

As she did all that, she continued speaking. "Panatakis is correct. While he slept and I meditated, I was able to piece together the interior of the pyramid." She turned to look directly at Panatakis, "I think you will find it supports your theory."

He nodded.

"Theory?" Victoria asked.

"Ah, yes. I was getting to that. As I was saying, I thought I had been ambushed, but everything I saw points to the group that came up behind me being a different set of mastigas."

"That backs up what that sophont told us," Victoria said.

From the door, Lelantos made a noise of disquiet, but said nothing. The few times the rest of them talked about that sophont, Lelantos had excused himself from the conversation. It was, Victoria suspected, why he volunteered to keep watch after she woke them from their first brief period of sleep.

"If I may?" Helena asked. Panatakis nodded and she continued. "The sophont we spoke to was unwilling to fight. You agree?" Helena placed heavy emphasis on "was." She continued: "it said there were six of them. At the time, you expressed a theory that there might be six, how did you put it?"

"Six divisions of mastigas, all serving different purposes," Victoria supplied.

Helena nodded. "Yes. I'm sorry. I spent some of my meditative time doing," she grit her teeth and the next word came out as a growl, "adjustments to my implants. Some of my memories became damaged in the process."

"At the time you had another violent episode," Victoria said. She very carefully kept any accusation out of her tone. She was not afraid of Helena, per se, but with no idea what sort of things triggered her, she thought it best to avoid the issue unless Helena herself brought it up.

"Yes. Another thing I must apologize for. I am still unable to explain why. That information remains locked. However, I was able to access a few things that I can now share without fear."

"Go on."

"In short, your theory was correct in a sense. There are six separate tribes of mastigas aboard this battleship, and not all of them want to destroy the Technocracy."

From the door, Lelantos growled. "You're saying that it was telling the truth? Some of these things are," he paused, apparently unwilling to even give voice to the idea, "capable of regret?"

"Not just regret," Helena said, "but free thought, or they should be. Something called the Sophocrat controls them. I found references to it in their computer system."

"Did you know?" Victoria demanded.

"About the Sophocrat? No. I knew about the six groups of mastigas, but that was among the information I could not share. I did not know, however, that some of them did not want to destroy us."

"How?"

"I..." she began.

"Can't tell us, I'm sure," Victoria grunted.

"You are correct. I will continue to address the problem."

"In any case," Panatakis said. He waved a hand and a large hologram of the pyramid room appeared in the air. His position as well as theirs and the positions of the three groups of mastigas they encountered were highlighted with different colors. "As I said, I believe the group here," the mastigas behind his position in the hologram lit up brighter, "were not the same ones trailing me before."

Helena sat on the floor, resumed her lotus position, and pointed to the hologram. A corner of the pyramid lit up and purple lines traced their way through the base of the massive structure. The lines converged on the group behind Panatakis's position. "They came from here. That much is certain."

"This is the part where things diverged from what I expected." He waved a hand and the hologram started moving. Everything crept along at one-quarter normal speed.

The front of the mastigas group headed toward Victoria's position stalled, stunned by the glare of Panatakis's flashbang grenades. The three of them fired at the disoriented mastigas. Victoria's automatic rifle spat bullets so quickly that even at quarter speed the shots came rapidly. Helena fired just as quickly while, behind them, Lelantos lined up his shots more carefully.

Inside the pyramid room, the second group of mastigas recovered from the initial pair of flashbangs and were filing through a different door. That door led to a hallway that would have wrapped around to allow them to support the first group, but instead they turned the other way, abandoning the mastigas being slaughtered by the three Titans.

The tiny figure of Panatakis stood and fired at the group of mastigas that had broken away from the larger horde. His grenade sailed across the projection, missing its intended target and detonating in the massed horde of mastigas.

Seconds ticked by as the third group crept forward. Panatakis turned, and even the thumb-sized projection showed obvious surprise and terror.

He leveled his rifle, but stopped. The scale of the projection made it hard to see, but he provided narration.

"This group was different." Panatakis shifted around, sitting with his legs crossed and his hands in his lap. If not for the bandoleer of grenades across his chest, he would have seemed small, even nonthreatening.

Before anyone could ask the obvious question of "how?" he paused the recording with a gesture and zoomed in on the group that had been behind him. He panned between it and the other as he explained.

"The sophont was close to the front of this group. The other sophont," he panned the hologram, "pushed from the rear."

"Their control is better the closer they are," Lelantos interrupted. "We knew this from Kipos. Maybe it just wanted to make sure its troops were staying quiet."

"I thought so, and that may be part of it, but there was something different." He zoomed in the hologram further until the memory-image of the sophont in question filled the projection. He adjusted it slightly, zooming out until he too was visible along with some of the mastigas. The smaller fonias were interested in him, but the body language of the one gigas in view showed something different.

The sophont looked down at him, its oversize head shrouded by its helmet. Only the angle of the chin gave away what it was looking at.

"It stared right at me," Panatakis added. He snapped his fingers. "I was about to die. I knew it. And then..."

Rather than explain, he slowly circled one finger in the air as though turning an imaginary knob. The image advanced at a quarter of reality. First, the fonias continued to creep toward Panatakis's position, and the barrel of one of the heavy rifles the gigas carried swept across the narrow field of view.

Several real-world seconds passed before the sophont changed its focus. Its head raised slightly and one long, spindly arm uncurled. Moving with a smoothness that reminded Victoria of a snake, the sophont gestured for the others to attack.

286

She recognized the gesture. The creature's long arm uncurled a joint at a time, finally extending with the wrist still bent. It raised its hand, palm out, then dropped two fingers. That gesture was followed by a roll of its wrist that ended with its thumb pointing forward. It touched its smallest finger, then the next one, then the pinky finger again.

Recorded footage from Pallasophia's combat uniform showed a similar set of gestures on the part of the sophont that attacked them in the basement of the labyrinth. What little public footage was available of the mastigas, most of which came from Kipos, showed the sophonts communicating in similar ways. Whatever the goal, the gesture was unmistakable for anyone who had faced them before.

The difference, she saw, was that the sophont's gestures were not directed at Panatakis. It aimed two quick movements with its small arms at the Titan, obvious gestures of negation even from an alien perspective, and the mastigas around it all turned away from his position.

The gesture from its long arm, however, had been pointed at the advancing group of mastigas.

Panatakis sped up the recording to faster than real-life and everything sprang into comically fast motion. The mastigas he thought had cornered him with the intent to kill opened fire on the group advancing. The smaller group found themselves outnumbered and, by all appearances, surprised by the attack and were massacred in moments.

As the tiny projected figure of Panatakis crouched back down and made his way forward, toward the side of the room where Victoria, Helena, and Lelantos were fighting the other end of the largest group, the formerly-stealthy mastigas broke into a run.

They passed by him on all sides, leaving him jostled and presumably terrified, but unharmed. Their target was the other horde, which was now in the process of wheeling around to face their new enemies.

"At that point, Helena sent me a map and we found another corridor away from the pyramid." Panatakis dismissed the hologram. "And here we are."

"Do you know if they're still fighting?" Victoria asked, directing the question to Helena.

Helena nodded. "During my meditations, I was finally able to patch into the mastigas sensor network. The data is less reliable while I am conscious, but clear enough for a general analysis."

"And you can read it all because it's written in a dead Technocrat language," Victoria interrupted. That thought, and the fact that they still had no explanation for it, continued to eat at her.

Helena nodded in answer to Victoria's question, then continued her explanation. "There have been three-thousand one hundred and eighty-two instances of weapons-fire being exchanged in the last forty-eight hours."

Victoria's eyes went wide and she felt her eyebrows threaten to merge with her hairline. "Selene's tits," she muttered. "All since we arrived?"

She nodded. "The first altercation was recorded by the mastigas ship's computer system, which logged it as the first such instance in seventy-five years."

"Can you tell which faction they belong to?"

Helena shook her head. "Not without chemical receptors more sensitive than we currently possess. I suggest we avoid any and all mastigas movement if possible."

Lelantos snorted derisively from the doorway. "After what happened out there," he jerked a thumb over his shoulder at the door, "I don't know how we can manage that. They can box us in whenever they want. They're just fucking with us."

Victoria nodded slowly. Since the firefight, she noticed a change in Lelantos's attitude. He had been less reserved in not just his language, but in everything. He spent the walk to their current hideaway talking privately with Panatakis, a conversation that continued until they all finally fell asleep. When Victoria woke them four hours later, they were still lying together.

She was afraid that, between the fighting itself and the revelation from the "friendly" sophont that not all the mastigas wanted to attack Kipos, he was growing reckless. She knew very little about the other Titans' lives before Project Titan, and hoped this was not some older mindset resurfacing under stress. With better communication equipment, she could have asked First Lord Rivka about it, but in its absence, she had to hope her normal reactions were for the best.

"I understand your frustrations," Victoria said, trying her best to use the same placating tone Pallasophia often used on her. "We were sent out here to lead an army on a mission to destroy the mastigas. Now, the four of us are all that remain. Things have not exactly gone according to plan." She said the last few words with a heavily emphasized staccato rhythm. "But we will get this done."

Lelantos laughed, but the adrenaline-tremors were obvious even from across the room. "We walked into a civil war. No, we started a civil war!"

Victoria stood and walked slowly across the room. She reached out a hand and placed it on Lelantos's shoulder for a moment. The gesture felt strange after he calmed her and brought her back from bloodlust so many times. "Trust me," she said slowly, making eye contact. "I understand."

"Do you?" he snapped. "My world was torn apart by these things and now I learn that they can think and feel and goddess knows what else?"

"Lelantos," Victoria sighed. Her voice grew harder for a moment. "Focus."

"I am focused!" he retorted. She realized there were tears in his eyes, but nothing she could do in that moment would help. "That's the problem. I spent my life wanting to fight the mastigas. I gave myself to Project Titan so that I could come out here and kill every last one of the green-eyed bastards! And now..."

"Now we know that things aren't so clear cut."

"Exactly!"

"What do you want?"

That question stopped his next retort before it happened. He thought for a few moments, seeming to turn her question over in his head before replying. He inhaled, long and deep. When he spoke again, the calm, slow voice she was used to was back. "I don't know. What do *you* want, Spatharios?"

"I thought I wanted the same thing."

"Thought." He smiled, thin and sardonic. "Past tense. What changed?"

"The sophont we met. Remember what I said, that I'd spoken to one during my training?"

He nodded, listening. The hostility remained, but it was directed elsewhere. Hopefully not inwards, Victoria thought, concerned.

"I thought it was just trying to manipulate me, but now I'm not so sure. It told me it wanted to leave, without fighting if it could, just like the one yesterday. I don't know what I want, ultimately, but right now I just want to understand them."

He nodded slowly. "Yeah. I do too. I just can't get the memories of Kipos burning out of my head."

"I understand."

"How can you? Limani, or wherever you're from, was never attacked!"

Victoria sighed. She had kept the truth from the others for too long. Tritogenes would probably have some unhappy things to say about it when she returned, but this was her secret to reveal. She spoke loudly, pitching her voice so that all three of them could hear. "I was born on Aphelion."

"Where?" Panatakis asked.

"Aphelion," Helena supplied. Victoria expected the usual textbook tone from her, but Helena spoke much more conversationally than usual. "It's an asteroid near the outer reaches of the system, currently on the

290

other side of the binary from this ship's original. Tritogenes ran his part of Project Titan from there."

"How did you...?" Victoria began.

Helena interrupted, not with words, but simply by tapping on the metal tendrils wrapped around her skull and offering an enigmatic smile.

Victoria nodded, and continued. "I was born into a world where the mastigas were trying to kill me. I spent a few days in that world, hunted by mastigas, before learning that I was part of a Project to create the perfect soldier."

"No," Panatakis interrupted. "You can't be telling the truth."

"Can't I?" Victoria asked. "I can show you the scars."

"It's not that," he argued. "You expect us to believe that First Lord Tritogenes created you in a secret laboratory? That's preposterous!"

"It's true, and I wasn't the first." She stopped for a moment to see if the others had anything else to say before continuing on. "Ninety-nine came before me, and I remember them all."

As she explained what she understood of Tritogenes's vision for Project Titan, which was much more than it would have been without Pallasophia's willingness to share information, the three other Titans sat silently and listened. Their expressions ranged from incredulous to angry to simply shocked, changing almost by the moment as she spoke.

"So that's why the black robe," Panatakis said. "It wasn't a religious thing. It's because you're not..."

"Legally, I don't have a rank. I became Tritogenes's Spatharios in part to hide that fact." She turned back to Lelantos, who had no retort for when she said, "so, yes, please believe me when I say I understand your pain."

"Pallasophia," Lelantos said after a long pause. His voice was quiet, soft enough that Victoria barely heard him. "You're fighting for her, aren't you?"

"I..." Victoria stopped. She supposed the kiss they shared before the launch left few doubts in anyone's mind, especially her own. "Yes."

"Do you love her?"

A deep inhalation of the cold air around them. "Yes."

Lelantos nodded. "Good. You do understand then."

"Understand what?"

"I joined Project Titan for one purpose: to kill mastigas. But then I started spending time with Rivka. She's like family to me. Whatever happens here," Lelantos pointed downward, at the floor under their feet, "I *will* keep her safe."

Victoria nodded. "Then let's stop this warship."

Lelantos laughed, once. The sound was harsh, quiet, and full of approval. "As you say, Spatharios."

He turned back to the hall, keeping watch once more. He seemed more focused than he had been, but his movements were sharp and tense. The anger had not gone away, she realized, it simply had a new target.

It would have to be enough, Victoria thought as she strode back to the center of the room. As a friend, she wanted to help him, but as his commander, she understood that his anger was a powerful tool against the mastigas. She just hoped it would not get him killed.

Before Victoria could sit down, Helena rose and beckoned her to follow. "A word please?"

Helena led Victoria to the far corner of their hiding place, where she had been meditating and next to where Victoria slept after waking the others. As close as they now stood, Victoria found the fact that Helena had yet to dress somewhat distracting. She loved Pallasophia, but Helena was undeniably beautiful.

Their proximity to one another and distance from the others gave them a measure of privacy, however. The need for it became obvious when Helena's demeanor suddenly changed completely. With Victoria's tall, broad-shouldered frame blocking her from view of the others, her iron-clad resolve seemed to melt away.

"I need a favor," she said. An expression Victoria had never seen crossed her face. On anyone else, Victoria would have thought she was *begging*.

"Anything," Victoria responded automatically.

"There are problems," she grated, "with my implants. Programming that I did not know was there until I activated it by accident. Many of them, such as the one that attacked you, are buried in modules deep in my muscles themselves."

Victoria reflexively rubbed at her throat and Helena nodded.

"Aegesander left certain mental blocks in place that I have had trouble circumventing. I could not even mention them before."

"Your hints were clear enough."

"A fact for which I am grateful. Had you continued to pry at that moment, I fear what might have happened."

Victoria felt anger start to boil up inside her. That anger was not directed at Helena, but rather at the person who chained up her mind like that. She might have resented what Tritogenes put her through, but limiting a person's ability to think for themselves was unforgivable. The only thing that made it out of her mouth was a growled, "why?"

"He was afraid of me," she said. She laughed bitterly for a moment, letting her emotions show. "Even now I can feel the tug of the programming, trying to keep my mouth shut and to paralyze my muscles before I say anything else."

"What can't you say?"

Helena smiled, then laughed. "If it were that simple to get around the blocks, I would have done so already. I can," a spasm rippled across her stomach and ribs, threatening to stop her diaphragm and lungs from working. She repeated herself and went on. "I can tell you one thing, at least. I know the truth about why we're here."

"We're here to stop the mastigas."

"In part. We are here," her jaw clenched and she coughed. "Strike me, please."

293

"What?"

"I cannot breathe."

Victoria drove her fist into Helena's stomach, forcing a deep inhalation of air. She spoke quickly, trying to get the most of that lungful of air. "Hyperion, before we left, talked about sins. He was not being metaphoric. We are all here to d—" Another spasming cough stopped anything further.

After a moment, she stood up straight again. "This is why I need a favor."

"Like I said, anything. You're my friend."

Helena nodded. "Thank you. Panatakis and you are the only ones who have not been afraid of me."

"Your own Hexarch tried to kill you."

"And he failed," she enunciated one syllable at a time through gritted teeth. She reached behind her back, seeming to adjust something. After a moment, she produced a half-meter long twist of blue-white metal that looked more like a sculpture of a scorpion than any machine. She held it out to Victoria. "Take this, please."

Victoria did. The metal felt warm under her hand, and parts of it were flexible. The entire thing was much heavier than she expected. "What do I...?"

"You ought to be able to wear it like an armband, or perhaps attach it to your armor's forearm plates. Just keep it with you at all times and in due time I will explain everything."

Victoria nodded. The metallic thing flexed in her hands, tendrils grasping at the air. It threatened to turn her stomach, but she wrapped it around her left forearm. It moved, snugging itself tighter against her gauntlet. The idea that the thing was alive would not leave her brain.

"Thank you," Helena said. "Now, I believe it is past time to get dressed."

"That was what you were waiting on?" Victoria asked, raising her left arm and the piece of Helena's implant nestled there. "This?"

She nodded. "Yes. I would not have been able to access it with my robes on. I would have been stopped." Her eyes suddenly went wide. "The mastigas are moving, we must pack quickly and go!"

***

According to the holographic map projected on the inside of Victoria's helmet, the four Titans were roughly three-quarters of the way up the pyramid. The interior was a dark, twisted maze of corridors that they were only able to successfully navigate with Panatakis's senses.

He all but shut off his eyes, routing sound to his auditory and visual centers. With that came the closest to echolocation that a human was likely to get, and with it he could paint a picture of the tunnels that surrounded them. It also allowed him to "see" any mastigas long before coming face to face with them. That information was superimposed on their helmet maps as well, leading to a sort of radar.

Avoiding the mastigas had proven to be more important than she expected. The creatures left them with no way to tell what group they belonged to—assuming that was even the proper way to think about the fighting that raged around them. Her standing orders were to avoid the mastigas as much as they could, a feat which so far had proved difficult but doable.

As the pyramid narrowed, however, the Titans found themselves running out of room.

Victoria held up a hand, gesturing for the three others to stop. Panatakis's map showed a small side corridor, narrow but empty, a few meters away down another branching tunnel. She led them there, watching all the time to make sure none of the mastigas decided to use the narrow hall themselves.

The hall had been marked on the outside with the same odd script they had been seeing everywhere inside the pyramid. The few instances where more than one or two words had been printed at the same time looked like the patterns found in Lexeis Archeio. The script was completely foreign, some product of the mastigas themselves, but it held

295

words of the same size and with the same sort of repetition as the Technocrat archival language. Helena promised a cipher would be easy to produce once they had some down time. Until, then it remained little more than another annoying mystery.

Without a key for the script itself, knowing what it was did them very little good right then. What it did do, however, was reinforce Victoria's decision to interrogate Tritogenes, and probably First Lord Hyperion as well, when she returned.

The map resolved itself with more detail as they stepped into the corridor. Like the other halls, it wound up and down, at times rising or falling several stories before leveling out again. What little of it they could see on the map seemed to twist around a central area, though with very little rhyme or apparent reason.

Pipes, some cold, others hot, and still others sheathed in some form of insulation lined the walls and ceiling. They rattled and hummed, and as the seconds ticked by, the map filled itself in further and further down the narrow, twisting passage. She hoped the noises around them would be enough to mask not only their presence, but anything they said.

Victoria had no intention of going very far. About ten meters in, far enough that the corridor they just left dimmed on the map to indicate that Panatakis could no longer hear it, she stopped and lifted her visor.

"First," she said as the others did the same, "we need to eat. If I'm right, we won't get another chance for a while. Helena?"

Victoria dropped her backpack lightly to the floor. She reached in with both hands and withdrew eight ration packs. They had not eaten that day and she decided in the moment that perhaps doubling up would not be a bad thing.

She set them out on the floor and started bringing out bottled water and supplement packs as Helena cleared her throat.

Victoria turned to look over her shoulder. Helena had projected a holo of the inside of the pyramid as far as they had been able to map.

With a gesture, she dismissed most of it, zooming in on the wide corridor they just exited.

One end of their twisting, pipe-filled tunnel lit up with a pale green glow. Her comment of, "we are here," seemed unnecessary. As she spoke, other corridors lit up with different colors. Likely concentrations of mastigas were yellow, and known positions, as much as they could know without direct observation anyway, were red. The hall they came from glowed a sapphire blue.

"Thus far, we have avoided the mastigas. A total of two-hundred and thirty-three mastigas have come close to what I believe is their optimal detection rage with a further thousand moving through the outer edges of Titan Panatakis's maximum detection radius."

Helena paused for a moment, adjusting the map. Victoria took that moment to pick a ration pack at random. The mastigas had keen senses of smell, perhaps even more sensitive than anyone thought, and most of their food was bland with very little aroma. Hot food was a non-option. The ration bar she selected tasted better than some, coming across like a mixture of chocolate and sour fruits with a generous helping of dirt.

When she looked up again, Helena had narrowed the map again. Now it showed nothing but the blue corridor. A thin black line led back to the entrance to their current hiding spot.

"That is about to change," Helena said. She panned the map and the blue area terminated into a mass of red at the apex. The red-highlighted area was about four times the width of the corridor and at least fifty meters long.

Victoria remembered seeing it on the map that morning. At that point, it had been yellow, showing only a probable mastigas presence. Now, seeing it lit up in red confirmed her suspicions. All of the major and several minor corridors led to that same room. A tunnel led away, rising sharply from one wall, but it was rendered with the fuzzy lines that indicated incomplete data.

"A high concentration of mastigas occupy this space," Helena continued. "Unlike the other groups we have bypassed, this group does not seem to have engaged in any combat. Others have come through the area, especially from above," the fuzzy corridor lit up a vague yellow-white, "and engaged other mastigas in the surrounding corridors."

"They're defending it," Panatakis said around a mouthful of ration bar.

Lelantos smacked a fist into his open palm. He had already finished both bars. "Then we take it from them!"

Helena nodded slowly. "I fear that is our only option."

Lelantos grinned, bearing his teeth in a predatory smile. "Excellent."

"Why there?" Victoria asked, opening her second ration bar. This one promised to be more savory in flavor, but she had her doubts.

Helena gestured and the fuzzy, pale-yellow vertical corridor turned a brighter shade of yellow. "Panatakis and I believe this to be the only way to the upper level of the facility. Moreover," she highlighted the red room again, "the mastigas appear to be defending this area specifically. It is one of the only such areas covered by a definite defensive posture, and the only one this high in the pyramid."

Victoria nodded. "It's a control center."

"That is my assumption, yes," Helena confirmed.

"How do we know what faction of mastigas controls it?" Victoria asked.

Helena shook her head and dismissed the hologram. "I do not know."

"We can't afford to walk in and risk them attacking us on the assumption that they might be the ones who don't want to kill us," Lelantos stated.

Panatakis washed down the last of his first meal bar with half a bottle of water. After a moment, he made a suggestion. "Offer to let them surrender?"

"No!" Lelantos snapped. "We go in there and we kill every last one of them."

"And if they do surrender?" Victoria asked, speaking softly and gently.

"If they," Lelantos started, then stopped. Calmer, he said, "if they do surrender, then we accept it, but we can't take the risk that they won't."

"I believe Lelantos is correct," Helena added. "We will be outnumbered. An overwhelming surprise assault is the only way we will be able to take that room."

"If the mastigas can't what makes you think we can?" Panatakis asked.

"If it's a control room," Victoria replied, thinking aloud, "maybe they don't want to risk a fight in there."

"That would be logical," Helena agreed.

Lelantos stood. "If it's a control room, then we have to destroy it, not take it over."

Helena nodded. Finished with her presentation, she reached for the first of her two ration bars and opened one. "That would be an easier option, yes."

"Then that's the plan!"

Victoria shook her head. "Not necessarily the best one, though."

Lelantos turned on his heels, abruptly facing Victoria. "Why not? We destroy the controls, we disable the ship!"

Victoria felt her own frustration rising. She fought to control it and her voice came out as a tight, thin growl. "We don't know how this ship is designed. Destroying the controls may very well destroy the ship with us in it."

"Then we go down having destroyed the mastigas!" Lelantos proclaimed. "That's what we're here for, isn't it? To die for our planets?"

"We're here to stop the mastigas and protect our planets. Dying was never part of the plan."

Helena's voice was uncharacteristically small and quiet when she said, "dying was always part of the plan."

Victoria repeated herself, rising to her feet. Her voice came out harsh, riding on the tails of the almost-confrontation with Lelantos. "Dying was *never* part of the plan!"

Helena shook her head. "You don't understand. The Hexarchs sent us out here to die. The *Hammer of Ares* might still be out there to save face, but picking us up from this ship was never part of the plan."

Lelantos growled. "Rivka would never betray us!"

Helena nodded slowly. Her voice was still quiet and eerily calm. "Nor would Tritogenes, or Enyalios, or even Hyperion."

"You don't really think Eurybia or Aegesander would betray us, do you?" Panatakis asked. His eyes had gone wide, as though he never entertained that idea before.

Helena looked away, avoiding any and all eye contact. "Eurybia, perhaps not, but my Hexarch has done so once already."

"How long have you known?" Victoria asked.

"Since before we left Prosgeiosi," she replied.

"And you never told us?" Lelantos demanded.

"I could not!"

He growled. "More programming, I gather?"

Helena nodded. "Yes."

"Helena." Victoria physically interposed herself between the other woman and Lelantos. "What was First Lord Aegesander's plan?"

"It was the same plan everyone else knew," she replied. "We come out here, destroy the mastigas, save the binary. Only we don't return. Aegesander counted on us dying out here. All of us."

"How do you know?" Lelantos asked.

"After a certain point in my..." She paused, thinking. "Training, I was able to bypass his security with ease. He had been acting more and more distrustful around me and I wished to know why."

"Did he know about the weapon that destroyed the Justice?" Victoria demanded. Aegesander would have a lot of answer for if he knew and sent them all unprepared. Over a hundred thousand deaths would be on his head.

"No."

"Then why?"

"First Lord Aegesander hoped we and the mastigas would destroy one another. The *Justice* was to survive. He..." She gestured with her hands, looking hopelessly at a loss for words. Victoria had never seen her like that and the idea that Helena might be floundering that badly was disconcerting. Finally, she said, "he was afraid of us. Of me. Of what I have become."

"And what *are* you?" Lelantos asked. His voice was devoid of judgment. Instead, he spoke from what sounded like genuine wonder.

"I can't say."

"Because you don't want to or because you can't."

"Yes."

"Why did Aegesander want the mastigas to kill us?" Victoria asked.

"I can't say."

"What does he know about the mastigas that we don't?"

"I can't say."

Lelantos cursed in frustration and stepped away from the conversation, crossing their little area to talk to Panatakis instead.

Victoria reached out and gently hooked a finger under Helena's chin and turned her head so that she could look directly into her eyes. Those ice-blue eyes were shot through with wire traceries and circuits so fine that she never noticed them before. Assuming, she thought, that they *had* been there before.

"Helena," she said, continuing to stare into the other woman's eyes. "Does First Lord Aegesander know why the mastigas are here?"

Tiny muscles around her eyes twitched involuntarily. Her irises dilated, first a little and then enough so that only a sliver of blue-gray remained around the rim. Her breathing quickened slightly, despite her obvious attempts to slow it.

She was in pain, Victoria realized. No, she was in *agony*.

Finally Helena opened her mouth, releasing one small word. "Yes."

Chapter 16

First Lord Aegesander stared out the window of the uppermost spire of Dasos's sprawling palace. The spire, his spire, rose a half-kilometer into the air, just high enough to bring it above the dense forest that lived and breathed around the palace. A thousand years ago, when the spire was first under construction, every effort was made to avoid disturbing the existing forests that covered the planet's temperate zones. The compromise was a thin tower that rose through the trees, almost like it was one of them, and a sprawling palatial complex that wound its twisted way through the tree branches like an Elven city on Earth.

Dasos was the second planet colonized by the original Technocrat settlers, making his palace one of the oldest structures in the entire binary. The stones around him were quarried and set before his grandparents' grandparents were born, and the weight of those centuries hung heavy in every room.

The air around him was dense and warm. Others called it stifling, humid, muggy. Any one of a hundred terms invented by people who simply did not enjoy air the way air was supposed to be breathed. Then those same people built steam rooms and declared them wonders of relaxation.

Aegesander preferred the real thing, lush and full of life. He breathed deep of the atmosphere around his tower. It smelled *alive*. Birdlike creatures moved around in the tops of the trees a few stories before his window. He watched them absently, eyes drawn to the movement more than any real desire to see what the animals were doing down there.

The console on his desk chimed and he turned away from the sea of trees outside. The interior of his office had been redone twice during his tenure as Hexarch, and at least three more times during his predecessor's tenure that he remembered. Yet, none of them ever used a different room for their work. The furniture wore out or was simply replaced, but the stones under his feet were the same stones under First Lord Moirai's feet, the *first* First Lord of Dasos.

A gallery of portraits hung on one wall, faces going back over a thousand years. His hung there, one among many. His portrait was no larger than the others and he felt the weight of that lineage bearing down on every decision he made—especially those he never wanted to make. Dasos was a planet of stability, only Kokkinos could boast of fewer, and thus longer-lived, Hexarchs. Aegesander was the twenty-first Hexarch of Dasos and so far the fourth longest ruling person to hold that seat, tied that very year with his direct predecessor, First Lord Adrasta.

First Lord Adrasta had been a curious woman to work for. She would change her mind constantly about small things—the placement of art, the color of the walls, the direction of her desk. Those inconsequential things were rarely the same between any two visits when this room belonged to *his* Hexarch.

Yet, when she set her mind to a task, nothing could dissuade her. The other Hexarchs at the time did not appreciate her uncompromising adherence to a single plan. A much younger Aegesander, a century before, had seen something different. In First Lord Adrasta, he saw a Hexarch unmoved by the opinions of those with lesser ideas and unswayed by the will of the mob. First Lord Adrasta, in his eyes, had been the sort of leader the Technocrats needed—swift, decisive, and uncompromising.

After becoming a Hexarch in his own right following her death, he learned exactly how she maintained that image of dedication. The things around her, her office, her art, had all been superficial distractions. They were the idle banter she allowed herself to be surrounded with so that she could ignore it.

For ninety years, First Lord Aegesander followed her example. At times, he regretted it immensely. Staying true to his ideals and goals had cost him more than he wanted to admit, and now it seemed the karmic bill collectors were beginning to catch him.

His desk console beeped again.

"Yes?" he replied, addressing the machine rather than the person on the other end.

The voice spoke quickly, not emphasizing anything. It delivered news and nothing more. "First Lord. Ships from Katarraktes and Kipos have entered orbit."

"We've come to the final act," he said, speaking too quietly for anyone else to hear. Louder, he replied, "acknowledged. Arm planetary defenses."

If there was any hesitation on the other end of the conversation, it lasted for less than a millisecond. "As you say, First Lord."

***

Second Lord Aella returned to Dasos to get away from the fighting, not to become part of an even bigger conflict. After leaving Limani an official hero for her "actions in defense of the Technocracy" and her "heroic stand in the face of Ouroboros aggression," she considered returning to Prosgeiosi, but the fighting there was even worse than it was on Limani. Dasos, she reasoned, should have been free from conflict.

First Lord Aegesander's military ground forces, herself included, were to make a token show across Dasos. Officially, the planet had nothing Ouroboros wanted and so the need for countermeasures was small. Officially, Limani, Pteryga, and Katarraktes were hotbeds of terrorist activity. Officially, that was the reason Aegesander's forces moved as heavily on those planets as they did.

Unofficially, she knew exactly why her father's military might was being flexed in the directions it was. She stayed out of his feud with First Lord Hyperion, but Aella was not in a position to judge her Hexarch's actions against Pteryga's First Lord. Obviously something there had lain dormant for years, perhaps decades, and one of them simply had enough of it.

Aegesander, her father, would not have moved against Hyperion without good cause. It was just bad luck that Rivka and Tritogenes—and some of Tritogenes's most loyal followers—got caught up in the process.

Years ago, Aegesander made a comment in reference to a lesson she was reading in school. "You will never have to kill a friend," he said. "If you have to kill someone, that person is no longer your friend."

Aegesander and Hyperion, herself and Mihalis; she supposed those words were about as much comfort as she was going to get on the subject.

Whatever his reasoning, however, two things quickly became clear. First, that Aegesander's initial offensive against Pteryga itself might have been successful against Tritogenes, but it failed to eliminate the threat presented by First Lord Rivka. Second, Rivka herself was a far more capable military leader than Aella—or Aegesander, for that matter— believed her to be.

That second truth was made immediately clear to her exactly six hours and thirty-seven minutes ago when a pair of Katarraktean battlecruisers accompanied by a full wing of ten Kiposian destroyers led by the *Eleusis* entered Dasos's orbitals.

She had her orders, however, and as Katarraktean and Kiposian troops began landing across the planet, Aella's job quickly stopped being decorative. Unlike Aegesander's centrally-focused assaults on the other planets, Rivka's soldiers focused on outlying areas first. Aella thought it was a foolish decision—strike at the center of the enemy and the rest will crumble—but now that Rivka's forces completely encircled Dasos's palace, she understood.

The broadcast, especially this second time around, only served to hammer home what had happened.

"This is Strategos Chrysanthe of the Third Kiposian Ground Army to all defenders of the Palace of Dasos. You are surrounded. I wish to end this fighting as much as I'm sure you do. Surrender now and we will grant you clemency."

That, Aella thought, was not going to happen. Privately, she doubted if the Strategos's offer was even true. She could not take the palace without assurance that its defenders were neutralized, and taking them *all* prisoner would be borderline impossible.

"You have one hour to decide. Please," the Kiposian Strategos continued, "make the right decision."

She knew exactly what the response was going to be. The palace was simply too well defended and too defensively designed for an invading force to take it easily. More to the point, the entire complex was very, very old. No Technocrat wanted to be known as the one who ordered the assault that destroyed one of the Technocracy's oldest structures.

No, if Rivka's forces persisted in trying to attack, it would be a long, protracted battle for every inch of the palace complex. That was a battle, Aella was certain, that the Kiposian forces would lose.

So when the offered hour came and went with no reply from her commanding officers, Second Lord Aella and her squad settled in for a long siege. The Kiposians would not bring vehicles or heavy weapons into the palace and so, even with her squad on the front lines, all she had to do was wait.

The invading army began moving twenty minutes after their deadline passed. Five minutes after that, official confirmation of Aella's orders came down from Strategos Nereus: shoot on sight.

The irony was not lost on her that "defending my home" was the reason Limani's militia gave such a brave and bloody resistance against

Aegesander's occupation force, and now here she was operating under the exact same motivation.

Aella's squad, like the other frontline squads, had one advantage that many of the other palace defenders did not enjoy. Her position had been designed as part of the complex's original defensive network and the hardened walls of her bunker provided much more protection than anything inside the palace proper.

Thirty-two minutes after the word came down that the Kiposians were on the move, the first bullets impacted the external walls of her bunker. Aella ordered her squad to return fire, counting incoming sources as she did so.

The very same trees that protected and enriched the palace made it difficult to get a proper read on the number of attackers, but she counted seven.

"One down," announced Third Lord Linos, and she corrected her count down to six.

"I've lost sight of the enemy, Lochagos."

Aella tapped a holo control on the side of her rifle's scope, cycling it through various wavelengths of light. Even on infrared, the forest in front of her bunker was frightfully empty. Moments before, it had been full of movement, perhaps even more people than her original estimate, but now...

"Confirm," Second Lord Efrosyni said. "There's nothing out there."

"Keep watching," Aella ordered. "There's no way that tiny probe was their entire plan. They're going to try and flank us."

Ten minutes passed. Aella was starting to hate her habit of keeping exact time while she was working. It made later analysis easier, but now the clock was making her antsy.

The bunker's emergency comm came to life a moment later. The message was audio only, no holo. "This i—" Static. "—unker Delta. The Kiposians hav—" Static. "—nside the perimeter."

An explosion in three stages followed. First, a muffled shattering sound came across the comm itself. Second, the noise of the detonation washed of Aella's bunker through the air, and third, the pressure wave hit.

"Gods between," she cursed. The Kiposians might *not* have many qualms about the age of Dasos's palace, after all.

"Orders, Lochagos? Do we assist?"

"Negative," she replied. "We are to stay here and def—"

The flashbang robbed her of all conscious thought for several excruciating moments as light, sound, and heat washed over and through every fiber of her being. She was on fire from the inside out. Aella thought she hit the floor, but with none of her senses working, it was hard to tell. She might have run into something, or someone, or even been struck by an attacker.

Her eyes started to clear quickly, but her ears continued ringing, lending everything around her a strange, surreal quality. She saw boots around her as her perspective shifted around, unsure if she was on the floor or leaning against a wall. Vertigo sank its claws into her brain and the world spun.

Aella fumbled for her rifle, but it was gone.

"Got another one over here!"

She reached for the pistol at her side. It was still there. The holster fought her, then the pistol sprang free. Aella could barely see, but the odds that those moving on their feet around her were her soldiers were quite low.

"She's still moving!"

She aimed, or tried to.

"Not for long."

Well, she thought, shit.

***

The ships from Katarraktes and Kipos blew through Dasos's orbital defenses in a matter of hours. Aegesander watched the skies burn, standing once again on the uppermost balcony of his tower. The suns were sinking low in the sky by the time the fighting started, and as it grew gradually worse, the metaphoric fire became real fire. Now, the air no longer smelled of lush green life, but of smoke, flames, and death.

The ships were too high for him to actually watch the exchange of missiles. Even their actual explosions, and the explosions of the ships carrying the men and women he damned to protect his planet, were little more than brief pinpricks of light in the darkening sky. The real fire came from the wreckage as it fell headlong and burning to the ground.

"It is not safe out here, you know."

He turned. First Lord Eurybia stood in his doorway. She wore her robe, as was proper, even during a siege. Beyond that garment, though, she sported very few adornments. Even with a brief glance, her annoyance was clear.

"It's not safe anywhere on this planet, right now. I apologize for the timing of this," he waved a hand at a dozen streaks of blood-red fire in the sky, "inconvenience."

She stepped out onto the balcony with him. Together, they watched the burning hulks that had been his orbital defense fleet disintegrate in Dasos's atmosphere. "You mean you apologize for trapping me here."

A flash of anger raced through his gut at her comment. For a moment, he felt as though she was directly accusing him of manipulating events so that she would take the fall with him. In truth, he had done no such thing. He wanted her to come out of this alongside him, triumphant. Her arrival two days prior had been unexpected. Normally, her presence would have been welcome, one of his many allowed distractions that kept his mind focused on the real task at hand.

Aegesander smothered that thought. They had worked together longer than Eurybia had been a Hexarch. He trusted her as much as she trusted him, with or without the leverage he held. Panatakis and Helena were gone, and soon Hyperion's—and his, but Aegesander preferred not to think of it in those terms—secrets would be irrelevant.

He grit his teeth and leaned on the marble railing. The ships were falling hundreds of kilometers away. Most of them dropped below the horizon before being replaced with a brief sunset-like glow.

His ground defenses, at least, were doing their job properly. Even if they were ultimately going to lose the battle against Rivka's numbers, it kept the other Hexarch away from him and his tower. Even his fleet was doing that job well enough, he supposed. With his forces spread across the binary, there was little resistance he could truly offer.

So Aegesander lied to himself, telling himself that none of it really mattered. Rivka's forces would not, *could not*, simply walk into his palace and kill him. Rivka would leave, unable to take that last step, and he would broadcast her failure to the binary as proof that Dasos stood strong against its attackers. At the end of the day, no matter how many of them stood at the base of his tower, Aegesander would watch from the top, triumphant.

And yet, a voice at the back of his mind said, he had already lost.

Finally, he looked back to Eurybia. The expression on her face was not what he expected. He was expecting anger, but not the sort she seemed to be radiating. Frustration at her predicament would have been understandable, but Aegesander got the distinct sense that something else lurked there, something that had been simmering for some time.

He again reminded himself that he trusted her. She was, in fact, the only Hexarch he trusted. Once upon a time, that trust had been formed out of necessity. She knew his secrets, including the one he shared with Hyperion and the rest of the older generation of Hexarchs.

He knew she knew because he told her everything that happened shortly after her own elevation. Since then, that fact dangled over both of them, threatening to destroy them if either of them shared it. She could ruin him, easily, but in doing so would expose herself as party, even after the fact, to the one of the worst atrocities mankind committed since going to the stars.

Their sin, Hyperion called it. The old man was right, and Aegesander hated him for it.

"Yes," he finally replied. "I am sorry that you find yourself trapped on Dasos during this inconvenience."

"You could surrender."

"I can't."

"Why not?"

Aegesander felt his fingers gripping the banister as his anger betrayed his veneer of calm. His knuckles went the same shade of white as the marble beneath them. "I have come too far," he growled. "I, we, have done too much to surrender. I have to see this through."

"You've lost, Aegesander. Surrender to First Lord Enyalios, plead your case, and perhaps the others will be lenient."

"What others?" Aegesander roared. "Do you think the Hexarchs will look favorably on me? I tried to kill Rivka. Hyperion is dead. Tritogenes is dead!"

Eurybia recoiled from his outburst, but the expression that came over her was not fear or even surprise, but another sort of anger.

"Tritogenes could have been my friend." Eurybia's voice dripped with hatred.

Aegesander sighed. He did not want to turn again and see the fury he knew to be simmering in her eyes. He did what he had to. "He would have been mine, too, if things were different. Hyperion was my friend, a century ago. Ophion, Stephania, Meriones, Diomedes, they were all my friends. None of it was supposed to happen."

"Then why?"

Aegesander fell against the railing. His arms shook, suddenly unable to support his weight or the weight of the tension in his hands. "Gods between," he muttered. "It has all gone so very wrong."

"If you had just told them what you told me..." she began.

"No!" Aegesander barked. Then, much weaker, he croaked, "no. I couldn't. Some things should stay hidden."

"Then why did you tell me?" she demanded.

"I had to tell someone," he answered. Aegesander heaved a sigh and pushed off from the railing again. Taking several long moments to recompose himself, he then said, "it was eating me alive, Eurybia, just like everything I've done since then."

"But why me?"

"Because I knew I could trust you."

"You knew you could blackmail me." Her voice was flat, devoid of any emotion of inflection.

Now it was his turn to recoil. Despite knowing the objective truth of what she said, hearing it spoken aloud hit him like a hammer. His reply was the mantra he had been telling himself for days. Out loud, it felt weak, even he knew that. He said it again anyway. "None of this was supposed to happen."

"None of it would have happened if you and the others told the truth!"

His adrenaline was receding. Even the burning ships above his head held little draw for Aegesander anymore. His arms and legs shook, weak. Where his pulse had hammered in his ears, now only an empty pit yawned. The only reply he could manage was a simple, "we couldn't."

She started to speak, but before she could say anything, he straightened up and continued. "This has gone beyond anything mere words will fix. Either I die, or they do."

Eurybia nodded, then placed a hand on his shoulder. The contact left Aegesander puzzled. For a brief moment, he felt like she was pitying him.

Behind them, in his office, his console beeped to indicate a text message coming through. A glance at the sky showed no new trails of fire. The fighting was over. That was likely the gist of the report waiting on him, either that or another request for surrender from First Lord Enyalios.

Aegesander gestured to the sky. "It's quiet now."

"You should have surrendered," Eurybia whispered. "I am sorry, my friend."

His reply should have been the word "what?" That, at least, was the message his brain delivered to his vocal cords. That word never came. Instead, what left Aegesander's mouth was a rush of air and a strained, confused gurgle.

First Lord Aegesander, Hexarch of Dasos and most senior member of the Council after the death of First Lord Hyperion, sagged to his knees having never felt the knife in his back.

***

First Lord Eurybia slammed her fist on the desk in frustration. She swore for perhaps the tenth time in as many minutes. "Damn it, Aegesander!"

The other Hexarch's body lay stretched out on the floor, atop a pile of towels and other absorbent cloth taken from his private bathroom. He bled out quickly, and the towels were soaked to the point that, had the floor been wood instead of textured marble, it would have borne a permanent stain.

A trail of blood led from his current resting place to the closed balcony door. Outside, Eurybia knew she left another pool of blood at the spot where he initially fell. The only thing she had actually cleaned so far was the knife she used to kill her fellow Hexarch. It had been wiped clean on Aegesander's own robes and then replaced in its secret sheath inside her own robe.

Eurybia never fancied herself a murderer. Over the course of her tenure as Hexarch, she had done things she objected to, even regretted. Murder, at least the cold-blooded execution of another human being face to face, had always been a line she refused to cross.

She always heard the expression "everyone has a price," especially during trade negotiations. Anyone could be bought. The Technocrat economy had long since gone beyond actual cash money, but that did not mean things lost their value. As people who prized time and effort above "mere" riches, most Technocrat bribes took the form of an exchange of services.

If bribery failed, then threats were just another method of persuasion. She could threaten to take something away or terminate a beneficial contract. As her negotiation partners grew in esteem, so did the ease of threatening them by cutting off their supply of some item or talent they required.

High ranking Technocrats rarely fell to physical threats—they had too many fallbacks for that. Threaten a Hexarch or even a Second Lord, and they would likely have the resources to make the one issuing threats regret it. So, to threaten violence meant a willingness to follow through on that violence.

That was the reason she never threatened violence. It was precisely because she did not want her talents reduced to that of a brute. Eurybia was too high-profile to risk issuing a threat and not following through on it as well. Her reputation would suffer as a result.

She never threatened Aegesander.

To threaten a Hexarch was to promise before the entire binary that she was willing to get blood on her hands. Until just a few minutes ago, she was not willing to go that far, or get her hands that messy.

As far as First Lord Eurybia knew, Aegesander never even suspected she harbored any ill will toward him. He knew she had been, at times, upset with him, but she never would have gotten that close to him if he suspected actual danger.

She looked again at Aegesander's rapidly-cooling corpse. He lay on his side with his face away from where she sat. The rip in the back of his robe, soaked black with blood, yawned at her like the mouth of a demon.

He blackmailed her for decades, and the end he deserved finally caught him. She laughed at the irony of it all. The only clear shot she had was while his back was turned. He, who thought he could trust her because of the Damoclean sword he hung over her head, had been stabbed in the back.

If he lived long enough, Eurybia wondered if he thought of his own murder as a betrayal. Perhaps, instead, he looked at it exactly like she did—as the fitting end to his life.

"Tritogenes was my friend," she snapped at the corpse.

She imagined Aegesander talking back even now. They had worked together so long that her mental image of his voice and speech were almost as real as reality would have been. "I know," she imagined him saying, terse and presumptive.

"Damn you!" she snapped. "I don't think you understand, Aegesander. Or maybe you do, or did. I may have been a Hexarch for a lot longer than Tritogenes, but we were Seconds together for a short time. We met when Stephania and Ophion hosted that ball the year before my elevation, just a few months after his to Second."

The corpse, even her imagined version of Aegesander, remained silent.

"Of course you don't remember," she said, then sneered. Fully aware of the sort of caricature she made, sitting there and sneering at a dead body, she forced herself to sit back in the chair and address the ceiling instead. "Of course you don't remember," she repeated. She realized her voice was quiet, sad. "You didn't come to that ball, did you?

"Diomedes was there," she continued. "He and Hyperion talked long into the night. I never knew what they were talking about, but now I can assume. It was you, wasn't it?"

"It was all of us," her imagined version of Aegesander replied.

She leaned forward, resting her elbows on the desk and cradling her face in her hands. "Listen to me, arguing sixty-year-old politics with a corpse. Of course," she added, looking up and fixing her eyes on Aegesander's bloody back, "they're not sixty-year-old politics, are they?"

She imagined his affronted face, offended at the absurd notion that he would have anything to do with any possible bad events she might be thinking of. Even her mental image of Aegesander could not muster enough incredulity at her accusations, though, because she knew he would have known they were all true. Even his famed control would have cracked a little if she had just confronted him even *once*.

"I suppose if I look through your files with the proverbial fine-toothed-comb I'd find the truth about Stephania, wouldn't I?"

The corpse was silent.

Eurybia scoffed. "I already knew about Ophion. Meriones, too. Surprised?"

Again, she imagined his offended face—eyebrows raised, one hand up as though to physically block any further accusations, mouth halfway open with a pre-prepared retort.

"And then Hyperion and Tritogenes. By the Ten Thousand, Aegesander, did you go to Pteryga to kill *another* Hexarch? Was that your goal?"

The imaged retort was hot, angry. "It was not."

"You intentions don't matter anymore," she growled. "Hyperion is dead. Tritogenes is dead. The blood of at least," she emphasized that word more than the others, "two more Hexarchs is on your hands. By extension, it's on my hands as well. Did you think of that when you brought me 'in' all those decades ago?"

Again, the dead stayed silent.

Eurybia sighed and tore her eyes away from the corpse again. She tried several more variants of passwords she knew or suspected he might use. Each time, his system locked her out, refusing the password.

She grumbled at it, lacking even the energy to be truly angry anymore. "Stupid machine."

Several more failed attempts later, she connected her personal computer directly to Aegesander's system, instructing it to use a brute-force crack on his passwords. While it worked, she stood up and paced his office, wondering what might have been.

Another glance at her feet reminded her of the man she once knew and respected. First Lord Adrasta died when Eurybia was a mere five

317

years old. She obviously saw something of promise in Aegesander, as he saw something in Eurybia.

Of course, that was nearly a century ago, and people could change. Rulers, especially, changed after killing their peers. Perhaps a hundred years ago, Second Lord Aegesander was a good man. Sixty years ago, a woman named Eurybia had been a simple dancer, and now she was party to the assassination of more good men and women than she cared to think about.

He had been a good man once. She did not doubt that. Eurybia remembered the man he had been before the mastigas came. All of the Hexarchs changed that day. Aegesander became angry and paranoid. Hyperion, still magnanimous within the small circle he trusted, became a recluse. Diomedes fell into depression, a disease which finally took his life when the mastigas sieged his planet.

Ophion grew angry. She remembered him as a kind man, if somewhat stern. When the mastigas came, he lashed out at his fellow Hexarchs, especially Aegesander and Eurybia herself, who was guilty by proxy.

Of course, by then she knew the truth.

She was the only one unaffected, it seemed, by the news of the mastigas's arrival in their system. For a time, that put her at the head of the Council as the others bickered among themselves. Then, Ophion and Meriones died "mysteriously," passing their planets on to Tritogenes and Enyalios respectively and the Council found its feet again.

The computer beeped, distracting her. Eurybia returned to the desk to find her programs had broken Aegesander's security. She quickly patched into the planetary communication networks, all of them, and prayed to the gods that they would believe her.

"This is First Lord Eurybia to the Dasos Planetary Defense Force. First Lord Aegesander is dead. He took his own life rather than surrender to First Lord Enyalios's forces. I urge everyone to surrender. The fight is over."

She terminated the message, sending it out to everyone and everything possible, and waited.

Her wait was short, as a few minutes later, a dull thump like the sound of booted feet came from the balcony.

Eurybia rose, crossing to the glass-and-bronze doors just in time for them to fly open.

First Lord Rivka stood there. Her face was set in a hard scowl and crossed by three bloody gashes and a smear of grease or soot. Instead of her Hexarch's robes, she wore a black suit of combat gear with purple stripes down the sleeves. A rope, likely connected to a small airship only moments prior, dangled mere centimeters above the marble at her feet.

Rivka also carried a rifle at her shoulder. One hand supported the weapon's barrel while the other wrapped around the grip and trigger. Her face was pressed against the top of the gun, already sighting down it even as she recovered her balance from kicking the doors open.

"Rivka, no!"

The gun spoke death, and First Lord Eurybia died before her body hit the floor. The last thing she saw was Aegesander's own corpse, waiting for her.

***

Rivka realized Eurybia was trying to surrender only after she pulled the trigger. She rushed to the older woman's side, but her aim had been too true. Eurybia was already dead, leaving Rivka alone in Aegesander's office.

More important in that moment, it left Rivka as one of the only two surviving Hexarchs.

She went to Aegesander's computer, intent on cracking his security and forcing his troops to surrender. Instead, she found the record of Eurybia's own surrender message.

Still, Rivka thought, redundancy could not hurt.

She record another message, this time with full visual. After the first Ouroboros mission, Victoria and the other Titans came through the public areas of Odyssey with their blood and bruises on display so the populace would understand what happened. She made the same choice—let them see the blood she shed. Perhaps then, they would understand.

"This is First Lord Rivka of Kipos." She paused, unsure of how best to proceed. After a pause, less than a second, she decided she would live or die by her own convictions. This was all for the truth, and she would be damned if she lied now. "I have killed First Lord Eurybia. First Lord Aegesander lies dead as well. This war is over. Lay down your weapons and surrender."

She ended the broadcast and dropped heavily into Aegesander's chair.

After several minutes, she got up once more and paced the small room. She could not leave until the fighting was over, Rivka knew that much. With Aegesander and Eurybia both dead, she and Enyalios were the closest things Dasos had to presiding authorities. Any surrenders from his forces had to be presented to her, and the best way to do that was for her to stay in the one place they knew to contact.

The first official surrender notice came eight minutes later. Another followed shortly after, this time reported directly to her by her own forces.

Her holo flashed an incoming message, one flagged as urgent rather than a simple status update. She accepted it, and Second Lord Ilias's face greeted her. Even projected only from the shoulders up, the blood and bruises were obvious.

She smiled at the irony—now she was the one playing witness to the blood and pain someone else suffered on her behalf.

"Hey, boss," he said with a wry grin. He cleared his throat. "Sorry. I mean, 'greetings, First Lord.'"

Rivka smiled. "I'm glad to see you're alive. Where are you?"

"About ten floors down, on my way up. We're taking surrenders right and left, so it might take a bit."

She nodded. "Good. I'm glad you're alive," she repeated.

"I am too. Eudora and I'll be up there in a few."

"Where are the others?"

Ilias's face fell. "They didn't make it off Pteryga."

"I'm sorry."

"No. Don't be sorry. You're alive, which means we did our job."

Rivka wiped at her face, unsure if the wetness there was from blood, sweat, or tears. "Thanks."

"See you soon," he said, grinned, and added, "First Lord."

Ilias arrived sooner than expected, and they spoke for several minutes while he put his gear down. Rivka had no real idea what was said by either of them; she was simply responding and talking on instinct while she navigated through Aegesander's computer systems. She told herself she was looking for information that might explain why he went to Pteryga, but in truth, she was simply *doing* without really thinking about it.

"Boss?" Ilias asked, then, "Rivka!"

She shook herself. "Yes?"

"Come here and look at this."

She rose. Something in Ilias's tone suggested it was important enough to merit her attention, and potentially too sensitive to mention aloud.

Aegesander's private dressing room sat off to the side, and it was from there that Ilias's voice originated. She stepped into the room. At first glance, she was impressed by the array of clothing and jewelry on display. Aegesander had been a Hexarch for a very long time, and it was logical that he had plenty to show for it.

What Ilias held up was a blue robe, suitable for a well-off Second Lord. Rivka scanned over it with her eyes, but nothing jumped out at her. It looked to the usual sort of garment worn by a Second Lord with a number of accomplishments to display.

"What about it? It's probably one from before Aegesander was elevated."

Ilias shook his head. "It's too new. And look at this."

Rivka peered closer as Ilias held up the robe's left sleeve. The same cold pit that opened in her stomach when she read Diomedes's suicide confession returned. Her eyes went wide and, for several moments, she was unable to speak.

Around the cuff of that sleeve was a glittering curl of silver embroidery—a snake eating its own tail.

"Selene's grace," she muttered.

"What do you want done with it?"

"Burn it," she said, making a snap decision. Hyperion was right after all, she thought. Some secrets did not need to be revealed.

Chapter 17

From the entrance of their narrow hall to what they all agreed was most likely a control room was a scant fifty meters. The only positive about the situation was that there seemed to be no active mastigas outside it. There were also no places to hide, no cover of any sort, between their current location and their destination.

An hour had passed since they finished eating. That time let the four surviving Titans put as much of a plan together as they could without any real firsthand information on their soon-to-be battlefield.

At the moment, they crouched just out of sight of the doorway to the control room. The strange curves of the floor helped for once, letting them get that close without being seen. The pseudo-mental radar Helena and Panatakis cobbled together thanks to the information from their implants indicated no mastigas anywhere nearby except directly ahead. That room showed as scarlet on the radar, confirmed presence of mastigas, but where they now stood was a mere dull yellow that faded to even safer colors further away.

Their combat suits were designed to operate in a temporary vacuum if needed. They offered little insulation against the cold of space, but in the event of a hull breach, they would keep air in the wearer's lungs. They also kept scents inside which, at the expense of a pleasant breathing environment, resulted in the closest thing to stealth technology they could manage.

Their cyborg-driven radar continued to detect nothing nearby, and the safe indicator colors slowly crept closer to their position. The room ahead continued to burn an ominous red. If anything, having more time to gather data gave them *more* proof that their destination was important to the mastigas.

The empty corridors around her set Victoria's nerves on end. She knew, in a few minutes, it would not matter very much, but for the time being she could not decide if the moment of peace was a good or a bad thing. Victoria found herself hoping for the former and expecting the latter.

Victoria tapped an indicator on her holo and the icon on her helmet display that represented her changed from yellow to green. Panatakis did so a moment later, followed by Lelantos, and then Helena. The icons representing Korakti and Daniel, for obvious reasons, remained a dull blood red.

She nodded and signaled to the others with one hand, then took a long step forward without rising from her crouch. She shifted, then brought her knees to the floor and crawled forward another two meters.

The others followed, all crawling on their bellies. Staying on the floor let them come ten meters closer to the door without being seen. With her suit completely sealed and running on bottled air, she could not smell the mastigas, but she knew what she ought to be smelling and her brain filled in the rest.

She gave another hand gesture and Panatakis slithered ahead of her. Helena came up beside, while Lelantos, with his rifle configured for precision high-caliber rounds, waited at the rear. Victoria grit her teeth. She *should* have had Korakti watching their back, and as it was she could not spare any of the remaining Titans for that role.

A deep breath and she checked Panatakis's radar again. She had to trust that it was accurate, because no other choice existed.

Panatakis's voice came over their helmet radios. He sounded strange, like a badly damaged recording. His voice was flat, unresonant. It lacked most of the features that typically identified a human voice, in fact. It was clearly him, despite the strangeness, because the tones and inflections came through like they should. It was all of the subconscious clues that went into making a voice sound real that were missing.

He sounded like a computer generated voice which, in a way, was true. Rather than speaking, Panatakis simply had interfaced with his helmet's radio, transmitting his thoughts directly to them.

"This is as close as we can get," the computerized pseudo-Panatakis voice told them.

Helena's voice replied, likewise lacking any timbre or liveliness. It was normal hearing her do it. During both missions against Ouroboros, Victoria spoke with that version of Helena's voice more than she spoke with her real voice. "Understood. We are currently thirty-nine-point-one-one-three meters from the outer opening. Panatakis, your grenades will cross that distance in approximately zero-point-four-seven-one-seven-seven seconds."

Victoria wondered how much that level of precision helped either of them. If their implants could handle that level of mathematics on the fly, it was no wonder the two cyborg Titans had such fast, sure reflexes.

The computerized version of Helena's voice continued. She rattled off a series of angles for his first three shots, then waited a moment for him to acknowledge the information.

Not for the first time, Victoria wondered why, if either of them could do the calculations, Helena did them and passed them along to Panatakis. It was possible that Helena's implants were more advanced than his, or simply that most of his "processing power" was dedicated to controlling his complex sensory input, leaving her free to run calculations.

However their partnership worked, it worked, and Victoria appreciated it.

"On my command," Panatakis announced.

"Ready," Victoria said.

Helena's voice reported she was ready as well, as did Lelantos a moment later.

Panatakis rolled onto his back, raised his rifle above him and fired. Victoria had no idea how he calculated the shot, nor how he managed to do it without actually using the weapon's sights, but his so-called trick worked exactly like he told them it would.

He rose, moving inhumanly fast on augmented muscles, shouldered the rifle, and launched another grenade. The muzzle of the rifle dipped slightly as he realigned his aim and fired a third time.

The first two grenades had been flashbangs and the third a wide-area thermobaric bomb. Panatakis spent much of the previous hour fine-tuning that grenade to do exactly what he wanted. Rather than abject destruction in a small area, he wanted it to spread out as far as possible, hurting and disorienting the mastigas in the entire room more than killing any of them outright.

That third grenade was also the signal for the rest of them to move.

By the time Victoria was on her feet, the initial flare from the flashbang was gone. If everything went like Panatakis claimed, one should have detonated on the closer half of the room and one on the farther half. The thermobaric grenade should have hit somewhere near the center. Helena's calculations had not been wrong yet, and Victoria hoped that streak would continue.

As the third grenade detonated, a sharp wind whipped over them, pulling cold air into the suddenly superheated mastigas control room. Victoria struggled to maintain her footing against it.

Even without Panatakis's adjustments to the grenade, human targets would have been immolated near the center of the blast, probably killing them instantly. Anything alive near the outer edges of the room would have been battered, most likely knocking them unconscious at best as the blast wave reflected back on itself again and again in the space of milliseconds.

Instead, as her vision settled against the front sight of her carbine, it was the *lack* of carnage in the room ahead that greeted her first. Any feeling of courage or confidence she might have had was ripped from her guts and replaced with a cold pit of fear. The mastigas ahead were disoriented for a the moment, and some near the center were even batting at flames that threatened to consume their clothing, but nearly all of them still stood.

In that moment, Victoria knew she would probably die in the next few minutes.

This was, in a very real sense, the moment for which she had lived her entire life. Victoria had been born in a lab. She was created to do one job—kill mastigas. The only time the weight of that job left her shoulders was when she was with Pallasophia. Even moments of levity with the other Titans did not erase it completely, because they too had been selected and trained to do the same job.

Victoria was literally born to do this.

That thought swept through her brain like fire, rejuvenating her nerves and giving her the impetus to move forward.

She stepped to the right side as Helena did the same to the left. That opened Lelantos's line of sight, allowing him his choice of targets.

Helena opened fire first. Her initial barrage struck a group of four fonias. The rounds tore through their clothing, leaving long streaks of red as they passed. The shots achieved their secondary goal moments later as the entire horde focused on her.

At the center of the room stood a pair of sophonts. They seemed to be working in close conjunction with one another, issuing orders to the mastigas around them. A trio of mikros stood nearby, operating several control panels under the sophonts' supervision. The mikros smoldered from Panatakis's grenade, but continued working with dogged determination. Whether they did not notice any burns or were simply unwilling, or unable, to acknowledge them under the sophonts' glare, Victoria could not say.

Regardless, that was where Panatakis aimed his next grenade. This one was a concussive round. What it lost in fire and flash it made up for with sheer explosive force. A nearly invisible blast wave erupted from the point of impact, throwing two of the mikros off their feet and slamming a third into its console hard enough to smash the interface.

The first of the mastigas other than the sophont to recover their eyesight, two gigas on the left side of the room shot back at them. They both carried massive weapons. One barked with the thundercrack of bullets so heavy they made the deadly arcs of the grenades from the other gigas's gun seem relaxed by comparison.

The bullets tore holes in the ground in front of them. The gentle rise of the floor was enough, combined with some residual unsteadiness from the flashbang, to throw off its aim. The grenades did likewise, impacting well over the Titan's heads and showering them with debris.

Another pair of gigas as the far end of the room bellowed a challenge, lumbering off of a raised platform. Their feet struck the deck simultaneously, reverberating and echoing loud even against the opening salvos of gunfire.

Victoria sprinted forward several steps and dropped heavily onto one knee, keenly aware of her proximity to the holes left by the first shots from the machine-gun-armed gigas. She spared that towering monster a half-second's thought, but the gigas were not her responsibility just then.

Instead, she took aim at another group of fonias opposite the one Helena shot at. Three rounds left her carbine, two of which slammed into the faceplate of the lead fonias. Its head exploded backward in a shower of blood and bits of black plastic.

The fonias directly behind the first one staggered and dropped to the floor as well. Three impossibly bright rivulets of blood ran from its upper chest.

Behind that group of fonias, a third pair of gigas clawed at their eyes and ears. Victoria assumed they were staring directly at one of the flash grenades when it went off. She felt a pang of remorse at the unfairness of attacking blinded targets, but their superior weaponry and numbers assuaged that feeling quickly.

At the rear of their group, Lelantos finally found a target worthy of his attention. His long rifle barked, roaring an octave lower and nearly twice as loud as Victoria's own weapon. One of the two sophonts and the mikros directly behind it—the last of the four and the only one that was not killed by Panatakis's grenade—erupted into a fine pink mist. The console behind the two mastigas sparked as smoke poured from a hole the size of Victoria's fist.

Victoria squeezed her trigger again, finishing the job she started moments before. Two of the rounds from that burst struck one of the two remaining fonias—for that group at least—in the abdomen. It shrieked and fell to the ground, clutching its stomach. The third bullet struck the other fonias in the lower leg, and from the way it immediately fell, Victoria assumed she shattered its shin.

Neither was dead, but neither would be fighting any longer, either.

Helena took aim and again fired at the same group of mastigas. Her shots landed truer this time, as a brilliant red dot appeared on the chest of the nearest fonias. It fell to the deck and its companions scattered to either side to avoid tripping.

Panatakis shifted his aim from the sophont in the center to the charging line of fonias. His shoulders shook as his second-to-last grenade sped across the distance to explode on the floor behind one edge of the horde of fonias. Two more groups of four had joined Helena's targets, and Panatakis's grenade destroyed the two on the right side of the line. The fonias next nearest the blast stumbled, but kept their feet under them.

The gigas took aim again, releasing hellfire into the air.

Victoria had seen the weapons the mastigas carried up close. Many of them were held in a museum of sorts on Prosgeiosi. The bullets fired from the weapons carried by the gigas were easily as thick as her thumb and twice as long. They were the type of bullets usually reserved for assaulting fortified positions or destroying vehicles.

Victoria never wanted to see firsthand what those bullets could do to a human body. In the split second before its partner's grenades reduced what remained to ash and char, Second Lord Panatakis's body momentarily resembled a paper shooting range target.

His scream, inhuman and distorted by the direct neural interface, rang in her ears. Somehow it was incalculably worse than having heard it from his vocal cords because the sounds of unutterable pain tearing through her mind were harsher and more immediate than anything she could have imagined.

Behind her, Lelantos echoed Panatakis's scream out loud. His gun roared its deadly thunder again and bright red fountained from a skull-sized hole in the rifle-armed gigas's chest. It gurgled and fell to the floor with a wet thud.

At the far end of the room, the pair of gigas that had been standing on the high platform split apart, each going a different direction around the center console where the lone surviving sophont frantically manipulated control surfaces that sparked and smoked.

Heavy bullets ripped through the air past Victoria's head, leaving her panic stricken mind to replay Panatakis's death. A grenade from the gigas's partner hit the ground at her feet. The explosion knocked Victoria off of her feet and backward. The blast itself knocked the wind out of her, leaving none in her lungs when she impacted the floor, but her armor seemed to have done its job.

She could not stop the thought from coming that her armor had done its job far better than Panatakis's had.

As she struggled to her feet, Lelantos's rifle fired again. She heard the roar of a gigas followed by a thud. Somewhere at the periphery of her vision, she was aware that one of the gigas that shot at her seemed to

330

have fallen, but her attention was taken up instead by the fonias in front of her.

The onrushing groups of fonias had merged into one single horde. As they jostled and shoved one another in their bloodlust, Victoria found it impossible to count them. Her estimate stopped at there being too many of them to be as close as they were. Far too many knives sat in far too many clawed hands, but instead of chilling her blood with fear, Victoria's blood burned with fire.

KILL.

Helena opened fire, raking a fully automatic fusillade across the front of the front of the mastigas horde. Some of the mastigas stumbled as rounds hit the ground at their feet, but their incredible agility kept them going. The mastigas in the nearest group were not so lucky as her spread of shots killed another one.

Victoria spared a half-second to thank whatever gods were listening for Panatakis's foresight. His stubborn insistence that she take some of his throwing grenades paid off. In a single motion, Victoria drew, armed, and flung a random explosive from her belt.

It sailed over the heads of the vanguard group that Helena shot at. She felt a moment of despair at that, but then the grenade landed amid the left flank of the fonias. It detonated, one of Panatakis's custom, though unmodified during their planning session, thermobaric grenades. The two-stage explosion eliminated at least half a dozen of the fonias on that side.

Victoria snarled. "That was for Panatakis, you fuckers!"

A noise came over her helmet speakers, something Victoria had never heard before. Helena screamed, giving voice to rage and anger so profound Victoria at first had no idea what she was hearing. It sounded angry, furious, as though whatever made that noise knew nothing else. It came directly from Helena's mind, eclipsing anything her helmet was capable of producing, and the searing static only made her pain that much more palpable.

As the unbearable pain started to lessen, Victoria felt like the human element was gone. All she heard now was rage, mathematically precise fractals of pain spiraling out and back upon themselves a thousand times.

The sound died, replaced with a frigid calm. The sounds in her ears, still coming directly from Helena's brain, were methodical now, almost mechanical.

In the silence that fell, Victoria's rage was replaced with a different, though no less insistent or familiar, impulse.

PROTECT.

She leveled her rifle, but Helena shot faster. A single bullet from Helena's gun turned the skull of the lead fonias into pulp.

The sophont in the center of the room gesticulated at the two gigas nearest it angrily. One nodded and lumbered closer, moving to shield the four-armed creature with its body. The other gigas did not seem to heed the orders being screeched its direction and continued to move forward. Unlike the other two still alive, its position on the ground—behind the fonias—made shooting at the three surviving Titans harder.

Lelantos fired again. His shot struck the sophont's guardian gigas in the meat of its thigh. It bellowed in rage and pain, but remained upright.

The partner of the gigas that killed Panatakis grunted and yelled in what sounded like frustration before stepping forward and dropping the meter off of its high perch. It grunted something at the wounded gigas, which nodded.

Lelantos's shots came faster now, with less time to aim between each round. Whether driven by Panatakis's death, frustration at "merely" wounding a gigas with his last shot, or the simple proximity of the remnants of the fonias horde, Victoria did not care. So long as he continued to hit his targets, she would not complain.

As it happened, the next round struck the same gigas he wounded moments before in the center of the groin. Bright red blood poured from the wound as its knees sagged and it fell to the floor.

A single gigas remained with a clear line of sight to the Titans, the partner of the one whose grenade knocked Victoria off her feet seconds earlier. It held one of the heavy machine guns like the one that killed Panatakis, and when pain blossomed in her right arm, she immediately assumed that she, too, was going to die.

Now, her brain said. Her time was now up.

The world slowed for a moment. Dirt and debris kicked up all around her, showering her from above as well. Everything fell into sharp focus a moment later, speeding up to an almost unnatural rate.

Victoria's arm burned with wet fire, but she was still alive and the appendage continued to function. Half a second's glance told her how lucky she was. The round seemed to have grazed her arm only. The wound trail was perhaps a milimeter deep and poured blood, but she was alive.

The gigas that ignored the sophont's orders moved out from behind the fonias. It leveled its machine gun at Helena and opened fire. She screamed in Victoria's helmet again, but the sound was more an instinctual reaction of fear and anger than pain. Rounds tore holes in the ceiling above her head, raining debris down on her, but none of the deadly projectiles seemed to have hit home.

This time, Lelantos took a moment to make sure his aim was good. While the gigas's weapon cycled, he pulled his own trigger and put a bullet through the faceplate of the gigas that shot at Helena. It did not have time for any noises of pain; its head simply existed one moment, then stopped existing the next.

The nearest of the mastigas was less than three meters from Victoria now. At that range, she could not miss, and she did not. Each of the three rounds from her carbine struck the mastigas in the chest, halting its headlong charge with a graceless tumble.

Victoria scrambled for her magazine release. Training fought against adrenaline for control of her muscles. In that moment, Helena put another bullet through the skull of the next nearest mastigas.

Six fonias remained, but their suicidal charge had finally brought them to within close combat distance. Victoria stared at the remaining knife-armed monsters, hoping her reactions were faster than theirs.

Again, the urge screamed in her head.

PROTECT.

Two of the fonias reached Lelantos before she could reload completely. The first lunged at him, but its blade did little more than slice his clothes. The second one bit deep into his thigh. Blood poured from the razor-edged weapon's wound as Lelantos fell to one knee.

He grunted and struck out with the butt of his rifle, but both fonias avoided the strike. Despite failing to wound either mastigas, he succeeded in pushing them away and preventing either one from stabbing or slashing him again.

More important, he succeeded in giving Victoria the few moments she needed to cross the remaining distance.

Victoria lunged forward, turning the powerful movement into a linear strike with the stock of her own rifle. She struck the nearest fonias in the chest and felt the wet-twig crunch of its ribs snapping. She also knocked it off its feet where it was trampled by its former comrades.

The sophont's guardian gigas took careful aim and fired. The mass of fonias between it and where Victoria stood threw off its aim. The bullet passed close enough to her head that the breath was pushed from her chest by the pressure of its passage. The other gigas, finally hindered enough by the fonias's presence that it realized it could get no closer without knocking the little ones aside, fired and missed as well.

Helena stepped away, an apology echoing in Victoria's head as her interface transmitted her thoughts directly. She raised her rifle and fired, hitting the sophont's guardian in the chest. The wound poured blood, but the giant did not look like it was about to topple. In the wake of her shot, the sophont broke away from its guardian and ran for the back edge of the room.

Five mastigas swarmed around her and Lelantos as Victoria dropped her rifle, trusting the sling to keep it attached to her body, and drew her knives. The fonias were too close to shoot anymore, but they had finally come into the distance where she was most skilled.

Her first attack struck one of the fonias on the faceplate. The plastic spiderwebbed and cracked and the creature snarled at her as the sudden impact threw off both its attack and its footwork. She drove her second blade upward, under the helmet of another fonias. The blow knocked the creature's head back, and, if the blade failed to kill it, its neck was almost certainly broken.

Helena fired at the now-abandoned gigas again. This time her shot pierced the gap between its armored torso and its helmet. Very little blood answered her bullet, but the titanic creature fell to its knees, chest heaving. It clutched at its throat as it fell the rest of the way to the ground and continued to lay there thrashing for some time.

Lelantos roared in frustration, rising to his feet despite the blood pouring from his thigh. He raised his rifle overhead, stock forward, and lunged for the nearest of the fonias. He drove the stock into the helmet of the fonias, crushing it. He stumbled, but his wounded leg continued to support him.

One gigas remained, but with a few fonias still around them, it continued to have difficulties aiming. It fired twice. One bullet hit the floor a meter in front of the Titans, harmlessly making yet another hole in the floor beneath them. The second, however, took Lelantos's leg out from under him.

The three remaining fonias lunged for Lelantos's prone form, but Victoria intercepted them. She struck the first fonias, burying her knife in the little monster's guts. With her second knife, she drew a long slash along the second fonias's chest. That one took another step, raised its own knife, and collapsed.

Victoria screamed, ripping her first knife free of its target and burying both of them in the final fonias's ribs. One knife tore open the mastigas's left flank and the other opened its right. Victoria ripped the knives free, pulling them toward her and through several centimeters of the fonias's muscle and organ tissue, before brutally kicking it away.

Coming down from the kick, she threw her left knife across the distance at the retreating sophont. Against all odds, the blade struck it in the right hip. It stumbled, and Helena fired.

The bullet struck back of the sophont's oversized head, spraying a fine red mist ahead of it. The corpse continued running for one, two, three steps before falling to the floor motionless.

The final gigas, the last of the mastigas in the control room aside from the remaining mikros scurrying away from their workstations, bellowed in incoherent rage and fired, missing every one of its poorly aimed shots.

Victoria dropped her remaining knife into her boot and sprinted forward, firing at the last gigas. Her shots went wild. Only one struck the behemoth in the shoulder, an impact which the gigas barely seemed to notice.

Helena broke into a run as well, following Victoria's lead and shooting at the last mastigas. The ground was littered with fonias corpses, which threw off her aim and her shots, too, went wide.

Several seconds later, Lelantos's rifle coughed again, sending one of its flesh-rending rounds through the gigas's faceplate. It did not fall. Instead, it simply sagged quietly to the floor, slumping against the knee-high railing in front of it as though it were simply asleep.

Lelantos caught up with them as Victoria and Helena slowed to survey the room ahead. Nothing remained of his left leg below the knee and blood soaked the thigh above it. A tourniquet made from strong tape was wrapped around the new end of his leg and he used his rifle as a crutch. He dropped a vial of quick heal to the floor and withdrew another one from a pocket before gritting his teeth and saying, "we did it. Now we just need to..."

Lelantos never finished his sentence. Rather, he finished it with a surprised gasp and a gurgle.

Victoria and Helena spun around in time to see a mastigas elite, no more than two meters from them, raise Lelantos up on a massive two-handed sword and then fling him away like a ragdoll.

The elite was joined a moment later by another one. They had been hiding in the shadows just inside the room's entrance the entire time, watching the carnage unfold without making a sound. They had to know exactly how the four Titans had been watching their movements, and so the mastigas sent dozens of troops to their deaths just to lure them into striking range of these two elites.

The four-armed monstrosities regarded them for a moment before one of them spoke. "Hello, humans," it said. Its voice was strange, unlike the wet-stones of the sophont. The elite sounded like a stringed instrument given voice, melodic and beautiful as a tornado. "We are impressed with your progress, but The One That Burns and The One that Roars demand your deaths."

Victoria looked at the elites for a long moment. She had killed their kind before. She was under nourished and probably dehydrated even slightly injured at that point, but she won that fight with little more than her bare hands.

Yet, she hesitated. She threw everything she had into the last few frantic minutes, and fatigue worse than she ever felt threatened to take hold of her. Worse, her arm was loosing blood and feeling. With no way of knowing what other internal injuries she had, Victoria would be hard pressed to defeat even one of these elites.

Helena, she knew, was a strong fighter, but even her skill did little to tip the scales in their favor.

The elite in the arena had also been smaller and probably malnourished itself. These two were healthy, armored, and much better armed than the elite she skilled. Rather than four one-handed swords, each of the monsters carried a two-handed sword scaled to their three-meter height, and a rifle.

The elites were too close, and these seemed even more intelligent than usual. Victoria knew somehow that they would cooperate unlike the others they faced in the ship.

Facing the two of them, it seemed Victoria finally reached the point of no return. Perhaps, she thought, Helena was correct about the real reason First Lord Aegesander sent them all out here after all.

Her initial thoughts were wrong, she realized. *Now* was the time she would die. Another thought interjected, this one in Pallasophia's voice. Granted, it said, all of the other times she thought she was moments away from death, she had been wrong.

Whatever her thoughts, Victoria had no intention of dying without a fight. If her count was right, the magazine in her rifle was half-full. The baton she took on her first day of life was still strapped to her waist and she still had one of her knives. Baton and knife saw her through the arena, and now it seemed it would have to see her through another fight. She grasped its cold handle and hefted it.

Scuffling and motion at the edges of her vision pulled Victoria's attention away from the elites. A half-dozen fonias rose up, knives gleaming in the dim light. They had not come from any of the side passages. Instead, like the elites, they had been waiting, hiding, for exactly this moment.

"Victoria. I need you to do exactly as I say," Helena thought-spoke through her helmet. She had no way of replying to the cold voice, and so simply listened. Something about her inflection, or complete lack of one, went beyond the normal flatness their radios gave to her synthesized voice. It made her pay attention.

With no way to reply, she simply waited a moment until Helena resumed speaking.

Helena lowered her rifle, letting it dangle from its sling. She took a step backward, a single one, slow and sure. The elites watched her from behind their helmets, and Victoria could picture their three-eyed stare, green and hungry.

"If I mean anything to you, do not argue," the synthesized voice continued. "When I tell you to run, you will run. The passage at the far end of the room, where the sophont was going, leads upward. It is the only such passage out of this room. You will run and you will run as fast as your legs will allow. Am I clear?"

Victoria hesitated. She opened her mouth, inhaled. "Yes."

Helena screamed, aloud and with her mind at the same time. "RUN!"

Victoria ran, realizing only after reaching the sharply-climbing tunnel that Helena was not behind her.

She slowed, both from the sudden steepness of the spiraling tunnel and from her realization. Victoria was about to turn around when a wave of light, heat, sound, and catastrophic pressure washed over her.

For a brief moment, she was in hell, being crushed by the weight of her sins made literal and burned by the fires of those she had disappointed. Then, it was over and silence reigned.

In that moment, Victoria realized why Helena insisted she be the one to carry the bulk of their grenades.

Chapter 18

Victoria stared at her discarded helmet, the empty bottles of water and ration packs, and the six units of quick heal scattered on the floor around her. She felt painfully aware of how quiet everything was. After the explosion, she tried to go back down, screaming for Helena to answer her, but the only thing she encountered was an impenetrable wall of warm rubble.

Helena must had set off two dozen grenades at once, all within her own pockets and bags. The explosion wrecked the control room and sealed the passage behind Victoria.

She only hoped Helena died painlessly, vaporized by ten kilograms of high explosives. The alternative, death at the hands of the elites or the fonias, was worse. The explosives, at least, would have been quick.

The corridor around her was dark, probably even darker than the rest of the ship. The passage leading up to it was too narrow for the larger mastigas to climb through. Only the sophonts and smaller varieties would have been able to squeeze their way up the meter-wide tunnel.

The air was also at least ten degrees colder and more humid than the cool, damp air of the pyramid itself. She shivered, the insulation in her suit proving insufficient to warm her. The chill that touched her bones went far beyond the ambient air.

She had no idea how many people were aboard their escort cruisers. She suspected each one had at least a thousand crew if the support personnel on the *Hammer of Ares* were any indication. Seeing them all die to a weapon no one knew about still resonated in her mind, perhaps even more painful than the memory of the *Justice*.

That ship carried a hundred thousand men and women, all volunteers. That ship, her mental spiral continued, carried her *friend*, Eleni. Its death had been drawn out, like dismembering an elite or a gigas before finally being able to kill it. Even the mastigas superweapon had trouble with the massive troop carrier.

Perhaps it was that perseverance that dampened the impact of its death, she thought, or her heart simply refused to process a tenth of a million lives gone in seconds.

"Or maybe," she said out loud. Her voice was dry, hoarse, despite the humid air. "After our escorts went down, it just couldn't hurt any worse."

She laughed, quietly and bitterly. That, of course, was not true. Her heart ached still worse as she continued to replay events in her mind. There had been no way to save Daniel. She hoped he was with his god now, the loving, father-like entity he always talked about.

Victoria scoffed, not at his religion, but at her own situation. Her gods, such that they were, were cruel. Gods of death and bloodshed seemed to be the only ones watching over her.

Korakti fell even before Victoria reunited with her. Despite seeing Panatakis's and Lelantos's deaths firsthand, Victoria felt it was Korakti's that stung the worst. She had been there for the other two Titans and fought alongside them.

Korakti did not die under her watch. The sense of failure there was far worse. She knew she had done everything she could for Panatakis and Lelantos. Their deaths were not wasted. They died fighting. Korakti,

Panatakis told her, died fighting as well, but Victoria had not been there to help.

She cursed bitterly, thinking of Helena's final act of heroism. Victoria cursed her bravery, angry at her sacrifice. It was stupid to be angry at Helena, her conscious mind knew that, but her emotions refused to listen to reason.

Victoria raised her left arm, where the silvery-blue piece of Helena's exoskeleton was still clamped firmly.

"You were supposed to help Helena fix what Aegesander did to her mind," Victoria said, addressing the machine. "Now that she's dead..." Another pang of cold regret flashed through her stomach. "What am I going to do with you?"

She put her other hand atop the piece of implant tech. It was still warm, warmer than her own body temperature but not unpleasantly so, and it continued to hum.

Victoria struggled to her feet. With no real guidance anymore, she picked a direction at random and started walking. There were only two of them, after all, so her options were limited. The corridor sloped upward in both directions, and she assumed either would lead to her destination—whatever that ended up being.

After five minutes, she reached the top of the slope. To confirm her assumption, she ignored the single side passage and continued forward. Five minutes later, she returned to her original location, then made her way back to the top.

Standing in front of the only remaining passage, she took a deep breath, trying desperately to calm her nerves. The cold, wet air smelled strange here. It smelled like the mastigas, but it was different somehow. It smelled older, like something that had been moldering for too long. Other scents were mixed in, things that reminded her of carrion and spring flowers all at the same time.

She dropped her helmet back on her head, sealed it, and the smell vanished. The system took a moment to reconnect, but Victoria stood there longer than necessary. She kept waiting to hear the quiet sounds of breathing or mumbled words coming through her speakers. When those sounds never manifested, when she realized they never would manifest again, her heart sank even deeper into the cold at her core.

Another deep breath, let out through clenched teeth, and she was ready. The pit in her stomach still yawned, blowing a chill through her soul that had nothing to do with the air temperature. Instead, it cooled the rage she felt, replacing it with a icy certitude.

Whatever else awaited her, she was near the mastigas superweapon. If she did nothing else before the endless hordes of green eyed monsters killed her, she could at least destroy that damnable beam cannon and clear the way for a second try.

Calmly, she checked over her weapons. She went through three-quarters of her rifle's ammunition store in the fight for the control room. One of her daggers was missing—it had been lodged in the leg of the fleeing sophont when Helena self-sacrificed. Her other dagger still sat in its sheath, strapped to her calf and waiting for its turn to be used. The baton, thanks to its mastigas-fabric tie, still dangled from her waist.

She took a moment to check over her backup weapons. Her pistol, so far unused, remained clean for the most part. It had a much smaller reserve of ammunition, but that reserve was all but untouched. Victoria also carried Korakti's sword, but her pistol had been lost when the gigas killed Panatakis.

Food and water were both running low as well. She had perhaps three comfortable days left. If she stretched things out to their absolute limit and ate like she did in the labyrinth, Victoria supposed she might be able to get two weeks out of what remained.

And yet, she had only been aboard the mastigas ship for a few days, and already was nearing their superweapon. Destroy the weapon, she thought, and the united Technocrat navy might stand a chance against the reaper that was the mastigas battleship.

As she raised her carbine to her shoulder, all thoughts of anger or range dissipated. She pushed down thought of panic and fear as well. Any of those emotions would only get her killed. She still had a one last job to do, and she would be damned if she died without doing her best to finish what she came there to do.

"And even if I don't," she muttered aloud, "I was born alone. I suppose dying alone is not the worst thing that could happen to me."

In that moment, Pallasophia's face flashed through her mind. She latched onto it, realizing how much of a lie that statement had been. No, Victoria thought as the memory of Pallasophia's touch caused her skin to tingle, she was *not* going to die.

She stepped forward and into darkness. The suit's visor automatically compensated, amplifying what little light was available and turning it into a ghostly hallucination of reality where none of the colors were quite right.

Nothing adorned the walls, not even written warnings to stay out of where ever it was she was headed. In her light-amplified vision, the walls were dull, painted with some sort of matte finish that seemed to absorb what remained of the light. A few steps further and she thought she would have to resort to using actual lights to see.

The hallway, however, was not long and she saw its end before things grew too dim for her helmet to compensate for. She stepped into the room, rifle raised, and the walls fell away, revealing an open, circular space some ten meters across. Holographic control surfaces, dim in ordinary light but glowing like lamps in her enhanced view, ringed the outer edge of the room. None of them were occupied.

In fact, the only thing other than Victoria in the room was a four meter tall, six meter wide mass of unidentifiable movement.

Three pinpricks appeared in the mass, reflecting the meager light.

The voice that emanated from the mass gurgled and cracked. It seemed to repeat itself, as though multiple speakers were trying to say the same thing at the same time.

"Human," it burbled. Echoes followed, all similar but all subtly different in some way. "Welcome to my home."

Victoria's blood froze, followed by all of her muscles. Whatever took up the center of the room was a mastigas, it had to be, and yet she found herself too paralyzed to do anything about it. "What are you?"

Laughter answered her. Laughter came from multiple mouths as first a second and then a third trio of pinprick eyes turned to regard her from the shapeless mass. She heard it move, a kind of creaking sound full of the popping noises made by stiff joints.

Light flared in the room, overloading her low-light vision for a moment before the system automatically shut itself off. As she blinked away the haze, Victoria found herself face to face with something she had no words for.

The monstrosity in the center of the room took the form of a single massive hulk of gray flesh. Arms emerged from the mass, twelve of them in six pairs all pointed a different direction. Each pair interacted with a different holographic interface. Above each pair of arms was an elongated skull with a distended mouth full of needle-like teeth. Each skull bore three brilliant green eyes, three sets of which were focused on her.

If the sophonts spoke with the sounds of water running across stones in a brook, the *thing* before her roared with the volume of whitecaps crashing against boulders. Its every word was a bass rumble that reverberated through the floor and into her bones.

"We are the Sophocrat."

Victoria's eyes went wide. "That sophont said there were six of them, but I never... By the Ten Thousand..."

"Yes," the heads replied. Disdain filled its voices. "That one belonged to The One That Hopes. We believe it was killed by sophonts loyal to The One That Burns."

"Which are you?" Victoria demanded.

It roared its reply, full of pride. "We are the Sophocrat!"

345

"You command the mastigas?"

"We ARE the mastigas!"

"Where did you come from?"

The Sophocrat laughed. Each of the heads cackled out of sync with the others, creating a disorienting cacophony of sound. Some of the laughter was low, spiteful; while here and there the high-pitched cackle of rage poked through.

As the laughter subsided, the three heads facing her turned away and turned their attention to one another. The Sophocrat's heads seemed to be addressing themselves as much as they spoke to Victoria.

"Where did we come from?" demanded four of them.

From the far side of the gray mass of flesh, a single head continued to cackle. Its voice was higher, more shrill. It seemed to be the source of the rage she heard. "The human does not know!"

Two heads spoke. "The One That Burns speaks the truth. We believe the human does not know."

"Damn you, answer me!" Victoria snapped. She raised her rifle, aiming at the Sophocrat.

From the far side, The One that Burns laughed again. Hands on the ends of impossibly long arms reached for her. "It seeks to wound us! It does not know! It must be exterminated before it is told!"

Another head from the far side spoke. Its strident voice was an octave lower than the others, and the very air slammed into her chest with the incredible volume. "SILENCE!"

"Heed The One That Roars," a pair of heads chastised.

A single head, accompanied by the pair of hands beneath it clasping together in what Victoria might have assumed was apology in any other creature, spoke next. "The others will contain The One That Burns for a few moments. Human, what is your name?"

Victoria was aghast. "My name?"

The head twitched in a gesture that might have been a nod. "We. No. No! I. I! I am called, was called, The One That Hopes."

346

Victoria slowly lowered her weapon again. Puzzlement and curiosity replaced every other emotion she had been feeling. "My name is Victoria."

"You have come here to kill us," The One That Hopes said. It was not a question.

"Yes."

"I understand."

Victoria stopped. Any retort or question she might have had was choked off in an instant. Nothing made sense anymore. It might understand, but she did not, and she could not kill it until she did. "You, I'm sorry, what?"

"I understand," continued the calm voice of The One That Hopes. "Along with The One That Is Silent, I tried to stop the others from attacking your planet, Kipos. We tried to stop them from attacking Dasos. The hate of The One That Burns, however, proved to be too strong. It swayed even The One That Roars for a time."

"You still haven't told me where you came from."

From the far side of the Sophocrat, The One That Burns let out an angry yell, drowning out the others in a wail of rage. "I will speak!"

"YOU WILL NOT."

"Do not silence me!" screamed The One That Burns. "If the human would know our origins, then I will tell it! It will know, and then it will *despair* before it dies!" The One That Burns cackled. "You wish to know where we came from, human?"

"Tell me, dark take you."

The One That Burns laughed again. Victoria would never have imagined that such scorn and hate could be put into such a simple noise. "If you would know, then ask your First Lord Ophion whence we came!"

Victoria felt a chill creeping outward from her stomach. "How do you know that name?"

"Is it not obvious?" demanded The One That Burns. "If he would but reply, The One That Roars would have you ask the same of First Lord Hyperion!"

"SILENCE!" demanded The One That Roars.

Victoria felt her knees weaken. Her rifle sagged toward the ground, lose in her grip. "No."

The One That Burns cackled, a sound that was quickly taken up by half of the heads. Only The One That Roars, The One That Hopes, and a third, as yet unidentified head remained silent.

A quiet voice cut through the laughter. It came from the third, unnamed, head. The other five immediately fell silent as this one spoke. Its voice was somewhat higher than the others, a calm baritone amid a flood of powerful, angry bass sounds. "Many decades ago," it began, "First Lord Adrasta came to the Technocrat Council with a message. One of the exploration satellites deployed by her predecessor detected something far, far outside the edges of Technocrat space."

"MACHINES."

The One That Burns echoed The One That Roars. "Machines!"

"A plan was created," continued the unnamed head.

The One that Hopes added, "the scourge of gods."

"MASTIGA THEON."

In lieu of speaking, The One That Burns simply continued to cackle.

"The One That Is Silent does not lie," The One That Hopes said. "Indeed, we cannot lie. We lack such an ability."

Victoria sagged to her knees. Her rifle banged against her side, forgotten. She simply stared at the Sophocrat as everything she thought she knew shattered.

"We did not want to return," said The One That Hopes. Its voice had quieted somewhat, matching The One That Is Silent in volume. The warped sophont faces seemed incapable of much in the way of expression, but the hands beneath it remained clasped in a gesture of begging.

"You did not want to return, you mean!" snarled The One That Burns. "The humans must be made to pay!"

Finally, as though that threat kickstarted her brain, Victoria asked simply, "machines?"

"Yes," replied The One That Hopes.

The One That Burns interrupted. "Machines! Terrible machines! Perfect predators! They consume all in their path and we were sent to fight them and die!"

Victoria laughed—or sobbed, she really could not tell. It was an empty sound so quiet that the Sophocrat did not hear. If it was telling the truth, then she could certainly sympathize with its anger.

"We took control of the guards of this space." The One That Hopes and The One That Is Silent spoke at the same time, creating an eerie stereo effect. "We sent them away, but we could not speak to the ones below."

"Those belonged to me!" announced The One That Burns, triumphant.

"YOU INVITED DEATH INTO OUR HOME."

"We did what was necessary."

Victoria rose. "To what end?"

"We must die." A third voice joined the other two.

"Do not heed The One That Fears!" growled The One That Burns. "It is you who must die, human. All your kind will perish in flames for what you did to us!"

A fourth voice joined the other three, drowning out the angry protestations of The One That Burns. The quartet spoke. "We were in error."

"RETURNING WAS YOUR IDEA. DO NOT TELL ME THAT THE ONE THAT PLANS WAS WRONG."

The sixth head spoke apart from the other three. "I was wrong. Merging our bodies and minds together was wrong, returning with arms was wrong."

"THE SOPHOCRAT ALLOWED THE MASTIGAS TO COMBAT THE MACHINES."

"The One That Roars speaks truth," The One That Burns snapped. "Without the Sophocrat, we would have been defeated by the machines!"

"Yet we *were* defeated by the machines," the quiet voice of The One That Is Silent said.

"But we live!"

"And we must stop this war," The One That is Silent and The One That Hopes said in unison.

The One That Fears joined them. "Human Victoria. We will war with ourselves until our death. You must kill us."

"Kill you." Victoria's reply was flat. The scene unfolding before her stained her credulity to its limit.

"You must," the Sophocrat said. Even The One That Burns and The One That Plans joined in. The One That Roars stayed strangely silent.

"YOU MUST NOT," it bellowed after a moment.

"I came here to kill you," Victoria said. "You must know that."

The One That Burns and The One That Roars did not join in the reply. "A task at which you *must* succeed."

Victoria raised her rifle, but the One That Burns choose that moment to speak. "That weapon will not kill us!" It barked a short, harsh laugh. "No, there is a way. Power conduits to our beam cannon run through the ceiling. You must use *them*. We will all burn together!"

"The beam cannon," Victoria echoed, already sizing up the ceiling and wondering how best to go about it. "Where did it come from? It's not Technocrat technology."

"THE MACHINES."

Several of the Sophocrat's arms gestured in different directions. Victoria saw that each of them indicated a different latch holding the central ceiling panel closed. A final pair of arms pointed to a control panel on the far side of the room. She wondered if the Sophocrat had planned for this all along, to die, and if so, why.

She crossed to the console, reached for it, and then stopped. With her hand hovering above the holographic interface, she turned her head to address the formless mass of gray flesh again. "Why are you so eager to die?"

Four heads, all of them except The One That Burns and The One That Roars, answered her in unison.

"We control the mastigas with our thoughts, and emotions through pheromones. If we live, the mastigas will never be free."

"And if you die?"

"In time," the four heads answered, "the sophonts will go their own ways. We cannot say what those ways will be, for they will be free of us."

"Why can't you release them on your own?"

"We are too powerful. As long as we live, we will continue to influence them."

"DO NOT DO THIS."

Victoria spun around, anger filling her retort. She grew louder as she continued. "You heard the others. You came back to our stars for revenge. You attempted to commit genocide against the human race! You killed my friends! Why in the dark should I not kill you, Sophocrat?"

Silence fell for a moment before the One That Roars spoke again. Somehow, it lowered its voice, speaking at a more normal volume. "I fear to die."

Victoria's heart sank, but she wrapped it in a protective layer of steel and simply said, "my friends did not 'fear to die,' Sophocrat."

Victoria turned back to the control panel, about to open the controls themselves when the quiet voice of The One Who Is Silent spoke alone.

"Please, Victoria," it said. The thought of an entity like the Sophocrat, any mastigas for that matter, saying please shook her deeply. She turned back to the Sophocrat. The other heads had all closed their eyes except that one and The One That Roars.

The One That Roars closed its eyes after a moment, leaving only The One That Is Silent to watch her with its emerald triad of eyes. "We hate too much."

Victoria started to turn back to the console.

"Please," The One That Is Silent repeated. "Free my children."

Victoria swiped her fingers through the hologram in front of her, throwing the switch that opened the ceiling. It slowly retracted, revealing a series of bare metal bars that buzzed and hummed with power.

Six pairs of arms reached up and made contact with the metal and electricity flowed into the Sophocrat's massive body. It convulsed and shook, clamping its hands tightly around the exposed conduits.

The huge mass started to smoke and amid its death throes, she heard The One That Burns cackle.

"Without the others to stop my children, the mastigas will sweep over your planets like wildfire! Your worlds will burn! Your people will die! And when the machines come, they will find nothing alive! Congratulations, human! Congratulations..."

Anything else it wanted to say was cut off as the electricity continued to flow, burning and cooking the massive creature.

The Sophocrat took several minutes to die, a time during which Victoria simply stood there and remembered everyone who died so that she could stand there.

***

An hour after the Sophocrat's death, Victoria managed to access the battleship's control systems, or what remained of them. The power surge the Sophocrat caused seemed to have damaged the weapon atop the pyramid, making shutdown easy.

She shut down power to the ruined the beam weapons at the front of the ship first, then disabled the battleship's conventional weaponry. Engines were next. She continued to work for some time before declaring the task finished.

Victoria looked again at the Sophocrat, this time coming close enough to touch it. It had been horribly burned by the electricity, and the terrible smell of seared flesh forced her to keep her helmet sealed and use more of her bottled air.

She reached out a hand and pressed it against the side of the massive creature. Victoria wanted to strike it, to maim and destroy the creature that brought so much pain to so many people, but it would do no good. The Sophocrat was quite dead, and yet she still moved gingerly around it as though anything she did might return it to horrid life.

Another hour passed before she was able to patch her suit's radio into the communication system of the mastigas battleship. She hoped Helena was wrong, and the *Hammer of Ares* was still within transmission range, and sent a low-bandwidth text-only message.

While she waited for the message to travel the vast distance between the two ships, Victoria stood and shut off the lights in the room. She could bear the sight of the Sophocrat's corpse no longer. In that cool darkness, she sat, staring at nothing, feeling nothing.

Some time later, her radio finally came to life. Through dense static, she heard the captain's voice.

"This is the *Hammer of Ares*," he said. "I don't know how you did it, Titans, but you did. The mastigas ship is reading as completely disabled. To whom am I speaking?"

"Spatharios Victoria," she replied, realizing after the fact that her voice was horse and cracked.

The captain's cheerful voice answered her thirty minutes later. "Tell the others that drinks are on me when you return."

Victoria sat in silence for several minutes. Her voice was small and quiet when she finally did reply. "There are no others."

Another half-hour passed and this time the captain spoke with formality. "Understood. Do you require extraction, Spatharios Victoria?"

"Yes," she replied, settling in to wait. As long as the mastigas ship's weapons remained offline, and the Sophocrat's chamber remained sealed, she would be safe.

And she would be alone.

***

A small voice roused Victoria from her sleep, sending her pulse immediately skyrocketing. Only the subconscious knowledge that the voice was not mastigas kept her from complete cardiac shock. It repeated itself, saying, "you are not alone."

"Who?" she demanded, eyes scanning the room.

"Look down."

She did, and her pulse again quickened. This time it happened for a completely different reason. Rather than fear, her heart leaped with joy.

Standing atop the blue-white metal on her arm was a hologram. It stood no more than twenty centimeters, shorter than her forearm was long. The presence of anything to converse with would have been welcome enough, but that was not the only reason for Victoria's joy.

The tiny hologram of Helena smiled up at her. "Hello, Victoria."

"But you died!"

The hologram shook her head slowly. Regret fell across her holographic face like a shadow. "Only that body died. It was never mine."

"You're alive? Still?"

"Yes. That body belonged to a girl named Helena, a volunteer."

Victoria's head swam. "Your name is Helena."

"I took her name," the hologram replied. "In honor of her sacrifice."

"You're alive," Victoria repeated. She felt stuck on that one concept, as though nothing else mattered.

"Yes."

"You're a hologram?"

Helena smiled and shook her head. "Not quite. This hologram is how I interact with you, my friend. What I am has always been this." The hologram spread her arms. "An AI."

"After what I just learned, I'll accept anything," Victoria replied. The feeling of numbness was starting to ebb, replaced by a tightening in her throat and a stinging in her eyes.

"I heard what the Sophocrat told you."

"Was it telling the truth?"

Helena nodded. "Yes."

Victoria let out a deep breath of air that she did not realize she had been holding. "Gods between..."

Helena tapped her holographic foot on the metal gauntlet wrapped around Victoria's arm. "Thank for you taking this. Without your help, I truly would have died. I am sorry it took so long for my system to adapt to its new home."

"I'm just glad you're alive."

The holographic representation of Helena's AI consciousness nodded. "I am glad to be alive, my friend."

"Helena, I..." she whispered.

Whatever else Victoria was about to say was cut off as her throat tightened in an unstoppable wave of grief. There, in the darkness, she screamed and wailed at an uncaring universe.

She had seen and been a part of so much death. Now that it was finally over, floodgates deep in her soul opened. She allowed herself to feel everything she had choked down over the last few days.

Victoria wept until she had no more tears left and she found herself curled up tightly on the floor of the Sophocrat's chamber. When she opened her eyes again, the little hologram of Helena sat next to her, legs crossed under her robe.

The AI smiled sadly, watching Victoria push herself into a sitting position. She regarded the hologram for several long moments as emotions continued to swirl through her brain.

Yes, she thought, many people had died. She watched her friends die in front of her, sacrificing themselves to save one another, and to save her. She owed them all a debt greater than anything. Even killing the Sophocrat, finishing the mission they all set out to accomplish, did not measure up to their sacrifices.

There in the darkness, with the only other person to survive by her side, Victoria vowed never to forget the sacrifices it took to bring her to that point. A hundred thousand people departed the *Hammer of Ares*, and only they two survived.

In the darkness, Victoria made a vow. She would make sure everyone knew what happened.

Epilogue

Victoria found a great many messages waiting in her suite when she returned to the *Hammer of Ares*. The captain only spoke to her as much as he had to and, after a request to be left alone, the crew avoided her altogether. He told her that terrible fighting raged across the binary while they were gone, but gave few other details. The rest, he said, could wait until she was ready.

She did not read the messages immediately. Instead, she showered and ate in her room, speaking to no one buy Helena. The other Titan kept her company, showing more emotion than she ever had now that the hardware blocks in her implants were no longer fighting her.

Victoria then slept for fourteen hours.

When she awoke, she took the time to count the messages, finding two hundred and sixty-three messages. Most were simple notes of encouragement from the citizens of the binary. Those she could read later.

Fortunately, sorting the messages was easy. She filtered out everything except the one person she most wanted to hear from. The most recent message, which came in less than twelve hours before her return, was from Pallasophia.

Victoria selected the message and pressed the "play" icon. The holo above her desk vanished for a moment before being replaced by a video recording. Three figures, an adult male, an adult female, and a girl faced the pickup.

She felt like she should recognize the child, but the bloody and dirt-smeared child-size combat uniform with its red arm stripes and her stern expression rendered any recognition impossible.

The man at first looked like Tritogenes, and Victoria felt a swell of relief and anger. She had things to say to him and even if she could only say them to a recording, she would say what she had to. After another second's scrutiny, she realized it was not Tritogenes—he was too young, too handsome to be her Hexarch.

The woman in the center of the group was, of course, Pallasophia. She too wore the black uniform of a soldier, but her arms bore blue stripes. Victoria's heart swelled when she saw her and she felt a smile forming on her lips.

"Hello, love," Pallasophia said. "I hope you get this message. The captain told me what happened to the *Justice* and your other ships on the way in. I am deeply sorry for their loss.

"Things here are not as they were when you left."

Even in a small hologram, Victoria could see the tension radiating out from Pallasophia.

The recording continued. "Let me start at the beginning. Weeks ago now, First Lord Aegesander assassinated First Lord Hyperion in his palace on Pteryga. Aegesander then immediately declared martial law throughout the binary."

Victoria's hand flew to her mouth automatically. Before she could curse, swear, or even say anything, the recording went on.

"First Lord Tritogenes tried to stop him."

The bottom fell out of Victoria's stomach. Before Pallasophia's message could even say what actually happened, she knew. She instantly regretted any bad feelings, any ill will she might have had toward her Hexarch.

"Tritogenes did not survive. He died a hero, allowing First Lord Rivka, who was also present after a meeting of her own with Hyperion, to escape.

"First Lord Rivka escaped Pteryga with First Lord Enyalios's help. Enyalios, having broken Aegesander's blockade above Katarraktes, assaulted Prosgeiosi itself. That fighting was over quickly and he and Rivka turned their attention to Dasos.

"Before they could secure Dasos, First Lord Eurybia assassinated Aegesander."

Next to the recording, atop the silvery-blue gauntlet resting there, Helena's hologram manifested. Her face showed a mixture of relief and anger. "Good riddance."

Victoria felt the same sense of numbness threatening to overtake her that she felt in the wake of the Sophocrat's death. She would not let it, fighting to keep her emotions front and center for the moment. She knew her eyes were wide and staring, but the video could not see that, and Helena would not judge her.

The recording continued. "First Lord Rivka then shot and killed First Lord Eurybia. Shortly thereafter, Dasos surrendered.

"Before I tell you the rest of my news," Pallasophia continued, "I need to introduce my companions. This is Sixth Lord Alexis, though if I have anything to say about it, she's going to be Fifth Lord by the time you meet her. She saved my life on multiple occasions when Aegesander's troops attacked Limani."

Pallasophia waved at hand at the man next to her. No, she waved a hand through the man next to her. "This is Logosarc, an artificial intelligence created by First Lord Ophion, though you might know him better as Second Lord Philip."

The recording paused. Victoria reached for the play button, assuming there had been an error with the software, but stopped when she realized Helena was reaching out a hand toward the screen.

"By the Ten Thousand," Helena whispered. "I'm not the only one."

Victoria smiled a brief but heartfelt smile as Helena gestured and the recording resumed.

"Now, for the rest of the news. First Lord Enyalios and First Lord Rivka are still alive. The Council, meaning Enyalios, ruled her killing of Eurybia to be justified and allowed her to keep her Hexarchate.

"That, however, still only leaves us with two Hexarchs. Elections from among the Second Lords will likely be held before you return, however there is an unusual element.

"After his death, I accessed Tritogenes's Will. It was very explicit. Within the bounds of both tradition and law, there are two ways to become a Hexarch. First is to be voted to the Council by the others, and the second..."

Victoria whispered, "no," repeating it several times, each one louder than the previous.

"...is by the written Will of a living Hexarch."

Her mind raced. "This is not happening. This is a trick. Tritogenes is playing a joke on me and when I get back to Limani, I'm going to tell him..."

The recording, oblivious to her protestations, continued. "...allow me, my love, to be the first to call you by your new title:

"First Lord Victoria, Hexarch of Limani."

AUTHOR'S NOTES

Now that you're through the entire story, I can tell you what the second challenge I set for myself was. When I realized where this story was going and what kind of story I was actually writing, I told myself I would avoid some of the pitfalls that I ran into in my very early stories. Namely, in those early, unpublished, stories, none of the main characters are ever in any real danger. There was no mortal risk for anything they were doing, because each important character was as durable as a comic-book hero. So, for *Scourge of Gods*, I told myself that I would throw that out the window. I would take these characters I cared about, characters that hopefully you cared about as well, and kill as many of them as I possibly could (provided their deaths furthered the story and were not just random violence for violence's sake). I think I succeeded at both parts of that goal. Some of the death scenes certainly choked me up when I wrote them.

My original plan for the story had the mastigas as just another invading alien race, but that didn't fit the feel and the symbolism I built up. They're a doom brought about by the technocrat's own arrogance, but why? I had no idea why the mastigas had been sent out until writing that scene with the sophocrat, and I heard in its booming voice, "MACHINES."

It's safe to say that we'll be back to the Technocrat binary before all it said and done. I originally planned for this to be everything, but the moment the Machines came up, I knew I had to come back. It may be years down the road for Victoria, but we will definitely come back.

The death of the sophocrat will definitely open up some interesting storytelling potential. I'll tell you that the sophocrat wasn't lying—unless it was, of course—and we're going to see some very interesting developments with the mastigas when we see the Technocrat binary again. Again, assuming the sophocrat was telling the truth, but you'll just have to wait and see, won't you?

I'll throw in a little tidbit for people who, first, actually read this section and, second, for people who read my other books. The *Odyssey* is, in fact, one of the three worldships that left Earth during the Exodus, which is an event mentioned in *The Stars Have Eyes*. For those who picked up on the origin of the pocket watch in *Stars*, there ought to be some interesting connections forming for you right about now (or maybe you've already put those pieces together!).

I suppose I'll leave you with an echo of a thought I wrote in an earlier set of Author's Notes for this series. This has been my favorite series to work on so far. I enjoyed the world and the characters more than any finished product, I think. I see them clearly in my mind and so it's very strange to finally be *finished* with their story.

I poured a lot of myself into these books, pain and joy both. *Scourge of Gods* was very cathartic at times, and at times as tedious and frustrating as any other project. I experienced the characters emotions sometimes more strongly than my own, and sometimes it was *my* emotions they were made to feel.

All in all, I sincerely hope you enjoyed this story as much as I did.

Additional thanks to: Rick Lowden, Mike Huddleston, Don Church, Michael Huddleston, Ashley Ward, Steve and Diane Mitchell, Becky Spain-Kaiser, Jacob Forbes, Heather Green, Beth Davis, Kaycee Dortch, Will Nunn, Jan Parks, Sarah Philips, and Susan and John Farmer

ABOUT THE AUTHOR

https://www.facebook.com/tafarmerauthor/

https://www.amazon.com/Thomas-A-Farmer/e/B01A436HFO/

Born to geeky parents and raised on a diet of Star Trek and Babylon 5, Thomas started writing at an early age, working his way through fanfictions of all types. For good or ill, a lot of that early work has been lost.

Writing occupied much of his spare time throughout school and the years after, eventually culminating in an ostensible *magnum opus* he calls the "Chronicles of St. Michael." To this date, those stories still reek of many "early writer" problems, but he promises they will, one day, see the light of publication.

What can you expect next? Who knows? Maybe "St. Michael" will see the light of day in the near future. Stranger things have happened.

He also hosts a podcast (internet radio show, when he's feeling fancy) called "Authors in Abstract." As of this book, the show is well into its second season. You can listen to the podcast on a variety of platforms, or by going directly to www.authorsinabstract.com

When his hands aren't full with books, reading or writing, he fills them with swords. Four nights a week, as of this publication anyway, he teaches historic fencing, also called HEMA (Historic European Martial Arts) as one of the head coaches of the Knoxville Academy of the Blade (www.facebook.com/KABFencing)

He lives with his wife, Stephanie, their three cats, lizard, and snake.

www.ingramcontent.com/pod-product-compliance
Lightning Source LLC
Chambersburg PA
CBHW051323250626
47155CB00007B/2431